THE WEDDING DIARIES

Sam Binnie was the 2005 winner of the *Harper's*/Orange Prize Short Story Competition, and lives in London with her husband and two children. She is still embarrassed that she forced people to camp at her wedding. *The Wedding Diaries* is her first book, and she is currently writing *The Baby Diaries*, to be published in Spring 2013, and suffering flashbacks to the horrors of antenatal classes.

To discover more about Sam and the series, visit www.sambinnie.com or follow Sam on twitter @pantherbinn.

SAM BINNIE

The Wedding Diaries

AVON

AVON

A division of HarperCollins*Publishers*
77–85 Fulham Palace Road,
London W6 8JB

www.harpercollins.co.uk

A Paperback Original 2012

1

Set in Sabon by Palimpsest Book Production Limited,
Falkirk, Stirlingshire

Printed and bound in Great Britain by
Clays Ltd, St Ives plc

MIX
Paper from
responsible sources
FSC **FSC˙ C007454**
www.fsc.org

For J,

Bringer of sunshine

August 15th

Here's who knows about weddings: Abba. The Dixie Cups. Alfred Doolittle. All masters on the theme of matrimony, whether it's the oaths (I do), the venue (Chapel of Love) and the punctuality (on time). But can they tell me: what happens when you ruin the proposal?

It was the final night of our long weekend in Bath, an early birthday gift from me to Thom, and I was getting suspicious. Thom had been strange with me for the previous week – silent, jumpy, and staring at me when he thought I wasn't looking – and had been in an odd mood for most of the weekend. He seemed twitchy and insistent on going out for dinner when all I wanted was to sink into our hotel bed with room service and some TV, so I put two and two together and decided that five = looking for somewhere public to break up with me. I'd had passing concerns every now and again since February, when I'd ruined a Valentine's meal at a tapas bar by rifling through each dish looking for a ring that wasn't there. In the taxi to the restaurant my nerves were noticeable.

Me: Are you sure this is the restaurant you want to go to?

Thom: [silence]

Me: Oh Jesus. Please can we just go home?

Thom: [silence]

Me: Look! There's a homeless man. Are you sure you wouldn't rather take him?

Thom: [silence]

Me: Brilliant. This is *just* how I hoped my holiday would end.

I'd whipped myself up into a frenzy by this point, dizzily chattering away as we were shown to our table. All I could see was that we were tucked into a corner, out of earshot but still in eyeshot should a court case demand it. As we settled into our chairs I realised that, having been eyeballing me for the last week, Thom now wouldn't even look at me, and I began to panic. I started reading out the menu, describing each item in my cheeriest voice and making comments on the dishes with a joyful tone that kept sticking in my throat. Hurray! I was becoming my mother. When I summoned the courage to look at Thom again he was staring at me, apparently about to speak. At that moment someone started tapping a knife against a wine glass, and the restaurant went silent. A handsome, happy man rose to his feet.

Handsome Man: Sorry everyone, sorry. I'll let you go back to your delicious meals in one moment. I just need your attention for a minute. This beautiful woman here [gestures to woman apparently trying to eye-laser an escape route through their table] has made me so happy over the last two years. In front of all of you here tonight, I would like to ask her: Jen, will you do

2

	me the great honour of becoming my one and only wife?
Jen:	[blanching] Oh, Steve . . .
HM:	Come on, stand up, darling! Will you join with me in holy matrimony, and finally make an honest man out of me?
Jen:	I'm sorry, Steve. [picks up handbag] This isn't going to work. [walks out]
HM:	[after a long silence] Sorry everyone. Sorry. Please . . . [sitting down] carry on.

I turned to Thom and he was paler than poor Steve. He actually looked as if he was going to be sick. At that moment the waiter arrived to take our order, attempting to plaster over the dreadful event the entire restaurant had just witnessed. Thom blindly ordered for both of us, which was unusual but fine by me as my stomach seemed to be about to crawl out of my throat. He couldn't break up with me now, could he? He opened his mouth to speak, his tongue dryly clicking.

Thom:	Kiki, we've been together a while, and I've started thinking about where we're going—[voice disappears]
Me:	[gibbering] No! Don't think about it! Although you did say that you wanted to go to Berlin, didn't you? Let's go to Berlin! That's where we can go!
Thom:	[touching my hand, looking at me] Keeks. Please will you marry me?
Me:	Is that a joke?

I didn't intend to say something so horribly unromantic, and a better story will definitely have to be devised for the grandchildren, but after I realised that he was serious and

Thom realised that he wasn't about to relive the Steve and Jen Story from the sharp end I couldn't stop crying. Thom moved his chair next to mine and hugged me for a really long time. Every time I'd almost calmed down, he'd say something like 'This will be brilliant' and I'd start off again. The manager was so delighted that someone would actually have a positive experience of the restaurant that night that he sent over a bottle of champagne. When we staggered out of the restaurant arm in arm and quite definitely tipsy, I kept thinking over and over: I could get used to this.

August 16th

So this is why I've started this diary. It will be a lovely keepsake of the wedding as well as a handy one-stop notebook for everything that needs to be done; all of it will live here. This organisation thing will be a lark. I've also signed up to receive a lovely inspirational email each month; a wedding from great literature. Not bad, eh? This wedding will be the making of me.

After work, we rang Thom's parents in Australia, who squealed down the phone at us and promised not to call my parents for at least an hour or two, giving us time to break the news. Alan and Aileen are dream in-laws-to-be: funny, thoughtful, kind and on the other side of the world, having emigrated there on retirement three years ago. Thom's an only child, and Alan and Aileen said they knew they didn't have to worry about him so would go and warm their bones for a while, just outside Sydney. They love it over there: the weather, the food, and their neighbours, but they say they miss us.

Mum and Dad were over the moon when they heard our

news. They've always loved Thom (a little bit more than they love me, if my suspicions are correct) and jumped from their armchairs when Thom announced our engagement. Well, I say jumped: Mum leapt up and started kissing everyone while Dad's face glowed, then he carefully lifted himself from his chair to pump Thom's hand up and down and envelop me in a lovely Dad-hug. Mum was already crying, and when Dad whispered, 'Well done, my girl – he better look after you or he'll have me to deal with,' I was laughing and choking up a bit too. Dad might be six foot four and solid as an old brick shed, but he's the kindest, most gentle person you could ever wish to meet. He retired early from a very dull senior job in a law firm and, while all his cronies were perfecting their golf swing and talking about running for parliament, Dad saw a TV programme about fine-working silver, took a short course and was such a natural that he now teaches Jewellery Making at the local sixth-form and adult college. He produces such beautiful, delicate pieces, necklaces and rings and gorgeous Christmas ornaments for the Twins, all of which seem impossible until you see his long, fine fingers, and all of which go with his brilliant, lovely mind, and all of which make you wonder how he managed to spend all those years in a legal office. A girl couldn't wish for a better dad.

Once Mum had mopped her eyes a bit, she found a dusty old bottle of pre-mixed Buck's Fizz from some party back in 1987 and we all toasted one another.

Mum: Congratulations to you both!
Dad: We're so proud of you two. We wish you every happiness.
Thom: Tessa, John – if we can spend one day of marriage as happy as you have always been, I'll consider us truly blessed.

Me: I'm not particularly comfortable with public displays of emotion, but I will raise a toast to that. To my mum and dad, and the giant wedding extravaganza that will make their daughter as happy as they are!

Mum rolled her eyes a little at that but Dad chuckled, and on cue the phone rang: Thom's mum. Leaving the mothers to discuss hats (or whatever), Thom bundled me into the car to go and see Susie, just around the corner, after swearing Mum and Dad (Mum) to secrecy for the next half-hour. Susie's been my sister for about as long as I can remember, being two years older than me, and – if I block the time she cut all my hair off when I was four – has been my best friend for pretty much the entire time. Susie, Pete and the kids live in a lovely old terraced house, extended almost into oblivion by the previous owners, so although the front is tiny, it opens out into a huge warehouse space once you get inside. The front door is tricky to get through, though, being jammed with children's boots and coats, Pete's souvenirs from around the world and a huge window seat that doesn't fit in the hallway but Susie insists is necessary, glamorous hallway furniture. She's going through a Sunset Boulevard stage at the moment, so thinks a lilac velvet chaise longue is exactly what a terrace in North Finchley requires.

She opened the door to us in her apron (not only her apron, obviously) with hands covered in flour and her six-year-old twins Lily and Edward scampering around her.

Lily and Edward: Thom! Hurray!
Thom: Susie. Children. [picks the Twins up by their ankles and carries them off upside down to the garden]
Me: [faintly] Hi . . . children . . .
Susie: Come and have a drink.

6

Oh, Susie, so good with the drinks offers. After Mum's ecstasies, I could have murdered a Band on the Run. She held up her floury hands and kicked a foot towards the fridge for me to help myself. After rummaging around for a while, I gave her my most disgusted look.

Me: You don't have anything to drink, do you?
Susie: Ooooh . . . funny you should say that. I bought some vodka a few months ago—
Me: [snatching up a pair of kitchen tongs and brandishing them in her face] *Susie* . . .
Susie: No. We probably don't. Sorry!
Me: Is Pete around to do an alcohol run?
Susie: Since it's neither Christmas nor the Twins' birthday, I think it's safe to assume he's not.

Also, Susie: not so good with *possessing* the wonderful drinks she offers. But the few times she has, combined with the frequency of her offers means she is somehow still seen as a glorious homemaker. I blame Lily and Edward. Their charm and beauty distract from the true horrors of their mother's hostess talents. And since Susie's husband Pete is almost never at home to ease her household burden, frequently away with his glamorous travel agent job, the fact that her children still have their full complement of fingers/legs/heads ought really to be enough for us.

We chatted for a minute or two, until I reminded her of my weekend away with Thom. I knew she wasn't really paying attention when she asked for details since she was so busy rolling out scores of pastry cases for some school event; I repaid her with a mind-numbing parody of our mother's anecdotes, in the style of a particularly dry shopping list.

| Me: | . . . And then we looked at the baths, so that was five o'clock, then we went back to the hotel, then we changed and went to dinner, at seven . . . no, eight . . . no . . . was it? . . . No. Eight o'clock. Then we were at the restaurant. Oh. And then he proposed. |
| Susie: | [stunned] Is that a joke? |

And they say we Carlows are unromantic. Besides our inability with languages (Susie and I once took a trip to Italy in our teens and when our passports were stolen, discovered that the only Italian we'd picked up was seventeen different kinds of pasta) it seems we also face romantic situations with the same facial expression and tone of voice of someone asked to kick a piglet.

When she realised that I wasn't joking, she lifted a floury hand to her throat, then clasped my hands between hers. As she warmly expressed her joy and excitement with little giggles and happy sighs, and clutched my arms, I suddenly twigged what she was up to, and looked down to find myself covered in flour up to the elbows. She started backing away, chuckling, but I held up my hands – Peace – and promised that I only wanted to wipe the mess off her neck. When she gave me that fatal moment of trust, I grabbed as much flour as I could from the counter and ground it into her hair.

Thom came in with the children moments later to find me bent over the worktop as Susie held my ponytail and rubbed my face in the flour, both of us weak with laughter. Susie called the Twins over.

Susie:	[sternly] I don't ever want to see you doing this to another child, do you understand?
Twins:	Yes, Mummy.
Edward:	[thoughtful] But can we do it to adults?

Susie:	No.
Lily:	But we can do it to Aunt Kiki?
Thom and Susie:	*Yes.*

TO DO:
Dress
Venue
Food
Honeymoon
Find out if I absolutely *have* to invite own sister

August 18th

My colleagues at Polka Dot Books were exactly as supportive as I'd expected: Alice was excited, Carol suspicious ('And how long will you be expecting to take for Honeymoon?' Me, to self: Why is she making that sound like a disgusting illness?) and Norman apathetic. Carol's our Commissioning Editor at Polka Dot and one of the grumpiest people I've met, but she speaks with such a beautiful tone, like a cross Joanna Lumley, that I never really mind her irritable pronouncements, while Norman, Head of Accounts and taciturn to the point of muteness mostly, would be newsworthy if something caused him to react at all. Alice is my closest friend there, and a member of the Hamilton family, of Hamilton Industry fame, the tooth-achingly rich owners of 60% of the world's chalk mines. I still can't tell if Alice works here for a dare, or if she's trying to prove something to her parents. She got the job through connections, of course, her father being the godson of our boss's mother (this is what Alice's whole life is like), so I was tempted to tip her off the fire escape when she joined the company. She's always immaculately dressed in DVF or modern Chanel with a few choice pieces of Whistles and Topshop thrown in, and I've never, ever seen her with egg on her blouse or a large bump of hair sticking out the top of her ponytail. Her handbags alone would be enough to make a grown woman weep, but combine that with the face of an angel and the wallet of a Trump and Alice completely terrifies most of our authors (while others are completely in love with her – one a little bit of both), so she turned out to be a great guard dog for the office. It also gradually became clear that like many of those lusciously maned ex-Edinburgh Uni girls, she was great at publicity, pulling on her spiderweb to get our authors into great magazines and media slots, so we all had a meeting behind her back and decided we'd let her live. She's incredibly posh but undercuts it all with a deadpan humour that took me three months to get but now is my favourite thing about going to work each day. She can say anything – literally, *anything* – to our authors and to Tony, the boss, and they might blink for a second but will never, ever disbelieve her or question quite how filthy/offensive/untrue what it is she's saying.

But it was a surprise for my boss to be so gleeful. He doesn't really approve of personal lives.

Tony: What's all this fuss about?

Me: [nervous] Oh . . . It looks like I'll be getting married next year.

Tony: Fine. [suddenly paying attention] Really? That's brilliant! Brilliant! What great news!

Me: Ummm . . . yes?

Tony: No, that's great! Have you got much planned?

Me: Well, it's still pretty early, so—

Tony: Brilliant stuff. Good. Well, this couldn't have come at a better time. I've got a new book for you!

New book was selling it somewhat short. Through some hideous Machiavellian scheming that I definitely don't want to know about, Polka Dot Books have somehow landed model/soapstar/popstar Jacki Jones's book – and it turns out that since she too is getting married next year, it's going to be a wedding book.

I'm a humble editorial assistant at Polka Dot Books, a smallish publisher of very commercial titles (the books you'd see at the supermarket mostly) which was opened in the eighties by Tony's parents. They kept their small family firm under the radar by publishing nothing arthouse, nothing controversial, nothing groundbreaking, just making cheap populist paperbacks available to a hungry public. Tony's father died when he was young, but his mother, Pamela, is still around, and Tony lives in awe and terror of her. She, in her turn, has rewritten the importance of Polka Dot into something comparable to the Gutenberg press, defending the honour of her publishing house by criticising most of what we publish. She also holds the family purse strings, and is the majority stockholder here (rumour has it she gave Tony 10% of the company on his 21st birthday, certain – and correct in her certainty – that those shares would keep him attached to the Polka Dot where mere maternal threats might fail). He's worked harder than his 10% would warrant, some might argue, doing a fairly good job (although the office hasn't been repainted in almost a decade, at least it's still open) with little from her but an occasional visit to snoop at the books 'she's' publishing.

Since arriving here four years ago my duties have officially been limited to office diary management and author care (patting the authors on the head, making sure they know how to get in and out of a taxi, taking them to the BBC and showing them where the door is for them to walk through, giving them a snack and carton of squash when they get fractious) with a little bit of editing on the side, although actually I've done so much 'editing on the side' that Tony's been promising me my own titles for almost a year now. So I should be excited that I've finally got one, and such an exciting one at that. But the fact that Tony's given me a book to work on at all (and such an exciting one, etc.) has rather set alarm bells ringing. What's so wrong with this author or this book that Tony is happy – and I mean *happy* – to hand it over to his assistant? The thought that this is finally a charitable move on his part is quite literally incredible, so I shall have to wait and see why *Jacki Jones's Perfect Wedding* is so monstrous that Tony Cooper, big fish in this small Polka Dot pond, has washed his hands of it. At least I might be able to pinch something from the photo shoots, I suppose.

When I came out of Tony's office, Alice was smiling wistfully.

Alice: I was engaged once.
Me: [shocked] Were you?! When? How?
Alice: Thank you for your incredulity, Kiki. I was engaged when I was seventeen, to the first man I ever slept with. Mummy and Daddy didn't really like him, and it didn't last long. After we broke up, he kidnapped a girl who looked exactly like me but he got off on an insanity plea.

Her tale was so awful, but Alice's straight-faced delivery and shrug – what? Doesn't that happen to everyone? – meant that I couldn't stop laughing for fifteen minutes. She came out as gay in her early twenties, to everyone except her parents. She now lives with a man she describes as 'so dim it hurts to talk to him', sharing a two-bed flat and moving into one room when her parents visit. Soon after I met her, I asked her why she was with him. She said, 'I'm not *with him*, with him. Anyway, he's really kind, he has an amazing collection of obscure science-fiction novels and my mother loves him. It keeps them off my back.'

It's not a large company – Tony, Editorial Director; Carol, Commissioning Editor; Norman, Accounts; an Art team of three, Dan, Mark and Nayla; a part-time Sales team of five; Alice and two others, one freelance and one part-time, make up Marketing and Publicity; a marvellous Production duo; whichever intern we've signed up for the month (currently Judy the Intern, who, now I think about it, seems to have been here for*ever*); various other freelancers; and me. In the early glory days of Polka Dot Books there was talk of moving to a building with a reception desk where guests would be warmly greeted and actually assisted, rather than bumbling up the stairs until someone recognises them, but one thing after another meant we're still in this sad office block off Baker Street – a lovely location, but a structure that is surely only standing because the developers haven't decided what to build on top of its shattered wreckage. The office itself is some odd hybrid of Dickensian lair and supermarket warehouse: books are piled on every surface, blocking windows and propping open doors, but each book usually has either glitter or a sexy-looking weapon on the front and back (each with a heavily airbrushed author photo). These are not Booker winners. But they keep people reading, and they pay for a roof over my head. I'm a fan.

TO DO:
Venue – location?
Dress – book Suse to come
Investigate how cross Mum will be if I don't ask her to come
    dress shopping too
Honeymoon – New York? Berlin?
Buy bridal magazines

August 20th

Tony's very kindly ordered a pile of wedding books For Reference Purposes before I get to work on Jacki's book. I am indeed referring to them, not least to work out the things I need to get done over the next few months. Some more for the list:

TO DO:
Announce our engagement – email? Newspaper? Rooftops?
Engagement party – usual gang? usual place? Friday night?
Sort wedding date – August? (nice weather)
Choose a colour scheme – blues? Nautical but Nice? Pinks?
    Like a big bruise? Or . . . all green. The Wedding of Oz.
Ask Suse about colour schemes
Dress – decide what shape I want (fishtail, strapless, A-line,
    column, empire, spherical, whatever)
Find magazine images of veils, accessories I like (who has
    veil preferences?)
Music for reception – see if Thom would be happy for Jim
    to find local band?

August 23rd

Here, for the record, is how we met.

One day, seven years ago exactly, I'd come to stay with Susie and Pete during a university holiday, and was working at a terrible data-entry job, typing in the details of vacuum cleaner warrantees for seven hours a day. Susie – young, carefree, albeit recently married – had called me up and said, 'Stop moping over your horrible lists. No one should have to care about vacuum cleaner purchase histories. If you haven't met

14

your quota, you can hang yourself later. You're coming dancing with us tonight.'

There was a big gang of them going out, a group from Susie's radio station, all impossibly cool to someone still not quite officially in the big wide world, even though most of them were only a couple of years older than me. One of them had a birthday so they were all heading east to some super-chic bar, and Susie was insisting I join them. It was either that or an evening in with Pete (he was exhausted from his new job at a travel company) so I bolted back to the flat, threw on Susie's favourite dress, pinned up my hair, and was out the door before Pete could regale me with a hilarious double-booking anecdote. When I got to Bar Electric – a bar so cool they simply put their records on shelves along the walls, so their hipster crowd could help themselves – Susie's original gang had swelled to include other friends of friends, so I was tucked into the booth next to someone Susie didn't know, so couldn't introduce me to, while she went to get drinks. I had no eyes for the company though, because I couldn't take my eyes off a guy I'd spotted the second I walked in. He had to be the best-looking human being I'd ever seen in my life. Piercing blue eyes, a half-smiling mouth, thick, perfectly-not-styled hair, and (from what I could see) a killer body: this was the full cliché. He was amazing. I couldn't believe that not only had he not had me thrown out for looking at him, but he'd actually been looking back at me, talking to his friend, looking at me, turning back to the friend but constantly seeing if I was still looking at him. He was *amazing*. Susie arrived with my drink shortly after, which I necked in my nervousness.

This went on for a while, until, after chugging four drinks and ignoring everyone else at our table, I'd gained enough confidence. I told Susie I was going over. She goggled her eyes at me and told me to take care and to

15

be careful; she was pretty hammered too by that stage. I strutted over to where he was sitting by a wall of vinyl, and flicked through one box of records for a while. I could see a better lot higher up, and reached up as far as I could to access the Whitney Houston winking to me from its heavy wooden box. I stretched up past Handsome Man to show off my body at its best ('Look how slender and supple I am,' etc.) and just got my fingertips to it, pulling, lifting it down – and it teetered, overbalanced, tipped off the edge and punched its full weight directly into my eye socket. I screamed: 'Mother*fucker*!' and doubled over, clutching my hand to my face, while bar staff hurried up to pick up the box and check the records were OK. Susie rushed across to take me back to the table where she could check me over, and I got a quick glimpse of the exquisite discomfort on Handsome Man's face. As Suse sat me down, I saw him getting his coat and pals and leaving the place, unable to look in my direction. Susie was drunkenly flustering a bit, but out of nowhere came a pint glass full of ice and a bar towel. I looked up and saw a guy turning away, sitting back down at the other side of the booth and continuing his conversation with some of Susie's gang.

I poured a handful of ice into the towel and put it to my face. I watched him as he was talking. He was so *good* looking: not hip, not breathtaking, not someone who would stop you in your tracks as you walked down the street, but with a face that looked *good*. Someone you would trust with your dog, your grandma, your handbag, your life. 'When did *he* get here?' I asked Susie. She looked at me, laughing. 'Cuckoo, he's been here all night.' Just at that moment, he turned to me and smiled. And my heart disappeared somewhere out the top of my skull.

16

(Just for the record, turns out the Twins were conceived that night. *Who* had to be careful, Susie?)

Seven years ago today, Thom was out with his new work colleagues for his birthday. Happy birthday, you good man.

August 26th

I love our flat. It's tiny, absolutely tiny, but I like it. Our landlord is totally brilliant – he lives in Canada so if anything goes wrong he just sends us money to fix it – and you get brilliant light in the living room in the summer. The kitchen is big enough for one (two if someone gets a chair and sits on the landing) which is just how I like it, the bathroom has a bath *and* a shower, and the bedroom has a king-size bed in. This is everything anyone could need in a home. Add to that our neighbours downstairs – a couple in their forties always offering us their lovely cast-offs, including a beautiful enamel casserole and an Art Deco glass jug recently – and I wouldn't want to live anywhere else. Thom, I think, could stand to live a little further from my family; Susie's five minutes' walk away and my mum and dad three minutes' drive, but it's not like she's one of those creepy mums who keeps a key to all her children's homes and lets herself in to do the laundry and washing up. Although if I could guarantee we'd always be out when she came, that wouldn't necessarily be the worst thing in the world. I've lived in a few places since leaving home, but we all ended up in the same neighbourhood, which still surprises me.

We had a tough Sunday afternoon in the flat, dealing with all the various key points. Organising weddings is hard work.

Me: I was thinking about the wedding party. Susie and Eve for my bridesmaids?

Thom: Do you even like Eve?

Me: Thom! She's my oldest friend.

Thom: I thought as much.

Me: Have you sorted out your best man yet?

Thom: I thought Rich.

Me: Of course. And when shall we do this thing? August?

Thom: Why not? If we do it near my birthday I'll have no excuse for forgetting our anniversary.

Me: Right. Done.

Thom: Another beer?

Me: Sure. We've earned it.

TO DO:
Relax. This stuff basically organises itself.

August 28th

Christ. Who knew you had to make an appointment just to try a dress on? Alice asked me where I'd booked, then had to explain it to me two or three times before I'd believe her. Not to be measured, not to be fitted, just to pull on a dress to see if you like it. Jesus. I've now made appointments at two wedding dress shops nearby for early September. Susie's booked Pete to be at home for once so she can leave Lily and Edward with him, and we'll have lunch and cocktails either side of the fittings. Is it wrong to feel like I'm doing charity work when I manage to take Susie out without the children? Giving her a window back into Living as an Independent Adult? Anyway, I'm led to believe the dress will be the trickiest bit of this whole wedding; Mum has demanded photos of everything I try on. I wonder if she bothered with all this for Dad?

18

Or did she find a dress in her local shop, get a matching hat and let the pub know there might be more of them than usual for lunch? I rather think he might have encouraged the latter.

TO DO:
Honeymoon – get guidebook for Indonesia
Think about ceremony and reception
Food – don't forget a veg option
Buy some more bridal magazines
Hen night?

August 29th

For the sake of posterity, I shall explain who some of the people in this wedding are.

Me: Bride. Full name Katherine Joan Carlow. Editorial Assistant at Polka Dot Books. Likes: almost all food, books, picnics, *Elle Deco*, Thom Sharpe. Dislikes: capers, oppression by the patriarchy, being made to watch snooker into the small hours.

Thom: Groom, Thomas William Sharpe. Accountant at corporate accountancy grindstone. Likes: twentieth-century literature, Kiki Carlow, snooker. Dislikes: most of his colleagues, anchovies, spending over £10 on three wedding magazines.

Susie: Sister of the bride, bridesmaid. Mother of the Twins, wife of Pete (a man whose passport has more stamps than a child's tantrum, and whose children have been known to confuse him with a delivery man, such is the frequency with which he arrives bearing a large parcel for them). Former leading light in radio production, now a stay-at-home mum. Incorrigible.

Rich: Best Man. Thom's oldest friend, boyfriend of lovely Heidi, computer programmer and expert pizza maker. Always welcome at our house. Especially when bearing homemade pizza.

Eve: Eve. Mmm.

I met Eve on the first day of secondary school, on the bus from the local streets of our little primary school in Finchley to the big scary comp from which we would spend the next six years dreaming of escape. She was tiny – a blonde sparrow, with thick lenses in the plastic frames of her glasses and an own-brand rucksack worn on both shoulders like a hiker. The space next to her was the only seat available, so Susie (chaperoning her baby sister) signalled me into it while she stood in the aisle, chatting to her own classmates and occasionally involving me in their conversations. Gathering confidence under the protection of my glamorous older sister I deigned to talk to this speccy mouse, and following Susie's lead, was as friendly as could be. We ended up sitting next to each other in every lesson for the next two years, until one September, Eve arrived back at school with contact lenses, breasts, and a sharp blonde bob. The ensuing attention resulted in the school authorities declaring us a bad influence on one another – ha! – and we were reduced to only hanging out every weekend, the bus to and from school and two hours on the phone each evening. We stopped being friends at the very end of the Upper Sixth, when Tim O'Connell, the crush I'd laboured under for a year and a half, finally got sick of Eve pushing her new cleavage at him and snogged her. We didn't speak for months. This was the start of a pattern: we'd visit each other at university, I'd let slip about a guy I liked, then I'd find Eve kissing him (or more) in broom cupboards, dark corners of nightclubs, brightly lit kitchens, even, at one memorable house party, my own bed.

20

I'd be so hurt and furious that I'd have no contact with her for months, then I'd find some old photos, or she'd be mentioned in conversation, and I'd start thinking: is she so bad? Really? And it would begin all over again.

But with Thom, it was so different. For a start, I didn't even tell her about him until we were moving in together; secondly, Thom has never liked Eve. He doesn't like the way she speaks to me, and he's no great fan of her past conduct, either.

So that goes some way to explaining why the phone call announcing our engagement went like this:

Me: Eve! It's Kiki! I've got some great news . . .

Eve: George Clooney's leaving his pig for you. You've found Atlantis.

Me: Nope. It's—

Eve: Hang on. [crashes about, away from phone] No, darling, you have to go! No, now. I'm sorry, it's a work call and I simply *have* to take it. [back on phone] Sorry. Some guy. Incredibly hot but with the smallest hands I have *ever* seen. Can you imagine some tiny ventriloquist's dummy manhandling you? Dummyhandling. God, I've absolutely no idea why I let him stay . . .

Me: Eve! Thom and I are getting married! [silence] Will you be my bridesmaid?

Eve: [long silence] Kiki, darling, can I give you a call back later? Little Miss Muffet can't find his way out. Love you!

Thom's asking why I'm writing my diary so angrily. I'd better stop for tonight before this page becomes shredded paper.

TO DO:

Rest of wedding party – best man, maid of honour, bridesmaids, ushers, ring bearer, flower girl

Find out if Thom is allowed to carry the ring himself, being
a grown man and everything

August 30th

I took Thom out tonight to the bar where we had our first
date. It happened a couple of days after we met; he 'found'
my number (thanks, Suse) and called me within twenty-four
hours, asking if I'd like a drink with him. Just him, no
heavy storage, he promised. I felt self-conscious as I still
had not only an enormous black eye, but also an eye-patch
that the doctor wanted me to wear for the next week, to
protect the – I don't know – eyeball, or something. But
speaking to him was so lovely that I said yes. Sure. Thank
you.

The night of the date I despaired of ever finding anything
to go with an eye-patch. I toyed with going full-blown
pirate, but just picked my favourite summer dress and
headed off to the bar, hoping I could hide most of the
patch under my hair. I got there first, and took a little
booth at the back, facing away from the door so I wouldn't
be looking up every time it opened. Then suddenly I was
aware of someone standing at my table. I looked up. It
was Thom.

Thom: [pointing to his own eye-patch] Well, if *this* isn't just
a coincidence.

With that, I was hooked.

An engagement ring! I hadn't thought too much about it until now, but my hand certainly did feel a bit light without one. Who knew picking a ring was an extreme sport?

We were using up the last of our summer days off at a dusty antiques market this morning, trying to find a suitably beige-and-purple (Mum's favourite 'tones') watercolour for Mum and Dad's anniversary present. Then Thom turned to me, grinning, and said, 'Let's find a ring.' Turning around the dark and plain hall, I felt pretty pessimistic about the whole thing, but Thom's face was so hopeful it felt mean to not even look. At the very first stall the man behind the table gave Thom a little smile and pushed a tray towards us. Off to one edge of the tray was the most gorgeous ring I'd ever seen – a pale gold band with a small ruby and two tiny diamond flowers off to one side. When I picked it up to try it on, it fitted perfectly.

Thom: Do you like it?
Me: Like it? This is . . . *perfect*.
Thom: Then it's yours.
Me: But how much is it?
Man at stall: To you two? £400.

Thom was grinning at me, but something in my stomach had shrunk from that figure. Yes, it was lovely, but it was also only £400. Weren't engagement rings the one thing that you'd wear forever and ever? I pulled him a little bit away from the stall.

Me: Shall we look at some shops in town?
Thom: But you love this! [laughing] Do you think it's too
    much?

23

Me: [queasily] It's just . . . aren't engagement rings supposed to cost one month's wages? It's got to be an extra-special piece of jewellery, to show how much . . . your husband . . . loves . . . you . . .

Thom: If that's what you really want, Kiki. [turning to vendor] Sorry mate. Looks like I was wrong.

It turned out that Thom had snuck over to the market a few days before, spotted the ring and, knowing I'd love it, asked the guy to keep it for me. Thom told me all about how special he knew I'd find it, with its own personal history and a unique story that no ring in a jewellery shop would ever have, of how it was originally made for a young wife by her new husband, with stones to signify passion and constancy for their life ahead. Unfortunately, he didn't tell me this until he'd turned off the light after finally coming up at midnight; he'd driven us home without talking and had been watching the TV in a terrible silence, until I'd lost my nerve and slunk off to bed alone. I'm writing this now in the bathroom by the shaving light, wondering whether my dearly beloved is tempted to call off the whole thing. Oh God. What have I done?

TO DO:
Dress – still needed?
Venue – as above?
Honeymoon – see if Susie is available to accompany me on the solo holiday I may need to get used to, in my new single life

September's Classic Wedding!

Everybody was asked to the *fêtes* of the marriage. Garlands and triumphal arches were hung across the road to welcome the young bride. The great St Michael's Fountain ran with uncommonly sour wine, while that in the Artillery Place frothed with beer. The great waters played; and poles were put up in the park and gardens for the happy peasantry, which they might climb at their leisure, carrying off watches, silver forks, prize sausages hung with pink ribbon, etc. at the top.

Vanity Fair
William Makepeace Thackeray

September 2nd

Thank bloody God. Thom went back to the market the next morning and bought the ring without telling me. I hadn't said one word to him since we'd left the market the day before (besides a whispered but heartfelt apology when I finally got into bed with him after writing this last night) and felt nauseous all the next day – what a horrible way to behave! When he came home last night with a poorly hidden smile and a tiny parcel of ring, I was full of promises and apologies, leaping at him like an overexcited puppy.

When I wore the ring to work today, Alice was in raptures over it, and even Norman raised an approving eyebrow. Carol could only muster, 'Couldn't afford a new one?' which earned a guffaw from Norman. He might not give two figs about your weekend plans or the small talk of an office, but I have my suspicions that he may actually be human after all.

Tony gave me Jacki Jones's email address so I could get in touch with her to start planning the book. Her agent is also her fiancé so I'm to avoid letting him know anything about the book, which, I have to say, is probably just about the worst business sense I've ever heard. Still, her wedding has been set for April next year, and the book will be rushed out to hit the shelves three weeks afterwards. Tony's promised me a definite promotion if this book works out. Not only a whole new job title (not Editorial Assistant – oh no – now I would be *Assistant Editor*. Woop!) but more money too (which in publishing terms probably means only enough money that I can switch from 'takeaway' to 'eat in' at the café at the corner, but still). And if I ever want to make it out of Polka Dot's hallowed doors and into the world of the big hitters, I need something like this under my belt.

TO DO:
Find out what we need to do for ceremony and reception
Guest book and photo albums?
Ceremony music – piano?
Wedding cake – classic cake? Something different?
Ultimately treat someone else's wedding as a great deal more
    important to me than my own

September 4th

Right, time to think about the engagement party. With some brief research (three bridal magazines and asking around the office) the trend seems to be for garden parties and gift lists. I think we'll just try the Queen's Arms: it's close to us and Susie, and it's nearish enough to the tube that people can roll around after work without too much labour. We'll try for next Friday, and allow a few rounds to be bought if the Moneybags Crew turns up from Thom's work. Thom can tell his lot, I'll tell mine, and we can flip a coin for anyone who falls into both or neither camp.

27

Dress day! What joy, what raptures! Who would have known that white floor-length dresses are the most flattering thing ever? Well, maybe Elizabeth Taylor. I thought it best to hedge my bets by booking us into an affordable place, as well as a more expensive option. We thought we'd work our way up, so started just off Oxford Street at the cheap place. And when I say cheap, I mean the wedding dresses are a bit less than £1,000. £1,000! Hahahahahhahaha! *£1000!* The absolute most I have ever spent on a single piece of clothing is £210, on a beautiful Jigsaw dress that was the most stunning thing I'd ever seen but in practice made me look like a gammon with the string left on. The 'Cheap Dresses' were even more lovely than that, and I was hugely surprised by trying on – and loving – the most Bridey McBriderson dresses, strapless and flouncy and lacy and glittering, like big white cakes. Oh, they made me so happy (them, or the champagne they gave us. One or the other). I felt like a royal-iced angel, and wanted more than anything for the walls to drop away to reveal Busby Berkeley dancers that would high kick and lift me around and around in a bridal wonderland. Maybe *that* was the champagne. I came out in one dress like a tulle snowball.

Susie: Oh, to have and to *hold*.
Me: For *rich*er, or for *poor*er?
Susie: I'm *sickness* for how in *health* you look.
Me: *Death* will not *part* me from this dress.

We were sniggering so much by then that the nice lady encouraged me to maybe take off the dress, so I did just that, waving goodbye to the beauty as we headed off with light, giddy hearts to the Pricey Shop, sure that we'd already seen our winners and only anxious over convincing Thom that his salary honestly could stretch to £950 for a dress I'd sport for ten hours. But then . . . Oh, *then*. The Pricey Shop wasn't just full of the most beautiful dresses, but the most beautiful everything. The carpet. The chairs. The changing rooms. Even the women in white gloves who helped me in and out of each dress. They only laughed politely when I asked if I could move in with them there. I, however, sighed piteously when, after three dresses, Susie said she didn't have much time left in town – Pete had something on in the evening so she had to get back to get the Twins in bed.

Susie:	I'm sorry, Kiki, but he did ask me yesterday, and I have been out all afternoon.
Me:	All afternoon? Bloody hell, move over Emmeline Pankhurst.
Susie:	Don't, Kiki.
Me:	What?
Susie:	Don't give me a hard time. He needs some time to himself too – while we've been gadding about like bridal pixies, he's been slaving over a hot desk. Give the poor lad a break.
Me:	[swallowing rage, sitting down next to her and slinging an arm around] Of course. I'm only sad that we don't have time for the post-wedding-dress-try-on paintballing I had booked.
Assistant:	Excuse me, madam, we have one more that may be what you're looking for.
Susie:	Ah, the old 'one more thing' trick. Worked for Columbo.
Me:	I don't think that's the same trick as Columbo's.
Susie:	Your *mum* doesn't think that's the same trick as Columbo's.
Me:	That doesn't work either.
Susie:	Shhhh. Look. They're bringing it.

Then . . . The Dress. It was Perfection in the form of Fabric, like music you only hear in your dreams, like food you remember from your childhood; familiar yet foreign. A simple white asymmetric sheath dress, with an organza overlay gathered at one hip in a large flower, and a matching silk tulle veil with a satin trim. I'm trying to not weep as I write this, but it was *so beautiful*. When Susie saw me in it, even she said, 'Wow. If it had been a toss-up between that dress and the Twins, Pete and I might have a house with fewer crayon scribbles right now.' The only fly in this Ointment of Delight is the price. £2,300.

I haven't *quite* mentioned the price to Thom yet.

TO DO:
Sell kidney (or even better – see if Thom needs both of his)
   for wedding dress
If that fails, see if can barter one of the Twins instead

September 13th

God, I feel sorry for Thom sometimes. How does he bear working there? He told me, laughing, that when he'd been inviting people from his office, the reactions varied from 'Where's your list?' to a baffled 'What kind of venue is it?' I despair. It's A PUB. You might have heard of them? What a strange bunch they truly are. So we shall just wait and see which of them shows up, but in the meantime we've got a yes from Suse (although Pete may be in Malaysia, lucky guy), from everyone at work, from my lovely old friend Jim, Rich and Heidi, and Nick and Rose, friends from uni. Eve says she's got a hot date that night, but will swing by if it all falls through. I've dug out my gorgeous blue dress (dry clean only – number of times worn previously: one) and Sheila the Landlady has put some extra champagne on ice for us. Done.

September 15th

I finally got in touch with Jacki today. She hasn't worked out how to put hearts underneath each of her exclamation marks, but I do slightly feel like I've been molested by a giant glittery bunny nonetheless. This was her final email of the day:

From: Jacki Jones
To: Carlow, Kiki
Subject: Hey!!!!!

Hi Kiki!!!
I hope you don't think I'm loopy, but I'm totally completely excited about this project!!!; I know we can sort out all these questions you've got. Let's meet up!!! You're such a gem to be helping me (I think I'll have loads of questions) and I'm sure we can make this book as brilliant as the wedding itself!!!! Bring a list of everything you've been asking me and we'll find an answer for all of it!!:

I'm free tomorrow 10–12 – do you want to come to Leon's office?! How exciting!!!!

See you then,
J xxxxxxxx :)

I'm sure this will all be fine.
  : (

September 16th

Today's meeting went well, but I take it all back. It wasn't a fluffy glitter bunny; it was a fluffy glitter bunny ROBOT. Jacki is the most amazing machine – which is no great surprise, given her swift and inexorable rise from catalogue model to TV soap actress nobody to household name. She is efficient and professional, and incredibly, unbelievably fond of (shudder) All Things Girly. But she's lovely. It's just that conversation with her is slightly unnerving, like your washing machine suddenly insisting you deserve a pedicure.

TO DO:

Actually start looking at some ceremony and reception options

Check whether Jacki has her own staff for this wedding, or whether Polka Dot are expected to plan it for her as part of our 'publishing' deal

Start thinking about guest list

Discuss with Dad while Mum isn't about who we absolutely have to invite

Get Thom to ask Alan and Aileen who needs to be asked from the Sharpe branch

Do I have to invite the whole office? Does Thom?

Florist – visit local florist on high street, get rough estimates

Save the date cards – necessary?

Wedding cake – start collecting images of cakes I like from magazines (this may turn into a slightly food-porny book of cake pictures)

September 18th

Heyyyyy! Great

Sorry, I may have slightly fallen asleep writing last night. It was such a great time, is what I think I was probably saying. Three people from Thom's work turned up – Paul, Robert and a really sweet girl called Luisa who's just started there as an intern. She looked about fourteen but was incredibly nice and bought us a bottle of champagne because she felt so bad for 'crashing our party'. Susie was unbelievably drunk (having slugged most of that bottle) and started the dancing at 10pm, in which she was joined by Alice, Jim and Heidi. Someone had brought party streamers and we were all tangled up in them. Purely due to not wanting her to feel like I wasn't in the spirit of things, I eventually joined in too, grabbing Sheila the Landlady's hand and doing the Twist. Suse and I set that place on fire! Not literally. But we Carlows can certainly shake it. That's all I'm saying.

At one point, Thom and I found each other in the crowd, and managed to get out into the fresh air together.

Thom: This all seems like good fun, doesn't it.
Me: Are we really doing this wedding thing?
Thom: Looks like it.
Me: I'm really happy.
Thom: Me too. I'm glad you said yes. If you hadn't, I'd have had to go with my backup girl. And she isn't too bright. [taps head]
Me: You are so romantic.
Thom: [picking me up, hugging me really tight]
Me: Hulk *happy*.
Thom: Yeah, I suppose Hulk happy. And if you buy me a drink I'll show you how easy I am when we get home.

God, I ache today. Hulk *dance*.

September 25th

I haven't spoken face to face with Eve since I told her about the engagement – I thought she took it well (for her), but she didn't take it well enough to make it to the party (that hot date was a success, apparently). But I don't blame her. Weddings are never particularly heart-warming when yours is still broken, and I know she isn't really over Louis (soul of a cockroach, hair of a god); they'd been together for three years by the time she finally woke up and realised love doesn't mean trying to make your loved one go completely mental with jealousy. She dumped him on her birthday last year when he turned up to her party with a drunk girl on his arm. God, he was good looking, though.

When she rang yesterday asking if I was free at the weekend, I had to tell her we had plans at Susie's. But she was eager to see us all, and asked if she could tag along and bring her new squeeze, the date she'd missed our party for; someone she'd met through her work as a fast-rising star in the charity world. Eve's so utterly charming that although she started as an intern at her charity for London's vulnerable people only two years ago, she's rocketed up the ladder and now has her own assistant (who she says is so useless it's more of a curse than a blessing), business cards, and even gets to *travel* for work (mainly to other UK cities, admittedly).

Susie knows her of old, and it was only a barbecue, so there we were: huddled around the grill in Susie's back garden with Susie's lovely friends Maggie and Eric, trying to pretend summer hadn't entirely given up on us, as Suse

34

tried to remember which country Pete was in today. Then Eve arrived, carrying a giant bunch of peonies for Susie in one arm and her date on the other. When she pulled him into the back garden, my mouth fell open, and when I swung my gaze towards Thom, his had done exactly the same. Eve's new boyfriend – oh, how does she find them – was the very man we had witnessed proposing in Bath. Steve. Jilted Steve. Dr No. The Refused. How was that possible? How could fate be so kind/unkind as to bring him to us again? We just goggled at him for a while, but Steve, thank God, had no idea we'd seen him at the site of his knock-back. By his fifth bottle of beer, however, it was clear that Jen's rejection had caused him to jettison his social skills entirely. Susie and Maggie were really enjoying him in a car-crash sort of way until the conversation took a fatal turn.

Steve: That's all well and good, guys, but you can't really *trust* women, can you? I mean, I'm sure you had your reasons, Eric, but you can't say that you don't realise what a huge mistake it was to marry. Every day, right? [roars with manic laughter]
Eric: Actually, Steve—
Steve: You know it! All women are *liars*, cheats and deceivers. All they want is to grind a man under their heel, *grind* him *down* . . . *break* him . . . [sobbing]

Even Eve had the sense to look uncomfortable by that point, tearing herself away from an ill-at-ease Thom who she'd been talking to at the edge of the garden (had she been backing out of bridesmaiding?). She dragged Steve into the kitchen to 'help her with drinks' and they left without sticking more than a goodbye arm back in the garden. Susie told Lily and Edward that it was worth remembering that actually, women were particularly brilliant, and the Twins responded by rote: 'Gene Tierney, Aung San Suu Kyi, Marie Stopes and Marie Curie.' Susie patted them both on the head and gave them a fruit kebab. Something tells me we won't be seeing Steve again.

September 29th

Further emails with Jacki have confirmed that she has all her own staff for the wedding – the venue is booked, the dress is designed, the food arranged and even the hen party organised. From the little I've had to do with her, I'm not remotely surprised. But I am surprised to discover how much I like her: she's not only incredibly professional and sweet, but pretty funny too.

We had this correspondence yesterday:

> From: Carlow, Kiki
> To: Jacki Jones
> Subject: Engagement?
>
> Hi Jacki,
>
> Will you be happy to include details of how you and Leon got engaged in the book?
>
> Thanks again,
> Kiki
>
> From: Jacki Jones
> To: Carlow, Kiki

Re: Engagement?

Hi Kiki!!!!!!

I am more than happy to have that in there. But we may need to freshen it up for the readers! I'm not sure how much they'd like to hear about me just grinding him down until he proposed.

Jacs xxxxxxxxxxxx

TO DO:
Probably don't recommend Jacki's book to Steve.

October's Classic Wedding!

ROMEO
Ah, Juliet, if the measure of thy joy
Be heap'd like mine and that thy skill be more
To blazon it, then sweeten with thy breath
This neighbour air, and let rich music's tongue
Unfold the imagined happiness that both
Receive in either by this dear encounter.

JULIET
Conceit, more rich in matter than in words,
Brags of his substance, not of ornament:
They are but beggars that can count their worth;
But my true love is grown to such excess
I cannot sum up sum of half my wealth.

FRIAR LAURENCE
Come, come with me, and we will make short work;
For, by your leaves, you shall not stay alone
Till holy church incorporate two in one.

Romeo & Juliet
William Shakespeare

October 2nd

Oh Christ. I think I'd forgotten that we'd really have to invite
people to this shindig. Talked briefly with Thom about doing
it just with family somewhere quiet, and his face lit up. 'Yes!'
he said. 'We can do it so cheaply!' Then I remembered The
Dress and mumbled something about us having to learn to
be sociable. I've been working on it all morning, and so far
I've got:

Me & Thom
Susie & Pete (if he's in the country)
Twins
Mum & Dad
Thom's Mum & Dad (Alan & Aileen) (10)

Eve & her +1 of doom
Jim and his +1
Alice (& Gareth?)

Carol (& husband Vincent)

Norman from work & his +1? (Does Norman have a special someone? How can none of us know this? What goes on behind that silent façade?) (10)

Rich (Thom's best man) and his girlfriend Heidi

Dave, Jules and Andy and their +1s, and Ben & Hester (Thom's school pals) (went to Ben & Hester's very drunken wedding a few years ago but we haven't seen the other three since then)

Six boffins from Thom's uni course and their +1s (names from Thom – have only faint memories of them)

Fiona (my first boss) and her boyfriend Mark

Nick & his fiancée Rose, Tim, Clare and Sara (uni house-mates) and their +1s (haven't kept in particular touch with Tim and Clare, but can't invite some and not all)

Five of my course-pals from uni and their +1s (lived briefly with Lucy after graduation and see her about twice a year, but mainly get news of the others from her) (they were utterly hilarious at uni, though)

Ruby, Ella and Vuk (friends from travelling) and their +1s

Other Tom from terrible holiday job I did when I was 17, and his +1 (50)

6 aunts, 7 uncles and 15 cousins between me and Thom (mostly me), including the v entertaining wonder that is cousin Emma (28)

8 horrible sweaty men from Thom's previous accountancy division with their anorexic, thick-haired public-school girlfriends/wives

10 horrible piggy men from Thom's current accountancy division with their slimdim Eurotrash girlfriends/wives

2 quite nice men from Thom's current accountancy division and their also-nice girlfriends

1 horrible fat sweaty boss from Thom's current accountancy division with his brutal, cold-eyed wife, living in terror that she's about to be usurped by one of the Eurotrashers and she'll be left with only their eight-bed townhouse, the Courchevel ski lodge, the New York apartment and the villa in Nice to comfort her (42)

So, as it stands, that makes 140, and that doesn't include the 'family friends' I'm sure Mum will insist on. It's fine. We'll get that down. Jacki's will be over 400, she tells me, so really it's still a nice quiet number.

October 3rd

It turns out that venue hunting is basically just like house hunting, with the only difference being that I will never get to live in places with a ballroom and an east wing. The money is just as eye-watering, though, and the venues themselves make me queasy in the same way that Alice's Hermès handbags do: I don't *want* to pour a cup of tea inside it, but the mere fact of its existence in proximity to me means it *could* happen. And I might, could, burn down a wedding venue. One careless sparkler, one stray sky lantern, and England has lost one of its top beautiful buildings (but also an entire wunch of bankers and accountants, so maybe the *Daily Mail* will go easy on us after the event). Thom was supposed to come, obviously, but his work was so horrific this week that he has to go in this weekend too. He was hugely apologetic last night, but I can see how stressed he is, so I smiled and said I didn't mind at all, that I'd give him a full debrief and he wouldn't miss a thing. He suggested I take Susie instead, but when I called her she said Pete was due back from a trip from which he'd be really jetlagged and the Twins had friends coming over, so she was stuck there.

When he left this morning at 7am, Thom gave me a kiss on the tip of my nose and said, 'I hope you have a nice day. What about Alice?' I told him I wasn't sure she'd want to, but sent her a text to find when she woke up, giving her the rough breakdown of the day, and saying she could join me at any of the venues if she fancied. I got a text back immediately: WITH YOU IN 30 MINUTES.

She was as good as her word, and I made us a pile of bacon sandwiches to keep us going while she outlined quite how lucky I was that things had turned out this way.

Alice: I'm truly sorry that Thom can't make it today, but you are now in the safest pair of hands there is. I've seen it a hundred times, Kiki, people get swept away by a nice staircase or a draped ceiling, and their numbers and plans go out the window. I'm not going to have you signing up to some townhouse rip-off just because the lady spoke nicely to you.

Battle-ready, we aimed for three of my shortlisted venues today, and there was a definite fleeting thought at their prices that if this is a business they can sustain, something is seriously wrong with the world. Who has that kind of *money*? (Besides Alice and her family.) And why aren't they spending more of it on C-list celebrity autobiographies and cookery books that are tenuous tie-ins from successful but un-cooking-related television series? (See Polka Dot's *The Duchess's Diet*, with some poor model done up like a *Downton Abbey* extra.)

First stop today was Fairley House, a Georgian townhouse just off Hampstead Heath, its chequered path shaded by two elegant plum trees. The house looked beautiful from the outside, but was actually quite dark and poky inside. I had a horrible feeling in the pit of my stomach – how to tell them it wasn't right, without offending them or convincing them that I simply couldn't afford it. After five minutes and a swift tour of the space, Alice looked disappointed.

Alice: Thank you so much, but this really isn't what she's looking for.
Me: [shocked] *Alice*.
Alice: It's too small for us, the lighting's wrong and the flow-through from dining room to ballroom isn't ideal.

And that was it. 'Alice!' I said out of the side of my mouth, trying to smile coolly at the staff as we walked out. 'You can't just *tell* them that.' She turned and took my elbows. 'Kiki, this is their business. It's not their first born. You need to *focus*.' It's then that I realised that Alice was right, and I was lucky to have her. Sorry, Thom.

She was equally relentless with the other two places. One had mould in one corner of the main hall (Me: 'It's . . . vintagey?' Alice: [hissing] 'It's a bloody *airborne toxic event*') and the other was decorated like a gentlemen's club, circa 1905 (Alice: 'Still, better than a gentlemen's club circa 2005'). We were still without a venue at the end of our day, but Alice had some great leads for me; places in less salubrious areas of London, but central enough that I would still pay a reassuringly eye-watering fee.

October 7th

Rose rang me today, of Nick and Rose (the Noses as we think of them), due to marry in May. I do like them so much, even if they do have more money these days than seems sensible for anyone who is not a national public service. But they are actually very sweet, and I've known Nick for years, back when he was one of my university housemates with big City plans. Rose turned him from potentially a fairly revolting Banker Playboy into a middlingly revolting City Worker (slightly lower down the revulsion ladder) and although they still do things like buy new plasma flat-screens for every room because Sony have released a new generation model, they are funny and very thoughtful for Rich Folk. After small talk, Rose seemed to want to say something else to me.

Rose: Kiki?
Me: Yes, Rose? [thinking, Please don't ask about that time
        Nick and I kissed when we were nineteen. For every-
        one's sake]
Rose: [deep breath] I'd like you to be my bridesmaid. Well,
        one of my bridesmaids. What do you say?

I didn't say that I was deeply surprised and slightly perplexed, both by the offer and the manner in which it had been ordered of me. I screwed up my face, knowing she couldn't see me, and said I would be honoured. She's so lovely, but I genuinely cannot fathom why she would want me to be her bridesmaid. It is kind of her, though.

TO DO:
Subtly investigate whether Rose will make us wear the ugliest
   dresses she can find

October 8th

A strange moment with Carol today. She'd been having her usual conversation with charmless Simon, head of our Sales team, in which she battled to get some sales figures out of him during what he clearly saw as his brilliant one-man comedy routine. It ended, as always, with Simon's weary sigh that 'Some people don't have a sense of humour,' as Carol shook her head with tight-lipped resignation. Then Alice grabbed Carol and me for sandwiches at the café on the corner, and I thought while we were out of earshot of the office, now was the time to probe into Norman's marital status. But when I asked if – for my wedding numbers – he had a special someone, Carol went white as a sheet and said she wasn't hungry anymore, and we'd have to go on without her. Alice and I looked at one another, wide-eyed. Is there – Does she – *Are they* . . .? Must now *definitely* continue my investigation.

October 12th

I made a big pot of stew and dumplings as Mum and Dad were over at ours tonight. (Could stew be a possible wedding meal? Christ, no, not in August.) When we sat down to eat, Dad said thoughtfully, 'You might know that we gave your sister a little bit of money after they'd married – obviously there wasn't much expense on their wedding, bar the cider and doughnuts, but we'd like to offer you that same start, if you want it.' I leapt up to give him a hug, and remembered that I ought to thank Mum too. Dad just nodded his head and smiled at us both, while Mum fussed with her napkin a little, unsure of what to say at this rare moment where we were all happy. Thom said how kind that was, and maybe, Kiki, we could think about putting it into our house-deposit fund, as our wedding surely wouldn't cost a huge amount, would it? I hem-hemmed a bit, and asked as sweetly as I could how much we were talking; I knew Suse and Pete had got £3,000 seven years ago, so was enjoying the thought of some inflation working in my favour.

Bad news. Inflation is apparently not applicable within families. £3,000 might just cover the venue costs if we marry on a Tuesday in February. That house deposit is not going to be hugely swollen by this gift.

October 14th

Jim is one of my oldest friends, after Eve. Fortunately, that's exactly when I met him: after Eve did, meaning that she'd already had her claws into him and he'd developed an immunity. They are civil enough to one another, but I get the sense that they each like to pretend I'm not particularly good friends with the other one. More than anything Jim's a kind man, one who is small on dredging up the past and big on simply being nice, and who lives a low-key yet secretly glamorous life as a session pianist. At a small bar near his studio, his response to my engagement was notably different to his ex's:

Jim: Enough about my fascinating world of popstars and the soundproofing of recording studios. And we all know that it is fascinating. Tell me a little bit about yourself.

Me: Well, Jim. You know that fellow I've seen once or twice?

Jim: Thom. I'm aware of his work.

Me: It seems he wants to marry me.

Jim: Oh, well done! [sees my face] Sorry. Not well done. Well . . . engaged?

Me: I suppose that'll do. Why are women congratulated

	on their engagement like they've been tracking their prey with a blow-dart for several years?
Jim:	[opens mouth]
Me:	Don't. It's too depressing to continue down that line of thought. Do you think you might come?
Jim:	I'm sure I can't think of anything I'm doing that night. Whichever night it'll be. Do you want me to do the music?
Me:	Oh, Jim, that's so kind, but Thom and I haven't really discussed the music yet. I'm not sure if we're going with something more . . . music-y – dance-y – or something.
Jim:	Ouch! Maybe we should leave that discussion there, don't you think? Well, great news for both of you, tin-eared bastards that you may be.

Oh, he's some kind of good friend. Jim also reckons he's done a couple of gigs at country houses in the area and will find out if mates' rates are available for weddings there.

October 18th

Bloody hell! Investigations bear fruit: Alice confirms that Carol and Norman are, in fact, 'an item'. But apparently they are top-secret-hush-hush, and Alice only knows because she came back into the office late last night to pick something up, and found Carol and Norman smooching against the temperamental photocopier-printer. I felt my gorge rise a little bit, but Alice said I was a prude and we should celebrate Love In All Its Forms. Not when it's getting all over my printouts, I won't.

October 19th

Raff Welles came into the office today. He's an ageing comedy actor from the seventies, famous for catchphrases that may have swept the country at the time but now don't mean anything to anyone but the most hardened vintage TV and film fans. He's charming and softly-spoken, always dapper – he plays the role of ageing and forgotten star to perfection. But he requires a *lot* of reassurance. We bought his memoir (called *AutobiogRaffy*, which I quite like) for peanuts, in the hope we could build some retro-wave for him to ride, but our legal team is working overtime to check his dangerously risqué anecdotes (can Sid James and Raff really have had an orgy with seventeen young nurses?) and it's turning out to be more work than we can possibly reap in sales. And Raff is in daily, requesting comfort, validation, and encouragement, that his semi-pornographic recollections of semi-forgotten actors is absolutely what the reading public has been waiting for. Our average conversation goes like this:

Raff: [pokes head around door, stage whispers] Hello! Hello all! Sorry to bother you all, working so hard!
Me: [keeps typing in the vain hope he'll get the message this time] Hello, Raff. [silence] How are you doing?
Raff: Oh, Kiki, it's so kind of you to ask. I thought I should pop in and help you with this book of mine – do you think we need more on X's alcoholism/Y's fetishism/Z's drug abuse and sexual aberrations?
Me: [gripping knees with claw-hands under the desk to keep from shrieking] Really, Raff, your book is brilliant as it is. I think you've really captured the fun/darkness/cultural importance of those times, and it's best if we all focus now on what we can do to promote the book in March.

Raff: Promotion! Goodness! Of course, you'll need me out in front of the public again. Yes, you're quite right, I'll start thinking about appearances. I'm sure Wogan will want me again – he'd better do, after that party I threw him in '78. But are you sure this book is right for today's audience? I'm sure they can't care about me, can they?

Me: [momentarily tempted to answer honestly] Raff, this book is going to be perfect. Your writing is fantastic and it will be the perfect gift book for anyone who's ever watched TV. Honestly, Raff, just let us take care of this now. You've done a brilliant job with your book and you should be very proud.

Raff: Marvellous! Kiki, you are a wonder of the world. Thank you all! [leaves, entire room sighs with relief]

It doesn't seem like much, but when he's round to Polka Dot Books *every afternoon* I despair of him, then always remember Raff's six marriages – ending up again and again with the One Who Didn't Stay. I'm so happy with Thom, and I'm reasonably sure that neither industrial quantities of uppers/downers nor Hollywood producers shall come between us. And that thought makes me feel a little bit warmer towards poor Raff.

TO DO:
Get some invitation samples
Caterers – match to colour scheme? Fish if blue colour scheme, steak if pink, etc.
Start investigating any friends' special dietary requirements (so can ensure we don't invite them hahaha)
Look into photographers
Car or transport – will we need it, or will ceremony and reception be at the same place? How far will it be? What's available?

October 22nd

Speaking of photographers, Jacki has requested 'Pedro' as the photographer for the book. They started their careers at roughly the same time and have travelled up the ladder together – but I imagine our profit on this book will be approximately 3p per copy, such are Pedro's fees these days. At least when Polka Dot Books goes bust we can all sleep on the streets under the beautiful glossy images we'll have produced. And I do look forward to meeting him.

October 24th

Alice and I are still searching for the right place, after having seen twelve venues. They all pull faces when I say we're looking at August dates, and some of them suck their teeth like plumbers as they flick through their desk diaries. 'August?' they say, as if I've asked whether they could manage tomorrow night. Some of them shake their heads at me – Sorry, love, I wish I could, their plumber equivalents would say – but some of them flick back and forth, back and forth, pretending to calculate something, before saying, 'Yes, I think we'd be able to do that.' I wonder if the fact that you can't cross a road around here without running into a wedding venue means that the demand isn't what it used to be, but there are several that can fit us in, even though I don't think they're quite right.

TO DO:
Keep looking

For the most part, the authors we work with – like Jacki – are lovely. They're professional, most of them having worked in the public eye for several years already; they're prompt, thoughtful, helpful and co-operative. Then there are the other 49%.

These authors would be a nightmare to work with even at a Trappist monastery. They are selfish, greedy, needy babies who need their hands holding and their noses wiped. Some of them are sexually aggressive (a knock on Alice's hotel room door at 11pm, a memoirist in a towel saying, 'It's a beautiful night. Would you like to come skinny dipping with me?' Alice: 'We're in Slough, not Thailand. I *think* I'll leave it, thanks'), some of them spoiled (I spent four days sourcing an antique tiara for one author. What's almost worse is how much she's worn the damn thing), some of them merely drunks. One of our authors, a 'towering master of suspense' (– *The Times*), insists that he must be chaperoned to every event we want him to do. It's not so much that he wants company, but that he needs someone to carry the bottle of whisky he requires for each appearance. We have to wrap it in a plastic bag so he can reach in, swig from it and not be spotted. Right. Because that's so innocent-looking. I've been to one party with him where he was so drunk, he offered another guest some wine, then carefully poured a glass's-worth into his cupped hand. When she didn't seem about to sip from his upturned palm, he looked puzzled at the situation he found himself in, then reached forwards and wiped his hand down the front of her friend's jacket.

I've had other authors for whom writing a book is the scales on which all their woes and successes balance. If it goes right, we are their best friends in the world, and our office is filled with chocolates, flowers, champagne. If things don't go according to plan, we are the Destroyers of Hope, the Evil Forces of Capitalism. When one author – let's call her Mary – received only a three-star review from *Time Out* magazine for her World War Two romance, she sent me an email saying simply: 'This makes me seriously consider leaving the country.' She spent the next three days making mock-inquiries into how she could write from France/Germany/Japan, until the *Telegraph* did a five-star write-up and suddenly this was a home she could never dream of leaving. Unfortunately, the positivity didn't last: when her expected review got bumped from a magazine, she called me at 2am, screaming: 'I'm going to KILL MYSELF and it's going to be YOUR FAUUUUUULT!' I listened for a while, then said, 'Sorry, who's calling please?' She was so taken aback that she halted her wails and her social conditioning kicked in. 'Oh, sorry. It's Mary. Who's this?' I briefly considered putting on an accent and claiming it was Ingrid, and who *was* this, but I told her it was Kiki, and asked was there something I could do? Her pace had been lost now, her stride broken, and she couldn't work herself back up again. She ended up talking for an hour and a half about how her grandmother had recently died and she wasn't coping well with everything. I listened to her until she started to nod off, and said we could talk more the next day. She hasn't mentioned it since.

November's Classic Wedding!

Lucy, the time has come and gone. I feel very solemn, but very, very happy. Jonathan woke a little after the hour, and all was ready, and he sat up in bed, propped up with pillows. He answered his 'I will' firmly and strongly. I could hardly speak; my heart was so full that even these words seemed to choke me. The dear Sisters were so kind. Please God, I shall never, never forget them, nor the grave and sweet responsibilities I have taken upon me.

Dracula
Bram Stoker

November 8th

Delights! Today was Jacki's first photo shoot for the book, and it was beautiful weather. We met at a studio in Chiswick with a gigantic garden, where the prop trunks and outfits were being unloaded from three giant trucks. It didn't matter much though, as Jacki's team were STILL working on her hair and makeup two hours after our official start time. By 12.30 we were all finally ready and in the studio: me, Jacki, Pedro the photographer, his team, her team, and the caterers. We had fifty-six dresses, thirty veils, forty-nine pairs of shoes and a whole case of tiaras, stockings, gloves, fascinators, wraps, boleros, boas, fans, parasols, pearls and diamonds, not to mention the props for the shoot: flowers, bunting, bird cages, fairy lights, lanterns, flags, wreaths, signs, puppies, topiaries, vases, tealights, place names, chairs, tables, sofas, marquees, tents, tiered cakes, cupcakes, invitations, save-the-date cards, tissue paper bells and balls, favours, pompoms and chickens. OK, fine, not chickens.

Pedro is a tiny, glamorous *monster*. He can't say a nice word to anyone who isn't famous or important (but is utterly charming to those who are) and treats Jacki like a trained monkey, but he takes the most beautiful photos in the world. I was making notes after lunch in the one corner of the studios that wasn't covered in lace and glitter, and he saw me.

Pedro: Katy?
Me: No.
Pedro: [apparently unaware I'd spoken] I'm tired, I need a little coke. Go and sort me out, would you? [seeing my face and getting *all* the wrong ideas] Ask my assistant for money, if *that's* your problem. [sneers, walks off]
Me: [wishing I had the courage to shout after him, instead of muttering] I'm not your fucking . . . *drug dealer*.

I was beyond furious, both with being put in this position and with the idea that I might be killed in the Colombian drug warfare I was reasonably sure occurred anywhere near any Class-A drugs ever, and thought of Thom having to go to our wedding alone because I'd been mown down in a W4 gun battle. I got so angry I marched straight up to Pedro and tapped his assistant gently on the shoulder before asking her if I could have a quiet word. Pedro gave me another smirk as she led me into the corridor, where I had probably the most embarrassing conversation of my life.

Me: Zoe. I really like my job, and there's so much variation and adventure and . . . colour . . . and Polka Dot Books are so honoured to be working with Pedro on this project, but . . . sometimes the job demands hit a wall, you know?
Zoe: Kiki, I'm really sorry. Has he propositioned you?
Me: No! No! Hahahahahahaha! No! He hasn't. He asked me to get him . . .

Zoe: Oh God, not a prostitute?

Me: No! Why, do you have to get him prostitutes? Don't
       answer that. Actually – maybe they'll help. He asked
       me to get him . . . some coke.

Zoe: Oh God. Kiki. This is awkward.

Me: Tell me about it. Where the hell am I going to get
       drugs in Chiswick at noon on a Tuesday?

Zoe: [not sure if I'm joking, clearly] No, Kiki. He means
       a coke. A drink. That's it. A coke. He's clean as a
       whistle drug-wise these days. He just likes being a
       total and complete prick instead. He's done this gag
       to a few assistants in the past. He thinks it's really
       funny.

Me: I'm fairly sure I'm about to die now.

Zoe, may heaven rain down blessings upon her for all
eternity, grinned at me and mimed locking her lips and
throwing away the key. I couldn't bear to be in the same
room as Pedro at that moment, so I walked to the corner
shop and bought six cans of Coke with my Polka Dot credit
card. There's something unbelievably forlorn about putting
four quid on your corporate credit card, but I was damned
if Pedro would have anything from me bar my extremely
efficient but ice-cold presence at his bloody photo shoot. I
left them on his table and ensured I kept as far away from
him as possible for the rest of the day – a feat not made
easy by the fact that I had to also remain within earshot of
Jacki at all times. This led me to spend almost an hour hiding
behind a pillar in one room, until Pedro shouted, 'Can
someone get rid of that bloody hairdo behind the post!' and
I walked out of the room without looking back, wondering
if Thom could marry me in prison once I've murdered a
celebrity photographer.

I stayed until 4pm when they'd switched to doing dress

shots indoors: they'll continue for the next two days there. I convinced Jacki that she didn't need me there for tomorrow at least, and I'd be back on Wednesday if she really wanted.

Don't tell me this job ain't glamorous.

TO DO:
Photographers are clearly nightmares – find out if we can take our own wedding photos (hold camera at arms' length and beam up into it)
Find out if I can get The Dress cheaper online
Find a wedding cake maker

November 12th

Jim's come through like a star. He called last night to say he's had luck with two of the houses he's gigged at. Wingfield Manor and Redhood Farm are willing to give us 20% discounts, meaning it would only be around £6,000 at either place. Now I need to frame this for Thom to make it sound as attractive and necessary as possible, and we will all be laughing (not least on our wedding day, surrounded by honey-suckle and rose sprays on the terrace of a beautiful old house while I pray no one's got drunk and attempted to throw an antique sofa in the lake, or whatever). Wingfield Manor is out of London a bit, towards Reading, but seems like a really charming old Brideshead Rejuvenated manor house; while Redhood Farm, while it looks utterly delicious from its pictures, is all the way out by Ipswich. Ipswich! That's basically Denmark.

Poor Thom has to work again this weekend. I'd feel a little bit cross but his job is making him so miserable right now that I know he'd do anything to not have to go in, and to come venue-shopping to the few remaining London venues with me. I'll take him in lunch both days, although I don't expect to eat with him – he'll just give me a frazzled thank you and a kiss, then he'll leave the food on his desk until 5pm when he suddenly realises he's starving, and vague memories of seeing me bring supplies will surface. Poor Thom.

I also know that in his absence, this is the kind of stuff I should be doing with my bridesmaids, but it's so depressing to always get the same response from Suse for this kind of thing, her stuck at home due to Pete's travels, and Eve's gone on a business trip for a fortnight. Even if Eve could come, I suspect she'd be trying to seduce the venue manager, or being cynical about everything I like. So Alice continues to be my man.

TO DO:
Flowers – decide what we want: boutonnières, posies/ bouquets, headpieces, centrepieces, runners, ceremony, etc.
Collect images of nice flowers
Research flowers in season in August
Wedding night – is there a bridal suite at the venues? Or a boutique hotel nearby?
Confetti – rice paper, petals, rice?
Wedding workout schedule? Work out how to pay for wedding hahaha
Also: plan workout for arms and abs (wedding dress danger zones apparently)

November 17th

Could this all be coming together? Is it as simple as that? Thom's being completely reasonable over the costs. Am I dreaming? Should it be so easy?

Thom's got a job that can pay for all of this, having joined his firm almost straight out of university, and he always seemed to enjoy climbing the greasy pole to senior accounting executive. Neither of us love the hours, or the colleagues, or the schmoozing, or really even the work ethic of parts of his firm, but since Thom gave up hope of getting something for which he could use his English degree, he's found a surprising clarity in numbers and a joy in managing them, corralling them into columns with sense and a purpose, turning symbols into someone's future (and not their bankruptcy). He likes helping people, and although this slippery career ladder has meant more money and tougher work, it's also meant the clients he's dealing with have leapt from emerging businesses with everything to learn and everything to lose, to multinationals who have the cunning of a business-school fox and the morality to match. It's still challenging work but in all the wrong ways, Thom says, and there are some days where all Thom wants to do is talk about where we'll live when he retires, which going by his ex-colleagues will be in his mid-forties. We won't be worrying about which child gets to go to university and which has to take an apprenticeship at the local black-smith. We're lucky – we have a car in London, a nice but tiny flat for just the two of us (rented), and we have a summer holiday and weekends away a few times a year. But we don't have an Aston Martin, and we don't go to those underwater hotels in Dubai, which is the absurd lifestyle I can see some people expect when they learn where Thom works and what he does. Instead Thom is always saving for something, insisting on Our Security in a manner that suggests he knows something incredibly grim about the future that I don't, but I know that the security he's building doesn't make up for how little he enjoys work now. It breaks my heart to see him, sometimes.

But he arrived home on fine form this evening, happy that he'd managed to sneak advising a small start-up businesswoman into his busy schedule, so I thought it was my chance to begin my delicate cracking of the tough wedding nut.

Me: Thom, there's something else I wanted to talk about, if you don't mind talking about the wedding right now. When I told Jim about our engagement, he said he'd talk to some of his contacts at the big houses round here, and two have offered discounts. They're really lovely and while their initial costs don't include food they are *really* beautiful, and the corkage fee at Redhood Farm is waaaaaay smaller than the other places I've looked at, and they bring champagne for the bridal party on the morning of the ceremony and can do it all within their buildings, and will organise the food from an external chef when you tell them what kind of food-mood you want . . .

Thom: Food . . . *mood*?

Me: Yes, food-mood, it's *huge* right now – and the photos at Wingfield Manor from previous weddings that I've seen on the websites are really amazing, and I think your mum and dad would *love* the gardens, and even you would approve of this place, really Thom, it's so nice. And although neither of them is exactly in London the trains are frequent and quick and there are *loads* of nice affordable places for people to stay nearby.

Thom: Kiki, it's fine. Let's do it. That's how these things work, isn't it?

Me: [rare silence]

Thom: And no, that's not a joke. Let's get this thing locked down.

60

So that's that. We're going next weekend to have a look at them both, and then we'll write the lucky venue a big fat cheque and I can stop fishing hairs out of the plughole (because my stress levels will decline and my hair will stop falling out, not because my hygiene standards will collapse).

November 23rd

Eve took me out tonight to a late night opening at the V&A, to make up for being away during the venue-hunt. In fact, I've not seen her since Susie's barbecue, although we've spoken a few times. I feel like she's somehow angry at me, but I don't know why, and I don't know why her nameless displeasure makes *me* feel guilty. I'm always scrabbling to make amends for something I haven't done.

Eve: How's the search been going?

Me: I think we've found our winner. Thom's coming this weekend to give the two finalists the once-over, then the deposit's paid and we're in.

Eve: That seems painless.

Me: Ugh. The number of places I've seen where I've been addressed simply as 'Bride'. 'Which one of you is *Bride*?' It's not painless. It'll scar me for years.

Eve: That sounds *dreadful*. Shall I tell you about some of the cases of homeless women and children I've been trying to get funding for this week? *You* could show them what a tough time *really* is.

Me: Ah, but if you'd been *with* me and not on one of your do-gooding missions away, I wouldn't be making these horrific claims on your sympathy.

Eve: OK. You're right, Kiki. You've taught me a valuable lesson I'll never forget.

Me: You're welcome.

We found our way to the ceramics rooms, and Eve linked arms with me.

Eve: Can we still do this even when you're married?
Me: I don't know. I'll have to ask Thom.
Eve: You joke, Kiki. I've seen it happen.
Me: You've seen a lot of things happen. I try not to think about all the things *you've* seen happen. Please let's not make predictions about my life based on the things you've witnessed in your job.
Eve: [makes wise face at me] You never know, Kiki, you never know.

I know you can't ever know, she's right, but when you're planning your wedding it feels nicer to at least pretend that your fiancé couldn't potentially be a control freak lunatic. I have no way of knowing the future, but it's classic Eve to make *that* the note on which she ends a discussion on my nuptials.

We spent the rest of our visit in the shop, wishing we could fill our homes with the prints, books and jewellery. While I chose a card for Dad's birthday tomorrow, Eve (of course) singled out the most beautiful object from the whole shop: a simple plate with a fish design, which I instantly lusted after once she'd picked it up. That dame has great taste.

November 27th

There has got to be a catch to all of this. First unlikely event: Thom didn't have to work this weekend. We visited both venues today, and Thom absolutely loved Redhood Farm.

62

We got up at the crack of dawn to manage them both properly in one day, and arrived at Wingfield Manor as the light was fading in and the mist rolled over the land. It was really lovely, light and pretty inside but something about the décor made me feel like I should be marrying in an off-the-shoulder meringue while my sister weeps blue eyeshadow down her cheeks. Put it this way: I would have gone crazy for it when I was seven. But after a few more hours in the car (it turns out it is *way* too easy to get lost in Suffolk) Redhood Farm was – like the dress – what I'd always been looking for without realising that I'd been looking for anything at all. It was charming and scrappy, full of colour and life and thoughtfulness, but professional and lacking in any of those dangerous witty little signs some wedding venues offer that make me want to abolish marriage altogether ('Make Way for the Mr & Mrs!'). It was aesthetically and emotionally everything I wanted for the day; laid-back, casual, gorgeous and unique. I knew we'd all feel comfortable here, every one of our friends and family, and Thom felt the same. The only thing he said, after taking me off to one side while the manager tried her best to look like she wasn't listening in, was, 'Are you sure this is the one you want? It's a lot of money, and I want this to be right for us. Is this really what you want to spend this money on?' I hugged him and said there was definitely no finer venue for us, and he smiled a bit. But to give him full credit, he didn't even cry when he – second unlikely event – wrote the deposit cheque for £2,000, just signed his name (I did check) and handed it over with a friendly nod. I'm so happy. This is going to BLOW EVERYONE'S TINY WEDDING MINDS (or something more fitting for gentle virginal white).

And on top of all that, it's Polka Dot's sales conference tomorrow. Fun times ahoy.

TO DO:

Block book accommodation locally – work out how many
    rooms we'll need

Make sure nicest rooms are reserved for Rowland & Fenella
    (Thom's boss and the wife)

Ceremony music – string quartet playing some Billy Joel?

Start taking skin vitamins

November 30th

Holy moly! I know Sales teams are notoriously tough but I
was not expecting that.

For a company of thirty people (only ten of which are full-
time), our 'sales conference' is really only a white wall, a
projector and some presentations in a room over the Stuck
Pig pub on the corner. It's normally fairly high-spirited, as
the people who don't usually work in an office together break
out of their cabin-fever and socialise with distant colleagues.
Plus we had fresh blood in the form of Judy the Intern,
keeping us on our toes as we all tried to behave like proper
publishers. The bar staff come up every thirty minutes or so
to top up our drinks, so by 3.30 it's usually pretty ugly, but
this year the drinks had been flowing faster than usual and
the Sales team really had it in for our books. They're a cynical
bunch, hardened by years on the road without colleagues
and convinced they are the lifeblood of Polka Dot, and they
refuse to pull their punches when talking about our titles.
It's probably the only chance they'll have to blow off some
steam about books they may find are not their cups of tea
– and normally nobody minds, since it does seem like quite
a thankless task to explain to a bookshop owner how much
they need the 500th incarnation of *Angel Hamsters* or *I'll*

Eat my Greens if You Don't Lock Me in the Shed Again, Mummy – but there was something in the air this year which made them much meaner than anything I'd seen before. Simon, self-proclaimed 'sales genius' and completely hammered, was declaiming to the room about some of the garbage he had to sell (never nice for an editor to hear; they clamp their lips and pretend they're thinking of something else), reeling off nasty joke after nasty joke about Jacki until I was digging my fingernails into my palms – just ignore him and he'll shut up – when he suddenly laid into *AutobiogRaffy*. Laborious as the publishing of a niche memoir may be, that book is Carol's baby and Simon really went to town on it, listing all the ways in which it was going to bomb. Carol's face was getting redder and redder, but she didn't say a word, just walked to the corner of the room, helped herself to a biscuit then busied herself tidying the books on the table at which Simon was perched.

Then Simon said, 'And books like that aren't helped by having *past-it* clueless old *jokes* like Norman working our numbers in the back office.' Carol turned to him for a moment, her face suddenly pale, before rearing back and pronouncing in her immaculate RP, 'Simon, you really are an absolutely un*bear*able *cunt*.' Carol then immediately burst into tears and Simon stood up, red-faced but un-bowed, still determined to prove once and for all that he was a prick. His audience turned away as one, and resolutely studied their printouts until Simon stopped drunkenly blustering and vomited down his Ted Baker suit. Carol kept crying until Judy led her away to the toilets and Tony declared we should probably leave it there for the day.

Dan from the Art team, eyes slightly boggling, turned to me and Alice and said, 'So that Carol – Norman thing is out in the open now?' I squealed, and demanded to know how *he* knew. He said that after work one night, Norman had asked his opinion on the necklace he'd bought for Carol's birthday, but sworn Dan to secrecy. I have *got* to start working late.

TO DO:

Find out if Redhood Farm have all their own tables, chairs, chair covers

If not, look at rental prices for furniture that matches our colour scheme

Pick a colour scheme

First dance – choreograph?

Clothes for ushers and best man – suits, ties, boutonnières, shoes, socks (forbid bright fashion/novelty socks) (unless in line with colour scheme)

Organise tastings for wedding cake at different bakeries

Arrange swearbox for Carol at the reception

December's Classic Wedding!

Grace went out and bought a hat, and dressing for her wedding consisted in putting on this hat. As the occasion was so momentous she took a long time, trying it a little more to the right, to the left, to the back. While pretty in itself, a pretty little object, it was strangely unbecoming to her rather large, beautiful face. Nanny fussed about the room in a rustle of tissue paper.

'Like this, Nan?'

'Quite nice.'

'Darling, you're not looking. Or like this?'

'I don't see much difference.' Deep sigh.

'Darling! What a sigh!'

'Yes, well I can't say this is the sort of wedding I'd hoped for.'

'I know. It's a shame, but there you are. The war.'

'A foreigner.'

'But such a blissful one. Oh dear, oh dear, this hat. What is wrong with it d'you think?'

'Very nice indeed, I expect, but then I always liked Mr Hugh.'

'Hughie is bliss too, of course, but he went off.'

'He went to fight for King and Country, dear.'

'Well, Charles-Edouard is going to fight for President and Country. I don't see much difference except that he is marrying me first. Oh darling, this hat. It's not quite right, is it?'

'Never mind, dear, nobody's going to look at you.'

'On my wedding day?'

The Blessing
Nancy Mitford

67

December 2nd

Dinner at my parents' tonight. Mum and Dad's house is nice
– it makes me feel like a child again – but is also dreadful,
because it makes me feel like a child again. So I can kick my
shoes off and lie flat out on the sofa, watching the TV side-
ways, but it means too that everything about it bothers me:
the fussy lampshades, the boring wallpaper, the general
porridgeness of it. Dad's added some nice touches since he's
been working at the college and got to know the local arts
community – there are vases and pictures where before there
were only terrible satin-finish school photos of Susie and me
– but I still feel it's basically the house that taste forgot. It's
not ugly, it's just . . . dull. It makes me want to paint my
house daffodil yellow and fuchsia, only because it's not the
1960s anymore, no one can actually afford a house around
here. I'm just waiting for my parents and Susie to die, and
I'll be laughing. (*After* the funerals, of course.)

Mum had made her supremely delicious chicken tagine
with four hundred different spices (you know I love you,
Mum; although it's not *entirely* because you're an amazing

cook, that really doesn't hurt) and it looked like we were about to make it all the way through the main course without anyone mentioning the wedding. Then Mum said: 'Kiki darling, have you thought about letting me make your wedding dress? We can go through my old patterns to find something you'll like. Those full skirts are easy enough to do, and we can add decoration to that strapless bodice that everyone has these days, if that's what you'd like.' I pushed my plate to one side and put my head on the tablecloth and tried to imagine myself somewhere else. Thom put his hand on my shoulder. 'Keeks, do you think that might be helpful? Isn't that a way for you to get exactly the dress you want?' I raised my head and blinked to force the tears away, while my BLOOD BOILED. I tried to stay calm.

'Thom, I've found exactly the dress I want. When you factor in the stress of fittings with . . . someone you know, and the reliability of the designer brand, doesn't it seem like a false economy to have someone else do it? Everyone knows what a mistake it is to get family involved in stuff like that. Doesn't anyone remember how messy it can be when a relative teaches you to drive?'

We Carlows all took a moment to recall our beautiful family car, and how much less beautiful it had looked after my first driving lesson with Dad. Dad, usually Forgiver of All Sins, hadn't been able to talk to me for almost a week after that.

'Fine fine fine!' Mum said with a false cheery voice. Dad massaged his jaw with a pained expression and Mum took his other hand. 'Are you alright, love?'

Dad winced a little, then smiled back at her. 'I am, Tessa, I am. A bit of a sore jaw tonight. Too much chatting, obviously.'

I laughed. 'Obviously, Dad. We can never get a word in when you're about.' I felt Thom and Mum look at one another, but was grateful enough for the interruption to not chase that glance down and kill it bloodily all over the dining table.

TO DO:
Check waiting times and delivery times on The Dress

December 6th

Am I simply having troubles with my priorities? Or am I a monster? A growing suspicion that it's the latter. Susie invited us over for dinner last night, for Pete's birthday and some early Christmas cocktails. For once she actually had both booze and Pete in the house, and was sloshing the former merrily into beakers as soon as we'd walked in the door. We toasted one another, with all the festive spirit mulled wine invites:

Susie: To friendship!
Me: To brotherhood on the high seas!
Pete: To the kingdom of Neptune!
Thom: To mermaids!
Susie: To milkmaids!
Pete: To *milkmen*! Speaking of which, Suse . . .
Susie: Are we blaming it on the milkman this time?
Me: [a bit tipsy already, laughing] Wait, what? Are you pregnant or something?
Susie: [pausing] . . . A bit?

Thom whooped and grabbed Susie, then Pete, and gave them huge hugs. I was a bit staggered – pregnant? Due in July? Which would mean next year would be entirely about the new baby? A new baby which would be there crying and sicking milk up during our wedding? Jesus, no, I am a monster.

Susie looked like she'd been slapped when she saw me hesitating, so I gave her an enormous hug and told her that she would be the finest milk-machine at our whole bash. She didn't really like that either.

December 8th

Thom had a horrible day at work today. They have a new client, a 'nutrition group' conglomerate that includes all the no. 2 soft drinks, chocolate bars and potato-based snacks in Europe and Asia. They are rich, and powerful, and from everything Thom says they have a massive potato-based snack on their shoulder (accountant humour) from missing out on the no. 1 spot in every field. Apparently they spent $17 million on a marketing push in Korea which saw them hit the top for a fortnight, before they went back to their familiar, uncomfortable second-tier position. The men who came to deal with Thom today are hardly people you'd invite to a house party – pigs at best, full-on pricks at worst – but he's always aware of how nice he has to be to them so that his company can get a little piece of their money, of which they'll give an even smaller piece to Thom to keep his brain working on how to make these men a little bit richer, etc. Put it this way: when Thom talks about his job, it makes me want to bake a thank you cake for Carol and Tony and Raff and Jacki. And today was even worse than normal, because today Thom was supposed to show them some fascinating little Monaco loopholes which would make them jig all the way to the bank, and he'd spent the last week checking and double-checking all the figures and the byzantine laws that help rich men stay good and rich, and had everything lined up in a snazzy little presentation for them, neat and clear and simple. But when the time came to start pointing his clicker – or clicking his pointer, whatever – he found that the screen was empty, as was the computer file, as was his USB stick. His secretary came in and had a go too, but there was nothing to be found, and after ten minutes of staring at the company's most handsome meeting room (while enjoying the finest coffee and biscuits money can buy and spending the time not tapping their feet in silence but comparing notes on their holiday homes and children's school fees) the Gloucester Old Spots starting getting their bristles up, saying at slightly louder than shouting volume, 'Bloody joke of an accountant, this one,' etc. *Quel charme*. Thom took a deep breath and apologised for the 4,000th time, then from memory gave them all the facts they needed and passed around the very detailed and very boring document he had prepared over the last few days. But they didn't want to know. Of course, they *did* want to know, and they'll be back in a week or so to get the plotting plotted, but men like that enjoy knowing that Thom will receive a royal ticking off, probably from a former school chum of theirs.

Maybe Thom's been hoarding all our money for his flight to Mexico when they all finally get too much. Maybe not.

December 10th

Alice and I enjoyed a – cough cough – extended lunch hour today, starting on our Christmas shopping. We'd elbowed our way into Liberty to admire the beautiful homeware rooms, when Alice spotted a sign, nudging me: 'Wedding Lists available here'.

Me: [sighing] Oh, Alice.
Alice: Uh-oh. Don't 'Oh, Alice' me. I think this was an
        error.

72

Me: I didn't even want a wedding list before, but just
         think. . .
Alice: I am thinking. I'm thinking that if your fiancé finds
         out I'm to blame for you wanting your wedding list
         at Liberty, I won't even be allowed at your wedding.
         And that will make me so sad. [pulls exaggerated
         sad face]
Me: [laughing] Alright, alright, I surrender. But a wedding
         list does seem like bloody good fun, doesn't it?
Alice: I'm not sure I like that look in your eye, young Kiki.

I promised I wouldn't do anything to get her banned from
our wedding. She looked sceptical. How many other things
have I not even thought about yet?

December 11th

Tonight was Thom's work Christmas dinner. Every year they
hire out one of the huge banqueting halls in a London hotel,
invite everyone in the company, from the big cheeses to the
secretaries, give everyone a plus one and access to an open
bar, and let mayhem commence. We were on a table of twelve,
and although officially I was seated next to one of Thom's
colleagues, he had swapped places to talk shop on the other
side. Instead, I was next to his wife, Della – of a month, she
insisted on telling me – while Thom chatted to the woman
on his other side. Despite my best efforts, my eyes were
drawn inexorably down to her hand, which waited, fingers
tapping, to show the enormous ring. She laughed when she
saw me looking at it, saying, 'It's subtle, isn't it? Well, I
thought I certainly deserved a reward.' I thought: maybe I'm
being unfair. Maybe she gave her husband a kidney. *I'd* want
a giant piece of jewellery if I gave Thom one of my vital

organs. Although maybe I'd want it shaped like that organ: a lung-shaped pendant. A liver-shaped brooch.

Della: We both work so hard that I thought it would be nice to have something to show for it, you know? We're working over eighty-hour weeks, we bought our first place together before the wedding, and I knew a year ago that I wouldn't just want some tiny little thing [flaps hand as if it's almost too heavy to lift] for the rest of my life. D'you know what I mean?

Me: [trying to laugh] I do, actually! [lifts up hand]

Della: [looks mortified] God, Kiki, I'm so sorry. I'm really sorry. That's a beautiful ring, anyway. Was it one in the family he had to use?

Me: No, Thom chose it for me. It is an antique, though.

Della: [putting her head on one side] Oh, well, well done you. Flying the flag for anti-consumerism.

Me: [taking a deep breath] Della. What do you do?

Della: Oh, I'm in the City. I'm a compliance consultant.

She saw my baffled/uninterested face, and proceeded to describe her job to me, but I tuned out after a while. Here are the highlights:

It's mainly about managing client relationships [I start wondering how many strip joints she's had to take those clients to] and ensuring their prime point of contact . . . blah blah blah . . . promotion of services within assigned accounts . . . blah blah . . . winning engagements . . . increased fee incomes . . . blah blah . . . supporting a new business direction . . . blah . . . allocation of resources for productivity levels . . . Ten minutes later I'd necked four glasses of wine and she stopped pitching to me, and switched gears to talking about how terrible it was that people were clamouring for any kind of financial regulations, and criticising bankers was a dreadful bore and utterly self-defeating. I suddenly felt very drunk.

Me: How exactly is it self-defeating?

Della: Well, all the banks will just up sticks and go to Dubai, or Singapore.

Me: And is that a problem?

Della: Well, the banks pay billions of pounds of tax every year, don't they?

Me: But do they pay all the tax they should? Do they make our country's life better?

Della: [scoffing a little] Yes, they employ thousands of people. Not everyone is a senior executive, you know.

Me: Of course, that's true. So why do senior executives get so much?

Della: Because they all work so bloody hard.

Me: But what is that work? What do they do? Why couldn't other people do it? Hasn't there been a study to show traders are no better at trading than a rolled dice? What do they *add*?

Della: Oh, Kiki, that's a bit of a socialist, naïve view of things. We can't just run the country on nurses and teachers, you know?

Me: Can't we? *Can't* we? What's the intrinsic worth of the City jobs? What do they do for us? If the company set up just to employ those people didn't exist, who would employ them? It's like ouro . . . orrob . . . oroboro . . . shit. Maybe not that. But their employable skills are in an *incredibly* narrow band, aren't they? [trying to hold up fingers close together, to indicate narrowness] They don't make tables, do they, or build houses? [I'm faintly aware

75

of Thom tapping my arm] Do they? Or do you? Does your bank build a house? [Thom drags my chair away, with me on it, and swaps it with his, leaving me next to a smart looking woman in her forties]

New lady: She's bloody awful, isn't she? I had to sit next to her last year, and she spent two hours telling me that public sector teachers are a drain on the country.

Me: [sobering up] Sorry, I'm Kiki.

New lady: Liz.

Me: What do you do, Liz?

New lady: I'm a teacher.

After that, I had a gay old time, sitting with Liz and chatting about our work and families. But I felt Della and her husband glare scornfully at me for the rest of the night, before Thom got me home and gave me *quite* the talking-to.

If that's what you want to call it.

December 15th

Bad days. Tony invited me into his office today *just* to remind me how much we'd spent on Jacki's book, how much that represented of our annual budget, how much space our Sales team had had to beg for in the supermarkets, and how, basically, the first book I'd ever officially been given for Polka Dot would be the deciding factor in whether any of us got a bonus this year. 'So you'd better make sure this *Perfect Wedding* is pretty perfect, yes?' If I didn't think that thought about four hundred times a day anyway, I would have brought it to Tony's attention that

76

no one at Polka Dot had received a bonus in the four years I'd been working there. But thank you for the added pressure. I sulked back to my desk and tried to go over the publicity plan with Alice.

Then his mother arrived.

I could hear her coming from the other side of the building, clattering up the stairwell, banging her oversized golf umbrella against everyone and everything she could, calling out, 'Anthony! *Anthony!*' like her forty-seven-year-old son was a runaway pup. She knew exactly where he'd be, and eventually made her way into his office after knocking piles of books over and pushing paper off any surface she could reach. The door slammed, but we could still make out every word she barked at him.

Pamela: Anthony, what the devil is this I hear about a bloody wedding book? What kind of trash is this?

Aha.

Tony opened his office door.

Tony: [nervously] Kiki! Would you mind stepping into my office for a moment?

Pamela, apparently, is disgusted that we're publishing the book of a *soap actress*, convinced that we're essentially becoming *Heat* magazine because we've got a celebrity telling us her wedding plans. I'm unsure what the difference is between this book and any of the other celebrity stuff we've done in the past – could it be that people may actually have heard of this celebrity? – but Tony had told his mother that *I'd* bought this book, that he hadn't been happy about this but I'd argued him round and it was on

77

my head. Pamela looked me up and down and gave a snort.

Pamela: I hope you know what you're doing, young lady.

Tony gave me a beseeching look. I toyed for a moment with the idea of pleading innocence, of explaining the unlikelihood of me being able to buy so much as a dictionary for the office, let alone a red-hot celebrity wedding book, and turning a mystified face to Tony for an explanation. But I also knew in the long run that yes, Tony would take the credit from Pamela if this book went right while I would take the blame if it went wrong, but Tony would not be able to defer my promotion again, once I took his side on this.

Me: I think we've got a great chance with this title, Pamela – the market's there, the product's good and the costings add up.

I suddenly thought: Shit, if she actually asks me about the costings I'm going to have to faint or something, as I hadn't seen a single figure on this; but she just looked me up and down again and shooed me out of the office. Phew.

Thom didn't have a good day either. After last week's PowerPoint debacle, the pig-men came back as predicted but Thom's boss, Rowland, has also made it clear that he's not in his good books. Thom suddenly has to put all the figures past him, and – horror of horrors – has to 'come and see him' each night before he goes home. There is no more humiliating discipline at that level, and none more difficult. Thom must time it perfectly – too early and he's a soft-handed workshy, too late and he's made his boss sit and wait for Thom to decide to go home, and probably ruined a perfectly good booking at the Ivy. He's

78

really struggling with this, so it's probably not entirely my fault that our conversation tonight went:

Me: How was your day?

Thom: Don't ask. Please, tell me about yours. Distract me from the horrors of the corporate crunch.

Me: [delighted to be asked] Well! Jacki's cakes were finally ready to be photographed today, and they were . . . amazing. There was one classic wedding cake with a giant silver crown on top, and one bombe glacé entirely covered with gold leaf, and forty tiers of cupcakes that were individually iced with Jacki and Leon's initials, and a six-foot wall of cake pops that made up a giant portrait of Jacki and Leon. Now, while I think it's got impact, I priced up the wall of cake pops and I think that, aesthetically, it might be a bit . . . *de trop*.

Thom: For CHRIST's sake, Kiki, can't you think of ANYTHING else? We aren't. Made. Of money. Can you please understand this? I don't want golden cake walls or a fountain of liquid sugar. This isn't bloody Willy Wonka, it's our wedding. Why are you so deter mined to make a joke of this whole thing?

Me: Wow. That joke *really* backfired. It actually was a joke, Thom.

Thom: [staring at the table] . . .

Me: Maybe . . . I'll just . . . go to bed. And think about the political situation in the wider world.

TO DO:

Take Thom out for a relaxing evening

Ask Norman if what Tony said about our bonuses is true

See if I can get The Dress tax-free in the US and ship back with someone over there for a holiday (Alice)

Rings – vintage to match engagement ring?

December 16th

At the wedding shop today for the final snaps before Jacki's wedding. I was cramming my notebook in my handbag when Reception rang to say my taxi was there, which was something of a surprise since I'd been planning to take the tube. Getting down to the street I found a black cab waiting with its door open – and getting in, I found bloody Pedro in the back, flicking through an issue of *Wallpaper* like he hadn't chewed me up and spat me out last time we'd met. He didn't look up but said, 'I thought you'd like a lift.' We rode in silence through the streets until we got to Pudding Lane, where Pedro leapt out of the cab and into the shop. I saw a cab pull up behind us, full of his assistants and equipment, and watched as Zoe got out and came over, saw my sad face peering through the cab window and put her head on one side, saying, 'Did someone leave you with the fare?' I was still so wiped out after Thom's overreaction last night that even these few moments with Pedro left me dumbfounded, so I got out and let poor Zoe deal with it. I heard my phone go, and fishing it out thought that I had a message from Jacki – delayed? Most unlike her – but saw it was actually from Judy the Intern. 'Did u no bout Carol n Norman? WOW!' What the . . .? Does anyone *not* know about this? Then Zoe touched my arm, and said, 'I know it seems like he's being a total dick to you, but as long as you're working with Jacki you're safe from his full venom. He knows which side his bread is buttered, Kiki. And it's not too much longer.'

Inside, Jacki was running about in a £900 silk and lace kimono while the lovely ladies of the bridal shop lined up rows of fizzing flutes of champagne on a giant silver platter. Pedro positioned his tripods in exactly the places that everyone needed to walk, so we spent the afternoon edging around the sides of the room like cartoon spies while he

80

snapped hundreds of pictures of Jacki in her dressing gown and sparkly bridal Louboutins (which, yes, I did look up later and yes, did cost more than *three months of my wage*) laughing and showing hints of her dress (a shoulder, an ankle) then close-up shots of the fabric of her dress that took for*ever*. Even Pedro started cooing when he got up close to the dress, admiring the beading and the weight of the silk satin. I felt a bit like crying when he made some joke about the nuns who stitched the beading going blind and everyone fell about laughing, but I just took a deep gulp of champagne and told the lady nearest me that I was getting married next year too. Her face lit up, and she said, 'Oh, will you be looking at some of our dresses?' I had to explain that my budget wasn't quite that of Jacki's, but she smiled kindly at me and said, 'But dear, we have a more affordable range as well,' and took my hand, leading me like a guardian angel behind one of the curtained-off doorways into a room of breathtaking dresses. I heard her say, 'I think this one is rather you,' and I turned around in what felt like slow motion and saw her holding out — of course — The Dress. The wonderful, beautiful, I-don't-really-need-to-eat-or-have-a-roof-over-my-head dress, perfect in its asymmetry and its edible sheaves of fabric.

That has to be a sign.

TO DO:
See if there's any way Mum & Dad's offering could be bumped up
Start selling Polka Dot's stationery supplies on the black market
Train as Raffles-like thief
Practise by pinching work kitty for Polka Dot's Christmas party tomorrow

December 17th

WHAT A GREAT NIGHT! Dinner, and singing, and talking – and WE ALL TALKED so MUCH and it was LOVELY! Dancing with brilliant Dan Alice Carol Judy everyone is FRIENDS and we're all going to make our BOOKS so SUCCESSFUL, and it will be BRILLIANT.

Shhhhhh . . . Thom wants to know what I'm doing but I *can't tell him about the dress* . . . It's bad luck for the groom to know about the dress before the wedding day *shhhhhhhhhhhh.*

I can't write this when I'm lying on the floor. GOOD NIGHT!

December 18th

Mum rang.

Mum: Morning!
Me: [taking a moment for some silent, beneath-covers sobbing] Is it?
Mum: [singing at me] Was somebody out last night?
Me: [trying not to remember Norman and Carol's karaoke duet after we'd left the restaurant] It was the work Christmas dinner.
Mum: Fine. Do you know if your cousins have got their invitations yet?
Me: [groaning] I don't. Do you want me to call their postman and ask if he remembers delivering it? That seems the simplest way of answering your question.

Mum:	So you have sent them out?
Me:	Oh! That's what I was forgetting. To send them out. To send out my wedding invitations. Oh well, I'm sure someone will turn up.
Mum:	Kiki. You have sent them, haven't you?
Me:	[taking a deep breath to control the nausea and the room-spinning] Tell you what, Mum. I'll ring Cousin Emma's postman, and ask him to give you a call when he remembers if he delivered it or not. Deal?

She let me go eventually, when I'd finally told her they were probably stuck in the Christmas post.

I should probably get going on those.

TO DO:
Invitations: design, produce, address and send
Don't tell Mum

December 20th

I went back to the first Wedding Shop again, the one I'd been to with Susie. The lady who opened the door to me recognised me, which also felt like a sign, and knew exactly which dress I'd come about. I apologised for not making an appointment and explained that I knew they must be busy, but I wanted to get my order in before Christmas. 'A Christmas gift to yourself?' the woman smiled as she typed all my details into the computer. I smiled back at her and tried to ignore my shaking hands. Adrenaline? I *know* this is the right thing to do. In years to come, when he thinks back to me walking down the aisle, Thom won't mind this money in the slightest. I handed over my credit card, and the deal was done.

I took Thom out for his 'relaxing evening' tonight; the Dogs. We each had a twenty pound note to bet as we liked, and I shouted us a burger and beer each. I was placing £2 bets, winning here and there, until I suddenly realised I had £40.

Me: Hey! I've doubled my money.
Thom: Are you going to make us roll around on your winnings in bed tonight?
Me: [considering] Mmmm . . . no, they're mostly coins. It doesn't seem very comfortable. But look at those profits!
Thom: Are you about to develop a gambling addiction?
Me: Would that be relaxing for you?
Thom: No.
Me: Then . . . no, I am not.

I took my mammoth winnings for some more beer and we went home to roll on the remaining cash (converted into two tens and a fiver).

TO DO:
Attend fitting in January
Second fitting in April
Collect dress in July
Find the money to pay for it somewhere along the line; not from betting on greyhounds

December 24th

I in *no way* spent Christmas Eve getting last-minute presents that I'd been intending to buy for months and never got round to. Pete will *love* a box set of *Buffy the Vampire Slayer* (an important influence for the Twins in their formative years) and Mum, I'm sure, could use another box of Turkish Delight (I buy her one every year). And Susie's just lucky the garage was open late enough for me to get her some screen wash and a disposable handwarmer. Which I'm *sure* is what she wants. Oh, plus a beautiful preggo dress and some medical-grade Ryan Gosling DVDs, for when she's in dire need of lifted spirits.

In the evening Thom and I went to the pub with Jim and his lovely band of music friends from the studio production team, plus Zoe and her stunningly handsome and remarkably sweet American boyfriend, Zac, both of them away from their families for Christmas. Zoe is so lovely, it breaks my heart how shittily Pedro treats her. That's it for this evening. I may have had a few ciders tonight and I need my Christmas bed.

December 25th

Merry Christmas, you handsome wedding diary, you. What a lovely day it's been! Thom woke me up with some aspirin, a large vat of orange juice and a giant sausage sandwich. That man is amazing. We lay in bed for a long while, listening to the Christmas Day service on Radio 4 for my nostalgia fix, and occasionally canoodling when my cider shakes subsided, until I could contain myself no longer and we abandoned ourselves to giddy Christmas Day merriment, rushing through to the Christmas tree and the presents underneath it. Most of them would be coming with us to Mum and Dad's in the afternoon, but there were enough under there to make me feel a) thankful that I had spent much much much more money and time than we had agreed on Thom's gifts, and b) like a tiny child desperate to open those parcels with my own name on. Thom mixed us a jug of un-Carlow-like super-fresh Buck's Fizz (hair of the dog – it's *medicinal*) and rang his parents for a Christmas Day chat, while I picked our first presents, for me and for him. To make this both more painless and to make my truly grasping nature a little more clear, let me break it down.

From me:

An old hardback edition of *Moby-Dick*
A jar of home-made tomato chutney that Thom loves
A silk tie
Silver cufflinks
A pair of handsome shoes that he'd been debating whether he could afford for months
A leather wallet

From him:

A roll of double-sided sellotape
Some of my own socks in a beautiful jewellery box
Some chewing gum, not even my favourite flavour
A Wispa (that was fine – I actually really like those)

I have to say, things weren't looking good for Thom – by which I mean I was trying to hide my tears, because crying over rubbish Christmas presents is both revoltingly immature and completely understandable – when he said with mock-casualness, 'Oh, hang on – is there one more thing for you there?' It was a little parcel, the size of a book. Heart leaping a little, I peeled off the paper to find a standard stationers' diary, plain black. 'Um . . . thank you?' 'Keep looking,' Thom said, 'oh ye of little patience.' So I opened up the diary, flicking through – and I noticed little slips of paper and envelopes stuck to certain pages. Looking up at Thom, I saw he was really grinning now, so I picked open one of the tiny

86

envelopes on February 14th and found two tickets to the cinema. In June, there was a formal invitation to a seaside picnic, and in October, a voucher for a Halloween costume of my choice. There were more scattered throughout, at least one each month, personal, thoughtful and utterly, utterly brilliant. At the front of the book on the details page, was a credit-card-sized golden card, with looping writing spelling out 'One filthy night of your life'; I looked at Thom and he said, 'Check the small print.' Turning the card over, I read: 'Definitely redeemable more than once'.

We made it to Mum and Dad's a bit late. My mum said it best when she opened the door to us and saw my face – 'Kiki, you're a very lucky girl.' If only she knew.

The rest of the day was spent in great glee, feeding Susie whichever Christmas treat she decided she wanted to taste at any given moment (brave Susie, pioneering gastronomer even in her delicate condition, forcing down sausage roll after marzipan fruit after mulled wine after stuffing ball after devil on horseback after mouthful of brandy butter after another sausage roll) and opening useless presents from Mum (a dog-shaped wall coat rack, a book on women in eighteenth-century Spain, and a really fat dark-blue candle that looks like her ugly blue sofa laid a wax egg) and lovely presents from Suse (a vintage tablecloth in the exact shade we drooled over in *Elle Deco* last month, a book on Marie Antoinette) and the Twins (a home-decorated jam jar filled with peppermint creams and tiny chocolate brownies). Mum gave Dad a new soldering iron, which he must have needed since he'd clearly been doing some overtime at his workbench at the college. He'd made a gorgeous mobile for Susie's foetus, with golden birds and horses swirling off each branch, ready for its arrival in the summer, and two

87

new silver and ribbon Christmas decorations for the Twins. Gawd bless us, every one.

December 26th

So twenty-four hours is still just about my limit at Mum and Dad's house. It's not the Twins' ungodly rising hour, nor the Boxing Day food-hangover. It's Mum's relentless passive-aggressive wedding tips:

1. Kiki, have you thought about what food you'll be serving? Chicken is quite a *safe* option, isn't it.
2. Kiki, have you decided who'll do your flowers? Because it does seem ridiculous to spend Thom's money on some stranger when I could do it for nothing.
3. Kiki, darling, I think Pam's daughter regrets so much not having invited the whole family to her wedding. It really was such a shame.
4. [confidentially, but at normal volume while everyone else sits in the same room mere feet away] Kiki, are you sure you want to go with such a big wedding? I know Thom's worried about the cost of these things.

I can't quite explain how much that woman annoys me. Is it that we've barely made a single decision yet, but she's already knocking our choices? Or that she wants us to have both a big-enough-for-all-her-friends wedding *and* a small-enough-that-Thom-won't-even-notice-it wedding? Or that Thom's paying for it all, like she needs to worry about the dowry she'll hand over to my new owner? Or that a kind offer ('Darling daughter, would you like me to do your wedding flowers for you?') instead comes laden with guilt, insult and presumption? GAH.

88

Thom and I had been going out for six months before he met Mum and Dad. Dad was welcoming and kind, and Mum talked without a break, speaking over Thom's answers to her questions and generally making me clench my fists under the table.

Afterwards, we drove back to his in silence. I tried to break it.

Me: Wow, look at those clouds.
Thom: [silence]
Me: Do you know that they mean a storm is coming?
Thom: [silence]
Me: I think that's so interesting.
Thom: [silence]
Me: Really, though. The world is so fascinating. There's so much in it, even stuff you didn't think you could be interested in. I think, if the right person explains it, absolutely *anything* can be interesting.
Thom: Except . . . *your mum?*

There was a terrible moment where we watched his comment slowly roll to a stop between us, then I sniggered, and he sniggered, then we both laughed so hard he had to pull the car over.

Thom packed our overnight bags, made our hasty goodbyes and stuffed me under his arm and out of the house before I said a few things that might make Father Christmas take his presents back. My word, it was good to be home. Thom thought it best if I checked my golden giftcard was still valid – and thus Christmas merriment was restored.

'I've come to say that we still have time. It can all be cancelled and corrected.'

'What? I don't understand anything. What's the matter with you?'

'What I've told you a thousand times and can't help thinking . . . that I'm not worthy of you. You couldn't have agreed to marry me. Think. You've made a mistake. Think well. You can't love me . . . If . . . it's better to say it.' He talked without looking at her. 'I'll be unhappy. They can all say whatever they like – anything's better than unhappiness . . . Anything's better now, while there's time . . .'

'I don't understand,' she said fearfully. 'You mean that you want to take back . . . that we shouldn't?'

'Yes, if you don't love me.'

'You're out of your mind!' she cried, flushing with vexation.

But his face was so pathetic that she held back her vexation and, throwing the dresses off a chair, sat closer to him.

'What are you thinking? Tell me everything.'

'I think that you cannot love me. What could you love me for?'

'My God! What can I . . .?' she said, and burst into tears.

'Ah, what have I done!' he cried and, kneeling before her, he began kissing her hands.

Anna Karenina
Leo Tolstoy

90

January 1st

Happy New Year, everyone. Mum and I had a horrible argument last night. We were all at Mum and Dad's for pre-dinner drinks before Thom and I stepped out with Susie and Pete, and we were cheers-ing one another and chatting about our plans for the new year. Mum hoped her hair would grow, Susie hoped her bust wouldn't, Dad wanted us all to be happy (same thing he wishes every year, except during one intake of students when our wellbeing was temporarily overlooked and he wished instead that the sixth-former who'd burnt a hole in the workbench with Dad's miniature blowtorch would decide to do mechanics instead) and Pete announced his intention to build bunk beds for the Twins himself, to which Susie only raised a sceptical eyebrow. I said I hoped my swanky dress would bring everyone's jaws to the floor, but then couldn't help noticing the strange silence that followed my words. It went downhill from there:

Me: What? What is it?
Thom: Keeks, you know we can't really afford it. Angelic
        as it may make you appear.

Me:	Of course we can! Everyone knows weddings are expensive, so we'll get a loan or something. It's fine! It's our wedding day.
Thom:	I know, Keeks, but it's more money than I think we should get into.
Me:	[like a small child but reasonably sure I still have some high ground] But it's our *wedding day*.
Mum:	Kiki, maybe you should listen to your fiancé.
Susie:	[to Pete] Uh-oh, no she di'int. Run. Run, Pete.
Me:	What did you say? Why is this anything to do with you?
Susie:	Seriously, Pete, leave my bag, let's go. We've got children to think of.
Mum:	Maybe Thom is right – maybe it's not a good idea for you to spend all that money on your dress.
Me:	[feeling fourteen again] It is NOTHING to DO WITH YOU! It is NONE OF YOUR BUSINESS. Why don't you just *LEAVE ME ALONE!!*
Susie:	It's too late, Pete. Grab Dad and we'll try to get behind the sofa.
Me:	SERIOUSLY, Mum. This is MY wedding – not yours, not Susie's—
Susie:	Why are you bringing *me* into this?
Me:	—not Mary's from tennis, not Keith's daughter's who's a doctor, and definitely not whoever's child's wedding you went to last year that had such amazing flowers that she'd done herself. OK? This is MY wedding, mine and Thom's, and you need to STOP trying to control every tiny aspect of it. It's OURS! Not yours! Not yours! Did you catch that?

Between Thom mentally cutting up The Dress and setting fire to it and Mum, as ever, eager to support whoever I'm disagreeing with, I *may* have lost it a teeny weeny bit. I told

Mum that she never cared about me, that I didn't want her opinion, and that I didn't even particularly want her coming to the wedding. When Thom tried to calm me down, I told him that he'd better be careful or I wouldn't want him at the wedding either. A dangerous silence followed that. Dad stood there, a bit blank and white-faced and kneading his arm, until Mum came over to him, talking quietly in his ear; when I started up again, she turned to me and yelled, 'Just *stop it*, Katherine!' She really must be serious if she'd broken out the Full Name Guns. We went home shortly after, safe in the knowledge that I had ruined the party for everyone.

TO DO:
Concentrate on what's important here:
Hair – hairdresser? Keeping it in good shape in the run-up?
Gift list – decide where to go (John Lewis, Liberty, Selfridges)
Convince Thom a gift list is a good idea
Wedding stationery – samples for invitations, save the date,
   Orders of Service and thank you cards
First dance – dancing lessons?
See if Mother of the Bride definitely has to be on the Top
   Table

January 2nd

I was out this morning at my annual January 2nd brunch with Eve (our tradition: I buy her pancakes, she tells me about her mind-boggling New Year's celebrations) and returned to the flat in the afternoon hoping for . . . not an *apology*, but *something* to show Thom was on my team. Thom was clearly expecting the same. We tried to talk to one another calmly but when I brought out this book and Thom saw all the magazine cuttings at the back, he drew back. 'Don't you want *our* wedding?' he said. 'Don't you want our friends and family watching us say we love each other? Why do you care about what these people say you need: toastmasters and bloody . . . disposable place names?' Thom gave a little smile. He was trying to keep us from fighting about this, but he was also definitely not getting the severity of his ignorance. 'This IS my wedding!' I said, holding his hands in mine. 'This is going to be so beautiful and so perfect. I'm only going to get one of these and I want it to be right!' Thom froze. 'Again. *Your* wedding,' he said. 'Maybe you'll let me know if I'm invited.'

We went to bed without speaking for the second night in a row. If anyone knows how to educate a man in the Ways of the Bride, please do let me know before I'm forced to knock on the doors of the Sainted Sisters of the Failed Wedding Plans and don my wimple (left over from a *very* messy 21st). But we've got enough weddings coming up this year – Jacki's; our university friends; Annie, my old pal from school – that maybe Thom might see things aren't as simple as he'd like to think.

TO DO:

Alcohol – white for starter, red for main, champagne for toasts and dessert?

Wedding website? Ugh. No.

Accommodation for wedding night – check out boutique hotels in Ipswich

Bridesmaids – what kind of dresses? Both the same, but in different colours? Same colour but different designs?

Find out what style Susie would be comfortable in a month after giving birth

Jewellery – vintage necklace or bracelet to go with engagement ring? Go back to the antiques market to look. Or ask Dad!

January 4th

I left work early today for my first fitting. Oh, how beautiful it truly is! I know it's such bad luck for a groom to see the dress before the wedding, but I think Thom would feel so differently about all of this if he could see how perfect it is. I was never a child who fantasised about weddings or princesses or fairies – Susie and I were too busy running a cut-throat grocer's shop from our living room, charging Mum and Dad all their hard-earned 1 and 2ps for empty cereal boxes and tiny hotel jars of jam – but this dress is everything I never dreamed of.

So I got back this evening on a cloud of air, thinking that if Thom could see me feeling this good about it, he'd be sure to come over to my way of thinking.

Wrong.

Thom: Have you been chatted up by someone on the tube again?
Me: Better. *Even* better than that.
Thom: Tony's given you your promotion early?
Me: Ha! No.
Thom: You got a free sample of food from outside a shop.
Me: No. I had my first wedding dress fitting!
Thom: [silence]
Me: Oh Thom, you're going to love it.
Thom: I didn't know you'd decided on one yet.
Me: You did! I told you about The Dress!
Thom: Yes, you told me it was £2,300, so I thought we were looking into Plan B.
Me: You want our wedding to be a Plan B wedding? Because – what? I'm your Plan B bride?

Thom: Hold on a minute – *that* doesn't even mean anything, and *don't* turn this around on me. What are you paying for it with?

Me: I've put it on my credit card until I've worked out where it will go in the wedding budget.

Thom: Where it will *go*? I can tell you where it will go – everywhere! It will go everywhere in the 'budget' – which, incidentally, is a word you use with no apparent understanding of what it actually means – because there will be absolutely no space for anything else. There will be no venue, no food, no music, and no money for our future because you and you alone decided you needed this dress, and who are you to listen to anyone else?

Me: Thom – please—

Thom: I'm sorry, Kiki, but this is unbelievable. What part of 'We aren't made of money' did you decide to completely ignore? Because it seems like all of it.

So that went well.

January 5th

No luck with Dad. I asked him if he might be able to make something for me for the wedding, and he looked uncomfortable. I laughed, and said of course, we would pay any costs if the material was pricey, that I'd do whatever I could to help. He chewed his lower lip, and said, 'I'm sorry, love. I'm just not feeling that creative at the moment. And I wouldn't want to muck something up that was so special on your big day.' After last night's fight with Thom, this is all I need. Could anyone care less about this wedding?

I've not heard Dad like that before.

January 7th

I could always do without Eve's birthday parties at the best of times, but things have been tense between me and Thom since New Year's. Having a birthday in early January is another example of Eve turning the lemons in her life (a birthday immediately after New Year's) into glamorous party-lemonade: every year she pitches it as 'A Hair of the Dog Party', and every year, too many people turn up for the venue she's arranged. So I thought tonight's bash might be a good excuse for Thom and me to drink and dance our cares away, get out of the house and forget about the wedding for a while.

I got dressed for it in the toilets at work, which is certainly my least favourite start to an evening; I had to cram myself into a stall the size of a family suitcase and manoeuvre myself into my best party dress while desperately trying not to blind myself on the coat hook protruding at eye height. Sweaty but decent, I poked my head back in to wave at Alice and Norman, then took the lift down, left the building and ran smack into Carol, weeping at the bus stop, looking like she'd really settled in for the duration of this hormone-maelstrom. I knew I couldn't get away without making at least a token gesture of concern, so I gave her arm a squeeze and asked if she was OK. I didn't put an arm round her, or take a seat beside her, but she was about to burst with news of her affair with Norman which we ALL KNEW ABOUT ALREADY, so she refused to take any notice of the International Body Language of Hurrying, and I found myself positioning my face into shocked-but-caring mode and sitting next to her while she told me far more about herself than I ever wanted to know about anyone. She told me all about how long it had been wrong between her and her husband, and how she and Norman actually had a lot in common, once they'd

97

started talking, which they'd done one evening when they were the only two left in the office, and it had just happened – she would *never* have planned this – but they hadn't wanted anyone to know so please, please, I mustn't tell anyone – the stress of keeping it from an office full of people (who secretly all knew) was tearing her apart.

It was forty-five – *forty-five* – minutes before I was allowed to get on a bus, which was then stuck in the most abysmal traffic the city's ever concocted so I didn't get to the bar until 8. Thom was already there, and it was clear from the state of him that he'd finished a terrible first week back at work too and had been unwinding pretty vigorously. He greeted me with a giant bear hug and pulled me over to the bar to get me a drink.

Thom: I'm sorry. I love you, Keeks.
Me: You do? Already? It does *not* feel like that time of the evening yet.

I was so tired but couldn't see Eve to wish her a happy birthday, so I just took a booth in the corner. Unfortunately I didn't see her assistant, Luc 'Complains' Compain, lurking in the booth either, and was trapped listening to his deadening French-accented litany of woes for half an hour.

Me: I'm really sorry to hear about your troubles, Luc—
Luc: Oh, GOWD! Iss not even like anyone list-*ens* to me when I know 'ow to fix these sings. Am one of ze young-est, cool-est pee-puhl in ze company, and may contacts are uh-mazing, but no one will list-*en* to mi. A know Eve's your frrrriend, and she is *fabuleuse*, but zat pless! 'Ow zey ever make any mon-ay for zeir chari-tubble acts is beyond mi.
Me: Do you think you'll move elsewhere?

98

Luc: A wissh! But A know zey need mi, so won't give mi
         a gowd reference to let mi go anywhere else. But zey
         won't give mi mowr mon-ay eizer. So A'm stuck
         somewhere zat A'm too gowd fohr. Kiki, iss such a
         bur-donn.

You know how some French accents just sound sexy no
matter what you're saying? Luc doesn't have one of those.
After half an hour Eve finally appeared, and with a smile at
Luc (which instantly started him simpering) set me free. She
hugged me.

Eve: Oh, it's good to see you.
Me: How's it been so far?
Eve: Five exes have sent flowers, one sent a gold bracelet—
Me: Wow, that's pretty seventies.
Eve: And Luc brought me in breakfast from the Wolseley.
         I didn't even know they did takeaways.
Me: Happy birthday?
Eve: I think I just wanted someone to give me the bumps.
         When did that stop being OK?
Me: It's so hard to get in an envelope.
Eve: So is a destroyed faith in humanity, but Louis
         managed it last year.
Me: Goose! This isn't a time for Louis. This is a time for
         me to buy you a *drink*.

We stayed by the bar chatting over our Bands on the Run
for a while, but both Eve and I were distracted by watching
Thom getting more and more drunk. He's not normally a
sloppy drinker, but he was keeping one firm arm around Jim
at the bar and talking fairly seriously to him with plenty of
finger-wagging.

Close to midnight, chatting to Thom's best friend Rich – we'd amalgamated all our friends years ago into one big group – I felt I'd stayed long enough. Between Carol's mid-life crisis and the relentless negativity of Luc's warm-up act to my evening, I was done. Thom must have sunk his body weight in whisky by now, so I knew I had to fish him out of whichever booth he was nodding off in to get him home. But I couldn't find him at any of the tables, or at the bar. Going back to Rich at the bar, I asked him to look for Thom in the toilets but when he pointed to the dance floor with a weird apologetic look on his face I suddenly got a horrible feeling in my stomach and turned in a sick slow motion. The crowd parted for a moment to reveal a slow-dancing couple in the centre of the floor: Eve's arms wrapped around Thom, stroking his back while he rested his cheek on the top of her head. I couldn't see for a moment, then was aware of leaving, unable to breathe, getting in a taxi waiting outside and telling the man to *drive*. Before he could pull away, Rich came rushing out of the bar. He said: 'Kiki! You know Thom's really wasted, don't you? You know he's asleep on that dance floor, right? Kiki?' I told the driver to GO and then I was home.

Happy bloody birthday, Eve.

January 8th

I rolled over in bed this morning, smiling without opening my eyes because today was a Saturday, and it was still early. My head wasn't that sore but something was nagging at me. Thom reached over and hugged me into him, and I shuffled closer. Then I remembered. I pulled away and got out of bed, into the bathroom and into the shower. Thom had gone when I got out: working again.

I know nothing happened. I don't expect Thom to leave me for Eve, and I don't think that he's about to start besieging her with messages of adoration. Nothing happened, I do believe that, and Thom has done nothing really that we haven't all done a bit when we're grimly drunk once in that horrible blue moon. But . . . still . . . it was *Eve*. I would rather catch him slow-dancing with my mum than her. I would even rather catch him slow-dancing with *his* mum, come to think of it. More than anyone, he knows my history with Eve, and the mucky self-hating and historical sentimentality which somehow coils its way around me to keep us friends. He's always said to me that she's like a snake, but he's always been one goat I've managed to keep out of her unhingeable jaws. And on top of all our bickering! Oh, Thom. Bother you.

January 10th

Conversations in the Polka Dot office today:

Alice: I hope that dimwit friend of yours grows up soon, or she's going to find she's awfully alone in a cold, cruel world.
Norman: [shaking his head incredulously across the office] What a silly billy.

I love my colleagues.

Thom and I haven't spoken much since Eve's party. One of us is always up at the crack of sparrow's and out of the house. It's not so much that I didn't want to talk to him: I wasn't angry, but just so hugely sad. Whenever my mind unfocuses from whatever I'm doing, I see them again together on the dance floor, and I *know* what Eve would have been thinking (old-style villainous music would probably cover it) and I think about pre-Eve-and-Thom-dancing days, and I consider them golden. Oh, *bloody hell*, Thom. I am 100% banning alcohol from the cold and loveless marriage I will hold you to.

January 12th

One of our most successful authors for the last few years has been Monica Warner, a women's fiction writer who has written the same book eight times (ah, but with a differently named heroine and hero each time, you see). She still sells, bafflingly, but her glowing, beautiful authoress persona hides the rancid evil dwelling beneath her Crème de la Mer-ed skin. She likes to come into the office and say things to ruin our days, but we like collecting and comparing them in a long-running game of Warner Poison Top Trumps. Our top five:

1. (To Norman, 58, Head of Accounts) I'll have a coffee, black with a teaspoon of honey. Do you need me to write it down?
2. (To me) Have you lost weight? You really are too skinny to make that dress look good.
3. (To Carol) Do you need a dermatologist, dear? I've heard that after the menopause it's the only way to keep your skin even half decent-looking.
4. (To Tony) I saw a tie like yours in *GQ* this month. My father would have said that you looked like a spiv.
5. (To me) Marrying? You? [peals of laughter]

She's never, ever rude to Alice, because Alice Knows People, people who (even after she married that Millionaire MP) aren't quite as close to Monica as she'd like. Alice is the real deal, goddaughter and cousin and classmate and niece of these folk, while Monica clawed her way up from civilian life and stands at the spiked turret with a crossbow, determined to take down anyone who may attempt to follow her.

I was in a crummy mood yesterday, still smarting from Eve's antics, so when Monica came into the office to talk about the marketing plans for her 'new' book and made some comment about my shoes (specifically, how some people need to be really careful that their shoe is in proportion with their leg, otherwise a heel can actually *shorten* the limb) I *may* have done some muttering under my breath. And that muttering *may* have contained both the words 'mutton' and, indeed, 'lamb'. And she *may* have heard. She looked at me for a little while, then when Tony came out of the office to greet her, took his arm warmly, in a manner which suggested that she was delighted to report that his blood sacrifice had been postponed for today, because someone else had stepped up instead. Curious but unconcerned, I answered with an unnecessary surliness when she appeared at my desk an hour later and asked:

Monica: Are you still getting married?
Me: Yeah.
Monica: And are you yet to sort out your little wedding cake?
Me: [slightly baffled, still a bit surly] . . . Yes.
Monica: Well, then you must let me recommend somewhere. Do you know Maison Edith on Thread Lane?
Me: Know it? It's *impossible* to get a cake there unless you're Kate Moss. Or the Queen.
Monica: Or me. Listen, you've helped so much over the years – why don't you let me put in a call for you?

103

I used to go to school with the girl in charge of wedding cakes there. Leave it with me.

Me: I . . . that's . . .
Monica: Thank you?
Me: Yes. Thank you.

Monica gave me a wink and swirled out of the office, and everyone turned to stare at Tony, standing in his doorway watching the conversation. Alice squinted at him, and said, 'What did you *do* to her in there?'

I was sceptical that anything was going to come of it, but this morning, like strange magical clockwork, I got a call from Maison Edith asking if I'd like to come in at the end of the month to discuss my wedding cake. Holy smokes. Then Thom came home with a beautiful bunch of scarlet carnations. He said, 'Kiki, I'm sorry that party was so awful. And I'm sorry a lot of that – urk! – *was my fault. Please can we be friends again*?' I'd wrestled him onto the sofa, and was sitting on his stomach while he pretended to flail for freedom beneath me. I said he had to swear that he would make me the happiest woman in the world. Gasping for breath, Thom wheezed out, 'Kiki, I look forward to our wedding so much. I . . . love . . . *you.*'

What a good day!

TO DO:
Look at some ready-made invitations
Makeup – anyone we know to do makeup on the day?
Accessories for bridesmaids – posies, jewellery, shoes
Hen night? Stag?

January 14th

My first treat from the diary: ice skating tickets, late night at Kew Gardens. The gardens themselves were beautiful: dark and mysterious, trees lit here and there, sparkling with frost, and gloomy hedgerows spooking everyone on their way to the rink. We swapped our shoes for skates, and hobbled across the meltwater-logged Astroturf to the ice. Thom and I clung to one another for a moment, dizzy from the kids skating past at top speed, twirling and whooping and near-missing one another, then we both pushed off and took little icy sliding steps, small at first but becoming swoops and glides soon enough. I couldn't stop with any real grace (I waited until I got close to one of the sides, then steered that way until I *thumped* into it) but was happy to just go round and round, ruddy-cheeked and woollen-hatted, sometimes holding hands with Thom and sometimes doing laps on my own. Then we skated slowly together for a while, watching the other people in the rink: the teenagers showing off; the parents with their children, allowed to stay up late for this treat; the old couple holding hands and going slowly around the rink edge.

Me: Will we be like them one day?
Thom: Despite what the adverts tell you, yes, we will age.
Me: Will we be as happy as they are?
Thom: How do you know they're happy?
Me: Because everyone knows that the family who skates together, stays together.
Thom: That's not how the phrase goes.
Me: But they do look happy, don't they? When was the last time you saw your mum and dad hold hands?
Thom: Kiki, they're in Australia. I can't even tell you if they've still got teeth, let alone if they hold hands.

Me: Fine. I just hope that . . . in ten and twenty and fifty
        years' time, we're still best friends. I love you.
Thom: I love you too, Keeks. But do you know what you
        might love even more?
Me: Nothing in the whole world.
Thom: Mulled wine from the bar.
Me: Wow. You *do* know me well.

January 20th

It turns out that I hadn't fully grasped that wedding invitations are the MOST EXPENSIVE THING IN THE WORLD.
Everything in the market is either wildly pricey and absolutely
exquisite (two colour letterpress, £370 for 100 – not including
envelopes, naturally) or horribly grim and completely affordable (like someone swallowed a wedding then threw it up
on a notepad). Just don't know what we'll do.

   Mum's birthday today, too. I went to drop round a card
and present before Thom got back from work, but they'd
gone out for the night. Lucky them.

January 25th

A tough day with Clifton Black. He's our author of men's
war books, which sadly don't sell as well as they ought
because they're fiction — much like Clifton's hints of his
own military career — and the market only seems to be
interested in war books that have come from men who have
definitely actually killed another man themselves. Clifton is
only ever seen in his army gear: he comes into the office
(thankfully forgoing smudges of camouflage stick on his face)
in heavy army boots and a clanking rucksack, filled with

106

God knows what. He talks in a barking military snap that I can only assume he's picked up from films, and addresses us all variously as 'Officer', 'Private', 'Captain', etc. It's pretty unbearable. But as far as we know, he's never actually been in active service, or even a member of the Territorials. One of his army boots is slightly built up, suggesting a leg not suitable for action, so I'm imagining his life – focused always on serving Her Majesty – has instead been lived through his books, with titles like *To Hell and Back* and *A Gun for Life* and *Bullets and Bravery* (yes, actually that). It's a terrible dance we do with him, where we know he's a fraud, and he must know we know, and dread us bringing it up (thank God our publicity department found out via a hurried call from his wife, rather than asking him outright) but we must always have this armed and dangerous elephant in the room even as we discuss the latest conflict he's 'covering', and ask whether he can think of anyone to give us a quote for his new book.

He was in today to talk about *Guns on the Run*, a look at the Gulf conflict through the eyes of his six-book (and counting) hero Grant Carter. We'd been talking for a while about the book jacket when he noticed my engagement ring.

Clifton: Bloody hell, my gal, is that a ring on your finger?
Me: Yes, Clifton, it is. Plans for next summer; I'll finally be made an honest woman.
Clifton: And is he fully aware of the mission ahead of him?
Me: Ha ha. Very good.
Clifton: Does he know the kind of forces he's up against?
Me: Ha. Yes.
Clifton: And have you given him any weapons? Need a bloody nuclear arsenal against most women these days. Poor lad. It *is* a lad, isn't it?

Me: Yes, Clifton. It's a lad.

Clifton: Good-oh. So what'll your name be once you're married?

Me: Kiki Carlow.

Clifton: [confused] The fellow's got the same name as you? He's not a relation is he? That can get damned messy.

Me: No, he's not a relation. We tossed a coin over whether I would take his name, close down my bank account, resign from my job and renounce my right to vote, or whether he'd just have to marry an equal human. Fortunately it landed on tails, as he says he really likes the free books from this place.

Clifton: Oh, one of *those*, are you. Well, good luck to him!

Me: Yes, Clifton. Quite. Shall we talk about using your military contacts to promote your new book, yes?

Fine, I didn't say that last bit. But I wish I had.

January 29th

What delicious, creamy, crumb-based larks! Off to Maison Edith today. For tastings! *Tastings!* Of *cakes*! And all you have to do is get wed (and have Monica Warner up in your grill with her toxicity for the last four years). If they advertised that first point more widely, those marriage rates would sky-rocket. Although, to be fair, the divorce rates would probably do the same, after everyone suffered their sugar come-downs. Thom and I took pity on my pregnant, sugar-craving sister and invited her along for the ride to Maison Edith itself: a stunning old Tudor house near Holborn, its windows stuffed with cakes and buns and gateaux of every kind, like the witch's house before the arrival of Hansel and Gretel. If that was what it took, I was completely willing to be caged up and fed sweet treats for the next few months, while Thom did all the sweeping and carrying. Actually, that isn't too dissimilar to how we live anyway.

We were greeted at the door by the most friendly young Italian man, who showed the three of us around each cake and explained our options if we didn't want to go with a standard tiered cake: towers of meringues, profiteroles or macarons, a deep fruit pie with our names on in pastry, or even a trifle with our initials in silver balls. We were all so excited to get digging in with the spoons, when he said, 'Ah! Here is Ma-ry. She weel help you with all theengs weddeeng. *In bocca al lupo!*' and gestured to someone behind us. As we all turned, Thom said to me, 'Did he say we were going into the wolf's mouth?' and the three of us saw Mary at the same time: a furious-looking, sour-mouthed, grey-haired woman who would not have looked out of place twirling her keys on a prison ward.

'*Girl* I went to school with', Monica said? That was quite some gamble, allowing me to meet someone of whom she was a school contemporary, age-giver-away that it is. If we're charitable, we can maintain that perhaps Mary was a Home Ec assistant and not a classmate at all. Which would explain how she appears approximately twenty years older than Monica. She looked us up and down, and said, 'Which of you is . . . "Kiki"?' I raised my hand, hoping I'd misunderstood her tone and she'd show a little more of Hansel and Gretel's friendly witch mode before she tried to kill us and eat us, but she just frowned and said, 'Come with me, please.'

We all got a bit giggly then, like naughty children, and followed her down the corridor pushing one another to go first, until we came to a giant taster kitchen with huge glass-doored fridges and massive steel tables, one with a tray filled with handfuls of tiny spoons and little disposable paper bowls. Mary stood on the other side of the table, and placed both her hands carefully on the surface. With a curt sniff,

109

she said, 'Wedding cakes are traditionally fruitcake. If either of you suffer from any *allergies*,' and she took a moment to consider this most revolting of concepts, 'then we can alter the recipe. Do you have any allergies?' We shook our heads. 'Fine. Then we can go ahead with the wedding cake as planned. You may choose the decorative icing, if you don't want white on white.'

She nearly got away with it too, but Susie was clear-headed with sugar-lust and called her back.

Susie: We were talking with your colleague upstairs—

Mary: Oh, yes, Mario. He doesn't work on weddings.

Susie: But he said we could have anything we wanted. Is that not actually the case?

Mary: Are you getting married too?

Susie: No, it's my sister and her fiancé here.

Mary: So . . . it's not your wedding, then?

Me: [sensing there may be more than crumbs spilt on the kitchen tiles any minute] No, it's our wedding. I think neither of us are huge fans of fruitcake – we came here to try and find some alternative that might work for us, and liked lots of the things Mario was suggesting. We're planning quite a unique wedding, and we're hoping to do things a bit differently, so a cake of some sort to match that would be great.

Mary: [huge sigh] Doing things . . . *differently*. Of course. What did you have in mind?

Thom: [taking up the baton] Please may we try the profiteroles?

Mary clenched her teeth in ill-disguised rage, then reached under the table to a hidden shelf and took out a warm choux bun glossy with dark chocolate with a tiny bit of cream bursting out. My mouth exploded with saliva just looking at it, but Susie reached across and put the whole thing in her mouth.

Me: You greedy hog. I hope that chokes you.
Mary: [sighing again, to me and Thom] I suppose *you'll*
        want to try one too?

It was like blood from a stone, but we did finally get to try everything we wanted. The trifle was beautiful, fruity and fresh with a rich eggy custard, and the macarons were meltingly rich, in a wild rainbow of colours. But in the end we chose a reasonably traditional option: a lemon and rosewater cake in two tiers, with garlands of tiny tea roses around each tier (Thom didn't really care about that bit). For the pleasure of Mary's company this afternoon and our lovely two-tier cake, we will be paying them £380 one day soon. Is Monica getting a cut of that? Cripes.

TO DO:
Start a wedding cake business to pay for our wedding cake
Find out if there's a trend for slightly wonky home-baked
    sponges instead
Think about cake-based vows?
Wait for this crazy sugar-high to wear off

February's Classic Wedding!

Meg looked very like a rose herself, for all that was best and sweetest in heart and soul seemed to bloom into her face that day, making it fair and tender, with a charm more beautiful than beauty. Neither silk, lace, nor orange flowers would she have. 'I don't want a fashionable wedding, but only those about me whom I love, and to them I wish to look and be my familiar self.'

So she made her wedding gown herself, sewing into it the tender hopes and innocent romances of a girlish heart. Her sisters braided up her pretty hair, and the only ornaments she wore were the lilies of the valley, which 'her John' liked best of all the flowers that grew.

'You do look just like our own dear Meg, only so very sweet and lovely that I should hug you if it wouldn't crumple your dress,' cried Amy, surveying her with delight when all was done.

'Then I am satisfied. But please hug and kiss me, everyone, and don't mind my dress. I want a great many crumples of this sort put into it today.' And Meg opened her arms to her sisters, who clung about her with April faces for a minute, feeling that the new love had not changed the old.

Little Women
Louisa May Alcott

February 4th

Jacki came into the office this afternoon to get some writing done. She's so funny, and was exactly what I needed; she keeps up a running commentary while tapping away at a little laptop she carries everywhere in her gigantic Mulberry handbag. We made tonnes of lists – chapter headings, things we need to cover (where to get the best bra for your wedding, what emergency items your maid of honour needs to carry around with her on the day), a small chapter on things to avoid (d-i-v-o-r-c-e, inviting exes to the wedding) and notes for everything she wanted to tell her readers about her own wedding prep and the day itself, from how Leon proposed to wedding night lingerie. Fine, it wasn't *Anna Karenina*, but I admired the fact that she wanted to write it, and that she genuinely wanted to put helpful things in there too. She wouldn't only recommend the lingerie she wore, in the upper hundreds, but insisted on putting in tips for every budget and look.

She went up in my estimation four million times more after Tony toddled from his office and burst into our room, saw what we were doing and rubbed his hands with glee. 'Ah, Jacki, I look forward to seeing your diet section as well – all the brides want to be in great shape for their wedding day! I could do with a few tips myself,' he said, rubbing his stomach for good measure. Jacki smiled so sweetly at him, like she was receiving a wonderful gift from this tubby, balding, charmless man, and said, 'Oh no, we're not doing that here. We want every girl to be happy whatever she looks like!' Tony hesitated for a moment, then recognised the flash of steel in Jacki's eyes and left the room, with 'Good, good, good . . .' trailing behind him. Here's what we ended up with instead of a diet chapter:

Looking the Best on Your Wedding Day

Can you climb the stairs without falling over? Have you eaten a piece of fruit this month? Do you see your toes when you look down? Then relax!!!! You can spend six months eating just olives and grissini (I like to think of this as the Cocktail Bar Diet), and walk down the aisle a size six, only to feel grim and dizzy all day and balloon to a size thirty on your honeymoon, or you can find a dress that bloody well fits you and shoes you can walk in, and stride into your church/synagogue/register office/other to see the face of the person who wants to marry you and live by your side forever and ever. Look at that face and think: did he/she ask me to marry him/her because they hoped I'd stop eating and change my shape and probably my temperament dramatically? Or maybe – just maybe – does he/she love the person I am inside?!

So. Eat some fruit, find a good corset, dance your socks off and smile at how good you'll look in photos when you've got someone who loves you standing beside you.

God. I love this woman.

February 6th

All of us over to Susie's for her birthday lunch today.

Mum: [rubbing Susie's back] Happy birthday! How are you feeling, 'Mum'?
Susie: Urgh, please don't do that. It's so meta.
Mum: What's 'meta'?
Susie: It's meta when your own mum calls you Mum. It feels like I'm in a science fiction film.
Pete: Don't touch her today, Tessa. I went to give her a kiss this morning and she tried to mace me with her deodorant.
Susie: Is *this* how I planned to celebrate my thirtieth birthday? I might be a little hormonal. But none of you have a – [looking around to check the Twins aren't about] fucking *alien* growing in one of your internal organs right now. Do you?
Dad: Hem, hem. Language, Susan.
Susie: [grinding her teeth]
Pete: I'll get the cake.

I don't think Suse is having the best of pregnancies. I think she misses the heady days of her youth, when the celebration for a birthday of this magnitude would have lasted a week and taken in several different countries. I gave her a hideously expensive stretch-mark cream and a gorgeous maternity pillow, and tried to distract her with flippant talk of venues

115

and the absurdity of honeymoon flipflops, but she looked like she was going to eat me so we all went home.

February 14th

On our first Valentine's Day together, I invited Thom up to my revolting student house (after bribing my housemates to stay out *all* night), made him a romantic meal and got so drunk I blacked out on the sofa. Last Valentine's tapas disaster meant that we spent the following six months having careful, two-steps-forward-one-step-back conversations about whether we both wanted to marry, and whether we wanted to marry one another. Which isn't half as romantic as it sounds.

But tonight was a perfect romantic date. In my Christmas diary, Thom had tucked two tickets to a double-bill of *Crocodile Dundee*s I and II at a tiny cinema in Hampstead, and we were enjoying two enormous burgers in a café around the corner before the films started. I'd just given myself a mayonnaise moustache – never not funny – to make Thom laugh when Eve and her date-for-the-night appeared in front of the café, done up in expensive clothes. I looked for a fraction too long, and Thom turned to see what I was looking at, which then caught Eve's eye. She gave us a huge smile, said something to her date and pulled him into the café after her, coming over to our table and surveying our greasy napkins and my mayonnaise face. 'Kiki! *Thom*. What a . . . romantic place. This is what saving money for a wedding looks like, right?' she laughed.

She'd been keeping a low profile, so it was the first time I'd spoken to her since her party, and I found I didn't have a great deal to say to her even now. I smiled because it was impossible to not smile at Eve when she'd turned her charm on, but she sensed the mood. 'Right kids! Enjoy your night.

116

Tim's taking me to Nobu, so I shall leave you to it – although these fries look amazing. *Sure* you wouldn't prefer to eat here, Tim?'

For a moment, I could really see the struggle within poor Tim: the slim chance this is what Eve really wanted, versus the idea of having to join these people whose body-language screamed 'Please don't'. With a polite smile at us, he simply said, 'Eve, we'll be late. Nice to meet you both,' and swept her back out the door and off to an evening of sushi and caviar.

Thom: Bloody hell. That was close. Kiki, you've got a little something [points to his upper lip]?

Ah! *L'esprit de l'escalier.* Always too late, I thought that I *should* have said to Eve, 'That's not a good date. *This* is a good date,' and pulled out our *Crocodile Dundee* tickets. But she probably wouldn't have got the reference.

February 16th

Jacki asked me if I'd come and meet her for a lunch today. We agreed on a delicious little French place off the Strand, where we got a cosy dark-green booth in the corner and a waiter who never left us alone. She looked a bit worried, so I asked the obvious.

Me: Jacki, are things OK?
Jacki: With me? Of course, love!
Me: And with Leon?
Jacki: Of course! He's great! He's off getting fitted for his suit. He's like a bloody peacock at the moment, strutting around asking me which kind of fabric he looks better in.

Me: Then, if you don't mind me asking, Jacki, what's wrong? I am never one to turn down lunch with anyone, and it is a real pleasure to see you, but . . . well, *are* you alright?

Jacki: Oh, doll, it's nothing. Let's order one of everything on the menu and forget all about it. Tell me about your wedding. Tell me where you're going to live afterwards, and how many children you'll have, and how many of them you'll name Jacki.

Me: Mmm . . . It's fine as long as neither of us mentions it; probably apart as we'll have fallen out over the necessity of rings or something; none if things continue the way they're going; and all twelve of the cats I'll get instead.

Jacki: Kiki, that's so kind. Can I come to the christenings?

Me: Absolutely. Getting cats into a font is much harder than it sounds. I'll need all the help I can get.

Jacki: That calls for a drink. Waiter!

We both jumped as he was already next to our table, but he settled our nerves with two Amaretto Sours followed by a bottle of Merlot. Shortly after our starter arrived we were greased enough for Jacki to tell me what was really going on. She said what was playing on her mind was how excited she was about her wedding. It was tough for her to think of anything else, and all her dreams were swathed in veils and tulle. But she was worried that her thoughts never really went past that. She didn't fantasise about her life married to Leon because her imagination just stopped at that point. What was wrong with her?

I ordered us two more Sours and told her this: if Leon could stand by her side when she became so obsessed with her own wedding that she *published a book on the subject*, then she wouldn't really need to worry about their future life together. I was pretty tipsy by that stage. But she looked thoughtful for a really long time, then took my hand and said, 'Yes, Kiki, you're probably right.' Then she described something she was planning for their wedding night that made us laugh so hard the manager asked if we would like our bill yet.

I'm actually feeling a bit queasy now. More later.

TO DO:
Stop the room spinning
Check at least one of us did actually pay the bill

February 20th

We've block-booked a sweet little hotel round the corner from Redhood Farm that's offered our guests a good rate for our party. Rich, Thom's best man, has confirmed that his girlfriend Heidi will be at the wedding, although she's slightly nervous about being so far from their hospital when she'll be eight months pregnant with their first child – although we've been shown to secrecy about the pregnancy for the next month. I told her that Thom's dad is a retired vet but she didn't seem that reassured. Where's her sense of adventure?

TO DO:
Music – jazz trio for drinks, Ceilidh band for the dancing later?
Caterers – anything but pâté followed by chicken. Pork? Soup?
Book hair treatment to keep it in good condition (one a month from March)
Makeup – ask at Space NK to see if anyone available for freelance work
Flowers – see if that amazing florist I always notice in Soho

can do a small posy, three boutonnières and a few centrepieces for decent price

Find out why florists insist on referring to wedding flowers
as 'blooms'

February 25th

I met Eve tonight, at a new little restaurant off Covent Garden.
It was so little that even though we were seated opposite one
another, I was almost in her lap, but it was incredibly trendy
and I'd heard the pulled pork was to kill for. Aptly, I thought,
as I watched Eve browse the menu and gritted my jaw.

Eve: I'm going to buy us dinner because I think you're
        cross at me.
Me: Why do you think I might be cross at you?
Eve: Why do I think that, or why might you be?
Me: Eve, I couldn't really give a shit about semantics right
        now.
Eve: OK, we've got *that* to be going on with. [silence]
        Yup, this is a bad one.
Me: What do you want me to say?
Eve: That you understand we were all drunk? That it was
        just my birthday and you know I didn't mean
        anything by it? That it was stupid but you still love
        me anyway?
Me: No. But I might manage, 'Bring me one of everything,
        please, she's paying'.
Eve: [clasping hands together under her chin] Oh, you *do*
        forgive me!
Me: Throw in a cocktail and we'll talk.

And we did talk. We had a hilarious time – Eve really
does make me laugh. Eve updated me on her work, telling

me about this great link they've set up with a local bakery, Bake Away, to encourage both young apprenticeships at the bakery and home cooking, and how she's got to get up at 4am tomorrow to meet the head baker there, which somehow cancels out all her good feelings about the project. I told her all about Jacki, and Leon, and their amazing wedding plans.

Eve: They won't last a year.

Me: You're so cynical it must actually affect your taste-buds. Does *everything* taste sour to you?

Eve: Oh, you're so heart-warmingly naïve you must never need a coat. It all balances out.

We hugged at the end of the night, and Eve promised to send over a loaf from the bakery.

The service began. The explanation of the intent of matrimony was gone through; and then the clergyman came a step further forward, and, bending slightly towards Mr Rochester, went on. 'I require and charge you both (as ye will answer at the dreadful day of judgment, when the secrets of all hearts shall be disclosed), that if either of you know any impediment why ye may not lawfully be joined together in matrimony, ye do now confess it; for be ye well assured that so many as are coupled together otherwise than God's Word doth allow, are not joined together by God, neither is their matrimony lawful.'

He paused, as the custom is. When is the pause after that sentence ever broken by reply? Not, perhaps, once in a hundred years. And the clergyman, who had not lifted his eyes from his book, and had held his breath but for a moment, was proceeding: his hand was already stretched towards Mr Rochester, as his lips unclosed to ask, 'Wilt thou have this woman for thy wedded wife?' – when a distinct and near voice said – 'The marriage cannot go on: I declare the existence of an impediment.' The clergyman looked up at the speaker and stood mute; the clerk did the same; Mr Rochester moved slightly, as if an earthquake had rolled under his feet: taking a firmer footing, and not turning his head or eyes, he said, 'Proceed.' Profound silence fell when he had uttered that word, with deep but low intonation. Presently Mr Wood said – 'I cannot proceed without some investigation into what has been asserted, and evidence of its truth or falsehood.' 'The ceremony is quite broken off,' subjoined the voice behind us. 'I am in a condition to prove my allegation: an insuperable impediment to this marriage exists.'

Jane Eyre
Charlotte Brontë

March 1st

An invitation brainwave. Where could I find someone who creates gorgeous, affordable designs to a strict brief every day? No, not just Topshop's design office. Polka Dot! Our lovely art department have to do everything from glossy magazine ads to sparkly book jackets, so I was sure with the right payment one of them might be willing to help out. Sure enough, Dan agreed. Mark had broken up with his girlfriend the week before and Nayla was swamped by the forty-eighth redesign for evil (hang on – maybe not evil? Can't cope with this new uncertainty) Monica Warner, but after a short bit of haggling, Dan settled on payment of one carrot cake for the invitation. I told him I wanted something quite classic, fresh and simple, but with a wedge of humour. 'Are we talking . . . Rosalind Russell film?' he said. I knew I had my man.

That was yesterday, and already he's *totally* delivered. There were a couple of tiny tweaks but Dan had produced a really gorgeous design, sparky and modern and clean. I ran to the stationers at lunch and got printing and guillotining those suckers, and returned home tonight with a stack of lovely expensive-looking invitations and a large pile of envelopes (there's one in the back for your historical perusal). All of which cost me £12 and a carrot cake. Thom gave me a high five when I explained the whole thing, then sagged when I handed him the address book and pen. He does have very nice handwriting.

As he wrote, Thom and I were having a totally necessary and reasonable conversation about who we know that has great hands, when I had a sudden thought: the wedding bands. I fished out my trusty bridal magazines to get browsing for inspiration, but when Thom asked what I was working on, he swiftly pulled them from my hands and said, 'I think that's my task, if that's alright. Do you trust me?' I reassured him that as long as the rings were circular and hollow, and matched my ring, and my dress, and didn't clash with jewellery I wore at any other time, and were classic enough that I could wear mine forever – Thom stopped me there: 'Got it. You trust me.'

TO DO:
Start taking vitamins for good skin
Just get hair mask from Boots? (for good condition on wedding day)
Gifts for the wedding party – Thom, me, bridesmaids, best man, ushers, parents
Helium balloons? Canister?

March 4th

Miracle of miracles, all the invitations posted this morning (thank you, Polka Dot franking machine). Otherwise, it was a horrible day at work – Norman and Carol were sniping at one another all day, until Tony finally called out from his office, 'My GOD, will you two just get a bloody room?' There was an excruciating silence, then Carol stormed out, sobbing. Norman suddenly became hugely interested in the sales sheets on his desk, but Alice raised one eyebrow at me, moments before Carol came in again, opened the printer drawer and throwing the ream of paper at Norman. Tony stepped out of his office for a moment to say, 'Did I hit a nerve?' then wandered back in and slammed the door. 'Prick,' said Norman. Fair enough.

TO DO:
Wedding pearls?
Teeth whitening? Will my teeth have to match my dress?
Hair colouring and styling
Fans for the guests if a hot day?
Favours – bags of sweets? Fortune cookies? Biscuit cutters?
   Diamonds?

March 5th

A joyful break from everything. Another of Thom's treats tonight: a forties-style swing night at a little underground club near Soho. He insisted on meeting me there, having mysterious errands to run, and when I got to the door he was waiting for me with a little parcel in brown packing paper and string. Inside: a red lipstick, a brown eyeliner ('To draw the seams of your stockings') and a hipflask of brandy ('Medicinal'). So we swigged from the hipflask, drew on my seams and headed straight inside, where they were giving free lessons to all the new dancers. We joined them once our medicine had kicked in. When I attempted some of the moves I laughed more than I had in months; let's just say that I'm no threat to Ginger Rogers. But it was a great, great night.

March 7th

First responses already in. Norman said he will be solo, as, separately, did Carol, giving me a meaningful look as she did so. Alice said, 'Wooooop! Count me in. But I'm not bringing Gareth, you clown.' I reassured her that she would still be welcome even without her pretend-boyfriend and that she could even bring an actual-girlfriend if she wanted, and she said she would think about it, but be there either way. Susie and Pete said they would come if we could guarantee someone else would take charge of their kids for the day.

Another wedding in two weeks – Annie and Stephen. Annie is a very old friend, since I met her even before I met Eve, but we never really kept in touch. We were close at primary school, in and out of one another's houses and together all the way to puberty. Our paths diverged when she got a job at a local stables and I blossomed into a terrible teenage cliché, snogging boys and drinking kiwi-flavoured 20/20 at discos. I'd see her around sometimes, crushingly wholesome, with happy anoraked friends while my crowd smoked roll-ups at the bus station and coloured in our nails with black permanent markers. But such is the wonder of modern technology that she tracked me down to invite me to her wedding. I really have no idea what she's like now, apart from the fact that she and I have *very* different taste in wedding stationery.

I remember that she liked holographic stickers, and building Lego hospitals in which our toy animals would be healed. It seems unlikely that she's still into that now, so Thom and I played it safe and bought a set of wine glasses from their wedding list. If she turns out to still have the same interests, I'm really going to regret not just sending over some silver hologram balloons. Fingers crossed.

From the snaps I've seen, I can't help comparing Stephen

to a young Keith Chegwin. But Annie looks nice now. By which I mean normal. I hope.

TO DO:
Bridal fascinator – as well as veil? Instead?
Shrug or bolero to go with dress? Vintage markets? Feather shrug? Gloves?
Paper boat place names?
Gifts for the groom – atlas? Smythson notebook? Silk pyjamas?
Favours – edible? Ornamental? Jewellery for women, cufflinks for men? Classic sugared almonds? Balloons? Crayons?
Remember most guests will not be six years old
Honeymoon!

March 8th

My birthday!! Good times. Pub with Thom and Jim and Eve and Zoe and her boyfriend and Alice and everyone (although poor Susie too knackered to make it out). Thom made us pancakes for breakfast, and gave me a gorgeous bracelet and an antique globe this morning, rolling his eyes when I opened the globe. He said, 'It's what you asked for. But the first time I find it tucked away in a cupboard, I'm getting rid of it.' He ruffled my hair, muttering, 'Ridiculous object.' Hopefully he was referring to the globe, not me. Nice to see Zoe and her crazily handsome American boyfriend have become friends with Jim since Christmas (Jim's studio is round the corner from their flat and they've stayed in touch). Even Eve was in fine form, and stayed miles away from Thom. Happy birthday me!

March 9th

Susie officially hormone-riddled. She gave me a fright though; when I went over on a visit this evening to receive my birthday gifts she looked a bit pale, and was tucked up on the sofa under an old blanket, watching Grand Designs.

Me: Are you alright, Suse?
Susie: Yeah, I'm fine. I'm really tired.
Me: Hormones?
Susie: [sighing audibly] Not *just* hormones. I'm not feeling brilliant at the moment.
Me: Have you been to the doctor?
Susie: Yeah, I went this morning. She said everything's fine, but maybe I should slow down a bit.
Me: That's what you get with baby number three.
Susie: [silence] What's that supposed to mean?
Me: Nothing! Just . . . maybe you should take it easy. You've got two already and you need to take care of yourself.
Susie: What – I've got two already, so it doesn't matter what happens with this one?
Me: [laughing] No! *Suse*! Come on – of course I didn't mean that. Didn't the doctor say the baby was OK?
Susie: Sorry, do you even care? It's quite obvious that the wedding is the *only* thing *anyone* is allowed to care about anymore, and you've made it perfectly clear that our baby is not a particularly welcome member of the party—
Me: Susie, of course the baby is welcome. I was surprised, the way you sprang it; I didn't know you and Pete wanted another one—

129

Susie: Who fucking cares if we wanted another one or not? How is that your business? If it doesn't come with a veil or confetti, it's impossible to find space in your subconscious at the moment anyway! I'm so sorry, I clearly should have discussed with you whether our unborn foetus matched your colour scheme. It was totally selfish of us to continue living our lives when you have this wedding to plan. So sorry.

Me: How am I being selfish? You've got your happy little life, and I'm living mine. Just because you and Pete decided to have your quirky, independent little wedding without bothering to actually involve anyone who loves you, doesn't mean that I have to do the same thing.

Susie: Involving anyone? Who are you involving? You're involving Thom's wallet, and that's about it! You won't let Mum do a single thing—

Me: *You* didn't even invite her to your wedding!

Susie: So what? I'm not the one pretending that I'm doing this big family event for purely selfless reasons—

Me: Susie! Can you calm down, please?

Susie: Can I calm down? Can you *piss off*, please?

Pete came in then, hearing us shouting, and in the nicest possible way repeated Susie's request. As he took me to the front door, he said gently, 'Give her a day or two. She really isn't feeling great at the moment.'

She chose to have this bloody baby. *She* can call *me*.

TO DO:
Bunting?
Manicure?

130

Disposable cameras?

Party poppers?

Practise hair (on my own, since sister is now insane)

March 14th

A few more invitation responses. Fenella, the cold wife of Thom's horrible sweaty boss, sent me a beautiful handwritten Smythson card saying they would be delighted to join us, and two of the thick-haired girlfriends sent identical responses. But booooo, brilliant cousin Emma can't come, as they can't get babysitting overnight and couldn't really bring baby Jacob along. Jim says he's really excited, although more about the 'massive knees-up' that will be our wedding than about being given an excuse to visit Ipswich. Fair enough. Other Tom (from dreadful holiday job) says it seems unlikely that he'll be there, as formal weddings aren't hugely his bag, but he does promise us a huge present to make up for his absence. Fiona and Mark say *they'll* be there, as do all Thom's school friends and my coursemates (bar Lucy who I've yet to hear from). Good going, so far.

Tony, meanwhile, has taken to hovering over my desk, as if he can pick up signals of how well *Perfect Wedding* will sell simply by eyeballing my computer. He sighs deeply whenever it comes up in our weekly meetings, and looks expectantly at me while I pitch our marketing and sales ideas and describe the new content Jacki's still providing. But Tony never seems happy. I was copied into this email from Pamela:

From: Cooper, Pamela
To: Cooper, Tony
CC: Carlow, Kiki
Re: Wedding book

Anthony,

Please can you ensure that this book docsn't compromise the company in any way . We have a lot riding on this, according to Norman and we need to bear in mind that it could have a vital bearing on our future stability.

Pamela

I can see why they had typing pools in the past.

I couldn't stop thinking about all of that as I got ready for Jacki's hen night tonight. A month before the wedding, thirty of her closest friends in the world (and me) went to the Soho Hotel where we had dinner, drinks, and barrels of popcorn for a private screening of *Die Hard*. A bloody brilliant choice, I might add. It was enormous fun, as we all heckled Alan Rickman, analysed Bonnie Bedelia's hair and cheered Bruce Willis's excellent comeback lines. After the film, we had the whole third floor to ourselves with massages, manicures and pedicures going on in each room, and B-list actresses and popstars rushing from suite to suite with nail polish and cotton wool. There may have been no paparazzi there, but there was the ever-present Pedro, snapping away at all the guests (except me). Jacki had also invited a whole bunch of friends from her school, women she'd stayed friends with even though they were stuck in a middle-England town and she was awarding statuettes at the Brits. Jacki's warmth made everyone feel comfortable, so a soap actress chatted to a single mum-of-two about the difficulty of kids starting school, and a star of the top ten shared travel tips with Jacki's primary school pal. We laughed so hard all night, and it was lovely to see how much all these people really cared about Jacki. And Pedro was a wonder – charming these women so no one looked nervous or self-conscious as he took pictures of them in various states of undress and tipsiness.

As the night was winding down (although from the sounds of it, one group was just starting on the mini-bar and sing-along) I told Jacki I would head home. She took me to her room and presented me with a party bag for the night. I didn't check what was in there straight away, but I caught a glimpse of Laura Mercier and Diptyque boxes. Bloody hell, I thought, this bag might provide me with presents for my family for the whole next year. Although, unless he is suddenly *really* into his skincare routines, Dad might be a bit disappointed.

Jacki: Have you had a nice time tonight?
Me: I've had *such* a nice time! Thank you again, Jacki. [suddenly embarrassed] Although you did have to ask me, it being my job, of course.
Jacki: But I would have invited you anyway, Kiki. It's been really nice getting to know you these last few months.
Me: Has it been instructive to see all those arguments you *shouldn't* have?
Jacki: [laughing] Are we ready to laugh about them yet?
Me: No.
Jacki: [mock-serious] No, it's not been funny at all.
Me: It might have been a bit funny. But I do think . . . I think as long as I can be with Thom. I think that's all I need. You know what that's like, though.

Jacki turned away and busied herself tidying up her makeup brushes as I put my coat on. Without looking at me, she said, 'I don't want to go down the same route as my parents, Kiki. They both gave me everything money could buy, but neither

Mum nor Dad cared about anyone else but themselves, and their reputations. What their friends thought they could do. They didn't love one another and they didn't love me. We had a house full of things, and that's all they cared about. I'm not going to live that life.'

I gave her a hug and reminded her that it was one thing she wouldn't have to worry about with Leon. She hugged me back and sent me on my way, off home to jog Thom's memory about exactly how much I loved him.

TO DO:
Confirm guests' travel – see if anyone needs to share lifts
Confirm with the hotel those guests who have booked with them
Stop feeling guilty about Susie being a loon

March 19th

Annie and Stephen's wedding today. I take back everything I said about her. She is still very much into her holographic décor, and she is definitely not normal. I really *hope* that's not normal, anyway.

The ceremony was fine. Her dress looked like it had been piped onto her from a fire extinguisher, and she had a giant sunflower behind one ear, as if she'd fallen into an Athena poster from 1987 and only just escaped alive. The service was unremarkable, bar a reminder on the back of the Order of Service of their bank details, for anyone who hadn't given to the gift list yet. I hadn't spotted *that* tip in *Beautiful Brides*.

But it was the reception that was the main treat. On arrival, I nudged Thom when I saw clusters of shiny silver balloons with holographic 'A&S's printed onto them ('I *told* you'), and was a little bit delighted that sometimes people still cling to something of their early identities. It was reassuring, and I felt close to my childhood friend for a moment. Then Thom, who had gone on ahead to look at the table plans, came back to say, 'I'm not sure if you should see this or not.' At the invitation of the best man, we all headed into the dining room: every table was covered in a silver holographic table-cloth, every chair had a giant shiny silver holograph bow, and there was a huge gold and silver banner behind the top table, saying, 'Annie & Steve – Love Eternal'. 'That's a bit . . . weird, isn't it?' said Thom in my ear. I didn't know what to say. We took our seats, shell-shocked and dazzled.

Annie and Steve were outside having their photos taken by the world's worst wedding photographer ('OK, now can the bride look at the groom, and the groom look off into the distance? Lovely') but arrived in the dining room not long after, and were given a standing ovation by the seventyish guests as Annie led Steve to the top table. We were at the second table, right next to them, and I gave Annie a wave and a thumbs-up as she took her place, and she smiled and waved back at me, open-and-closed hand, like a baby. The waiters came out from the kitchens with our starters, and the man to my left reached for a bottle of white wine at the centre of our table. Thom was opening the red as the waiter put our food in front of us; a bowl of what looked and smelled like Heinz Tomato Soup. I looked over at the top table to see how Annie would protect her dress, and saw that the six guests on the top table were being handed delicate dishes of French Onion Soup, with tiny heart-shaped croutons floating on the top. Checking the other tables, I saw that only the top table had the good stuff: the rest of us had tomato soup and a basket of sliced white loaf in the middle. I nudged Thom under the table and signalled to him the striking discrepancy, and he rolled his eyes slightly. The red wine having gone around the table, Thom finished it into my glass and caught the eye of a waiter: 'Could we get another wine, please . . . No? No, nope, never mind, nothing . . .' Thom's voice faded away, neither of us surprised now that Annie and Steve would provide only two bottles of wine for each table of eight.

The delights kept coming. Main course for the top table: rack of lamb with dauphinoise potatoes and what looked like an asparagus and green bean side. For us: dry chicken with breadcrumbed potato croquettes and peas. Pudding for the top table: Eton mess. For us: bowls of strawberry blancmange with squirty cream and some hundreds and thousands.

After they had finished their puddings and we were still picking bits of clotted blancmange out of our teeth, Steve stood up, tapping his glass. We all got comfortable, gripping our glasses of tap water for the toasts, and Steve said, 'Ladies and gentlemen: the cash bar is now open!' And that was it. There was a stunned silence, which the DJ took as his cue to start up the dancing with '(I've Had) the Time of My Life'. Annie and Steve hurried to the dance floor and I tried to make up my mind which was worse: terrible speeches which went on for hours, or no speeches at all. I did feel slightly cheated, and was desperate to hear their justification for the meal choices (unlikely speech content, admittedly).

After dancing together for fifteen minutes ('Dancing Queen', 'Summer Lovin', 'Angels') Steve left the dance floor and disappeared upstairs. After half an hour with no sign of him, and as Annie looked like she was flagging out there ('Love Shack', 'Baggy Trousers', 'My First, My Last, My Everything', 'Time Warp') I took it as my cue for me and Thom to go and pay our respects.

Me: [shouting over the music] Annie! You look so beautiful!

Annie: [also shouting] Hi Kiki! Thanks so much for coming!

Me: Thanks for inviting us!

Annie: I hear you're getting married soon too!

Me: Yes, this is Thom!

Annie: Will Steve and I be invited?!

Thom: [squeezing my hand, hard] Oh, Annie! We haven't even set a date yet!

Annie: Really? I thought Kiki's mum said—

Me: This is such a lovely wedding, Annie! You're giving us so many ideas!

Annie: Do you really like it? Steve thought it might be too much, but I think it's worked out well!

Me: Is Steve OK? He went upstairs a while ago, didn't he?

Annie: Yeah, I think he gets a bit stressed sometimes! He's gone for a bath – he might be back later!

Me: He's . . .? Right. Well, thank you so much for inviting us, Annie! It's so great to see you after so long!

Annie: Yes, let's meet up after all of this! We mustn't leave it so long next time – although of course there'll be your wedding!

Thom: [dancing me away] Nice to meet you, Annie!

Me: I'll call you!

When we'd danced all the way to the edge of the dance floor, Thom said, 'You didn't mean that, did you? You won't really call her, will you?' I said, 'Not bloody likely. She'll have me hand-making hologram favours for our wedding if I get too close.' Thom said I was too cool for school but he loved me anyway. Then we found a three-quarters-full bottle of wine on the top table, and snuck away with it to the gardens. I ended up quite enjoying that wedding.

March 25th

I had a day off today, to make up for all the extra stuff I'd had to do with Jacki lately, and thought I'd get some wedding shopping in. I know I can't tell Susie about it, but to prove how wrong she was about keeping our mother out of the wedding loop, I called Mum yesterday to see if she wanted to come and look at some possible decorations with me. Mum sounded slightly stressed, then immediately said begrudgingly, 'No, no, that's fine. I'll come.' I thought: You see, Suse? This is why I build an impregnable loop to keep Mum out of these things, but just said, 'Thanks Mum! Shall I see you at Oxford Circus at 11? Is that OK?' She grumbled a bit more, but agreed to meet me, and signed off with, 'I'm sure that'll be very nice, Kiki.' Hold on to your hat, Mum, this sounds like a wild ride.

We were both fifteen minutes late, thank goodness, but she arrived thirty seconds before me, just long enough, apparently, to call my phone four times to find out where I was. Tentatively reassured by my actual presence that I hadn't been kidnapped, we started our trawl of the shops. It became instantly apparent – as if we hadn't known this before – that our tastes were diametrically opposite: she loved union flag bunting and glittery fake flowers ('Aren't they *fun*!'), while I favoured pastels, tarnished silver, fat ribbons and old glass. She kept bringing things to me, too, like a simple-minded Labrador in Laura Ashley, saying, 'This is nice? Don't you want one of these? Sheila's daughter had a set like this on each table.'

I thought of Susie, bit my tongue and smiled at Mum. I lasted an hour less than I thought I would and had to make my excuses to get home early, but to keep her happy, I'd ended up coming home with the perfect decorations for a high-camp super-patriotic sweet-sixteen. Thom told me he kind of liked the look, and I had to break it to him that everything was going back the next day. 'Even this?' he said, twirling a blue-lace-and-white-ribbon garter above his head.

'Especially that.'

March 30th

Bloody Susie. Still no word. Just because *I'm* missing *her* does *not mean* that I'm going to be the first to pick up the phone. She's an idiot.

Speaking of responses (or lack of), most of them in now, amazingly, although some of them were bad news. My friend Lucy can't come – she sent a passive-aggressive message that she's moving house around that time, and since 'some of us' don't have jobs at multinational corporations she'd be struggling to afford a hotel. I'm assuming she's being a dick about Thom's job, rather than mine, otherwise she's been wildly misinformed. All my old housemates can come – good – and almost all of the Accountancy Massive. *Oh hurray*. Ella and Vuk can come, but Ruby can't, since she *was* seeing Vuk when we all travelled together and now Ella is. Nice number reducer. Thom's cousins can both come, and mine are still dithering. Thom's two favourite boffins, Phil and Malcolm, have also given their yes vote. Real hurray! But I am surprised and disappointed by how many people say they can't come because of expense, hinting subtly or not-subtly-at-all that we should have organised the whole thing around them. I despaired:

Me: I don't understand – aren't people pleased to be invited to these things? Isn't it special that we want to share this with them? Why is everyone being so mean? Why can't everyone be nice when we've invited them to our wedding day?

Thom: I know you've put so much effort into this, and this will hopefully be the only wedding you host, but . . . think how many we've been to over the last few years. How much have we spent on presents, and clothes, and hotels, and drinks? And we've liked everyone whose wedding we've been to—

Me: We didn't like Annie and Stephen.

Thom: And some of the people we've invited from my work haven't even met you, let alone seen you enough to be glad of the expense of it. And in August, most of my office shuts down; those Caribbean holiday lodges aren't going to visit themselves, you know. Everyone might love a wedding, but not everyone even *likes* being a guest.

Am I marrying the least romantic man in the world? Could he care less about his own wedding?

A nice evening with Thom, in which I was more inspired than ever to show him how much this wedding meant to me and how perfect it was going to be for both of us. In high spirits, we were snuggling on the sofa like old days. He had his arm around me as we watched an old Buster Keaton film and talked over the jangling piano score about where we'd go on our dream holiday.

Thom: Bali.

Me: Japan.

Thom: The Maldives.

Me: Sardinia.

Thom: Mmm . . . Would you settle for Paris?

Me: Ooooh, when?

Thom: For our honeymoon. Wasn't that what we were talking about?

Me: Yes, but . . . I thought . . .

How could I admit that I thought he was surprising me with a little pre-wedding treat, and that yet again he was turning my wedding dreams into Euro-ashes. Paris? For our honeymoon? Paris where we'd been plenty of times before, where we'd gone as students, where Thom had thrown up a batch of dubious snails? Paris? Not tropical beaches and silent waiting staff to provide you with all the smoothies one newly-wed can drink; not million-dollar yachts and black-tie casinos; not Paradise but . . . *Paris*?

April's Classic Wedding!

When Charles visited the farm, they talked about preparations for the wedding, they wondered in which room to hold the dinner; they imagined the dishes they would need, and what should the entrées be?

Emma, however, yearned to be married at midnight, by torchlight; but Père Rouault wouldn't hear of it. So there was a wedding feast, with forty-three guests who sat eating for sixteen hours, which carried on the following day and into the next few days.

*

The elder Madame Bovary had not opened her mouth all day. She had not been consulted about either the wedding-dress, or the organization of the banquet; she went to bed early. Her husband, instead of following her, sent to Saint-Victor for some cigars and smoked until daybreak.

Madame Bovary
Gustave Flaubert

April 1st

With two weeks to go until Jacki's wedding, I took a much-needed afternoon off work today for my second fitting. Joy! That dress doesn't ever stop being the most beautiful thing I've ever seen. And also . . . bad times. Thom came home from work and wouldn't even give me a kiss. He stood across from me in the kitchen while I grated cheese for the lasagne, and passed a bottle of beer from hand to hand while he talked.

Me: [nervously] How was your day?
Thom: Complete garbage. It's a hateful place to work. But I've been thinking. And I think we need to talk.
Me: Is it about how beautiful my dress looked today? *Very*. Or is it about your suit? Because I think I've had a thought about the way we can make it vintagey, without having to dig you out some suspicious-smelling old actually vintage suit. There's this amazing—
Thom: Kiki, stop. It's this whole wedding. I don't think we have the money—

143

Me: But we've already paid the deposit! That four grand is gone! And we'll find the money, everyone does—

Thom: But I don't *want* to find the money. I don't *want* that money to go missing from the rest of our lives! Why are we always fighting about this? What's happened here? This whole thing is becoming a monster, and I don't know if I'm happy being part of this anymore.

Me: Wait, is this . . .? I'm loath to say it, but – well, it is April 1st . . .

Thom: *No*, this isn't a bloody joke, Kiki! Annie had a 'fancy' wedding. Annie and Steve had a *really* 'fancy' wedding.

Me: For the top table at least.

Thom: She will have spent months planning it, maybe years. They will have saved up, and saved up, and saved up, and all they will have to show for it is wedding photos with loads of flash reflections and all the tinfoil they'll ever need. Is that what you want? A stupid wedding that everyone laughs about, because you were too busy competing with God-knows-who to actually remember what this whole thing is about? Anyone can have a 'special' wedding, Kiki, like anyone can have a credit card and a massive debt, but what separates us from wooden spoons is that we can understand that these decisions will affect our future. Maybe it's time you woke up and understood that no one is going to wave a wand for you to have the million-pound wedding you think you need.

Thom slammed his bottle of beer on the counter, and it fizzed open and sprayed him. He didn't even laugh, just sighed and set about cleaning up. I put the lasagne in the oven, half-covered in cheese, and tried to help him clean up too.

Me: [trying to stay calm] Thom, I do understand all that.
        I really do. But you are providing me with nothing but
        problems instead of helping me make this a wedding
        for both of us.

Thom: Because it's becoming ridiculous, and I can't bear to
        see you behaving like this. Who *are* you? What are
        you *doing*? This shouldn't all be so difficult. Do you
        know what you've been like to your parents? Do you
        have any idea how you sound when you talk to them?
        When you just put your head down on the table
        when your mum is trying to talk to you, don't you
        have any idea how hard it is to be on your side? And
        I *want* to be on your side! Christ, Kiki, your mum
        winds me up too, but do you know how your face
        looked when your parents 'only' gave us £3,000?
        £3,000! Do you have any idea how much that is?
        What are you *doing*, Kiki?

Me: [letting out a small scream] *Thom!* You've had
        precisely *nothing* to do with organising this wedding
        so far, and if you think you could do so much better
        you are *more* than welcome to arrange this whole
        bloody thing yourself. One minute you're merrily
        writing a cheque for £4,000 and agreeing to £380
        cakes, the next you're saying we can't afford clothes
        for you or a dress for me!

Thom: That's not a dress, Kiki, that's a mortgage payment.

Me: [picking up this book, becoming louder] Here are a
        few things you might want to consider: venue details,
        food, booze, a band for the wedding – and the actual
        wedding *bands*, your one job so far – the dress, the
        veil, cars, flowers, decorations, favours, the cake, table-
        ware, photographer, guest books, confetti, disposable
        cameras, place names, bridesmaids dresses, accom-
        modation for guests, my hair and makeup . . . gifts

for the wedding party. Table plans. Orders of Service!
The wedding list! [panting a bit]
Thom: [silence] Why do we even need a wedding list?

I screamed. The evening did not end well. I threw a plate
at Thom. I'm so tired, and so frightened that this isn't just how
our wedding is going to be, but our marriage too. I'm lonely
every time I see Thom and I can't understand how to join us
up again. When he fell asleep, before I came to write this, I
took off my engagement ring and left it on Thom's bedside
table. I've realised what I need to do. I've packed a bag, ready
for the morning. I want so much to talk to Susie about all of
this, but she still hasn't called me. What is wrong with her?

TO DO:
Try to work out what the hell it is I think I'm doing

April 2nd

I think we need a little break. I don't want to lose Thom,
but I feel like we're both losing our minds slightly. I felt
faintly ridiculous when I woke up without my engagement
ring on this morning, removed in some dreadful soap opera
statement. But I couldn't take it back. I snuck out before
Thom woke up, and I didn't look at it or him as I closed
the bedroom door. And Thom was right. I do love that ring.
Almost as much as I love the person who chose it for me.
   I met Alice for breakfast, where she saw my sad little
weekend bag sitting like a kicked kitten under our table.

Alice: Ahhh, that's nice. Are you going away with Thom
         this weekend?
Me: Nope.

Alice:	*He's* going away with *you*?
Me:	No, Alice, I'm going to stay with my friends before Thom and I drop dead from stress over this wedding.
Alice:	[aghast] You're . . . *moving out*?
Me:	Alice, we're not divorcing. It's just driving us absolutely up the wall at the moment. The planning. Our 'ideas'. And I'm not sure I particularly like who I am right now. I'd rather stay away from Thom until we can be friends again, which I'm sure will be soon – as soon as he calls and we can sort all this out – but in the meantime I'm going to stay, for a few nights, with friends, who have beds I can lie in at night, and that's all. It's not even A Break, it's just me staying out for a while, so we don't break one another. It's just got a bit . . .
Alice:	Silly?
Me:	Maybe.
Alice:	But you're not breaking up?
Me:	I bloody hope not. What if I lost custody of you?
Alice:	And the Hamilton millions?
Me:	Exactly. Who would keep me in diamond shoes then?

Then Alice made a serious mistake.

Alice:	Why don't you just go and stay at your parents'?

I tucked my chair right next to hers, pushed her coffee away from her and listed for twelve minutes all the ways in which it would be neither sensible nor effective for me as a spiritual, growing person to allow my mother any idea of what was going on. She clearly couldn't care less about this wedding, unable even to muster a Mum-ish criticism about the venues I'd mentioned to her. Or was it more that, going back through the years, every time – *every time* – I would be upset by a falling-out with a friend, a mean girl at school, a rumour that I'd been caught up in, she would ask me one question: Well, what did *you* do for this to happen? I'd learnt soon enough to avoid discussing anything of any importance with her, and the idea that I would go running to their house for comfort, even though I wanted so much to see Dad and have him tell me how ridiculous it was, the idea that I would walk right into the lions' den of self-flagellation so she could tell me that I didn't deserve him, that all this was my fault, that I needed to apologise immediately, and – worse – if all this didn't get fixed, if somehow – GOD – somehow if I lost Thom, the thought that she had watched it all in slow motion, shaking her head at me and knowing better, was more than I could possibly bear.

Alice: Oh, right. I just thought they might have converted your room to an office or something.

I wiped my mouth and apologised. Alice patted my hand and said she knew I was going through a tough time.

Obviously I can't stay with Suse right now, so I've come to stay with Jim, oldest and wisest (and most musical) of friends. He hasn't even asked why, just let me in when I arrived, showed me my bedroom and told me the roast was in the oven. After the last few weeks of eggshells and rage, I wanted to cry at how lovely it was, but toughened up and gave him the Clifton Black books I'd swung by the office for. They're his secret vice, and if there's *one* thing I can do without harming anyone, it's feed a secret book vice. We sat in companionable silence for the afternoon, watching terrible TV – occasionally one of us would get up for another pair of beers – before Jim put a pizza and an old Tom Hanks film on and we ate and laughed ourselves queasy and then watched an old zombie flick until I realised I was going to be too scared to sleep. As we were going our separate ways for the night, Jim softly nudged me with his foot and said, 'Is this going to be like . . . that dark time?'

Thom and I had been together for two years when something went wrong. I don't know what it was, and to be perfectly honest, I don't care to think about that time at all. Maybe I should be plumbing those depths to save us from whatever is going on right now, but I can't. At the time, it somehow seemed like a mutual decision for us to split up, but when my brain tiptoes around those memories, trying not to look but still catching glimpses out of the corner of its lobe, I think I must have gone completely mad. I did some very strange things then. Those flashes of recollection suggest that I literally lost my mind. I was a walking hollow, functioning, but with no reference to the person I had been before. I'm amazed I could tie my shoelaces during that time.

It was fine in the end – ha! Look at us now! – and we got back together with a beautiful inevitability, and things were better afterwards than they ever had been before, but I know what Jim is frightened about. That . . . was not a good time.

Me: No, bud, it's not going to be like that. If all else fails I'll just settle for the shittiest wedding in the world. I'm not dragging anyone back there again.

TO DO:
Find out if it's too late to marry Jim. Or maybe Alice. Or Tom Hanks?

April 3rd

I know it doesn't seem like it, but, in normal circumstances, we hardly argue at all these days. (since Jim's question last night I've been thinking about it a *lot*). When we first moved in together, it was truly terrible. Thom had no idea how to put things in the cupboards: the cup handles would be pointing in any direction, and the plates wouldn't even begin to be sorted by colour. It was a bumpy ride, but he educated himself and things smoothed out. Then he suddenly realised that *I* was ridiculous, and forced me to learn how to hang my clothes up on mismatching hangers and put my shoes away in non-pairs. Then: we broke up. I can still remember so clearly packing up that flat, putting all my things in boxes, not able to move fast in case I shattered completely and scattered all over the floor, not able to look at him, putting away all those things I thought would be the bricks in building our future.

So we broke up, then after about six months, we got back in touch. It's fine! we both said, We're just friends! It's not complicated! But it was complicated, thank God, and we moved in together – again – two and a half years after we'd originally met, so close to my parents that I wondered if it didn't seem to Thom like I was hedging my bets. That time it was much harder. We didn't argue – I think we were both frightened to – but we weren't comfortable. I was embarrassed, somehow, about what had happened, having to tell both of our parents that we'd broken up, then that we'd got back together, and I was embarrassed that my faith in us had been shown up so clearly. To have believed so utterly in someone, and to be shown up as mistaken. I was so embarrassed for so long, until one day, as we had a lazy battle about buying some milk, I realised I wasn't anymore, and I loved him, and we were going to be OK. But we didn't really argue after that. So this feels . . . bad.

The *very* first argument we ever had was as ridiculous as first arguments ever are. What tips a happy new couple over into two bickering people? When you're in that first flush of love, how bad does the argument have to be to realise this isn't someone you want to be with? Ours was about *The Great*

Gatsby. I loved the book; the style, the sweep, the romance of it, but Thom thought it was flat and silly. What started out as a flirtatious warm-up to the evening's activity swiftly snowballed into something else.

Me: [laughing] You can't really feel that way, can you? It's a *classic*.

Thom: I can really feel that way, and I do. And I don't think classic status protects it from anything. At its weakest, it's just a list of clothing.

Me: Haha. Ha. [frowning at his stubbornness] No, really, even if you don't like it, you can recognise the quality of the writing, can't you?

Thom: Shall we talk about something else?

Me: [hackles up] I don't want to talk about something else. Please can you not tell me when I've finished talking about something?

Thom: [half to himself] Well, this is fun.

Me: I *am* still here, you know.

Thom: Are you sure you want to be?

Me: Thank God you're here to make my mind up for me. [picks up bag and coat]

Thom: Are you serious? Calm down, Kiki, don't go home.

Me: Calm down? Do you want to just pat me on the head and be done with it? *Don't* call me. [leaves]

Ironically, *The Great Gatsby* is now one of Thom's favourite books. I find it unreadable.

April 4th

I read in the papers this morning that Jacki's already working on her new album, of classic love songs 'reworked for the twenty-first century'. Before Tony could start jumping around my desk sweating at me that our author was getting distracted from her important book project, I'd drawn up a document to show how we could cross-promote between the album and the book and with clever marketing this could double our sales without us having to do a thing. Tony read it and grunted. I was dismissed from his office. But my GOD, Jacki works hard. How does she do all this? I suppose working side by side all day with the man she loves must help. With ten days until her wedding, her emails don't show a hint of nerves.

Speaking of which event, I'm still Jim's number one fan. Could I stay here indefinitely? It's so unbelievably nice to not have to talk about weddings, or think about weddings, or argue about weddings in my own time at least. Jim made us both lunch this morning, met me at the tube after work, cooked dinner and had me call a coin for whether we watched cruel Japanese gameshows or play Scrabble. Since we spent most of Sunday playing increasingly heated games of Scrabble with bottle after bottle of cider (last night I got polygyny, even after several gallons of that delicious appley poison. 38 points with a double word score. COME ON) watching cruel Japanese gameshows was a quiet, sober treat tonight.

Then I looked in my diary when I came to bed and saw that tonight was the night Thom had booked for us to go to the Planetarium.

April 5th

Thom called today. We talked for a while – I told him about Jacki's new album. He started singing Roy Orbison's 'Crying'.

Me: I miss you.
Thom: [in rough approximation of Roy Orbison's Texan

152

drawl] Come on home then. I've got a bed that's sure feeling lonely for you.

Me: Ugh, you make that sound really creepy.

Thom: No, that didn't really work, did it. But hurry up, Keeks. I could do with you being back. I can't work the boiler properly. And I love you.

Me: I'm afraid you're just going to have to put another jumper on. We need to make sure this isn't a fissure that'll lead to a canyon.

Thom: Kiki, it doesn't need to be this way. If you listen to your mum—

Me: *What?*

Thom: Hold on, you know I didn't mean that. But both of your parents are worried about where this wedding seems to be headed. If we all talk about it, we can make this work.

Me: Thom. I don't need this. Please.

Thom sighed, and we said we loved one another, then we said goodbye. Do we even like each other right now?

April 6th

I met Eve for a drink after work yesterday. She spent thirty-five minutes telling me about a guy on the tube who was trying to look at her tits until she undid her top buttons and told him that would be £50, please. She said she didn't know who she felt sorrier for, him or his wife – 'Although of course I didn't really feel sorry for him, the dirty pervert.'

At that particular moment, I felt most sorry for me. Bringing another pair of Bands on the Run from the bar, I took a deep breath and said as coolly as I could manage, 'Eve, can I come and stay at yours for a while? This wedding planning is so tricky when Thom and I are on top of one another and nitpicking. I wanted to get some bulk of the organisation done, then he and I can thrash the details out.' None of that began to cover the terrible air between us every time the W-word was uttered, nor how close I felt to losing him for good, but it was as close to the truth as she was ever going to get. Eve raised one eyebrow at me, but simply said, '*Mi casa es su casa.*' I slugged my Band on the Run and we went for a karaoke session. What *doesn't* seem better after belting out Elton John's hits at the top of your lungs? I'm eager to stay friends with Jim, so despite his hospitable objections, I'm going to Eve's tonight. It's that old saying about houseguests and fish: I don't particularly want these few days to stink our friendship up. I'm on the way over to Eve's now.

Still no word from Susie. Three months to go until that baby's out. And I don't even know if Thom's heard from her.

April 7th

I arrived last night in the pouring rain with shoes squelching, and hair dripping right onto Eve's Liberty welcome mat. She came at me with a gigantic fluffy towel, wrapped me up and handed me a mug of hot chocolate only slightly smaller than my head. 'Come in and watch some *All About Eve*,' she said, steering me to the sofa. 'Why are you watching a film about yourself?' I asked, delusional with cold and tiredness. I remember drinking half the hot chocolate in one swig; then Eve waking me up when the film was over and steering me off the sofa and up to her spare room. I woke up at 7 this morning, with Eve tapping at the door and brandishing a beautiful tray with a vintage cup and saucer and a Vera Wang teapot, and saying, 'Time for work, Sleeping Beauty.' I tried desperately to remember where the hell I was, then felt like crying when I remembered that I still wasn't home. 'Aren't I just the best company you've ever had?' I asked. Eve sat at the end of my bed, tucked her knees beneath her chin, and looked at me for a while.

'Kiki, you know you can stay here for as long as you want. We don't have to talk about anything that you don't want to talk about, or we don't have to talk at all, if you like. I am monastic like you would not *believe*. Just get your rump off my beautiful sheets, eat the delicious breakfast I've made you, and get to work before you lose your somehow-enjoyable job.' I thought it best to follow her excellent orders.

When I got back this evening, Eve had ordered an amazing Japanese takeaway, with grilled quail eggs and mixed tempura and a whole heap of udon; while I changed into pyjamas, she poured me a glass of some absurdly expensive saké. We spent the evening discussing all the people we went to school with, details of our dream party (with key use of the cuttings in this book, which I pulled out for the visual aids) and planning a business for renting dogs as party icebreakers. Sometimes, I can really remember why I'm friends with Eve.

April 8th

Christ alive. Eve is a *nightmare*.

We'd been spending a great Friday night going through her cupboards, sorting all the gorgeous finds she's sourced from flea markets, antiques shops, jumble sales and car boot sales into Definitely Keep, Let Kiki Have and Sell On piles. She's got such an eagle eye for this stuff, and I'm sure half the

155

reason she never keeps a man is that he might unbalance the visual beauty that is her home. I found a snow-globe with tiny numbers in instead of snowflakes, and thought of Thom and his terrible job, and all the numbers in his life that crush him. I said, 'I love these. No matter what's inside them, the kitsch outweighs the cheapness. In a good way.'

Eve took the snow-globe from my hand. 'I don't really understand what you're doing here, Kiki. I love you, and I'm really glad you're staying, and you really are welcome to stay for as long as you want – I could do with a housemate from time to time – but I really don't know what you're doing here. Do you know how much Thom loves you? Listen, I've been talking to someone recently – not a professional, someone I've met – and it's been quite shitty to admit that I am, mostly, pathetic. Yes, I have the nicest house of anyone you'll ever meet, and my hair is amazing all of the time, but what kind of person would have to prove herself by trying to snare a friend's man?'

I felt a bit sick. This wasn't really why I was staying away from my flat. I wasn't missing my own bath and bed and kitchen and sofa and fiancé just so someone else could make me feel so stressed I wanted to vomit.

'Kiki, *listen*. Thom has made it abundantly clear, time after time after time, that he cannot stand me. He's so polite, but I am fully aware of how he feels. And why wouldn't he? He can't turn around without finding me pushing my tits at him. I know he doesn't like me. At *all*. Do you know what he was saying to me at my birthday party, when we were dancing together? He kept calling me Kiki. There isn't a scrap of sexy-space in his brain that isn't taken up with you. And while I can understand that you're finding organising a party for 150 people stressful, you should be talking this through with – or ignoring it all next to – him, not me. Even though I love you.'

I had nothing to say to that. I can cope with being friends with Eve if we both pretend she was just drunk at her party, but I can't manage if she tells me that she's tried to steal Thom. Or if she then tells me how to manage the relationship she was, apparently, desperate to break up. I picked up my pile of Let Kiki Have things to go to bed, shaking, then had to turn around and say, 'Eve, what the hell is wrong with you? You need to fucking pull yourself together. You're fucking . . . *disgraceful.*' Eve sat with her face in her hands, and *she* had nothing to say to *that*.

April 9th

I'm home again. I stayed up most of the night thinking about what she'd said, thinking about what she's *been* throughout most of my life, and how since I met Thom I've seen her less and less, naturally, but each time the three of us were together she never once gave me the impression that she enjoyed herself or got on well with Thom, only that she wanted to be there, witnessing us, somehow. I must have fallen asleep a little after 4am, and dreamt of hundreds of doors closing off a long corridor, and my old History teacher saying she couldn't be my girlfriend while I was still engaged. I'm not sure what any of it meant, but I do recall feeling *really* cross about it in the dream. Eve was gone by the time I got up, having to rush off to some charity emergency, but she left my breakfast all laid out and a note saying 'Sorry x'.

I took the bus home. As we drove past the statue of the naked lady with the sword, I imagined how tough *her* life must be. Back at the flat by 10 this morning, I closed the door after me with an un-silent silence, trying to creep about in a way no one could possibly have missed. When that received no response, I closed our bedroom door and put some music on – again, unmissable for anyone in the flat. After ten minutes, I noticed the stillness of the whole place, and started registering things I'd seen on the way through: the pile of letters on the mat; the tidiness (although that may have been due to my week-long absence); Thom's brown suitcase missing from the top of the wardrobe. I had a sudden feeling in the pit of my stomach, and rooted in my bag for my diary. The dates were there: *Thom to Edinburgh.* I'd completely forgotten that Thom left this morning for a course and wouldn't be back until late next Sunday night, and I realised then how much I'd wanted him to be here.

April 12th

I took off from Polka Dot early today, to see Dad at the college. He was in the middle of one of his classes, but he saw me hanging around outside like some gloomy paedophile and called one of the assistants to take over for the last fifteen minutes. He bustled me into his office (a cupboard next to the Arts foyer) and made us both some tea.

Dad: What are you up to, little Katherine?
Me: [lump in throat]
Dad: [patting my knee] Like that, is it? Drink your tea, girl.

We sat in silence until the buzzer rang for the end of the day, and listened to the kids banging and calling on their way out. After a few minutes, I said, 'Dad, I think I'm an idiot.' He said, 'Well, that's true of most folk. What's your main concern?'

I told him everything that had happened, feeling no disloyalty to Thom because the telling made me realise quite what a minuscule crime Thom had committed. Poor Thom. Dad gave me a big hug and said we were all as bad as each other;

that nothing was as bad as it seemed, and at least the pair of us had our health. He said that we clearly loved one another, and that it ought to be good enough to fix all this silliness. I felt better, and like the biggest idiot in the world.

Now, Thom, please can you come home?

April 13th

Spent the last few days moping around the house waiting for Thom to come back and running off to do last-minute stuff with Jacki. She wants Polka Dot Books there for every stage: no purchase is too small to record and (unfortunately for me) photograph. I feel dizzy; Jacki's life is a tornado, with her at the centre, beaming at everyone through the chaos and activity. If anyone in the history of weddings has ever earned their honeymoon, it's that woman. Two days to go.

April 15th

OH GOD I'M EXHAUSTED. And terrified that the police are about to knock on my door. One can only assume that Jacki's *actual* wedding co-ordinators were replaced by amphetamine-fuelled robots months ago. Today was, finally, the day of Jacki and Leon's wedding. I'm not sure I can think about any of this at the moment. More soon.

April 17th

Right. I've had thirty-six whole hours in bed and on the sofa with dire daytime TV, a bag of brioches and several pints of lime cordial, and I'm beginning to feel human enough to talk about it.

I was due at Jacki's at 4.30am, to ensure that Pedro and his assistants had their way clear, and that Jacki would not have to worry about anything to do with the pictures and the last few bits of writing (I was going to do those after I'd eye-witnessed the whole thing). I got a taxi over and expected to find a dead silent sleeping house, but pulling up outside, every single light was on and the front door was wide open, with people already coming and going with lighting rigs, hampers, gifts, dress-racks and flowers. No one knew exactly where Jacki was (or at least, everyone told me somewhere that she turned out not to be) but eventually I found her, in the base-ment kitchen, the only place in the house that was still and quiet. I couldn't see her face when I first walked in, and when she lifted her head to see who was coming I was shocked to see how haggard she looked, how terrified. But she recognised me, and leapt up to give me a huge hug, talking away ten to the dozen like I hadn't seen her face just a moment before. She kept me close to her, one arm half round me like she always did with whoever she was speaking to, but when I asked if Leon was in the house she said, 'No, no love, he's at his mum's. Bad luck to see the bride on the wedding morning,' then took us out of the kitchen and all the way up the house to her bedroom, past flocks of people being paid Christ knows how much to do Christ knows what. Her room looked like Diana's funeral, piled so high with flowers I could barely see the furniture underneath. In one corner was a dressmaker's dummy, with her beautiful wedding dress on and her little Louboutins peeking out from the hem like the mannequin was all ready for her big day. There was a luxuriously wrapped parcel on the bed, about the size of a shoe box, with a giant bow on top and a label saying, 'For my Ladybird.' Jacki saw me looking, and said happily, 'It's his wedding present for me.' It was still only 5am, but her excitement was almost pushing me over. Then Pedro arrived – we could hear him barking orders to his underlings the second he walked in the front door – and I was relegated to the edges, directed to keep out of shot and not get in the light, so I pulled out my notebook and began trying to sculpt some of the things Jacki had said (or not said) into her hilarious marital prose. The hours sped by, because every ten minutes or so someone would come looking for another pair of hands to hold this vase/steady this ladder/move this pile of presents from room to room to room. Jacki and Leon would be having a post-reception reception here, so the house was being decorated just as carefully as the venue itself. Caterers filled Jacki's kitchen, and lighting designers called me down again and again to give my opinion at which side of the room the lamp looked better, God knows why. Finally at 11am, Jacki, with hair in rollers and face glowing, found me in a corner and demanded that I go into her room and try on a few things to get me looking a bit more weddingish. I asked her if she had any floor-length white dresses hanging about for me and she said, 'Kiki, love, you joke, but I bloody will do. Plenty of them. Slightly worried we might look a bit of a pair, though.' I loved the dress I was in at the time, so she found me a giant broad-brimmed green hat and some matching cropped gloves, then she stood back to consider my outfit and fished in her jewellery trunk to find a long rope of pearls. I balked, saying I didn't think I should walk around in something so precious, but she only laughed, and explained that these were M&S's finest. I was slightly concerned that I looked ever-so Miss Marple, but when I went to her wall-o-mirrors I was delighted to see that I looked more *Harper's Bazaar* than village fete, so Jacki clapped me on my backside and said that I would do. Then she went off to get her hair finished while I sat in her room and fantasised like a five-year-old about owning her wardrobe (bigger than our bedroom and living room put together) and all those things in it (worth, I suspect, twelve times more than any home we'll ever own). After half an hour of stroking her coats and picking up all her shoes I actually felt a bit of a deviant, so I tucked myself back in the corner to make more notes, anything other than I WANT HER SHOES I WANT HER CLOTHES I WANT HER HANDBAGS. When she found me again, she was in her million-pound Jenny Packham dressing gown and ready to get into her dress. She wanted me with her, so Pedro, Zoe, three assistants, two makeup artists, two hairdressers, plus the dress designer and her assistants, all piled into Jacki's room, where she was chatting to all of us, remembering everyone's names and putting everyone at ease. I think only I was aware of how hard she was squeezing my hand. Because she has the body of a Greek goddess, she was happy for Pedro to keep snapping while she dropped her robe, revealing her beautiful underwear, and allowed herself to be dressed by the designer herself, and when the dress was fastened and Jacki turned around to us all, I doubt I was the only person with tears in their eyes. She really was beautiful, a million miles away from the person I'd glimpsed at the kitchen table that morning. Hairdresser A fastened the veil in her hair while hairdresser B stood nearby spraying hairspray like she could fix this moment in time forever, and I actually did start crying then. This was all so lovely, so perfect. Wild horses wouldn't have torn this sentiment out of me out loud, but . . . she looked like an angel, like I wanted to look, like how all brides should look on the day of their wedding. She was amazing.

Then suddenly we were being bustled out of the door, into the cars: I was planning on getting into whichever car had space for me at the back of the parade, but Jacki called out from her grey Rolls Royce, 'Kiki! Get in here with me. You'll need all these details!' Pedro – ever the charmer – hissed, 'Don't you fucking get in there yet and ruin this shot,' so I pretended I had to re-tie my wedges until Zoe gave me the thumbs-up. Jacki didn't hold my hand this time but talked the whole way, about what we were seeing, who would be there, who she hadn't invited and whether the paparazzi would be there (No Jacki, I thought, they'll have decided to let you and Leon enjoy your one special day with some peace and quiet). I didn't have to hold hands with her to see how much she was shaking though, and thanking the stars for Susie's tip from months ago, I reached into my handbag and offered the vodka miniature I'd snagged from her hen night. 'It doesn't really seem dignified, does it, Kiki?' she reprimanded, unscrewing the lid and downing it in one. 'Holy *Christ*, that feels better.' We were at the venue now. She looked at me again, and said, 'Thank you, Kiki. Thank you for everything.' Then her bridesmaids were at the door, pawing at the handle to be the one who got her out, and Jacki was laughing and stepping out, smiling and waving sweetly to the paps as the cameras flashed and her fans called out to her. I sat in the car for a minute or two more, to make sure I wouldn't clutter up any of her shots and to get a few more notes down ('I was nervous on the way there, but every bride is!') then stepped out into a street which was suddenly eerily deserted. The paps had gone for a sly drink/fag break and the fans had trickled away to wherever fans go when their stars aren't there. A few stray photographers hung around to see if there were any famous latecomers to the festivities, but didn't even bother raising their cameras when they saw me opening the car door. Charming.

Inside, I snuck in at the back, flashing the ushers my invitation and sliding into a chair beside a girl with lips so glossed they looked like they were about to run down her chin. The service, naturally, was stunning, although the readings – done by those of Jacki's friends who possess hopes of an acting career – all seemed to be pegged at a *Hollyoaks* level of melodrama and joy. During the vows, I welled up a little: they were the simple, classic words of betrothal and oath, and something about the way Jacki said them made my eyes brim. She put such hope and faith into what she was saying, and I believed with all my heart that she would make this marriage work. Leon seemed a bit more affected by nerves, though, looking around the whole time he said his vows, laughing, taking Jacki's hand like someone had asked him to hold an old fish for a moment. When Leon finally said 'I do', the glossy girl next to me started sobbing, and the girl the other side of her hissed, 'Will you *shut up*, Karen. You're not making this any easier for anyone.'

I missed Thom so much. I don't even have Susie to tell all this to.

Then we were pouring like treacle across to the reception rooms. They were immaculately carpeted in white wool and every available surface was covered in glasses of champagne and tiny canapés in a hundred delicious flavours. When I caught a harassed-looking Zoe and she warned me quite how long the wedding photos were likely to take, I took a whole tray from a passing waitress and went to find Pedro and co. They were on the grand staircase, with hairdresser A and the makeup trio fussing around Jacki while the designer's assistant made minute changes to the way the train of the dress lay perfectly casually on the stone steps. Leon kept an iron arm around Jacki's waist, never letting go and smiling beatifically at everyone. Jacki saw me and waved, making the dresser groan as she leapt forward to correct the one millimetre the train had moved. Pedro turned around to see who Jacki was waving at, and reassured that it wasn't anyone famous or important bellowed, 'For *FUCK'S* sake, can we get some fucking professionalism here, people?'

Dick.

We didn't sit down to eat until almost 7, but Jacki and Leon gave their joint speech while we were eating (Jacki said she was too nervous to wait and wanted to be able to enjoy her food) and they were so charming and funny and loving – Leon described Jacki as 'the sun that makes my moon go round' which, while lacking any technical accuracy, is a very sweet sentiment – and everyone seemed ready to forgive his laughter during the vows, and being forced to make small talk to semi-famous strangers for five hours. The food was exquisite, tiny slivers of duck on a bed of vermicelli followed by a juicy, flavourful stuffed roll of pork, then a giant, immaculate eight-tiered wedding cake with Jacki and Leon's names embroidered into ribbon which wound around each tier and flowed in a giant bow from the top. It was so grand, I wanted to live in it. There were two other speeches, from Jacki's chief bridesmaid (an old friend of hers who recounted hilarious misadventures from their teenage Ibiza holidays together) and Leon's best man. His speech was . . . well, let's say I probably wouldn't want him to do a school assembly, but he was pretty funny, mostly. I didn't love the stuff about Jacki's mountains of money, but it ain't no problem of mine, and Jacki laughed harder than anyone.

Their first dance was 'You Look Wonderful Tonight', and they danced wonderfully. By the second verse, Jacki was waving the crowd onto the floor and I was swept up by a dapper old man who could shake it like nobody's business. I was the first to surrender, begging off at the fourth tune when I realised the aged groover was a great deal fitter than I was. Sweating but happy, I took a chair at the edge and watched the action for a while. Jacki was dancing like she'd done nothing but sleep in preparation for this wedding, rather than organising it and writing the book and working with producers on her love song album and heaven knows what else to maintain her career. She was whirling and laughing and jumping with her friends around her. Leon had retreated to the bar with a few pals, but kept looking over to watch her and smile.

At ten to one, I was at the bar arguing with the bartender about how to make a Band on the Run. He said it required Angostura bitters, but I was trying to tell him that I'd invented the bloody thing so it could have whatever I wanted in it. Then suddenly Jacki was next to me, saying, 'Same as her, Julian,' and I was suddenly getting the drink I'd requested. Jacki looked happy but exhausted, and she told me she couldn't wait to get all of this into the book back in the office on Tuesday – she's not even taking her month-long honeymoon in Mauritius until the book is signed off and sent to the printers on Friday. She'd already started making notes every time she nipped to the bathroom. She broke off and gave me a huge hug, and I could hear she was choking up when she said in my ear, 'Thank you so much, Kiki. I couldn't have done it without you.' I heard a hiss in my ear and pulled away to see Pedro glowering over my shoulder. He leaned past me to take Jacki's hands, and said, 'Jacki, my love, can I have a quick word with Kiki?' She gave us a big tired smile and blew us a kiss, then swept back to the dance floor with her gang of pals.

Pedro turned me to face him. 'Listen to me, you silly little bitch. I've worked with Jacki since she started in this fucking industry, and I'm not going to have you forcing your way between us because you're bored of that fucking backwater little publishing house. Do you understand me? You're a worthless little nobody, and Jacki is not your meal ticket. So just fuck off out of it, yeah? That's a good girl.'

He gave me a horrible poisonous smirk and skulked off to take more photos of beautiful people. I thought I was

166

going to throw up, and it definitely wasn't only the four slices of wedding cake I'd eaten. Where the Jesus Christ had this come from? Yes, I wasn't a huge fan of Pedro, but I'd always behaved professionally and had never given any indication that I wanted even the tiniest slice of his crazy fame pie.

It was . . . shocking. A punch in the gut from a mugger solely after my happy buzz, to feed his dreadful, all-engulfing insecurity. But why was I his victim tonight? I suppose he caught me making Jacki smile, while he could only do the catching and not the making, that bullying shit. I was so angry, so furious that he would talk to me like that – that he would talk to anybody like that – that he would try with his words to make me feel small, and worthless—

It took me a moment for my hands to stop shaking, and I thought of everything I could do. I thought: I could pour wine into his camera case. Or convince him that Jacki had already hired me as her assistant. Or give him a reasoned, biting analysis of all the ways in which his little speech had made him much less of a person than I would ever be. Whatever sweaty little drunken pleasure he'd got from it, he wasn't going to bloody keep it.

I scanned the room, finding him in one corner snapping some of Jacki's more notable guests, and made my way over. 'Pedro?' I waited until he was looking at me, his smirk still in place. Suddenly, my blood roared in my veins. I thought back to my years of training – growing up with an older sister – lifted my foot, and kicked him as hard as I could on his shin. Before he could say anything (or kick me back), I walked away and found Jacki on the dance floor, told her how much I'd enjoyed her wedding and what an honour it was to have been here, and let her embrace me again, knowing Pedro was watching the whole time. I got a taxi home, aware the whole way back that Thom wouldn't be there to wait

167

up for me, and prayed I wouldn't find the police waiting to arrest me for assault. Susie would *love* that. I thought:

Maybe . . . I'll ring her. Maybe. But I still haven't.

April 18th

Oh, *heavens*.

Monday, a day I've been given off after Friday's antics. I heard Thom get in late last night – when he got into bed he hugged me, and I wrapped my arms around him, but he was asleep in moments – and was aware of him leaping back out of bed extremely early for work. I heard the front door go at 7am, then pulled a pillow over my face and went back to sleep, sad at not being able to apologise to him. At 9am, there was a soft scratching at my door. A cat burglar? When I drowsily sat up (still full of a fantastic dream about being Prime Minister of 1960s France with Damian Lewis as my Chancellor of the Exchequer) there was Thom, scrabbling to open the door with his foot while he balanced a giant tray of breakfast. All my favourite things: an *Elle Deco* with the inserts already removed, Egg Bread with a dish of cherry jam, a teapot of fresh mint tea, a tiny bowl of Coco Pops, a tall glass of fresh orange juice and an enormous ketchup-y sausage sandwich. It was delicious, and thoughtful, and for me, and I couldn't hide the smile from my kind butler. I took his hand and said, 'Thom, I'm so sorry,' and tried to pull him onto the bed for a kiss, but he pulled away from me; 'Sorry, ma'am, that wouldn't be appropriate. Your itinerary for the day confirms that you will be collected at 10.30 this morning, and you will be required to wear Something Comfortable.' Then he left, only returning to poke a tiny radio into the bedroom, playing Elvis Costello. This really was bliss. I managed to push a few mouthfuls of everything down and roll like a doughball into the shower, and was prepped and ready for my day at 10.30 sharp, waiting at the front door and wondering what mischief Thom could be getting us into, when there was a hoot-hoot from outside. Oh, joy on toast! It was a soft-blue Nissan Figaro, my little fantasy felt-tip sketch of a car, with Thom himself behind the wheel, peaked cap on head and creepy eighties-chauffeur shades on his face. 'Your rented carriage, ma'am,' he intoned, stepping out to open my door. Never one to argue with a good spoiling, I climbed in.

Me: Am I being carried off into white slavery?
Thom: And leave me to pay for my books? No fear. I mean, no fear, ma'am.
Me: You'd better be a bit careful, or there'll be no tip for you, Jeeves.
Thom: I'm not that worried, ma'am. I'm the only one with the house keys.
Me: Touché, the Help.

I allowed him to sweep me off to our destination, which, after a long circuitous drive, turned out to be up the road at Alexandra Park. He parked up and directed me towards the trees by the lake; heading there, I could see someone on a blanket. It looked like they were flashing a light at me, but as I got closer I realised it was a pair of binoculars, and they were being held by Jim. From the way he leapt up when I was remarkably close, I could almost hear him say, 'Oh, *shit*!'; then Thom's guard ran off through the trees, leaving a tartan blanket and a big wicker hamper. When Thom caught up as I reached the blanket, he had removed his cap and pervert sunglasses. He knelt beside me and opened the hamper with a flourish, revealing not a Henry VIII feast of stuffed swan and badger cooked in stout (sadly), but (*maybe* even better) cushions, two glasses, a chilled bottle of Pouilly-Fuissé, a pile of my favourite books and – when I looked closer – a child's purse, clinking with coins, with a label saying 'For Ice Creams'. We stayed there for much of the rest of the day, Thom twice doing an ice cream run but otherwise reading next to me. We occasionally hooked ankles and swung our legs together, but didn't really talk, so happy to be happy. Once he put his arm around me, and said, 'Kiki, I really love you. I really love you.' I couldn't help but let him know that the feeling was mutual, and that I truly did think he was the bee's knees. It was the least I could do after he'd bought me two Magnums. I said, 'Thom, this is all very nice, but wait till you see what I've got *you*.'

Soon afterwards he drove us home again and that's *all you need to know about it*.

April 19th

Thom and I had a long talk before work this morning, about everything.

Thom: I'm really sorry, Keeks.
Me: Why are you sorry? This has been awful. Well, not the picnic part. Or the car. Or the breakfast. Or when you did that thing with—
Thom: Yeah, I thought you liked that. But the rest of it has been awful, hasn't it?
Me: It really has.
Thom: I don't want us to forget what this is all about. Ever. Not just this wedding, but with all the stuff we'll have to deal with: kids and work and houses and

170

... well, all that stuff. The stuff we've got to do together.

Me: Alright, Winston Churchill.

Thom: It doesn't make any sense to be dicks to one another.

Me: I don't remember that line.

Thom: I might not work somewhere like this forever, Kiki. What would we do then? I'm afraid you've become rather comfortable being comfortable.

Me: I know, I know. But ... this is still going to be a great party, and I'm doing this *with* you. So it would be better if we could do it together. So we both care about it, because everyone we both care about will be there. It doesn't have to be ... lavish, but it does have to be involving. Both of us. I'm not just going to invite you along to our wedding – it's a party for us *both*.

Thom: [silent for a while] Yeah, sorry Kiki. Let's not be stupid anymore.

Me: Let's make this a wedding no one will forget.

Thom: [looking at me] OK, Keeks.

As good as her word, first thing on Tuesday, Jacki was in the office with all her notes. I asked her if she'd spent her first day as a married woman making more notes and she laughed. She said, 'We really need to get those photos in from Pedro, so we can get our captions on each one and get them into the wedding pages. Because you'll need to know the space for the text, right?' Uh-oh.

'The thing is, Jacki, I'm not sure Pedro and I have the best relationship right now. I maaaaay have kicked him on the shin at your wedding.' Jacki started laughing, harder than I'd ever seen her laugh before, and asked me through her laughter what he could have done to deserve it. I felt a bit awkward – I wasn't about to dob Pedro in, but I couldn't think of a convincing lie fast enough. Jacki's laughter slowed down. 'Kiki, what did he do?' Christ, I'd better think of a lie fast, or Jacki's mind was going to be filling in the blanks with far worse stuff.

Me: It was nothing major. Really. I think he was a bit tipsy and probably pretty stressed, and I think I was in the wrong place at the wrong time.

Jacki: [definitely very serious] *Kiki*, what did he *do*?

Me: [wishing Jacki was still laughing, so doing the laughing for her] Jacki, I'm fine, really. I think he thinks that I'm some kind of celebrity social-climber, and . . . that was it, really. It's fine! Jacki, please! Do I look like it's upset me? I *kicked* him on the *shin*, Jacki. It's fine.

It was too late. Her face was completely white, and she was packing up her stuff and heading out the door. 'I'll be back later. Stay here.' I kept trying to tell her – it didn't matter – I was fine – please, let's forget about it – but she was gone. Five minutes later, back at my desk, Alice arrived in for the day. 'What the hell is going on out there?' she asked. 'Jacki is going absolutely ballistic at somebody. I would never have guessed she even knew some of those words.'

Whoah. Turns out she is one to have in your corner. But all her work is now done, and she is free to enjoy her honeymoon/married life/lovely fat Polka Dot cheque.

TO DO:
Music – maybe *just* a Ceilidh band, get quotes for shorter set
Flags? Seed packet favours? Ask Redhood Farm what favours they've had in the past
Streamers? Bird cages?
Naming a rose for our wedding day?

172

April 23rd

Speaking of which, it's the Noses' (Nick and Rose's) wedding in the next few weeks. It's been playing on my mind for months, although I've also been trying not to think about it – doing a continual double-think where I try not to imagine all the things that they might do differently to/better than us. Isn't that rotten?

Thom went on Nick's stag yesterday. They had an afternoon session at an 'urban golf course' – basically a dark cellar with a giant screen onto which they project a flat-looking course – followed by dinner at Nick's club and a night at the casino. 'See if you can seduce a rich woman into giving you some chips,' I called when Thom was leaving. He said it was unlikely he'd be doing any seducing with a gang of seven wasted men with him, but I just eyeballed him until he promised he'd do his best to come back with chips from a wealthy widow. This morning, he tells me that one of the highlights of the night was Nick's colleague turning up to the urban golf course, and when Nick, Thom and a few others were just trying to kick the ball as hard as possible at the screen, pulling out not only his own golf club, but also his custom-made golf glove. I can't wait to talk to him at the wedding.

April 26th

My turn now. I've just had an email from Rose's maid of honour about the hen party, next Friday. But don't worry about me having too much time to kill this weekend – it doesn't *finish* on Friday. Oh no. It only *starts* on Friday, and continues until SUNDAY NIGHT. Because who doesn't like to spend an entire weekend on one member of a wedding party prior to spending another entire weekend on the pair of them? I can't even back out as I'm one of Rose's bridesmaids. *Who let this happen?*

Maid of Honour hit us with this:

From: Helen Hudson
To: Fleur Riley; Bunny Gladwell; Rose Gold; Kiki Carlow; Greta Moore
Re: Hen Fun!

Hi Girls!

Everyone ready for the weekend? The house will be ready from noon, so Rose and I were thinking that we could have lunch at Paddington, then get the first train after that and catch cabs from the station to the house in the afternoon. I've found a really nice restaurant in the evening, in Cirencester, then we can come home and have a nice wine and DVD night (please can everyone bring one nice bottle of wine?). On Saturday, we've got a drawing class in the morning, lunch booked at the Lampley Hotel in Langton, then an afternoon at the spa and a really special treat in the evening – we've booked a chef to come and cook us dinner at the house! On Sunday, we'll take a walk to the pub for lunch, then in the afternoon there's chocolate-making in Gloucester, then we can all get the train back at 6ish.

Since it's Rose's hen, it's not really fair to make her pay, so I think if we have money for the kitty for meals, it breaks down like this:

Lunch in London £120
Dinner £300
Drawing Class £120
Lunch £180
Spa £240
Chef £300
Pub £180
Chocolate class £120
House £350

So let's say £390 each. Are you OK to send that to me? We can spend any leftovers on cocktails before the train home.

Thanks again, and see you at Paddington on Friday!
Lots of love,
Helen xxx

Not really so much with the OK. Definitely not OK. Something opposite to OK. That money is a summer holiday in Greece, or an amazing weekend in Paris, or a flight to New York. Is she *high*?

I made some calculations – if I could arrive late on Friday, citing lack of holiday allowance from work, then I could miss the lunch, and possibly even the dinner. But could I fake an illness that would get me out of the hen activities? And is there any more fun-repellent concept than a 'hen activity'?

From: Kiki Carlow
To: Helen Hudson
Re: Hen Fun!

Hi Helen!

Thanks so much for organising this; I think Rose will have such a great time.

Unfortunately I'm not able to get Friday afternoon off from work, and the first train I can get doesn't get into Cheltenham until 9pm, so I'll grab something on the way and meet you back at the house for some wine and a DVD.

On Saturday, I've heard there's a really charming market in Dunford Leas nearby to the house, so maybe we could go there rather than the drawing class? It might be nice to save our pennies for the fabulous hats we shall require for Rose's big day. And on Sunday, what about each of us bringing a game along, and we can play them post-pub back at the house until we have to head back to our city grind?

Thanks so much again, Helen – can't wait to meet you and all the others at last!
Kiki x

Bad, bad, bad idea.

From: Helen Hudson
To: Fleur Riley; Bunny Gladwell; Rose Gold; Kiki Carlow; Greta Moore
Re: Hen Fun!

Hi everyone.

It seems we've got a slight change of plan for this weekend – we're not going to the art class any more or the chocolate-making, but we will have a visit to a

176

market on Saturday instead. Can everyone please bring a game for Sunday, and we'll play those games instead of the chocolate-making.

I think since Rose is so special to all of us, and it's HER wedding, it might be a good idea for everyone to get into the spirit of things and understand that this weekend is for Rose, not for anyone else. It's a bit selfish of those people who think we have to do everything their way, and maybe it's time to think of Rose instead of thinking of those people who are supposed to be making it special for the bride.

See (some of you) for lunch on BANK HOLIDAY Friday, Helen xxx

Oh yeah. No work on Friday. This will be fun!

I showed the correspondence to Thom, and said, 'Look at this, Bunny. BUNNY. These are the people I have to go away with.' He just looked at me for a moment, then replied, 'KIKI. It's hardly Jane, is it?'

Fair point.

April 27th

Popped in on Mum and Dad tonight before I went away for the weekend, to bore them about Redhood Farm a bit more. Mum kept her lips tightly clamped together, so I was surprised when Dad made some kind of sighing noise when I was talking about the services they offered there. I was hurt and confused rather than angry – it being Dad, not Mum, after all – but Mum just bustled him out of the room and upstairs before I'd even said anything. They were gone ages and when Mum came back, she was alone. She told me Dad wanted a quick nap as he'd slept so badly the night before. It's rare that Dad's a daytime sleeper. Why was he sleeping badly? Mum went into the kitchen and made herself a cup of tea without even the merest peep of an offer. I took that as the sweetest of hints and scarpered home again, leaving the brochure for Redhood Farm on the table where she could poke through it at a later date to tell me all the ways in which it was the wrong choice.

TO DO:
Table plans and place cards – can I further bribe Dan in our
    Art dept to rustle up some more designs?
Orders of Service – same?
Ribbons for decorations?
Table runners?
Any day now, start taking those vitamins
Have a practice makeover at Selfridges
Decide on first dance song

April 29th

I'm writing this by the moonlight coming in the kitchen window. It's a little hard to write as my teeth are chattering so hard. I haven't really warmed up yet.

My plan worked perfectly, up to a point. I arrived at Cheltenham station at 9pm, then realised I needed to get another train to a smaller station, Leasby, which was just down the road from our house. My phone was out of batteries and I didn't know anyone's number by heart, but it was only a four-minute hold until the connecting train, so I got to the correct platform and waited. At 9.03, there was a station announcement: 'The train pulling into platform 2 is actually the 21.04 service to Bansham, calling at Cottingsbourne, Leasby and Marsh Hampton. If you wish to travel to any of these destinations, please travel to platform 2.' I grabbed my bag and ran, down one flight of stairs and up another, leaping across the platform as the doors starting bleeping closed. But something was keeping me from making those final few steps. Looking down, I saw my trousers caught on the jagged edge of a station bench – my lovely Zara trousers! – and I pulled with all my might, tugging against the ripping cloth in a frantic attempt to make the train. The fabric finally gave way with a shocking *rrrrrrrrrip* which sent my straining leg catapulting into a passing commuter ('What the *hell*?') and then my overbalanced upper body slamming into the doors, now closed. I heard a *pheeeeeeeeeeeeep* next to me on the platform as the railway employee a foot away from me the whole time raised his paddle and signalled the train on its way. He turned his dead eyes on me and said, 'Lucky for you that man didn't press charges for assault.' Assault felt like a dangerously attractive idea just then, but I hobbled down to the ticket office to ask about the next train. 'Not to worry!' said the grinning man behind the plexiglass. 'It's only an hour to wait! Maybe you'll be on the right platform this time!' Only the thought of the luxury bed awaiting me (and having witnessed the ferocity of the transport police and heard tales of how long they could detain angry travellers) held me back from just roaring directly at his face through the plastic wall between us. I smiled through gritted teeth, my eye tic-king, found an intensely uncomfortable cold metal bench to sit on for the next 55 minutes, and took my book out. 52 minutes and one numb rump later, another announcement: 'For all those waiting for the 22.04 to Bansham, calling at Cottingsbourne, Leasby and Marsh

Hampton, this will be departing from platform 3 – platform 3 for the 22.04 service to Bansham. Not platform 2!' I was beginning to wonder if this was actually a really terrible dream, but the train arrived on time, on the platform I'd been told, and none of the station furniture was determined to keep me from it, so I took my seat next to a snoring schoolboy in an ancient dusty three-carriage train and was grateful for it. After twenty minutes, I was disembarking at Leasby (still no train fittings holding me back) and walking across the platform, through the tiny station, and out. Out into the dark, empty road, without a taxi rank – or a car – in sight. I went back into the one-room station, and asked the woman behind the counter, shutting up for the night, where I could get a taxi. 'A taxi!' she chortled, as if I'd asked for a saddled elephant. 'Not at this time, not on a Friday!' Why were all these station staff so good-natured? Why did they find their own uselessness so entertaining? I showed her the address of where I was going, and she told me it was only a five-minute walk up the road. 'You can't miss it, love, straight out, turn left, walk for five minutes and it's the big yellow house on your right.' There was a subtle but unmistakable stress on the word 'big' and I saw myself as she saw me – some Londoner with fancy weekend bags, come here to drink wine and destroy the fabric of their community. Fine. I could play her game. 'Brilliant! Thanks so much!' I beamed. We smiled at one another until my face ached, then I remembered the red wine in my bag and I turned on my heel, out of the station and towards a corkscrew, a glass and a bed. I started off down the road, and the skies opened. And I mean *opened*. This wasn't rain, this was karmic revenge that must have hung about from a former life since there's no way I've done anything that bad in this one. I was drenched in moments. Trying my best to shield my bag (with my dry outfits in) with my hunched body, I continued up the road towards the promise of support. About a minute after I'd left, when the rain had filled my shoes and frozen my finger tips, a car drove past, hooting with great jollity, and the woman from the station waved gaily at me through the passenger window. If I'd had any strength in my body I would have hurled my bag at her, but I just smiled gaily at the retreating car, waving my free hand until it was out of sight, then let out a sob and started walking again. After fifteen minutes I arrived at the house, soaking wet, in torn trousers, late and hungry and cold, skirted round a car blocking the whole front path, and rang the door bell. Rose answered the door.

Rose: Kiki! Oh my God! Are you OK? Why didn't you call? Bunny would have come to pick you up. She ended up driving.

Me: [teeth chattering too hard to talk]

Rose: Are you cold? Why did you walk? Come in, come in! Fleur, can you get Kiki some towels?

Helen: She really needs to get out of the wet clothes – there's no point getting the towels wet if she's still soaking.

Rose: Kiki, drop your bag, come in, come in, just – no – don't hold on to your bag – just – *give* it to *me*—

Despite my arms being frozen around it and my lock-jawed attempts to explain why it needed cradling, Rose prised the bag from me and dropped it onto the hallway's flagstones. There was a muffled crack, and we all watched a burgundy stain spread across the bag's fabric. And through all my clothes. What a perfect first impression to give to all these new people.

Rose took me to the bathroom, turned the shower on and gave me a stack of warm, fluffy towels. I stood under it until I could feel my limbs again, then wrapped myself up in giant towels from head to toe. Waddling down to the living room, I saw the five of them snuggled on two huge sofas, watching *Grease*, my least favourite film of all time. Rose saw me, and shuffled over, introducing each of the others and leaving a nice space between her and bony little Helen for me to sit. I thanked her and said I was going to get dressed first. Rose looked at me apologetically. 'Oh Kiki, I'm so sorry. I had a peek in your bag and it looks like the wine got into everything. I'm sure we can lend you stuff for now, though. Come with me and I'll find you something to sleep in.'

Almost two hours and several dreadful musical numbers later, I was on the sofa in Rose's too-small pyjama trousers and Bunny's oversize Wham! t-shirt. I stank of red wine, since Helen had kindly just stuck my wine-sodden underwear on a hot radiator, without putting them into the washing machine on even the briefest of cycles. I went back to the bathroom and hand-washed what I could of my wine-y luggage, leaving my underwear and t-shirts dripping over the shower rail and taking a deep breath before heading back to *Grease*. Finally, finally, the film was over, and I asked the group which room was mine. Greta suddenly looked awkward, while Rose looked shattered. 'It's such a pain,' Fleur said apologetically. 'It seems there was a misunderstanding when we booked – although there's room for six, there are only five bedrooms. The sixth bed is the lounge sofa bed.' I turned back to the giant sofas, squashed and sweated into beyond all recognition by six grown women squirming and slouching. Helen then walked in with a smile and a pile of incredibly expensive but amazingly scratchy wool blankets. 'Here you go. Up early for the market!' She sneered at me and sniffed the air conspicuously. 'Mmm, boozy,' she whispered. 'Sleep *well*!'

I've struggled with the sofa bed, but something's gone awry and it won't fucking fold out. I'm just lying along the sweaty, squashy sofa cushions instead, with my head at a 90-degree angle to my spine and my feet on the other armrest. It's like a fucking dog bed. I'd better get under the scouring-blankets, if I don't want them to find me dead in the morning, blue with hypothermia, clutching my wedding planner. That would not be a cool way to go. Better luck tomorrow.

April 30th

I woke up at 6.30am when the chickens next door started calling to one another. My bed smelled like warm red wine gravy and I ached all over from sleeping scrunched up against one arm of the non-functioning sofa 'bed'. Wrapping myself in the least scratchy blanket, I limped to the bathroom, brushed my teeth, washed my face, rearranged my clothes on the radiators and cleaned myself up for the day of relentless, grinding fun ahead of us, before getting some top-notch grade-F TV watching in: some politicians interviewing one another apparently with zero signs of humanity between the pair; a fading celeb having breakfast cooked for her by an aggressively cheerful chef; some cartoons; a Paul Newman and Robert Redford film. *The Sting*! Joy. Slightly unexpected joy, but joy nonetheless. I tucked myself under the pub-smelling wirehair blankets and settled in for my clothes to finish drying and the others to wake up. By the time of the final scene, I was utterly immersed, despite having seen the film hundreds of times. A shot rings out and an impossibly handsome Robert Redford falls to the floor, while in the ensuing chaos, Robert Shaw is whisked away from his half-million dollars. I heard someone behind me. 'He's not really dead, *actually*.' I looked over my shoulder, appalled. Naturally, it was Helen, back again with the sneer on her face like it had camped there overnight. 'Don't worry,' I said, as cheerfully as I could manage, 'I've seen it before.' She reached past me to the remote and flicked the TV off. 'Well, you don't mind missing the end, then. Everyone's getting up now, so maybe we can get breakfast?' I stared at her for a few seconds, feeling like I'd been transported back to school somehow to face the meanest girl in the year, and shuffled to the kitchen to get out the cutlery and crockery. Half an hour later, I started hearing other people stirring. Helen had spent the whole time on the sofa, flicking through *Vogue*, occasionally looking over at me on the other sofa while I read my book, and sighing. Helen suddenly disappeared and reappeared moments later fully dressed and ready in dark designer wear, followed by the rest of the group. I was still in my borrowed pyjamas, but leapt up ready to dress while everyone was eating breakfast. Apparently Rose and the rest didn't eat breakfast, so they stood around in immaculate outfits while I pulled on some damp underwear and some warm, damp jeans. I was ready within a few minutes, in time to hear Rose saying to Helen, 'Thanks for getting all this stuff out anyway. It was really thoughtful of you.' I scrunched my face up and scowled at Helen, muttering, 'Dick,' realising too late that Greta, one of Rose's friends from her office, was behind me. But she just walked past trying not to laugh.

Since Bunny (a nickname, obviously; real name 'Clytemnestra'. Holy cow) had her car we decided to squeeze into it for the drive to the market. It was a ten-minute journey of agony, as I was squeezed against Helen and every bend in the road made her sigh dramatically, followed by little *ouch, oof* noises. The poor little butterfly. I was attempting to fold my own body into itself, but there was only so far I could go in sitting on my own knee. There remained some points of contact between us and they *burned*. Eventually we got to the appointed field: 'Gloucestershire's biggest antiques market every other Saturday!' Of course – *of course* – this weekend was not one of the weekends it fell on. Of course. The other five got out of the car, and rooted around the gate as if there might be a secret door to the antiques fair if they looked hard enough. Reassured that I really had fucked up, they wheeled about to stare at me, as I sat balled up in the back of the car feeling sicker and sicker. Then Greta laughed and said something to the others, and four of them came back to the car smiling. Rose said, 'We really don't need to spend our money on this now anyway. Not when I have access to Nick's bank account next month.' There was a moment when I wondered if she was serious, then with a cold shrug I realised she was. Greta turned to me, flaring her nostrils slightly and tilting her head infinitesimally at Rose. Then she said, 'How about we go to Langton and kill some time until lunch?' All back in the car, Helen had managed to manoeuvre herself to the other side of the back seat, so I was actually allowed to pull air into my lungs without Helen's gale blowing down my ear. In Langton, things were quiet, but the local museum was open and a whole street of my favourite shops: chemists, charity shops and sun-bleached homeware stores. I felt a gush of misery within me for Rose's terrible hen and Helen's total bloody-minded awfulness, but Fleur, a sweet girl from Rose's schooldays, gave a theatrical gasp when she saw the museum's sign. 'Hold your horses – a teacup museum? I. Am. In. Heaven.' We filed in and paid our £1.50 each, and tried to drag out the two rooms for as long as possible by playing Favourite Cup, Cup You'd Most Like to Break, Cup You'd Give to Your Mum, Cup You'd Marry (tenuous hen game number four hundred and twenty-nine) and If I Were a Cup I'd Be . . . I chose a cup with two handles and a large walrus moustache; Greta went for one that looked like it had melted in the kiln; Bunny and Fleur both went for mugs that would not have looked out of place in my grand-mother's display cabinet; Rose picked one with a large rose on – seriously – and Helen simply said she needed to find our

185

restaurant and walked out of the museum. Greta called after her, 'If you don't get your hand stamped, you can't come back in!' and even Rose laughed.

We finally conceded defeat and went to find Helen, who was standing outside the museum with a thunderous expression. 'I found it,' she said, pointing across the road to the Lampley Hotel. We were seated in the velvety dining room within minutes, and the waiter came with a bottle of champagne before we'd even cracked the food menus open. Bunny had recommendations for us all, having been here before with her grandmother, and gave lavish descriptions of the cheeses, the pâtés, and the fruity duck mousse.

Me: I have *got* to try that duck mousse.
Helen: Will you be *able* to afford it?

There was an intake of breath from everyone else when she said this and I let out a quick sigh of fury and shock. Helen is such a fucking . . . *plum*.

The food was as delicious as Bunny had said, but the mood was slightly cowed by Helen's furious eating, biting mouthfuls from her fork like a cross fox in DKNY. A meal that should have lasted for two hours in the right company was over after forty-five minutes, as we all refused dessert and hurried outside before we infected the other customers with Helen's menacing temper.

Next stop was the spa. Everyone was extra sweet to me, mostly because Helen was being so deranged but also because I suspect they were just nice people, and I was touched, but whatever tiny chamber of my heart might have been in this whole weekend was beginning to crumple away. I wanted a giant Band on the Run, a clean, flat, human (not dog) bed, and no Helen snarling in my face. Was that too much to ask? As we changed into our swimming costumes and thick white robes, Greta noticed my flagging spirits and came over. Putting her arm around my shoulders, she addressed the group. 'Good news, folks. My mum's old college buddy owns this place, and has given us all a free treatment each. Ta-dah!' She turned to me. 'Kiki? First dibs?' There was a pointed coughing from Rose and Helen, and Greta swiftly added, 'After the bride, of course,' but squeezed my shoulders in solidarity. From our six possible treatments, Rose had taken the facial and left me with a massage, a floatation treatment, a hand treatment, a leg wax, or a manicure. I took the massage, thinking it might knead my sofa-bed knots out, and the list passed around the group. Helen and Greta agreed to toss for the final appointment, which saw Greta take a manicure and Helen left with leg wax. I felt triumphant as we filed to the booking desk to fill in the paperwork for our treatments, but when we sat back on the armchairs, white puffy robes making me feel sleepy and good-natured, I felt really bad for Helen's pointy little disappointed face. When our names were called, I said, 'Helen – do you want my massage? I feel a bit sore anyway and might go in the sauna instead.' There was a brief flash when she looked like she might thank me, but instead she nodded and said, 'Fine, if that's what you want.' Greta shook her head at me and even Rose looked embarrassed but I didn't really mind. I cancelled Helen's wax, picked up all the *Vogue*s and a stray *Empire* that had somehow made its way in, and made myself a comfy nest on one sofa while the others disappeared off. Forty minutes later, they began emerging from their various treatment rooms, comparing soft faces and hands and coconut-smelling limbs. There was a crash and a muffled roar from Helen's room; the door flew open, and a giant nectarine rolled out, pinky-orange and round and furious. It was Helen. Through a tiny, puffed mouth, she hissed at me, '*You . . . did . . . this.*' I looked around at the others, stunned.

How could her fruity transformation be anything to do with me? 'Oh God,' said Rose. 'Your allergies. What happened? Didn't they know?' Helen lifted a bloated arm and pointed her chubby finger at me. 'No,' she said, 'they *didn't* know because *someone* was *so kind* that they gave me *their* appointment. They had her details instead of mine. How *could* they have known that I was allergic to almond oil? Only someone who *knows* me would have that kind of information.' The finger was still pointing at me, and I was starting to feel like she might come and push it into my eye socket.

'Jesus, Helen, I *don't* know you. I hadn't even met you before last night!' It didn't help, and Helen waddled away with another muffled roar while Rose, Bunny and Fleur chased around after her like fruit flies as she swatted them away, enraged.

Greta: Shit. That did *not* go well.
Me: Yeah. But think how delicious the juice will be when we squeeze her.
Greta: [silence]
Me: Too soon?
Greta: No, I'm just enjoying that mental image.

We found the others again later, minus Helen who had been sitting in the ice room for the last forty-five minutes in the hope that it would reduce the all-over body swelling. Rose said that the in-house medical team had looked at her and reassured them that Helen would be back to normal in the next four to five days. She also said that Helen really didn't want to see anyone right now, and her boyfriend was driving from High Wycombe to pick her up.

I did feel terrible that she was having this rotten time – I wouldn't wish that kind of allergic reaction on my worst enemy – but I also couldn't help being overjoyed that she was off. It made it so much easier to be sympathetic and helpful to her and about her. I ran off to reception to get some paper and a pen, and we wrote a very sweet note to her, hoping she got better soon and thanking her for a great weekend. I did not write: And a special thank you for stepping away from my weekend entirely, you loopy bridesmaid demon. But I might have liked to. We slid it into her locker, then dressed and were back in Bunny's car before you could say, 'Let the fun commence.'

Back at the cottage, we opened some wine and cleaned ourselves up before the chef arrived. We were pretty merry when he got there, and our card game (Beggar My Neighbour – best game ever) was so involving that not one of us offered to help him in with his baskets of fruit and veg, cold boxes of meat and bags of dairy goods. After checking if any of us had any allergies (Rose let out a tiny giggle, then looked really shocked at herself), he whipped up a scrummy feast: five super-light mackerel soufflés; five tiny lime sorbets; five little poussins from which we ended up sucking meat off their tiny bones, served with an orange and beetroot salad and roast butternut squash; five dark, dark chocolate mousses with squashy, tart raspberries buried at the bottom; then he presented us with a huge cheeseboard, crackers and grapes, and left us to it while he cleaned the kitchen.

Me: This guy is *good*.
Greta: [whispering] Fleur, you should find out if he's single.
Chef: [from kitchen] I'm not single.
Fleur: [sad] He's not single.

We played various childhood card games for most of the rest of the night, although it turns out that Rose is a bit of a lightweight and there are things about Nick that I can now never un-learn.

I've really enjoyed this weekend. Yes, Helen will almost certainly try to poison my food at the wedding, and yes, I've now registered I'll be having my own hen party and yes, that thought now fills me with a strong sense of nausea, but I've grown pretty fond of this bridal gang. Which, considering most people don't live anywhere near their friends and family anymore, must be the point of these horrifying occasions. And I have met Greta, who is *definitely* a keeper. If I can just make it through tomorrow without hospitalising any of the others, maybe I can be convinced that hen parties aren't the Pit of All Evil, after all. And thanks for this nice bed, Helen.

May's Classic Wedding!

She did not want to go to the wedding, but the other girls came and took her with them. Whenever her turn came to sing, she would step back, but finally she was the only one left and was obliged to sing a song. As she began to sing and her voice reached Roland's ears, he jumped up and exclaimed, 'I know that voice! That's my true bride. I don't want anyone else.'

Everything that he had forgotten and everything that had vanished from his mind suddenly filled his heart again. So the faithful maiden married her sweetheart Roland. Her sorrows came to an end and her joy began to flourish.

'Sweetheart Roland'
The Brothers Grimm

May 1st

No one else in hospital! Victory. Just a very nice morning having a long breakfast at the local pub, before we all headed home. Bunny gave me and Greta a lift, as we live reasonably close to one another, and we managed to not discuss Helen's lunacy the whole drive back, which *I* think deserves some kind of medal.

Thom was pleased to see me when I returned. He was in the shower, but swept the curtain back when I came into the bathroom and reached out to pull me in with him.

Me: I hope that's some kind of joke.
Thom: Naturally. For your information, I'm really enjoying having this shower all to myself. [soaps self lasciviously] How was your weekend?
Me: I arrived seven hours late on Friday with luggage soaked in red wine, I didn't have a bed and had to sleep on a sofa, I made them cancel an art class so I could take them to an antiques market that was closed, and the maid of honour got such a bad allergic

reaction from a spa treatment that she had to go home. Oh, and she blames me for everything.

Thom: I look forward to the wedding.

Me: Strangely, so do I. How was your weekend?

Thom: I worked on Saturday and went for a run this morning.

Me: Whoah whoah, too many details! Hold *something* back for the Christmas newsletter.

Then Thom insisted I removed my clothes and see quite how good that shower really was, and exactly how much he'd missed me. I should go away and ruin people's hen weekends more often.

But by 3.30, I couldn't take it anymore. I told Thom I had an urgent errand and had to borrow the car; I drove to Whetstone's fanciest deli, picked up a gorgeous bottle of hand-pressed apple juice and a big bag of pine nuts (the only craving she had with the Twins), and headed round to Susie's. She opened the door and smiled at me.

Me: A May Day mayday?

Susie: That better be whisky in there.

Me: Good to see you too.

She let me in; we talked non-stop for three hours about my hen disaster, her ankles, her back, my dress, her sleep, my work, until Pete came back with the children from Victoria Park. And all is well in the world.

Thom saw my face when I got home. 'You and Susie friends again, then?' I just shrugged, and beamed. Too giddy to write more.

193

Nick and Rose over to dinner tonight. An absolute feast, of which Rose ate almost nothing ('Have to make sure we'll fit in the dress!' It took all my self-control not to say, 'All four of us? Ho ho ho,' since it was such an unforgivable Dad joke) and even Nick just poked the food around on his plate a bit. Thom said, 'Lost your appetite, Nick?' and Nick darted a terrified glance at Rose, who said with forced jollity, 'I hope not, or your suit will be too *big*!' Suddenly we were entertaining some boxing pros, living at the edge of a fighting class and petrified of tipping the scales at a new weight. 'You must be the same, right, Kiki? As my bridesmaid? You'll want to look your best!' There was a slight edge of threat in Rose's voice all of a sudden. Thom and I looked at one another, faint terror in both our faces. He gently kicked my ankle under the table.

After the initial chat about work and our families, Rose said that I must surely – like her – only be able to think about weddings at the moment. She kindly took the decision from my hands and talked of nothing else from the moment we sat down at the table until I got up to take our plates away. Nick immediately stood up too, knocking his chair over, and picked up a single plate and carried it to the kitchen ahead of me.

At the sink, Nick looked at me. 'It's just really important to Rose. All this wedding stuff. She just wants it to be perfect for everybody.' I patted his hand. 'I really love her, Kiki,' he repeated. 'She just wants it to be perfect. For everybody.' I sighed with him: 'Yeah, Nick, weddings are pretty crazy.' I looked at the chocolate torte I'd made for dessert, and he gave a tiny head shake. I put it back in the fridge and started slicing up some fresh pears and cherries for a fruit salad. Nick looked relieved.

After they'd gone home, Thom and I sat on the sofa together, not speaking for a few minutes.

Thom: Well.

Me: That was . . .

Thom: Wasn't it.

Me: Maybe they . . .

Thom: Here's hoping.

Me: But she . . .

Thom: I know.

Me: OH MY GOD.

Thom: What?

Me: [savouring the moment] We've got a *whole chocolate torte* in the fridge.

Thom: I'll get the forks.

This is not a fun time for Nick, I think.

TO DO:

Table plans and place cards – advice from Redhood Farm if Dan's designing?

Start drawing up rough lists for table plans

Check with Redhood Farm their minimum/maximum for seats at their tables

Find out whether Nick and Rose would actually prefer to sit apart at our wedding

May 4th

I didn't mention to Rose last night that I was seeing Greta today. Greta and I have been in touch since Rose's Hell Hen (which really wasn't that bad at all), but I'm not sure if she'd be delighted to have turned two strangers into friends, or if she'd see straight through us as the mean girls clubbing together in the face of her (extreme, alienating) efforts. But it was really good to see Greta – she was as hilarious as I'd remembered, as we sat over cold beers in a pub garden, telling each other more about ourselves and making plans for the future. It was one of the best dates I'd ever been on.

May 5th

I had a long conversation this afternoon with the caterers Redhood Farm recommended to us. I really wanted something quite low-key and casual, going with this beautiful summer vibe of Redhood Farm; the woman I spoke to was able to advise me on the dishes that work best for different occasions. In the end we settled on a light pork rillette, poulet rôti and our wedding dessert. So . . . pâté, chicken and cake.

Shit.

May 6th

When I got in to work today, I found this email from Rose. Is this her revenge? One can't help but feel Helen must have been doing some work on her – I *think* she used to be quite sane. But let's thank goodness again that I've agreed to be her bridesmaid.

Hurray!

From: Rose Gold
To: Kiki Carlow, Nick Lord, Bunny Gladwell, Fleur Riley, Mummy Gold, Helen Hudson, Greta Moore
Subject: Action plan!

Hi girlies (and Nick, my almost-hubbie)!

I know this might look a little scary, but it's the best way to get this all done effectively and efficiently.

Here comes the Big Day!

R x

Order of the Day

0730 Photographer arrives for candid shots, flowers for wedding party arrive

0800 Rose breakfast – egg white omelette, fresh orange juice, wholemeal toast (plain), mint tea

0845 Hairdresser arrives – Mummy first

0945 Rose to shower

1000 Hairdresser – Bunny

1020 Hairdresser – Fleur

1040 Hairdresser – Greta

1100 Hairdresser – Kiki

1120 Hairdresser – Helen

1140 Hairdresser – Rose

1200 Caterers arrive at venue – Nick to direct

1230 Rose makeup
     AND bridesmaids into dresses

1315 Rose into dress

1345 Rose, bridesmaids, Mum shots

1400 Photographer leaves for church

1415 Nick, Tim and ushers, church shots

1430 Nick and vicar go through service and paperwork

1430 Car arrives at house
     Toast with bridal party

1445 Rose and Daddy leave in car

1448 Ushers bring everyone into the church

1450 Church shot
1452 Bride arrives
1457 Daddy and Rose shots
1500 Rose and Daddy enter church
1600 Service ends, everyone leaves church
1615 Ushers bring everyone to confetti shower
1630 Family formal shot
1645 Wedding party shots
1700 Everyone shot
1715 Cars arrive for wedding party
1720 Comfort break for Rose
1745 Drinks served at the reception
1750 Bride and groom shots
1830 Tim announces dinner
1930 Tim announces father of the bride speech
2000 Tim announces groom's speech
2020 Tim's best man speech
2030 Tim announces bride and groom
2035 Cutting of the cake
2040 First dance
2100 Socialising!
0100 Taxi for bride and groom

Of course Big Day was capitalised. Of course. Because it's not only her big day, is it. It's a Big Day for the world. Naturally.

Five minutes later, Nick, bless his cotton socks, sent this reply:

From: Nick Lord
To: Rose Gold, Kiki Carlow, Bunny Gladwell, Fleur Riley, Mummy Gold, Greta Moore, Helen Hudson
Subject: Re: Action plan!

Hey all.

If it helps at all, I can move our scheduled 17.00 earlier.

It was almost – almost – enough to stop me writing back to her, but I was drowning in work, in my own wedding plans and the undeniable fact that weddings seemed to turn everyone mad. And she was being a hysterical idiot. Is someone going to have a stopwatch on the day? Can the happy couple only socialise from 2100 hours? I couldn't quite bring myself to condone this lunacy by being her dancing monkey, even if it was her wedding day. I sent her email to Susie and Thom; Susie wrote back, furious, saying, 'She's a MONSTER. Is it too late to say you can't go? Tell her Mum needs us. For your dress or something.' Thom said, 'Oh good God. But think of it this way: the enormous good karma from doing this will cancel out all those times you used up the hot water in our flat.'

Something about Rose's behaviour nudged both Thom and me: for Thom, it was a reminder that, on the grand scale of things, his bride wasn't a complete loon yet. And for me, it was that Thom felt exasperation about this kind of behaviour, just as I did. I took a deep breath and crossed my fingers that this wouldn't come back and bite me. I wrote Rose the nicest email I could, explaining that (slight porkpie) Saturday morning was when we'd scheduled my mum to come to the final dress fitting, and it was really hard to get these things organised with everyone as I'm sure she knew, so I'd be round at noon to do absolutely anything I could to help. I said I knew that whatever time I arrived, it would be a great day, and that I was really looking forward to it (big juicy porkpies). And yes, I know I'm also being a fiend. Just not as much as her. It was either that or kill her.

She wrote back shortly afterwards:

199

From: Rose Gold
To: Kiki Carlow
Subject: Re: Action plan!

Kiki, I totally appreciate that your mum wants you to
go, but it means you can't get your hair done.

I'm trying not to have a tantrum about this, but do
you think you actually want to do this? It feels like
you just can't be bothered to make any effort,
particularly after my Hen (Helen told me all about it
later). I don't know whether you feel that we should
all be paying attention to you because you're getting
married this year, but I'm getting married too! This is
supposed to be the biggest day of my life! I so want
to share this day with someone who actually cares
about me, and I feel you just don't want to share in
my happiness. I am always going to remember this
day and I don't want to always be reminded of your
lack of support or interest. I know that you have a
wedding to plan too (believe me!) but you're MY
bridesmaid. It's actually a really big responsibility, and
it would be great if you could show even the tiniest
bit of excitement.

Thanks, R

Oh, Rose. I think Helen has broken you.

TO DO:
Check the Nose wedding list again and see if any weapons
on there. Otherwise, wrap up a tranquilliser dart and
hand it to Nick, with a label saying, 'You may need
this.'

May 10th

My favourite pair of authors was in today: Ann Tate and Charlie Greer, chefs who met in the kitchen of her restaurant and were married six months later. They produce books together now, little windows into a world where everything is tasty and lickable. They've both got meat on their bones, too, from all the hog-roasting and ginger-syruping, but they have that creamy plumpness associated with pre-Raphaelite portraits rather than a chicken-skin-and-idleness diet. I love them so much (or at least want to take them home and chain them to my kitchen) but they are awfully nice too, breaking every cliché about successful chefs; they're polite, calm and thoughtful, and while Ann swears blind she can only maintain her calm because she makes Charlie do all the work, Charlie will explain regretfully that his good moods are only possible since Ann does everything for him. And it's not, despite my sugar-high as I write this, simply because they always bring a delicious cake into the office when they visit. I like seeing them because they really do enjoy one another's company. Today they brought in a coffee and walnut cake, in three shades of buttercream-cake-walnut, and one flavour (or two slices, whatever) of deliciousness.

Whenever we publish one of their books (their new one is called *Pat-A-Cake* and has a pastel photo of them working together on a gorgeous cherry gateau on the front) Alice calls round all her contacts and places them well: while there's none of that filthy fighting and occasionally bribery that comes with the big celebrity guns, the bookers always seem genuinely pleased to have them as guests. Ann and Charlie bake for everyone they visit (including the crews for each show) and make no demands of anyone but some tea and plates for their treats. Have I said before? *Sometimes*, I love my job.

They came in today with a proposal for a whole new series of books, in a completely new field: Crime. They've written the first three chapters of a detective thriller, featuring a pair of amateur chefs called Steve Mortar and Emily Pestle, who solve the crimes using their particular kitchen skills; calculating when the murder took place by studying the rate at which the body had been slow-roasted in a hot room, etc. It's undeniably tongue-in-cheek, but very well done.

TO DO:
Put a pestle and mortar on wedding list?
Eat more of Ann and Charlie's cake

May 13th

The Twins' birthday today. After work, Thom and I took round a pile of books and enough Lego to build an aircraft hangar, and we all ate more ice cream and jelly than seems sensible. I'm wobbling as I write this (but not as much as Suse, although I'd lose an eye if I made that joke to her face).

It was probably a foolish idea to eat quite so much, as it's the Nose wedding tomorrow. The bridesmaids' dresses Rose and Helen chose for us are – as is always the touching tradition – both ugly and unflattering, and mine is staring at me from its dress bag in the corner of the bedroom. Susie came round after the Twins had gone to bed to laugh at it, saying between breathless teary laughter, 'But . . . you look . . . like a *cube*!' I said, 'Really? You really want to do this? At seven months pregnant, you want to talk about body shape?' She took off her shoe and threw it at my head.

But I am ready to bear witness, toast, and jive like it's

going out of fashion. As long as Rose trusts me to do my own hair like I do every single day of my life, it should all go pretty smoothly.

May 14th

Well, that was . . . strange. Nick and Rose's wedding was beautiful, but also . . . I don't know. Something *not* perfect? Is that possible? I realised I'd been a bit mean, and headed over to Rose's house for my military briefing at 9am, prepared to explain that Mum had cancelled our imaginary appointment. When I got there, Rose was sitting with tear marks down her face and a slightly woozy look in her eyes. Greta was there in her equally unflattering dress, and gave me a hug when she saw me, explaining that Rose's mother had crushed a pill into Rose's drink to calm her down a bit. She'd be fine for the ceremony, but just wouldn't offer much sparkling bridal repartee for a couple of hours.

Her father had hired a Silver Phantom to ferry them around, while the bridesmaids (me and Greta giggling, Bunny and Fleur, plus Helen, with a very serious and dignified expression) and mother of the bride had two huge black Mercedes. The journey was tense, as Helen clearly had yet to forgive me, but when we got to the church, I saw how beautiful it was, picture postcard perfect; and as Rose climbed out of the car she really did look lovely, albeit just like *every other bride ever* in a strapless white full-skirted gown. After the service (when I was allowed a brief wave at Thom, in the pews) the wedding party all got back in our big wedding-party cars to a huge country house a few miles down the road, where we were greeted with banks of pink roses and lilies and trays of champagne. It was clearly an expensive wedding, full of money and thought, but somehow . . .

Somehow, something. Or nothing. Was there anything missing? Not quite, as the Noses really do love one another and I could not imagine anyone better for him than Rose, and yet . . . also . . . a bit. It was so lovely, and they even had the gift table that I dream of but I know Thom would *die* rather than permit, full of Martha Stewart-esque gift parcels; they had lovely, safe, crowd-pleasing food; a first dance tune that was fine (hilariously, also 'I've Had the Time of my Life'), which they swayed awkwardly to in the tradition of all couples ever (why does that first dance always make couples look like they loathe one another? Everyone seems to believe they shouldn't be seen to be speaking to one another during the dance, so all conversation is conducted from behind gritted teeth, making the whole thing appear like they're having a furious row); the photos took forever and were full of those same boring 'OK, and can the groom turn slightly more towards the bride . . . yup . . . and can the bride lift her chin a bit . . . yup, OK, a bit closer to the groom . . . yup . . . great . . . and can the bride put one hand on the groom's arm . . . a little higher . . . lovely. That's lovely. And one with the groom down on one knee? Niiiiiiiiiice' wedding shoot platitudes as at Annie's wedding. I had a good time, I really did – Thom gets on well with the Nose crowd and it was so nice to see Bunny and Fleur again, and Greta and I danced for hours, and we at least had unlimited drink at our table, which meant even Thom ended up on the dance floor, twirling me round and dipping some of our party ('Is *that* what you call it?' I said in my best innuendo voice when we saw one another briefly). But when we poured ourselves into the taxi at the end of the night, I had a sudden terrifying thought: was that fabulous wedding . . . *boring*?

May 15th

It keeps going round and round in my head: is our wedding going to be like that? I've spent hours poring over confetti choices and ribbon catalogues, wedding candles and wedding biscuits, fireworks and keepsakes and bubbles and place card holders. But does order and preparation produce perfection? Or is perfection what we witnessed there? Did we just feel like extras at the event exactly because the wedding had been directed to within an inch of its life?

So we had some actual fun today to make up for the Nose wedding. Thom's more stressed than ever as he's having to deal with the redundancies of some of his colleagues, so his workload is even greater than normal, but Jim made our day with a lovely BBQ at the park for his birthday. About thirty of us came, all bringing beers and bread and meat and cheese, and Jim had brought a ball and it ended up in a rowdy football game with all thirty of us wrestling and tripping one another over and obstructing the opposition in a revolting manner, while Rich's increasingly pregnant girlfriend Heidi refereed from the sidelines. In a brief half-time break for spoonfuls of melted frozen gateau and more beer, I talked to Zoe and her boyfriend Zac, now the best of buddies with Jim since Christmas.

Zoe: Kiki, it's really nice to see you away from the Pedro-cloud.

Zac: Can you believe that guy? I thought my boss was a dick but Pedro takes it to a whole other douchebag level.

Me: Sadly, I find it all too easy to believe Pedro. In the world of celebrity, he is but small fry on the Total Dick scale. But it's so nice to see you too, Zoe. Thom and I were actually wondering if you guys would come to our wedding, too? It's in August – if you fancy it, I'll send you the details.

Zoe: Hey! That sounds good; we'd love it. Thank you.

Zac: Did Zoe tell you, we got engaged a year ago? But Pedro won't give Zo the time off.

Zoe: Zac!

Zac: What? *You* don't work for him, do you, Kiki? Are you going to tell him I was complaining?

Me: Is that true, Zoe? I *think* that may be illegal.

Zoe: We'll get round it. Don't worry, either of you. Look how much your faces are worrying! Stop worrying. If you love someone, you have to let them find a way to plan the wedding without worrying about their prick of a boss. That's what my grandmother always used to say.

Christ. Pedro's even more of a scumbag than I thought. But it's the field Zoe wants to work in, so she can't leave without him blackening her name (as he's done with previous assistants). And Zac's family are all in New York, so a wedding couldn't be done on a spur-of-the-moment Saturday morning. Plus, Pedro's working hours are so long and so erratic that she could never rely on happening to have the day off at the time they'd booked their wedding. Christ, he's a horror.

But the whole picnic today was brilliant. It was the perfect antidote to Nick and Rose, and Thom and I returned home with scuffed knees and a great beery buzz. Joys.

TO DO:

Check Redhood Farm providing menus

Book meeting with their wedding co-ordinator to co-ordinate each phase of the day

Confirm photography spots in the grounds

Check spots for musicians

Check lighting in the dance area

Underwear – corset? Basque?

Alcohol – find out about getting cocktail bar – staff from
  Queen's Arms?
Would need:
Bar
Alcohol
Equipment
Staff
Glasses
Games?

May 20th

I'm not sure how long I can stay in publishing, let alone
at Polka Dot, when I have to deal with some of our authors.
Taz Taylor is a hairdresser to the stars, and only marginally
less of a prick than Pedro. Until today, that is. He's doing
a book for us called *Lord of the Hair*, a mixture of gossipy
stories about his clients and hair care tips and styling. He's
not my author, he's Tony's, but Tony was out of the office
on the day that Taz was supposed to be doing signings of
his book at the Dorchester Hotel. When I got into work,
I could hear my phone was already ringing as I hung up
my coat. It stopped as my answerphone picked it up, and
three seconds later started ringing again. This time I got
to it in time, and found Taz's frazzled assistant Cara on
the phone.

Cara:	Hi, is Tony there, please? This is Taz Taylor's assistant.
Me:	Hi Cara, it's Kiki. Tony's not here at the moment – can I help?
Cara:	Oh *Christ*, Kiki. The signing's due to start in an hour, and Taz has decided he can only do it if

	he's sitting at a specific antique mahogany desk. He says all other furniture makes him look fat.
Me:	Cara. Where's the desk?
Cara:	[beginning howling] We don't know! He's seen it once but can't remember where.
Me:	Shit. Can't he sign standing up? Or . . . in bed? Very sexy-celebrity-fuck-you?
Cara:	No, he . . . hold *on* . . . [sounds of a struggle]
New voice:	Who is this?
Me:	It's Kiki. How can I help you?
Taz Taylor:	You get me my fucking desk, or you can kiss goodbye to this signing. You hear me?
Me:	Absolutely, Mr Taylor, we'll get that desk over to you within the hour.

He'd already hung up, that grubby little scumbag, but I'd had an idea. Who did Taz Taylor worship more than anyone else on Earth? Madonna. And where had Madonna stayed on one tour in London? The Dorchester. Giving him time to move away and start screaming at someone else, I rang Cara back and explained the plan, then called the hotel and told them exactly what we would need.

Fifty-five minutes after, four porters brought a mahogany desk down from the Audley Suite to the Pavilion, as Cara recounted to Taz how we had called all round the city and contacted every antiques dealership in West London, until we'd discovered – fancy that! – *the* very mahogany antique desk that Madonna had loved so much when she'd stayed here. The manager, accompanying the desk on its journey, added that she'd loved it so much that she'd wanted to buy it from the hotel, but it was a very special design from an era that prized the perfect proportions of the human body in furniture, and a very, very rare antique. They'd turned down her kind offers and she had been seeking its twin ever since.

Taz did the signing. But thank Christ alive that Jacki always said she'd rather sport an eighties wet-look perm than have him do her wedding hair.

TO DO:
How to make our Redhood Farm wedding unique from Nick & Rose's: magician?
When making wedding decision, remember a useful rule of behavioural thumb: WWTTND (What Would Taz Taylor Not Do)

May 29th

Another Thom trip! Less to write about this one. A weekend in a beautiful B&B outside Cambridge, during which Thom managed to forget his horrible work-stress enough to do a lot of rigorous testing that the gold giftcard was still valid.

(It was.)

June's Classic Wedding!

In the midst of the turmoil, preparations went forward for Scarlett's wedding and, almost before she knew it, she was clad in Ellen's wedding dress and veil, coming down the wide stairs of Tara on her father's arm, to face a house packed full with guests. Afterward she remembered, as from a dream, the hundreds of candles flaring on the walls, her mother's face, loving, a little bewildered, her lips moving in a silent prayer for her daughter's happiness, Gerald flushed with brandy and pride that his daughter was marrying both money, a fine name and an old one – and Ashley, standing at the bottom of the steps with Melanie's arm through his.

When she saw the look on his face, she thought: 'This can't be real. It can't be. It's a nightmare. I'll wake up and find it's all been a nightmare.'

Gone with the Wind
Margaret Mitchell

June 4th

Today was the most fun I've ever had doing imaginary shopping. We picked our wedding list with super-futuristic hand scanners, running around the shop and scanning everything that caught my eye (grabby) or that Thom deemed useful (yeah, *sexy*). Wedding list, you say? Indeed. The conversation about this whole process was *stunningly* pain-free. Last week over dinner, I'd really dug myself in for a long session of haggling, but actually:

Me: Thom, I've been thinking about a wedding list. I know you didn't like the idea before—

Thom: Oh God yeah – I can't bear the thought of guests spending money on things we'll never, ever use. Did you see some of the stuff the Noses were given by people who insisted on going off-list?

Me: Um . . . what?

Thom: I think it's a really good idea. But two conditions: we have lots of cheap options, and we only give out details if anyone asks.

Me: Um . . . OK. That was weirdly easy.

A few days later I was still carrying that shell-shock around with me when we hit the floors, clutching our scanners like weapons of mass selection. Thom looked at my excited face and reminded me: 'Kiki. Nothing too huge. Small things for any friends who want to get us something. Deal?' I squealed and sprinted down the escalators to the crockery department, and started zapping all the gilt-edged bone china I could lay my lasers on. After a minute or two I heard a polite cough behind me. Thom. With a heavy heart, I started deleting those £75 plates and bowls from my zapper, and moved over to the boxes of crockery: £60 for the full set. Boooooooooo. I guess I should probably have waited for him to leave the floor before I started scanning the £6,000 rugs, too.

TO DO:
Calligrapher to write the place names, seating plan, table names?
Toasting drinks – shot glasses with pomegranate seeds and ice cold gin? Peach bellinis?
Wedding day kit for Thom – razors, balm, socks, little note
Shirt for Thom – embroidered collar?
Underwear – go for fitting at Rigby & Peller
Jewellery – look into vintage tiaras or jewelled hairpins, since Dad can't help
Confetti cones from old book jackets?
Shoes for the wedding – Louboutins?

June 6th

Thom came home from work an odd shade of grey. I went to kiss him but he took one of my wrists in each of his hands

212

and sat me down on the sofa. I was frightened, as a hundred terrible possibilities raced through my head.

Thom: Kiki . . . I've lost my job.
Me: Oh, God.
Thom: I'm so sorry.
Me: Thom! Why are you sorry? I'm sorry for you! Oh Thom, are you OK? What happened? What did they say? Are you alright?
Thom: I'm fine, Keeks. I'm pissed off, but it was hardly a bolt from the blue.
Me: What happened? Are you OK?
Thom: I'm fine. Really. That sweep of redundancies over the last couple of weeks; I thought I was safe, that it was over. I should have known I was still in the firing line. Ha! Literally. All that shit about the PowerPoint, and having to check in with Rowland every night. I should have seen this was coming, there'd been rumours for ages . . But what about the wedding?
Me: What *about* the wedding? What's that got to do with it? They weren't sponsoring it, were they?
Thom: Err . . . they kind of *were*, actually. That salary they've been giving me – that was going to be covering all that stuff at the wedding.
Me: But – we *can* still get married, can't we?
Thom: [hugging me] Of course we can! Please still marry me? It just means that it'll have to be a lot smaller. We can go through your lists and work out what we can still afford. Kiki, I'm sorry, but Redhood Farm might have to be rethought.
Me: [trying to hold it together] Oh, Thom, don't worry about that! It only matters that you're OK.
Thom: Kiki, it's alright. I'm fine. You can talk about the wedding if you like.

Me: We can fix this. I'm sure we can. We can make this all OK again. [dying inside. But *will not* cry]

We talked for a long time – about cutbacks whispered about for a long time at the company, about the souring relationship between Thom and his boss, about how long Thom had been unhappy there – really unhappy, not just unhappy because he isn't an astronaut or a zookeeper – and how really, really, once the shock wore off, he was happy, although frightened, but happy that this meant he would have to take action about the situation and work out what he really wanted to do with his life. He apologised for being so stressed at me over the last few months.

While I write this, I try not to think that Thom may have known this was coming. I try not to think about anything, especially not the possibility that I won't have my dress, or the caterers, or Redhood Farm, because every time I do think about them I forget that this is Thom's problem and some-thing I need to support him through, and instead I find that I am a horrible person, and almost crying again.

June 7th

I had plans to see Greta tonight, but was going to cancel to be with Thom. He said I was being ridiculous and he didn't want me becoming a shut-in just because of his joblessness. Why is he in such good spirits about this? I did as he commanded and met Greta for dinner in Chinatown. She greeted me with, 'You did *not* tell me how hot your fiancé is. How is *he* keeping?'

Me: [starting to cry] He lost his jo-o-ob.
Greta: God. Kiki. I'm so sorry.

214

Me: No, I'm sorry. Please don't think I'm a crier. I never cry. Don't judge me.

Greta: [laughing] I'm not going to judge you, Kiki. Are *you* OK?

I felt ridiculous enough that I managed to stop crying, and tell her everything. About Thom's horrible job, about my dreadful inclination to immediately think about our wedding, about the pressure it was putting on him, about how I thought I was becoming a terrible person.

Greta: Have you drafted any emails with a minute-by-minute breakdown of the day?

Me: No.

Greta: Are you getting to your wedding by helicopter?

Me: No. But that sounds good.

Greta: Have you slept with Thom's brother?

Me: No. He doesn't have one.

Greta: Shame. But I guess you're in the clear.

I hope she's right.

When I got home, I told Thom about his new fan. He said, 'Oh, *reeeeeally*?' in his most perverty voice, clearly delighted with his conquest. I've got to show him *some* ray of light in his life.

June 8th

I went over to Mum and Dad's after work today, to tell them about Thom's job. I was nervous – I didn't want them to worry, and I certainly didn't want them echoing Thom's concerns about going ahead with the wedding we could no longer afford – but in the end I never got to tell them at all. Mum handed me a pile of bridal magazines from her friend's daughter in a most distracted manner (no lectures about not reading them while drinking a cup of tea or tearing anything out before she'd called her friend to get her daughter's permission) then went up to see if Dad was awake yet (he was having another nap). She came down again to say that he was still asleep. I asked her what on earth she'd been doing to the poor man to exhaust him like this, and Mum stared at me like I wasn't really there. Tough crowd. I didn't fancy breaking the news to her alone, though, so I made my excuses again and went home.

I really need to talk to Susie about this. What's up with those two?

June 10th

Home isn't great right now either. I think Thom's still slightly in shock. He doesn't sit around in a dressing gown watching *Loose Women* and eating pickled onions from a jar; instead he's up and dressed by the time I leave the house each morning, tapping away at the computer or making lists and phone calls about which he is most mysterious. I'm waiting for the crash. I think this denial is about to come and bite us all, big time.

I ventured a comment that may well go down as the least popular suggestion since Herod suggested cutting down on the baby population:

Me: Thom – it might be too soon to be searching for silver linings for this whole thing, but won't your redundancy money mean that we *don't* have to worry about the wedding?
Thom: How come?
Me: You were there a while, weren't you, and those places

216

don't throw you onto the street with only the coppers from their pockets, do they?

Thom: So what, you've spent that money already?

Me: [gulping] No, of course I haven't spent it, but you said that we'd have to find some kind of solution to you not having a job anymore, and it seems . . . a bit . . . like we've got . . . a solution? [fading off]

Thom: Kiki! I don't know *when* I'll find another job. I've got rent to pay here, and bills, and I've got to eat, and I've got no idea how long I'll be doing all that on the money they've given me. And even if I found a job tomorrow, how many people get given that kind of money? Imagine what we could do with it! That's a flat deposit! And you want to spend it on one day's dress and dinner?

Me: You had me at '*Kiki!*' I get it.

Thom: This wedding will happen. You need to just remember who we are.

I brought him through a bowl of apple crumble and custard (his favourite comfort food) and sat down on the floor to rub his feet. I waited a couple of minutes before saying, 'All I know is, I am the best. Wife-to-be. EVER.' Thom just said, 'You're an idiot.'

June 12th

Shit. Oh shit oh shit oh shit.

OooooooooooooaaaaaaaaaaaaaaaaaaAAAAAAAAAAAAAAAAAAAAAAAAAAAAAAAAAAAA.

This is what happens when everything seems to be working. This is what happens when you think it's allllll sorted. That

217

everything will go according to plan and you can start dusting off your hands and relaxing.

You start making apple crumble and saying you're a brilliant wife-to-be, and the next thing you know, there IS NO WEDDING. This has not been a good day. Is this diary about to become not a record of my happy marital plans, but a final memorandum before the last days of the human race? Because THAT IS WHAT IT'S BEGINNING TO FEEL LIKE.

I called Redhood Farm's recommended caterers today, to ask if they might be able to do a cheaper menu for us than the one we'd discussed. They couldn't. In fact, they so couldn't, they asked if they could help me find another caterer, as they'd had a request on that same day for a much bigger event and thought it might be better for me to work with a smaller, more affordable catering company. They fired me. My wedding caterers fired me. Writing this down again, can this really be right? With an awful sense that this probably wasn't the day to do this, I rang my dress shop next. The beautiful, beautiful dress shop. The dress shop full of lovely ladies and plush sofas. The dress shop which has since closed down. Obviously. *Obviously*. With the magical symmetry of threes, the phone rang as I was calculating whether to cry in bed, or go the whole hog and throw myself into the Thames. It was Mary from the cake shop! Of course it was! Checking that I still wanted my five-tiered fruitcake. In a fit of hysterics, I wailed that I didn't want fruitcake and hadn't ordered fruitcake. She suggested that maybe I should go elsewhere. I said I didn't have time to find anyone else. Sweet Mary told me with all the charm she could muster that this wasn't her problem. I fired her. I realise *now* this was evil Monica's evil, evil revenge for the Mutton Lamb muttering and even if I'd got a cake out of them, it would probably have had raw rabbit hearts or something inside anyway. So we were now cakeless, dinnerless and dressless. And neither Susie (napping, the lazybones) nor Thom (who knew?) were picking up.

When Thom came home from another mystery outing I was sitting shell-shocked on the sofa. He prised the March edition of *Martha Stewart Weddings* out of my clenched fingers and asked if everything was OK with my dad. Yes, I said, unable to get beyond my pain. Susie? Is it your sister or the baby? Your mum? I was beginning to feel faintly ridiculous by now, so my subconscious decided to compound the matter by sending me flouncing out of the doorway screaming, 'No, it's MY life and it's RUINED and this WEDDING is OVER!' Because nothing makes you feel better than behaving like an eight-year-old.

He had the enormous good sense to leave me to stew in my own foolishness, coming in later to offer me food. Always wise.

Thom: I've cooked some deeeeelicious pad thai. But I couldn't find any salt – can I have some of your tears for it instead?

Me: How can you be so cruel? If you weren't so handy around the house I'd have found myself a loveless relationship with someone who cared as much about this wedding as I do.

Thom: That person doesn't exist, Kiki. And let's take a look at dinner before we start talking about my cruelty and your lovelessness.

Me: Hang on – what's that ridiculous poker face you've got going on there? Is that . . . is that a *pun* alarm going off? If I walk into the kitchen and there's one

219

of your ties on a notepad, there's going to be a serious talk, young man.

Thom: *Would* I?

He would, and he did, even sprinkling chopped peanuts delicately over his construction. Pad tie. Brilliant. But, smart man, he swiftly fished out the real meal and we sat down together to slurp noodles and mull over the future of our wedding.

Thom: Kiki, what are we going to do?

Me: I think . . . I think that we've got no caterers, we've got no cake, and I've got no dress.

Thom: Do you still want to get married?

Me: Very, very much, Thom. To you in particular, ideally.

Thom: Then I think we should. If you can bear it, we can make this the best wedding in the world, which it always would have been since you will be marrying me.

Me: No, uh-uh – *you* will be marrying *me*. But I suppose you're right about everything else. I just need a few days to mourn The Wedding That Wasn't.

Thom: I understand, Kiki. [whispering] I'm so sorry for your loss.

When I came to bed he'd taken some black tights from my drawer and tied the bridal magazines with a giant mourning bow. He'd also wrapped a black hairband around his upper arm. I can see he's taking my grieving very seriously.

TO DO:

Try to pretend that money doesn't matter

Research whether joblessness is likely to result in groom eating all of the wedding cake

Research whether joblessness is likely to result in groom eating all of the wedding guests

Research how this wedding is even going to happen without
   a dress, food or money
Check Thom really is OK

June 18th

A fabulous date from Thom's diary to lift our spirits after the
last few weeks of terrible luck. He bundled us off to the station
this morning, carrying a huge rucksack and reminding me too
late of all the things I'd probably try to bring if he didn't make
us leave so early. At the station, he presented me with a thermos
of tea and a crossword book for the journey, and we spent a
happy hour bickering over capitals of the world and possible
cryptic solutions. When we got off the day had turned from a
grey just-out-of-winter dawn to a here-comes-summer morning.
And, even better, we were at the seaside for it. Joys. We spent
a perfect, lazy day, sitting on a rug and talking, occasionally
heading to the water to cool our feet, then back to the rug for
more bites from the picnic Thom had brought and to talk
about nothing: what we might do at the weekend, how my
work was, what he'd heard from his old colleagues about the
place now. When we headed back to the station and ate our
fish and chips on the platform, from the paper, we were
exhausted from the sea air in all the best ways.

I do feel better than before. Thom's still tying black
mourning bows around everything – I opened the fridge this
morning to find a long black sock bound around the milk
– but I think this will work out. We'll find that money from
somewhere. It will be nothing like the Nose Nuptials: I want
ours to truly be something special. Thom suggested photo-
copying our faces with Polka Dot's equipment and pasting
them onto balloons to give our ceremony the personal touch.

*   *   *

But I am worried that Thom really is having a breakdown. He's still getting up with me each morning, putting on his suit and heading out to the tube. When I ask where he's going he wiggles his eyebrows mysteriously, denying any interview but saying he'll keep me posted. Is he like those jobless Japanese salarymen who don't don their smartest suits to sit in the park and feed the pigeons for eight hours a day?

TO DO:
Focus on venue – ask Redhood Farm for other caterers and
   cake makers

June 19th

Thom's mum rang last night. She said they're both so worried about him.

Aileen: Kiki, you know he'll never tell us anything. Is he OK? Are you? Can you afford your rent? Do you need any help?

Me: We're OK, thank you. I worry about him too—

Aileen: Is he sleeping? Eating anything?

Me: He's eating everything. He hasn't had an appetite like this for years. And he sleeps like a baby. I've had to start keeping a knitting needle by the bed to prod him when he snores.

Aileen: So why are *you* worried, Kiki?

Me: He just seems so *normal*. He seems . . . *happy*.

Aileen: Do you think he might just *be* happy?

Me: I suppose it's not beyond all possibility.

Aileen: But you can keep a roof over your heads? You've got food in the fridge?

Me: We have, thank you. It'll be tight, particularly with

the wedding, but we're not in any danger of having to move in with Mum and Dad.

Aileen: Oh, I wish we could help you more, Kiki. It's terrible being all the way over here when something like this happens. I can't tell you how much worrying I do. Sometimes I feel it's all I can think about—

Alan: [in the distance] Aileen, the jacuzzi's waiting!

Aileen: [giggling] Well. You can't worry *all* the time, can you, love?

Me: You go. Or I'm flying over there and getting in there before you do.

God, that seems like a nice life right now. If one more thing goes wrong I'm going to bloody do it.

June 25th

I called Redhood Farm to ask if it was possible to get any more discount. No, they said. Fair enough, I said. But could we have a tiny bit longer to pay off the balance? No, they said, it's due by Friday, or we keep your deposit *and* you lose the venue.

That was on Monday.

It's now Saturday.

They won't give it back.

They say it was in the contract we signed, that they are permitted to keep the deposit against the likelihood that they can't fill the date with another party. So, with my lost dress payment, that's over £4,000. *£4,000.* That's over a thousand morning coffees. Or a lifetime of Lancôme mascaras. Or most of our wedding fund. Or our entire honeymoon. I don't know what to do. Thom's got no job and we've just lost £4,000 and it's two months until our wedding and we don't have *anything*. Oh GAAAAAAAAAAAA.

TO DO:
Swap vitamin skin pills for cyanide pills (probably fine, as I would never remember to take them anyway)

June 26th

I woke in misery this morning, so asked Thom if he'd come with me to the park. We took some stale bread and took turns trying to land pellets on the back of the birds in the pond, until one of the park wardens suddenly arrived behind us and tutted loudly. I was laughing so hard that Thom had to guide me away.

Thom: Thanks for that, Keeks.
Me: For getting you barred from the pond?
Thom: No, for the walk. I have a nice time with you.
Me: I'm sorry about your job, but I am glad that I'm a girl who can still show you a good time.

Thom pulled me into a headlock and said not to worry my pretty little head about big man issues like jobs. I tried to give him a Chinese burn and he chased me out of the park, all the way home.

Jacki came in today to have a first look at her finished book after her long honeymoon. We'd arranged to send over the twenty books requested in her contract, but she said that we'd all worked so hard on it that she wanted to be with us together when she finally saw it.

She came into the office clutching a giant bottle of champagne, tottering on enormo-heels and hugging all of us. I led her to our meeting room where Judy the Intern had spent the afternoon putting up balloons, streamers and fetching a vast white cake with 'Jacki and Leon – Together Forever!' in pink icing across the top from the bakery round the corner. Jacki actually gasped when she saw what we'd done – rather gratifyingly, I thought – but then looked in danger of bursting into tears, so I busied her into the room and got started on popping corks and congratulating her. The book itself was gorgeous – a matt satin mint-green hardback with a funny-but-gorgeous photo of Jacki in a veil on the front and a potted CV on the back ('Jacki Jones: model, soap actress, popstar . . . and now bride?') and a few juicy hints of all the details she'd managed to cram inside. I doubt anyone would believe that she'd written the whole thing herself (with a little help), but I know what a labour of love (ha!) it's been for her. And the book is just like Jacki herself – commercial, beautiful, funny, and top quality. Everyone was huddled in twos and threes with copies of the book, admiring Pedro's photography and the lavish wonder of the pages and pages of wedding extravagance, even though we'd all been looking at it ever since it came in a few weeks ago. All of this stuff, all of this beauty, all of these snaps of this perfect, precious day – Jacki will only have this once, with her flawless occasion documented for all time, while I will have . . . what? Some supermarket confetti at the local register office? A home-made cake with a holiday snap of us Blu-Tacked to the top? One of my holiday dresses with a 'my other dress is a wedding dress' badge on it? I'm fully aware there is something ridiculous about this, but, bloody hell, I WANT MY WEDDING.

June 30th

This is exhausting. I'm so tired. We've done the fighting, we've done the making up, we've done the coming-to-an-agreement-about-doing-our-wedding-my-way. With his redundancy, Thom's got more than enough to worry about at the moment, and I don't ever want to make him feel that he was ever just a paycheque to me . . . but I also know how much we *need* this wedding to start our lives together right. I want to do it properly. I don't want some forgettable register office legality. I want us to have a *good time*. A bit of colour. I don't want to start our lives together in some half-cocked pale imitation of a celebration.

And I think Dad's not well either. Every time I call he's either asleep or in the bath. Has Mum poisoned him with a bad batch of curry? I'll go round at the weekend.

I don't know why I'm still writing all this. It's gone from notebook and memento to . . . something else. A record of all my errors. A keepsake of the people who have let me down. A souvenir of how my wedding didn't happen. I feel like I have no one else to talk to right now. With two weeks until her due date, Suse understandably isn't particularly interested in our wedding, Thom feels a million miles away, Alice has surely reached saturation point when it comes to my 'wedding issues' and I can't bear to attempt to engage my mother in any meaningful discussion on the subject.

I don't know if this wedding will go ahead. I don't know what's happened here. Like school days, these should be some of the best days of my life: all that hope and excitement ahead of me. But, like school days, this is actually completely shit.

TO DO:
Work out what any of us are doing here.

July's Classic Wedding!

We came to the door of the suite. 'I think I had better deal with this alone,' he said; 'tell me something – do you mind how soon you marry me? You don't want a trousseau, do you, or any of that nonsense? Because the whole thing can be so easily arranged in a few days. Over a desk, with a licence, and then off in the car to Venice or anywhere you fancy.'

'Not in a church?' I asked. 'Not in white, with bridesmaids, and bells, and choir boys? What about your relations, and all your friends?'

'You forget,' he said, 'I had that sort of wedding before.'

Rebecca
Daphne du Maurier

July 1st

When I got home tonight, Thom had just had Susie on the phone, in all sorts of terrible moods. Apparently she'd called to report that Pete had brought home completely the wrong type of bread and Mum had been on the phone at her asking if she'd had the baby yet. '*Yes* Mum,' she'd apparently said, 'I had the baby last week and I was waiting for you to call so I could tell you.' Thom tried to keep her on the phone until I got back, hoping I could lift her spirits, but when he told her I'd walked in that moment he was suddenly on the receiving end of a dial tone.

Me: [taking the phone] Hello? *Hello?* Oh God, what have I done now?

Thom: Oh, leave her alone. She's probably in labour.

Me: Ooooh, Mystic Thom speaks of the mysteries of women. You're so attuned.

Thom: She probably is.

Me: Oh, man. That would be brilliant.

Thom just nodded knowingly and went back to tapping out secretive emails at his computer. I tried to call her but she wasn't picking up, nor Pete, nor Mum. *Oooooh*.

TO DO:
Consider calling Susie in the morning to check she's OK
Also consider that maybe at this moment she's pushing a baby out
If she is OK, maybe see if she's able to look into the flowers?

July 2nd

In the end, I didn't call Susie this morning. She called me.

Susie: Morning!
Me: Morning. What's new with you?
Susie: Nothing. You? [sounds in the background]
Me: Suse . . . what's that noise?
Susie: Which one? The banging racket or the crying baby?
Me: The crying . . . baby?
Susie: That, my tiny-skulled betrothed little sibling, is your new niece, Frida Emily Carlow Miller. It turns out she was in my stomach *all this time*. Who knew?
Me: Bloody hell, Suse. If any of the nurses hear you baby Frida will be off to the orphanage.
Susie: Possibly.
[silence]
Me: OH MY GOD. You've had a BABY. Is it yours? Can you see her from where you are? Can I visit? Is it a baby? OH MY GOD.
Susie: Yes, I thought you'd say that.

I calmed down after a while, and congratulated them all on being bonkers crafty weasels, secreting herself away like a wild animal to birth her squirming infant, and she was happy with that comparison. They'll be home at lunch and Thom and I are permitted an hour's visit tonight *if* we bring foie gras and apple martinis for the parents. Which seems like a totally legitimate request from a nursing mother.

I could not be more excited. That clever old sister of mine. That beautiful baby. I'm so happy for them all.

July 4th

Alice brought in a tiny Tiffany bag and a little Bonpoint parcel today, and raised them to a great height before dumping them on my desk. She said, 'It's a rattle for the baby and some super-tiny outfits. They better make their way to your sister, Kiki – if I catch you wearing that baby toy on a necklace like some dreadful nineties raver I'll have Hamilton's private police force on you faster than you can say "But it looks better on me, officer".'

I love it when she's all rich and masterful. And when she allows me to convince my sister, albeit momentarily, that I love her child more than I love eating food and paying my bills.

July 5th

Susie says if I visit her any more frequently I'll have to start doing household chores round there, which I said was ironic since she certainly hadn't lifted a finger to clean the place up for the last week or so. As soon as I said it I thought I'd set her hormones off, but it was only when I said even Norman had asked after Frida that she started weeping

231

copiously. I offered to take the kids out so she could have a rest, but she said she was so happy not to have that wriggling baby in her womb anymore that she didn't know what to do. I think she's fond of Frida. I've said we'll add that baby to the wedding guest list *if* Susie finds her a giant pink bow for her bare baby scalp. Susie said maybe she and Pete might be busy on that date after all, but she would ensure Mum and *all* Mum's friends could make it.

TO DO:
Research if bridesmaids dresses are available in a 'dressing gown' design (as requested by Susie)
Venue – on a boat? At London Zoo?
Dress – see if Mum has any suggestions
Wedding shoes – something from LK Bennett
Music: for introducing bride & groom, first dance, cake cutting, father/daughter dance and final dance
Catch up with Dad, and check that he finds the father/daughter dance as creepy as I do

July 6th

Dad's in hospital. He's OK. He had a small heart attack yesterday afternoon. Mum told us they've given him clotbuster injections and ECGs that show he's much better than before. He's got to stay in overnight, but he's OK. He's OK.

We went to see him and stayed and chatted with him for almost an hour.

Me: [with mock indignation] You're fine! Do you have any idea how busy I am right now?
Dad: Well, it was either now or Christmas. And who else was going to put up all the Christmas decorations?

Me: Fair enough. [bursts into tears]
Dad: Oh, love. I'm alright. Plenty of life in this ticker, yet.

Then a frazzled nurse threw us out. He really bloody scared us.

That's all.

July 7th

God, he scared us so much.

Mum took him home today. He looked better, tucked up on the sofa, making gentle jokes with everyone, grimacing a bit but with colour in his cheeks, smiling at Mum and taking our flowers and cards with an expression which spoke perfectly of his embarrassment at the fuss. When we said goodbye I hugged him so tight.

July 8th

The phone rang as I was running out of the door to get to Mum's, with Thom jangling the keys at me, saying, 'Leave it, Kiki!' but I had a sudden moment where I thought – what if this is Mum? What if we shouldn't go to theirs? What's happened? But, even more shocking, it was Pamela Cooper.

Pamela: Hello, Kiki. This is Pamela Cooper calling.
Me: [stunned] Er . . . Hello, Pamela. Is this something to do with Polka Dot? Because it would be a

lot better if I could call you from the office tomorrow.

Pamela: No, no, don't be ridiculous. My son Anthony told me about your father.

Me: Oh.

Pamela: I thought that I would call on behalf of Polka Dot management, and say that if you need any time off, any time at all, you don't need to worry about a thing. You must be with your father whenever you feel you need to be.

Me: Er . . . Thank you.

Pamela: Don't thank me. Work is just work. It's not people. The sooner you young folk learn that, the better by far for everyone. Don't think I don't see you, beavering away in that office. I'm no fool. And you've got enough on your plate without Polka Dot making *you* ill too. D'you hear me?

Me: Really, thank you. I'm just going to see him now, actually.

Pamela: Well, stop chatting to me, silly girl. Off you go.

Thom: What was that? Is Polka Dot closing down?

Me: No. Weirder. Pamela Cooper just rang because she was worried about me.

Not sure if there's a recent head injury that would explain all this, but I was unnerved, and touched. This phone call came from a woman whose mantra is 'Profit Before People' so I am mystified to say the least. Maybe she'd been mainlining tequila at 5pm. Maybe someone had a gun to her head. Maybe she had a point. Mmm. I'll check in with Tony tomorrow.

July 10th

Oh God. Dad back in hospital.

He'd been at home and was fine.

They were watching TV, Dad asking about when Susie and I were coming over next. Then Mum said his speech went all broken. His face was off white like porridge, and he clutched his chest and stared at Mum. She said she called an ambulance and went with him. She called us and we all went to the hospital and hung around the corridors until they said we should go home. They were putting in stents to make his heart work better and there was nothing we could do for him. Thom and I are sleeping in Mum and Dad's guest room. I didn't want to leave her, or miss a call from the hospital.

We'd all gone to bed tonight when I heard a noise from the kitchen. I pulled on my comfortable childhood dressing gown and went downstairs to investigate. Mum was there, sitting at the table. I put the kettle on and made us both a cup of tea. Mum warmed her hands on hers but didn't drink anything. I put my hands around hers. We sat there until our teas had gone cold, not saying anything, and then we went upstairs together. She gave me a long hug, and I felt like crying.

Daddy, please be OK. Please don't go anywhere. Please. Please don't die, Dad.

July 16th

I haven't written for days; I couldn't. I couldn't think about the wedding at all, when all I wanted in the whole world

235

was for my dad to be alright again. Thom's been really sweet, checking me over each morning to see that my shoes are matching and I haven't forgotten to put a top on, but I've been fairly useless at work, coming back to the hospital to see Dad each evening when he's mostly been asleep, or completely zonked on whatever they're giving him and not so great at small talk. Thom's parents have been lovely too, calling each night to check on us all. Our July treat, theatre tickets, went to Alice as neither of us could face it.

July 17th

Dad looked better tonight, so much better. His skin is actually skin-coloured now, rather than wet-newspaper-coloured (which it was when he first came in), also something of a relief. Mum still hovered around him like a nervous fly but after a few minutes, he asked her if she wouldn't mind getting us all some dreadful hot drinks, please, and Thom (recognising the international code for privacy) offered his assistance. When they'd left the room, I asked Dad if he was about to die. He laughed, thank God, which was promising. 'No love,' he said, 'I'm not about to die. I hope. But I did want to give you these just in case, before you went and did anything rash like marrying.' He'd been fishing in his bedside drawer, and came up with a little blue velvet ring box. He put it in my shaking hand, and said, 'Open it, please.' I lifted the lid and saw two wedding rings, one slim and pale gold, one thicker and platinum, both fashioned to look battered and scarred and beautiful. 'Quite a special commission, this one. Hence why I couldn't take yours, you see. Sorry, love.' I gaped at him. 'Yes, it turns out that fellow you've picked up is quite eager to keep a roof over your dad's head too. Don't worry – I overcharged him grotesquely.' I didn't know what to say.

Two of the people I trust the most in the whole world sneaking behind my back. Pretty good.

Dad, I love you very much.

July 19th

Dad was allowed home this morning, so Thom and I were round with grapes and piles of convalescence reading earlier tonight. Mum's so shaken by the whole thing. Of course I knew this was hard for her, but I don't think I've taken a moment to consider what she was truly facing. Her husband of thirty-five years, gone in an instant.

Once we'd seen Dad tucked up safe on the sofa, I went upstairs to find his slippers; Mum was sitting on their bed with the slippers in her hand, staring at them. She heard me come in and looked up, pale.

'You know, Kiki, that my father wasn't at our wedding. When your dad and I were courting, my father was dying in his bedroom. He missed our wedding by a week. Your dad made me feel like he was building me a future because he couldn't keep me from the grief of the past.' She paused. 'He's always been my best friend, Kiki. He still is. I don't know what I'd do without him.'

She let out a sob but turned it into a cough, rubbed her face and said brightly, 'Right! Found the slippers!' Oh, Mum.

And Thom's busy-day mystery has been revealed. He admitted that Dad had got him a volunteer placement at the college, and that he's just been helping out wherever he's been needed. I think, having done so much corporate work, Thom's felt eager to do something for someone who doesn't have a second/third/fourth home, but I suspect once the wedding is done he'll be champing at the bit to get back into an office somewhere, after dealing with those bloody kids.

I'm so glad Dad is home.

July 20th

Once we'd visited Dad after work, we went to go and see Susie and that new little piglet again. Thom had bought a miniature keyboard and an Etch-a-Sketch for the Twins, and I parcelled up all the pâté and brie I could find for Susie and her giganta-breastfeeding-appetite. There was no answer to the front door, but I saw the side gate was open so waved Thom round as he locked up the car and we followed the path down the side of the house to the garden. I couldn't see Edward and Lily anywhere, but I could see Pete and Susie, hunched over baby Frida and squealing their lungs out with laughter. Susie was actually crossing her legs and holding her stomach in with one arm while she pushed Pete away with the other, and he was laughing so hard that he was doubled over, almost on top of her. Baby Frida watched with her giant marble eyes, and then Pete stopped laughing and kissed Suse so nicely that I thought maybe I ought to head back out of the gate.

They were so happy and so peaceful. If Pete spent the rest of his life looking after my sister the way he had so far, and was capable of making her laugh like that before kissing her like that, then he was OK by me, absent dad or no. But it wasn't just that. Suse and Pete's wedding had been at a register office in the middle of nowhere; at the age of twenty-two they'd disappeared on holiday and come back with mischief in their eyes declaring they'd brought us all back a holiday souvenir. 'For you each . . .' Susie said, fumbling in her bag, 'a photocopied . . . wedding certificate!' They'd wanted no fuss; there was little fanfare, no colour-schemed chair covers and certainly no panic about which wedding cake was particularly *en vogue* at the time (their wedding cake at the party we threw for them at the pub a week later was a pile of jam doughnuts with a horseshoe candle stuck on top) and yet, here they were, in a brief moment when Pete wasn't living his life elsewhere, happy as Larry simply being with one another. *They* were happy enough without a toastmaster playing a fanfare at the start of married life. So where does that leave me?

July 23rd

Saturday, and Eve called to ask if I fancied brunch. Never one to turn down the opportunity for some eggs Benedict and a pint of coffee, and not having seen her since my disastrous stay at her house, we met at a Soho café. It was so odd – for maybe the first time ever, I didn't feel defensive meeting her. The lack of it made me suddenly realise: every time I'd seen her in the past, I'd needed her to like me, and I needed to let her be the boss – I was nervous before she'd even spoken, waiting for her to remind me why our dynamic had become the way it was. Every time, something of that skewed relationship from our teenage years echoed between us.

But this time, it felt so different. I was furious, for a start. Furious for how she'd treated me, furious for how I'd let her, furious for her behaviour at her birthday party; furious for her treatment of Thom, that my dad had nearly died, that my amazing work project was over and I'd be back making lunch appointments for Tony, handling the books he didn't care about and pretending I didn't have a mind of my own, that my fiancé had lost his job completely and that he'd forced himself to do something he'd hated so much for so long, furious that Eve was still getting under my skin. I was angry before I'd even sat down. But then she began. Eve started by saying that she was sorry, again, really sorry. She'd been a dick, she said, and didn't want to be a dick anymore. She'd been talking to someone – about me and Thom and herself – I laughed and said, 'Is this person you mentioned a *therapist*?' The thought of Eve wanting – and asking for – help seemed impossible: a fox asking for its teeth to be removed. She smiled at me.

Eve: I nearly did. I was going to, but I found something even better.

Me: Slow *down*. Have you found . . . God?

Eve: I have, Kiki. I've found God and have been welcomed into his heart, and there's a peace there that I want to share with you.

Me: Oh . . . [faintly] good?

Eve: I'm *kidding*, you idiot.

Me: I was about to be sick.

Eve: You fool. It's a guy. And not any guy, but . . . he's nice. Don't you dare tell anyone. He's nice enough that I want to be a bit nicer, so he might hang around that little bit longer. And – you mustn't bloody tell this to anyone either – I actually quite like being nice, and I'm quite sorry that I've been a dick to you occasionally. Let's start again.

Me: [goggling in silence]

Eve: This isn't easy. Never explain, never complain, you know. After you'd come to mine for those few days, I started thinking about what I'm doing with my life. Who I am. Jesus, I sound like a wanker. But I thought you might like to know that I might be in love.

Me: Fine. As long as you're doing it just to impress a boy, and not because you've actually got a new outlook on life or anything.

Eve: A man. Not a boy.

Me: Haha! [singing] You've bee-en saved by a ma-an!

Eve: I haven't been saved by anybody. I don't need saving from anything. I just realised . . . I could just do what I wanted and not have someone I loved with me, or I could maybe take some advice sometimes and keep that person in my life.

Me: You must like him quite a bit.

Eve: I was sort of talking about you too.

Me: Oh, that's *terrible*.

Eve: What is?

Me: You've become a self-help book.

Eve: Oh, I never realised – this is *all* fine: you're a horrible person too. I didn't need to worry about you at all.

Me: You're a manual on how to love yourself.

Eve: Nothing wrong with a bit of loving yourself. It helps me get to sleep.

Me: There's a mental image I didn't need. I think we're finished here.

Eve: Listen. I hope you don't mind, but he's going to swing by in a minute. I wanted you to meet him so . . . maybe . . . he could come to the wedding?

I would have welcomed anyone Eve wanted to bring, anyway – she was my bridesmaid and friend, and I *did* love her – and then he arrived. Eve suddenly hissed, 'Oh shit – he's called Mike, by the way.' He was nothing like I expected. Bloody hell. He was . . . normal. A tiny little bit of a gut, faintly nerdy hair, but the nicest smile in the world. I'm not kidding. Sorry Thom, but this guy's smile . . . I got it. I really did. He gave Eve a kiss (long enough for me to get the picture – they were into one another, alright) then turned and gave me a handshake. I *love* handshakes! Love. Them.

Mike: Kiki! I've heard so much about you. I'm sorry to crash your brunch but I was nearby and Eve really wanted to introduce me, while I'm still fresh out of the box with this killer athletic body.

Me: It's so nice to meet you. I've heard almost nothing about you due to Eve's unusual new secrecy, but she seems so happy on whatever you're giving her.

Mike: Give her a few weeks and I'm sure I'll be the sad toy she doesn't want to play with anymore. You can have her back then.

I've never in my life heard any man speak about Eve like this, and certainly no one has ever got a handle on her so fast. But instead of rolling her eyes at him, Eve laughed, blissful, and held his hand. She never looked at Louis like that – they were always in fierce competition, so smiles were doled out on a point-scoring basis, or after a triumphant put-down. I'll be delighted to invite him to wherever our wedding ends up being. *If* it ends up being.

July 24th

Mum called to say it would be nice if we came over to see them, but not until the afternoon when Dad had had a chance for a nap, and not all at once. Susie and Frida went over there for a light lunch, and Thom and I were permitted to go over for a roast in the evening. Dad kept insisting on how well he felt, but we were all handling him with kid gloves. After dinner, Mum and Dad suddenly seemed slightly nervous.

Mum: So, you two, we wanted to talk to you.
Me: Dad, are you OK?

242

Dad: I'm fine, love. It's something else we wanted to talk
        to you about.
Me   [aghast] Are you two getting a divorce? *Please* don't
        be getting a divorce . . .
Mum: Kiki! Of course we're not getting a divorce.
Dad: It's nothing bad, love. Some friends of ours mentioned
        that the school field is available for hire this summer.
        You can have access to the facilities there, too, if you
        want, for a small bit more.
Me: The school? Over the road? That school?
Mum: Why would you think we're getting a divorce?
Thom: That sounds great, John. What kind of price are they
        after?
Me: Hang on – my old school? Opposite here? Or do
        you mean a lovely old grand public school? The latter,
        yes?
Dad: For the field alone, it's £100 – for the field and
        whatnot, you'd be looking at £250. What do you
        think? £250 will get you from 5pm on the Friday,
        right through to the Sunday afternoon.
Mum: A divorce, Kiki. What a terrible thing to say to your
        parents.
Me: Mum, I wasn't *hopeful*. I was . . .
Thom: Hopeless? [to Dad] That sounds brilliant.
Dad: Of course, at that price, we can help you out with
        the cost.
Me: Can we slow down for *one* second? I remember that
        school. The dark corridors and the scary assembly rooms,
        and the teeny tiny toilets. We can't get married there!
Dad: It's been totally refurbished, Kiki. It's a lovely place
        now, with proper facilities and everything.
Me: But the toilets are tiny!
Dad: I wouldn't have suggested it if I didn't think it would
        work, love. Listen, my friend Mike is over there now,

we can go and have a look, and you can make your mind up once you've seen it.

Thom: Brilliant. Kiki?

Me: [feeling the crushing ball of inevitability mowing me down once more] Fine. Thanks, Dad.

Mum: [quietly] Divorce! Honestly. Where does she get this?

Dad took Thom and me over the road to the school, shuffling over while Mum called terrible curses after us if we let anything happen to him. His pal was there directing workmen round the back, and left us to it once he was happy that Dad was getting on OK and we knew our way around. We went into the school through a little fire exit, propped open for the men, and saw in the half-light the rows of classrooms. How could the smell not have changed in twenty-odd years? It was so unmistakably a school. Dad said, 'Come round to the playground, you two – that's the bit you'd be at.' He explained that we'd have the sports field off the playground, plus the toilets, school kitchens and power supply in the buildings at the edge of the field. I could see the playground through the big doors as we approached. Heavy grey tarmac and a big brick wall, both of which used to cause scuffed knees and elbows as the kids had shoved and tripped one another during break. We followed him outside in the dusk, to where a big grubby grey tent was erected at the near end of the school field, with big grubby men coming in and out, carting pipes and wires and wheelbarrows of other grubby junk back and forth. I could make out a bit of scrubland behind the tent, and the half of the playground that had been dug up to access the pipes beneath it with grubby metal fences around the holes.

Dad: Listen, love, this will all be gone in a week. It really will look very different in the sunshine, with this all cleared away.

Me: [struggling to swallow the misery-lump in my throat]
        Dad, this is fine, thank you. It'll be great. It won't
        be licensed for weddings though, will it?

But Thom had an idea: head to a register office the morning
of the wedding, get hitched with some legal backing, then
come here for the 'real' wedding with all our friends and
families.

Dad's checked with his friend, and the school is available on
our wedding date. It'll cost us an extra £100 to get the place
cleaned after we leave, on top of the original £250, which
makes Redhood Farm's £700 corkage fee alone look like
sheer bloody robbery.

TO DO:
Check the register office can do our date
Decorations & lights
Marquee
Dance space?
Tables & chairs
Food
Flowers
DRESS

July 25th

Oh. I had never been to a register office before. It's certainly
very municipal. The plug-in scents of fake flowers filled the
air, and the walls were covered in plastic frames full of legal
notices and fire drill information. The registrar we saw was
so friendly and helpful though, but that didn't stop my nerves
when we had to take it in turns to remain silent while the

245

other one answered questions. Thom had to give my date of birth and occupation while I kept thinking don't make a joke don't make a joke don't make a joke . . . We got through that much without Interpol bursting in and declaring our marriage a sham, and then the spanner hit the works. Our Saturday is fully booked, and has been for months. The registrar said as kindly as she could that summer Saturdays get booked up almost as soon as they became available – she would let us know if she had any cancellations, but wouldn't we consider an appointment on Friday afternoon instead? I took a deep breath, and said, 'Friday would be perfect. As long as we're married, that's all that matters. Thom, is Friday OK with you?'

I got home and stayed locked in the bathroom for almost an hour before my breathing stopped sounding like I was about to burst into tears. Which I was. Oh God. Is our wedding going to be conducted at mini-desks while we serve tiny bottles of milk? Will our wedding flowers just be plastic rentals from the register office?

If I stay in here writing this, maybe someone out there will come along and fix it all.

TO DO:
Research whether the local fried chicken bar delivers
Florist – find out if we can just put some bits of hedgerow in jars
Lighting – ask if someone's willing to stand in the corner and turn the lights on and off occasionally to add atmosphere
Tell everyone to not even bother coming
Stop feeling sorry for myself

July 26th

We met Rich and Heidi after work for a film and dinner. Heidi had picked a screening of *West Side Story* (the power of pregnancy – neither Rich nor Thom raised a dissenting peep) so it meant the meal afterwards was punctuated by Heidi and me hiccupping as we struggled to contain our emotions.

Thom: Heidi, would you like a starter?
Heidi: I – hic – would, thank you, Thom.
Rich: Kiki, you?
Me: Yeah, I think I will. [shuddering sigh]
Rich: How's work at the moment, Kiki?
Me: It's good, thanks, although my boss Tony . . . sorry, I just can't stop thinking about Tony and Maria.
Heidi: [openly sobbing]
Thom: Kiki wasn't even this sad when her dad had a heart attack.
Me: [weeping] It's troo-hooo-oooo.

Thom warned me afterwards that, unless I buy them off the internet, we are now never, ever having kids.

'

We've counted again and again, and both money and space makes it pretty clear that even sixty people is pushing it. When you factor in those of us actually in the wedding party (my family, Thom's family, Eve and Rich) we're looking at around forty-five other guests.

Alice has made her feelings clear about bringing her faux-boyfriend along, so I'm glad to be able to invite our designer Dan along instead, since his lovely invitations kept me going all those months ago. He was so touched, and as he's single too at the moment, he and Alice have agreed to escort one another as work buddies. I asked Alice what will happen when she meets someone she really *does* want to live with. She said, 'Why do you think I've been working here? All those pennies go into my Disinheritance Fund.' As ever, I'm unsure if she's joking.

It looks like it will be:

Me & Thom
Susie, Pete & 2 (3-ish, really, but Frida doesn't quite count yet)
Mum & Dad
Alan & Aileen
Eve & lovely Mike
Rich & Heidi

Jim & +1
Alice & Dan
Rose & Nick
Greta & +1
Zoe & Zac
Carol & Norman

Fiona (old boss) & bf Mark
Sara (uni housemate) and her +1
Ben & Hester (Thom's school pals)
Malcolm and Phil (Thom's two favourite boffin-pals from uni) and their +1s
Paul and Robert, Thom's two decent ex-colleagues and their +1s
Other Tom from terrible holiday job I did when I was 17, and his +1
Ella and Vuk (pals from travelling)
Chuck and Matt (Thom's snooker-playing buddies) and their +1s

Cousin Emma & her boyfriend Rocky, plus baby Arthur (our favourite members of the extended family, by a giant length, and who also live down the road from Mum & Dad)

Aunt Pepper and Uncle Joe (cousin Emma's mum and dad,
    and the best of the extended family after Emma)
Elena and Stuart (Thom's cousins) and their +1s
Audrey and Graham, Elena and Stuart's parents
Jacki and Leon? I really don't want her to feel that I'm
    inviting her for any reason other than I'd like to share
    this with her. But is she weddinged out? No, I will invite
    her. She is completely brilliant, after all, and if anyone will
    inject some fun into the day, it's her.

And that's sixty.

There's no saying I'm heartbroken about not celebrating my
nuptials with the pricks who made Thom jobless, but I'm not
quite sure how one words these un-invitations. I don't think
any decent-minded printer would permit Thom's suggested
phrasing, but since it's only Dan and me producing these
beauties, I was sorely tempted. But I've settled on matching
the disinvitations to the old ones for Thom's crowd and the
distant aunts and uncles we never really wanted, and an
updated version for our close friends and family. (I've tucked
them at the back of this book for posterity.) Ta-dah! Easy
peasy.

TO DO:
Orders of Service – write with Thom. Might Dan help us
    again?
Ceremony readings – poems? Songs? Anything from any of
    our authors?
Wedding cake – ready-made?
Abandon all-Haribo diet
Admit defeat over vitamins
Remember to eat an apple occasionally

July 27th

BRAINWAVE. I sent an email to Ann and Charlie, our cookery authors, today.

> From: Carlow, Kiki
> To: thecooks@tateandgreer.com
> Subject: Wedding Cakes
>
> Hi you two,
>
> How's everything coming along with *Dining with Death?* I've really enjoyed the chapters I've seen so far.
>   I know it's such late notice, but I'm getting married at the end of August and wondered if you could recommend any bakers – our wedding cake plans have fallen through.
>
> Thanks so much and best wishes to you both,
> Kiki

It's the best I could do without writing 'PLEASE MAKE ME A CAKE'. Fingers crossed.

July 28th

> From: thecooks@tateandgreer.com
> To: Carlow, Kiki
> Re: Wedding Cakes
>
> Hi Kiki,

250

Glad to hear you're enjoying the book. It's so different to working on a cookery book but we're hoping all the food-related deaths don't put customers off the restaurant . . .

Regarding wedding cakes, we wish we could help you ourselves! But between Dining with Death and our summer event bookings we're totally swamped. In the meantime, I know the wedding rep at THE place for wedding cakes in London, Maison Edith. Shall I put you in touch?

Lots of love from both of us for your upcoming wedding day,
Ann x

Dammit.

July 29th

All invitations (and non-invitations) done and in the post. I hope no one is hugely put out by the change of plans – I've checked with the hotel everyone was staying at near Redhood Farm and they *will* give refunds (furious as they clearly were), and almost everyone we've rolled over to the new wedding either lives in London or has someone they can stay with here.

Jacki came into the office today. I've been speaking to her on email recently but I haven't seen her since our little party when she collected the finished book; she came in today to sign some copies for a competition we're running. It was a genuine pleasure to see her, I realised, and we chatted for ages – trying to ignore Clifton Black barking in Tony's office about getting his new book out to the Forces – as she asked me about Thom and our plans, and even about Mum and Dad, and Susie and the kids, and some of our other authors who I in *no way* was indiscreet about to her. She thanked me for the invitation, and said she really hoped to be there, but her schedule was crazy at the moment, and please would I keep a spare chair and a piece of cake for her, just in case. She kept asking me questions, listening to my despair at my own wedding falling apart, and telling me funny stories about her wedding day that I hadn't known about, or things she's been hearing since publication from other brides or newly-weds, and I thought, 'I'm really going to miss you.' Finally she got all the books signed, then suddenly looked a bit apologetic. 'Kiki,' she said, 'look. I'm more than happy to come in here and sign these books for you – any time you want me to do stuff like this, I'm happy to, and I hope we'll stay in touch, but there's something I need to tell you.' For some reason, I was convinced she was going to tell me she was dying, which goes to show you *can* have too many Bette Davis films in your life, but what she actually said was worse. 'Kiki, I don't want you to think that I'm mucking Polka Dot about, or that I'm wasting your time. But I want you to hear this from me. I don't know how popular this book is going to be when the readers hear that Leon and me are getting a divorce.'

My jaw dropped for a moment before I took her up in a hug. It felt for a moment like she might be crying, but when she drew back she kept hold of my hand and just sighed really deeply, dry-eyed but exhausted-looking.

'Those jokes from the best man weren't too far off the mark. Leon was with me for my money.' I reassured her that with her pre-nup, she must know that wasn't true.

Jacki sighed again, like she would split in half with it. 'Oh,

Kiki. I knew it for months. I've really always known it was that way. It wasn't a secret between us. I knew that this wedding – and this book – would help my career, and he knew my money would impress his girlfriends. I thought, once we were actually married and living together under the same roof with the rings on our fingers, he'd change his mind and realise we had a future together. It just didn't work out that way.' She laughed, bleakly. 'He didn't even give me that present on my wedding day. I did that. I thought . . . if I worked hard enough at all of it . . .'

It seems that Leon didn't stay at his mum's the night before the wedding – he was with the lip-glossed wedding guest who had sat weeping next to me through the ceremony. And with the guest's cross sister on the wedding night itself. Poor Jacki. He'd barely been home since, only coming back to get fresh clothes or match diaries so he would be there for the main events in her life: they'd agreed he'd keep quiet for six months. He'd been counting the days while she thought every morning would be the one she'd wake to find her handsome prince kissing her. No dice.

Jacki looked at me. 'Kiki, if it's what you really want, you know I can help out, don't you? If one good thing can come out of this whole thing – I've got so much money and it's only sitting there.'

If it's what you really want.

That phrase echoes down the years; Dad checking that I really do want the bike that's a bit too big, but I insist and fall off it, taking off most of my left knee and keeping me a nervous distance from all bikes for the next ten years; Mum, saying, 'Darling, are you sure that dress is the one you *really* want?' and within moments we are screaming at one another in the middle of a shop, another outing together ruined; Susie saying sweetly, 'If that's what you really want!' when I tell her on my seventeenth birthday that her new

253

boyfriend can fuck off, and she does just that, disappearing to the pub with Pete while I stay at home, playing Cure albums and promising that everyone will regret their treatment of me in a few years when I am on *Time* magazine's Twenty Amazing People Under Twenty list; Thom. Thom crushed, putting the ring back in its tray, saying, 'If that's what you really want, Kiki.' It's here, right in front of me, the wedding I really, *really* want, waiting to be taken from this kind woman, fairy godmother in my hour of need, and all I have to do is say Yes (please), and that wedding will be mine, everything fixed. But I look at her crumpled face, all the sparkle knocked out of her by her giant, shiny, glittering wedding to a man who won't ever realise how stupid he is to let her go, and I remember Thom, and I think of how I've learnt one thing: 'If that's what you really want' is life's wonderful alarm bell to tell you that you're being a terrible idiot. I smile at Jacki and take her hand and say, 'No, but thank you.'

July 31st

Just less than three weeks to go. Having utterly abandoned Martha Stewart's wedding checklist (Book master of ceremonies! Check bridal gifts have been sent! Order monogrammed thank you stationery!) I thought I'd browse some forums for any last-minute tips. (If you're looking for some affordable foliage for your wedding day, why not try the back of a funeral home! Can't afford favours? Ask every guest to pick up a bag of sweets from a petrol forecourt shop!). Error, error, *error*. Rather than helpful tips, these forums have opened up a world of pain, a world I don't ever, ever want to face again. I have truly looked into the heart of darkness. There's a certain tone on there that is remarkably reminiscent of Rose's planning emails – It's My Day, And I Can Basically Do What I Want. And If Any Of You Call Me On It, I Won't Speak To You For Years And I Will Always, ALWAYS Feel Like I Have The Moral High Ground. Between our grandmother's generation and ours it's like something slipped – something that was originally 'Oh, poor thing, of course the bride might be nervous on her wedding day, being unlikely to have seen this many people, having never been let out of the schoolroom/kitchen before', has somehow become 'The Bride is absolutely, positively allowed – nay – *encouraged* – to behave as if this party is the only thing anyone will ever be invited to, and she can be a total monster to everyone who has ever passed five words with her because that adds to the magic of the day so much more than if she somehow was just relaxed and happy albeit a bit worried that there might not be enough drink for everyone'. How did this happen? How did we let ourselves get into this state? There are women on these forums asking if their sister, who's recently had a miscarriage, has a right to be upset that the bride's asked her to sit at the children's table. Women who have had arguments bad enough for the grooms to cancel the wedding because she didn't want his parents on the top table, because it was *her* parents who paid for the event.

I read one woman's story, about her fury and crushing disappointment ('all I can do is cry') that her husband made the mistake of booking their honeymoon in her current, actual name, rather than her imaginary married name. She grieves that her honeymoon, while enjoyable, will always be slightly ruined by that name on her ticket being not magically transformed into that of the man she's marrying. Obviously – *obviously* – a completely legitimate complaint. A complaint akin to one's families being torn across a religious divide, or one's husband being sent to war, or being forbidden from marrying the person you're in love with by your own government. The nightmare of a bridesmaid getting pregnant out of step with your plans, or a mother pleading to wear a hat she likes despite the fact that the one you've chosen is *all* you want to make your wedding perfect . . . These are all equal concerns. Definitely equal and totally valid.

Enough. My best friend, who I want to spend the rest of my life with, lost his job and his first concern was my tantrums, over a dress I'll wear for a few hours. My dad was hiding his heart medicine and having minor heart attacks while all I could think of was the crockery I needed or the candles I wanted or how to match the napkins to my fake eyelashes. The wedding I was inspired by and jealous of was a complete lie, and that strong, funny woman is crushed by the twin weights of betrayal by the man she loved and the expectations and assumptions of an audience baying for more – more glitter! More glamour! More expense! More wedding!

Can I be human again? Can I forget everything that's happened? Is it too late to have a great party for everyone we love and who is kind enough to come and see us promise that we'll try to be nice to one another for as long as we both shall live? Oh, that could be a *really* good time.

I've got someone I love more than anyone else in the world, and he loves me too. How could I want a single thing more than that? What is it that's really important?

TO DO:
Convince the man I'm trying to marry that I'm definitely not a dick
Plan a wedding

August's Classic Wedding!

The wedding was very much like other weddings, where the parties have no taste for finery or parade; and Mrs Elton, from the particulars detailed by her husband, thought it all extremely shabby, and very inferior to her own. 'Very little white satin, very few lace veils; a most pitiful business! Selina would stare when she heard of it.' But, in spite of these deficiencies, the wishes, the hopes, the confidence, the predictions of the small band of true friends who witnessed the ceremony, were fully answered in the perfect happiness of the union.

Emma
Jane Austen

August 2nd

So many lovely responses to our invitations already. My adorable and very, very funny (and very much favourite) cousin Emma says she and her boyfriend can now come, as the baby can manage that journey no problem, plus her parents will be there to help out with him so they can let their hair down; Other Tom says it sounds like this is a bash he can get behind and he will be delighted to join us; and lovely-Greta-who-was-the-best-thing-about-the-Noses-marrying says that she has recovered enough from previous weddings this year to attend our spousal picnic-bash. Alan and Aileen are really excited about travelling for three days to get to their only child's wedding, going from their hilarious almost-daily calls to us. Mum wrote a really, really nice card too, saying that they're looking forward to it so much. She'd also written:

It's a tough job to organise a party for so many people when you have such a lot of other things to think of at the same time, but you're doing it so well. This will be a wonderful event just perfect for you two, and we're so honoured to be invited.

Which was nice.

And last night, while we were watching a very old *Quantum Leap* episode, Thom turned to me with the air of one who doesn't really want to know the answer, and said, 'Out of curiosity, how much are the Orders of Service costing us? I know that nice letterpress stuff you like isn't particularly cheap.'

I was glad to be able to turn to him with a triumphant air.

Me: Oh, Thom, how little you know me. I have found
        Orders of Service that will cost us approximately £3.
Thom: Each? Oh, boy.
Me: Oh, no no *no*, in total. And a coffee cake.
Thom: This seems like some weird new internet bartering
        thing. Are we going to suddenly be in the middle of
        a banking scam?
Me: No. Dan in our Art department is using those designs
        from our invitation to throw together an Order of
        Service. The £3 is for card to print them on, and the
        coffee cake is the only payment Dan would take.
Thom: I might actually be able to go halves on that.

Then he looked at me thoughtfully.

Thom: Kiki, how did you pay for your dress?
Me: Credit card. Don't. I know. I've only paid off half.
Thom: [laughing] But the shop's completely closed down?
Me: Yup, gone. Like a bride in the night.
Thom: But your money, Bride-in-the-night, is not gone. If
        it's on your credit card, you can get it back.

Me: [takes a moment to dance around the kitchen] Wait. You couldn't have mentioned this a little sooner?

Thom: Do you mean while I was being made redundant or when your dad had a heart attack?

Me: Oh, you kidder.

We toasted our luck with mugs of tea and my heart felt so much lighter. Then I baked the cake and brought it to Dan with the air of one who knows someone is about to do them a favour worth several hundred pounds in return for one small gateau. But he was on fine form, and once he'd located the artwork from the invitations, simply bashed out the Order of Service in half an hour, while I hovered over his shoulder like a nervous client. Have I ever been as interested in a book's jacket as I was in this? To be fair, probably – and nobody is going to be paying for one of these, so even if it looked like it had been thrown together with some ClipArt, no one was going to refuse to be involved with our wedding. But it did look lovely, thanks to Dan, with some text on the back to entertain the crowd while we're getting our vows out at the front. They were printed off in twenty minutes and completed before my lunch hour was even over. Now *that*, my friends, is Wedding Efficiency.

Thom gave them the thumbs up this evening, and we celebrated their success with a jug of sloe gin and a Thai takeaway from round the corner. This is totally the life.

Speaking of which, I really look forward to the hen on Friday. It's not huge – me, Susie, Alice, Rose, Greta, my old boss Fiona and Eve. Susie's found us a great restaurant which serves Brazilian food (she's never really got over her two months 'travelling' there after university) and a club nearby where we're on the guest list. I've picked out my finest dress, my tallest shoes and my glossiest handbag, and we shall enjoy tomorrow night with some sparkling conversation, fine food, sophisticated wine and some hip-shaking to the best tunes around. Oh yeah.

And speaking of cake – Eve has sent me the most helpful of offers, via Mike's job: baker. Baker! He's offered us any dessert we'd like. Will talk to him next week about possible plans. Delight!

TO DO:
Music – pull together all our favourite songs for a playlist at the reception
Alcohol – Calais run?
Make list of photos we'd like on the day for Susie
Check how Dad is

August 5th

WOOOOOOOOOOOOOOOOOOOOOOOOOOOOOOOOOO OOOOOOOOOOOOOOOOOOOOOOOOOOOOOOOOOO OOOOOOOOOOO!!!!! Lovely time with lovely freinds and dancing allllllllllllllllllllllllllllllll niiiiiiiiiiiiiiiiiiiiiiiiiiiiiiiiiiii iiight!!!!!!!!!!!!!!

August 6th

Oh God. Call off wedding. I'm dying.

August 7th

Slowly.
    Shh.

I can just about see now.

I spent all day yesterday crying at every advert on TV but now I remember . . . I remember Friday morning. I remember my working day on Friday, and I remember going to Alice's to get ready for our night out. I remember dinner . . . no. Wait. I remember the starter, and most of the main. I remember Rose offering everything from her own wedding that we wanted, and any help she could give. That made me feel even worse about being so mean about her. Oh God. I *don't remember dessert*. There was something . . . aflame? Did we have crêpes Suzette? No. Thom tells me that apparently Susie knocked over the candle and set fire to the tablecloth. Then we were asked to leave. OK. I remember walking to the club – the air must have sobered us all up a bit, because I have a clear image of Greta giving us all bottles of water in the club, then realising they were £5 each and taking them all back off us. We had our heads under the taps in the toilets for ages, and I remember dancing, feeling much better. Then . . . oh. Then Eve arrived late and bought us all tequila shots to apologise. Then . . . I have a memory of Alice taking the mic from the DJ, and giving a shout-out to everyone in publishing . . . I can remember the silence after that, and I remember hearing a song Thom and I danced to at an indie club when we first met, and texting him . . . Thom doesn't remember. What? I'm telling him that it was about half midnight. He didn't get it, he says. I'm checking my phone.

Oh.

Fuck.

I sent this:

I LOVE YOU! They playing Olivers ARmy and I THINK OF YOU I LOVE YOU FOREVER no words how i much love love love xxxx

To:
Clifton Black.

TO DO:
Find out about changing name after wedding. And before wedding. And changing jobs. And face.

August 9th

I met Mike today at lunchtime, to talk about our cake. I asked Thom if he wanted to come too, but he said that if he couldn't trust me with arranging a free cake from a master baker, I wasn't worth marrying anyway.

It was nice to meet Mike on his own. The more we talked, the more I understood why Eve was with him. He wasn't *charming* in a serial-seducing way, but was just very good company; kind, thoughtful, witty. My brain instinctively thought: *If I was single* . . . before it veered away at the ironic horror of that joke. I'll wait a while before I expect Eve to find that thought funny. She's clearly talked about us a lot, as he seemed to know everything.

Mike: So are you sure you're happy to leave it all up to me? I've got your major dislikes here . . . [points to notes, reading only: NO ANIMAL-SHAPED CAKES]
Me: Yee-es. There was one other thing . . .
Mike: [picking up pen again] OK, go ahead.
Me: [taking a deep breath]

I'veneverseenEvelikethisandifyouhurtherI'llhuntyou-downand destroyyou. [exhales]

Mike: Do you mean that?

Me: Not really. But you know what I mean.

Mike: I do. And I'm flattered.

Phew. I thought for a moment I'd lost my free wedding cake.

August 12th

At 8.45 this morning when I definitely should have been getting ready for work, the phone rang and Thom leapt out of bed to answer it. I would probably have preferred him to stay at that particular moment, considering what we'd been doing at the time of the phone call, but his face when he came back was (almost) enough to make up for it.

Thom: Keeks. Guess who that was?

Me: Clifton Black to confirm he's left his wife and is on his way over?

Thom: Close. It was the headmaster from Hendon Park.

Me: Oh God. Am I still at school? Is this one of those weird dreams where I haven't finished doing exams after all?

Thom: No. They've accepted me on a trainee teaching course. I'm going to be a teacher!

Me: I'm not awake yet. Of . . . accountancy?

Thom: No. English. I may not have mentioned it before—

Me: You definitely didn't.

Thom: —because I never thought I'd get it. Keeks, it means we'll have almost no money for a while. What do you think?

Me: I think it sounds pretty nice.

Thom: Can I get back into bed now?
Me: You'd better. I've got some congratulating to do.

Good work all round.

A bit later, after I'd done all that actual-going-to-work stuff, we did some proper talking. So Thom has abandoned the hard-nosed world of corporate finance altogether to embrace the soft paws of children's schooling. Well, I *say* soft-pawed, but he'll actually be dealing with secondary school kids, which means that if the school he ends up at is anything like my secondary, he'll spend every lesson trying to break up a row between the girls about whether Juliet was a prick-tease or not while the boys at the back shout out suggestive comments about who they'd like to tease with their prick. Although I didn't say that to Thom. I do know that it's something he's mentioned before, on drunken evenings of long conversations, always swearing off accountancy at the coalface of corporate greed to get back to his love of language. I'm so proud of him for sticking to his guns, and for not getting back into that pit that made him so miserable, and for doing this good thing. So it's three cheers for him, that clever, secretive son-of-a-gun.

Speaking of lessons, having learnt a valuable one from me, Thom set off on his stage with earnest resolutions to stay sober-ish. He and the guys (Rich, Pete, Jim, Ben from school, Malcolm and Phil from uni and Rocky, boyfriend of Emma) are going camping for a couple of nights, with some meat, a few boxes of beer and some camping equipment (of unknown quality).

    As Thom walked out this evening with giant rucksack on, Rich hooted the horn outside and revved the engine aggressively.

Me: This bodes well for a gentlemen's civilised weekend.

Thom: How do I know Clifton Black's not going to be round here the second I'm gone?

Me: I've booby-trapped all the entrances. I figure you've got little to worry about. [Rich hoots again] Well. Little to worry about on my behalf, anyway.

Thom: I promise not to go into any abandoned-looking houses if we get lost in the woods.

I've had a lovely night with Greta and Alice, *Casablanca*, a giant pasta meatball bake and a jug of Band on the Run. We sure know how to tear. It. *Up*.

August 13th

In Thom's absence, I was drinking iced tea with Susie in her garden when Mum marched round with her military expression on. Dad must be feeling better for her to allow him some time unsupervised. 'Right!' she said. 'I've got the print-outs of the dress you like – let's go and find something even better. Susie, Pete's going to look after your three, and you're coming too. Come on, girls, don't dawdle.'

With a whoop of glee, Susie and I had our shoes on and were waiting by the door before Mum even had the chance to chivvy us along. She drove the three of us round to Tally Ho corner, and took us into the smallest pokiest dress shop I've ever seen. It was a shop of Seconds, so if we found anything we wanted, we could take it with us straight away, rather than waiting three to six months to get it delivered. Surely just what I needed.

But as soon as we entered, I knew it wasn't. Wall-to-wall strapless meringues, with a floor-to-ceiling glass case in one corner crammed full of sparkling cubic zirconia tiaras. Mum and Susie had split up and were taking a wall each, as Mum looked back down to the printout of The Dress, and I felt a welling misery at the contrast between this dark, poorly lit little place and the angelic beauty of my vanished wedding shop. Susie looked at me and grimaced a bit, gesturing to the rack of meringues she was sifting through, then Mum cried out with a little 'Oooh!' Susie and I came over to see her Surprise Find, but when she pulled out the dress it was another strapless frock, with a slightly slimmer line to the skirt than most of the others. 'Look,' she said, holding up her clutched picture. 'It's the same basic shape as this one. I can tweak it to make it the same – it's so easy, Kiki. I can do this.'

In the old days, I would have raged at her, for not *getting it* and crowbarring her meddling into my wedding. It would be an ugly dress made clunky by an amateur's stitchwork, and I wouldn't look like a *Brides Magazine* model. But I was exhausted by my rage at everything that didn't need raging over, and I had a sudden idea of a startling new tack.

'Thanks Mum,' I said. 'That would be nice.'

She looked stunned, then gave me a big smile and a hug. 'You'll see, Kiki; your wedding is going to be wonderful.'

TO DO:
Chase remaining RSVP-ers
Check final headcount
Receiving line – ask Thom to imagine us actually trying to
    pull this off
Enjoy the two hours of laughter that will follow
Speech?

August 14th

At noon today there was a weary sort of knock at the door. When I opened it, Thom was standing there with a thousand-yard stare, while Rich and Pete had their backs to us, unloading camping stuff from his car. When Rich came in to drop the stuff in the hallway, I saw he only had one eyebrow, and a singe mark where the other should be. I looked at Thom.

Thom: Just . . . don't. Don't ask me anything.

After a three-hour bath, Thom finally managed to eat. As long as he doesn't expect me to clean any of those camping things up, whatever happened in the New Forest can, frankly, stay in the New Forest. This is the spirit I shall carry into our married life.

Dad, meanwhile, seems a million times better than even a couple of weeks ago. His colour's back and he's as busy as ever. I'm so happy. Once Thom was in a fit state, we headed back to the school to get a better look at it for decisions about where to put the tent and access points, and where to direct the wedding guests. I wasn't particularly looking forward to it – the less time I had to spend there the better, as far as I was concerned. As long as everyone turned up, and enjoyed themselves, and didn't get ketchup on my high-street wedding dress, that was fine by me.

But something had happened to the school in the last three weeks. We entered through the front this time, through the high-ceilinged hallway and the light, bright corridors, past colourful classrooms and giant, well-appointed kitchens. At the doors of the playground and school field, I could glimpse through the windows that the work tent had come down, and the pipes had all been completed and covered up. When Dad pushed open the double doors, I saw a very different venue.

Whoah. *Whoah*. This was absolutely and most definitely not the school I remembered. Instead of a scrappy dry field full of ankle-breaking holes and tripping hillocks, this was a smooth, green field of lush grass. I could see in the warm dusk that along one side was a long strip of meadow, full of waist-high flowers and grasses – the school's wildlife project – and along the other, bunting from their sports day hanging from tree to tree. The back of the school looked really lovely too. I'd never registered before that my primary school, as well as being the scene of many a childhood trauma, was a wonderful old Victorian building. It had been renovated beautifully, and instead of fading portakabins and clunky new buildings, the view from this side was like slipping back a hundred-odd years to when the school was new (even the wooden doors to the tiny little child-toilets).

Thom and Dad were grinning at me, both with a slightly expectant air. 'Crumbs,' I said. 'This *is* nice.' Just then my phone rang – it was someone from the registrar's office, apologising for calling out of hours but just wanting to report that they'd had a cancellation on the Saturday morning, would we like to move our slot? I checked with Thom, who gave the thumbs up.

And just like that, we are now *go* for one busy, beautiful Saturday.

August 16th

Another day, another day trip. First thing in the morning, Thom and I were at Heathrow to collect his bedraggled and jet-lagged but still good-natured parents (Thom's mum: 'Kiki, you are Bride Incarnate. Doesn't she look well, Alan?' Thom's dad: 'Like a spring flower, no less') and take them to a hotel near Mum and Dad. They refused to be put up by any of us, saying we had more than enough to worry about without having to check they had sufficient towels – his mum threw in, 'And my room service demands are very rigorous when I've been on a plane for days. None of you will fancy making me a steak sandwich at 3am when your fridges are full of carnations.' We took them up to their room and left them pottering about, promising to meet again tonight when they'd settled in. Then Mum ordered me and Thom off to the garden centre. She was too busy with my dress (gulp) to come with us, but said we had to look at all the flowers and plants we liked, then come back with a list that she'll share with her Women's Institute cronies. I'd taken some snaps from the flower market by the station too, and the garden centre was full to bursting with great lush plants and full pots of flowers, from tiny delicate sweet peas to fat calla lilies. We made our list, bought a little hosta for Mum to say thank you, and went round to deliver them both to her. She was all efficiency, with no space for nagging – she looked down the list and shook her head or nodded along with some internal checklist, then positioned the hosta on the windowsill and watered it, still making her mental lists. 'Alright, dear, that's all fine. Leave it with me.' She gave us both a kiss and a hug and we were out, Thom back home and me to work.

Thom: What's she taking?
Me: It's the uppers that were passed down to her from her mother. When I have events to organise, she'll pass the pillcase down to me. It's a Carlow chemical heirloom that we're very proud of.
Thom: I really don't know if you're joking.

270

Me: This stuff with Dad has shaken her so much. Of course it has. But haven't you noticed she looks about ten years younger? Having Dad home again, and well again – the pair of them are like teens in love. If it wasn't working out so well for me on the organising front, I'd say it was a bit gross.

Thom: Gosh, you really do have an enormous heart.

Me: I caught them *kissing* them other day. Shudder.

Thom: Well, I'm glad for them both.

Me: Me too. I'm thinking how we can harness her energy for the betterment of the country.

TO DO:
Check whether Mum is *also* actually on uppers
If so, check she has enough for wedding day
Write vows

August 17th

A great evening. At Jim's request, Thom, Susie, Pete and I spent it putting together a playlist of all our favourite songs in the world. Edward and Lily favoured early-era Beatles, while Thom preferred seventies denim rock and Pete's hits all turned out to be pleasingly camp – the Pet Shop Boys, Marc Almond and Donna Summer's disco hits. Susie rolled her eyes and told us all how happy she was in her lavender marriage. Between Susie's fifties jazz classics and my nineties pop, there should hopefully be a tune for everyone.

Going through that music felt so strange. Some songs made us all dance (Jimmy Cliff, mid-era Blur), some songs got instant vetoes (almost anything from Pete's hardcore clubbing years), and some were so fiercely evocative that they almost took my breath away. One song – Hole's 'Violet' – took me back fiercely and instantly to my teenage years, to those nights where I would sit in a darkened room, listening out for Susie to come home again from a happy night with her friends, not sure who I was or where I could fit in the world. And here I am, with a lovely sister and her happy husband, three whole nephew/nieces, two parents who are alive and love one another, a job I enjoy despite my boss, and Thom. Thom. Thom, you make my heart leap every time I see you. You make me happy to be alive, every single day. You make me smile and make me want to be the very finest person I possibly can be, because you are that rare gem – a very, very good person. *You're* my favourite tune in the whole world.

TO DO:

Table plans and place cards – abandon entirely, but ensure Susie doesn't sit directly next to the buffet or no one else will be allowed to eat

Give Mum final numbers for food

Final measurements and fitting for dress with Mum

Check Mike's OK with numbers for cake

Ceremony music – ask Jim to play something nice when I walk down the aisle

Fairy lights?

Get those lovely silver-white wedges from Topshop

Makeup – buy new mascara

Borrow some clear nail polish from Mum

Write vows

August 18th

A half day at work today, to check everything is OK before I'm on holiday. Hold on. Not holiday. Honeymoon! Alice gave a lovely speech at noon, describing how different life will be for me once I'm married: compulsory couples nights, no longer allowed to socialise with single friends, weight gain on both sides, and a sudden unexpected passion for DVD box sets, so we don't have to talk to one another. She got a cheer and applause from Norman, Carol, Judy the Intern and the Art and Production teams, while Tony looked slightly uncomfortable as he handed over a card and a beautifully wrapped parcel from everybody. 'Open it with Thom,' Alice said, widening her eyes lasciviously. Then Tony beckoned me into his office.

Tony: So I hear Jacki's divorce is going ahead.
Me: Yes. I'm sure you could have done with knowing that was going to happen when you went ahead and bought the book.
Tony: Too bloody right. But the thing is, this divorce has done nothing to harm sales whatsoever. The massive coverage we've got from the whole thing – when sales otherwise might have rolled over and died by now – means that *Jacki Jones's Perfect Wedding* is one of Polka Dot's bestsellers of the year already. You've seen the figures: this book of yours has already earned back its advance. Which means . . .
Me: Which means . . .
Tony: Congratulations, Assistant Editor. I'll have all the details for you when you get back, but I thought you'd want to know before you went.
Me: Thanks, Tony.
Tony: Well, it was my mother who pushed this one through. You can decide if you want to thank me once you've seen the books you'll be working on this autumn.

So with that I was bustled out of his office and through Polka Dot's front door, sent on my way to marry and make something of myself, off to the giant supermarket round the corner from Mum, to meet her and Thom to get food for Saturday.

They were both there, Mum ready with a trolley that was all but revving. We went down every aisle, and ended up getting another trolley too for all the salads, fruit, breads, wine, and various other ingredients for Mum's food master plans. She said she'd ordered all the meat she needed from the butcher and would pick it up tomorrow morning, then worked through her long, long checklist, adding any suggestion we made and crossing off other dishes, before heading for the tills. The boy behind the till widened his eyes at the sight of our two trolleys lined up together like a little train of greed, and Mum smiled and said, 'It's for their wedding. My daughter's getting married on Saturday!' I thought he'd give a token grunt and scan our things with his head buried in the till to avoid small talk, but he charmed Mum entirely with his interest and suggestions for the day itself. It turned out his sister had just got married and there'd been talk of nothing else in his house for the past eight months, so he was full of great tips for serving the food and what had gone down well with their family. They got on so well while he was scanning everything that it was touch and go whether Mum would invite him along on Saturday, but she settled on shaking his hand and telling him what a blessing he would be on his own wedding day. He nodded sagely and mouthed 'GOOD LUCK' to us with a big smile. Unbelievably, the whole bill came to £500. £500! To feed and water (or wine) sixty people, compared to the £3,000-plus at the venues we'd looked at before.

We stuffed Mum's car and ours with the groceries and headed back to their house to begin preparations. Alan and Aileen met us there, and Mum soon had us working the knives and beaters like pros, as she referred to nine different recipes pinned up on the notice board she'd cleared especially, flitting between each of us (and Susie, who'd come for moral support and was instead put to work, allowed at least to sit down) and giving us precise instructions, plucking bowls and boards away from us then replacing them with new ingredients and instructions. Mum led me upstairs at one point for my last fitting, denying me a mirror but pinning my dress surely and confidently in tiny areas of tuck and dart I would never have noticed. 'Yes, Kiki, we're just about done here. You will look lovely.' I thanked her, but she said we hadn't finished with the food yet and I could work my gratitude out in the kitchen as child labour. So we all worked until 10, then Mum said her freezer and fridges were full, and that was enough for today. With aching backs and hands and more than a couple of blue-plastered fingers between us, we were allowed back out of her kitchen and home to our beds.

In our flat, as we were getting under the covers tonight, I remembered the gift from Polka Dot. Taking the parcel out of my bag and putting it on the bed, I looked nervously at Thom.

Thom: If this is the Polka Dot backlist, I am not going to be writing the thank you letter.
Me: If this is the Polka Dot backlist, I'm not going into work again.

It wasn't. It was a big gift box, filled with tissue paper. When we pulled back all the paper, there was a picture frame, and inside the picture frame – oh! Our amazing Art Dept strikes again. They had taken the jacket from an old 1950s book of poetry, *Poems for Love*, and adapted it. The credits on the front now read:

and the old imprint name was replaced by the Polka Dot logo in tiny letters in the corner. Those clever beasts.

I went to add it to the list for thank you cards, and thought I'd check on our wedding gift list since I'd been too busy to look for the last few weeks.

Me: Oh, Christ . . . Thom, I think there's a bug in our list.
Thom: [getting out of bed and coming over to see with a groan] What's the problem?
Me: It says that not only has every single thing from our list been bought, but we've also got over £2,000 worth of gift vouchers.
Thom: Hang on a second. Look at the buyers and see who's been duplicated.
Me: [checking] *Holy* . . .
Thom: That's . . . not . . .
Me: Oh my God. That's not a mistake.

It seems that the wives and girlfriends of the accountants who no longer employ Thom felt so bad about his redundancy that they took their Black Amexes to town on our wedding list. Every little scrap has been bought up. And when every tiny item had been bought up and there were no huge TVs or designer sofas on there, the wives and girlfriends had to go for vouchers: £400 from Charles and Clara; £200 from Guy and Sara; £500 from Rowland and Fenella, Thom's boss and his frosty, terrified wife. Apparently not so frosty. Well, well, well. That will keep us in napkins and affordable crockery for many, many years to come.

TO DO:
Final dress fitting with Mum
See if she needs any more help with food
Check all the glasses have arrived
See if I need to do anything about the flowers
Check guest book and pen
Check enough balloons and ribbon
Write vows

August 19th

I had a teeny, weeny, minute moment of breakdown today. Thom was cha-cha-cha-ing round the kitchen to some jazz on the radio, when I suddenly started crying. I wailed, 'Thom! I *do* want to be married to you more than anything, and we are so lucky, and I can't wait to be your wife and for you to be my husband, but . . . I still want a beautiful wedding and everything seems to have gone wrong. I don't think it's a sign of anything other than that we aren't multi-millionaires, but it's so bloody exhausting to have been faced over and over with why it's going to be smaller, or cheaper, or more split-into-several-days, or designed entirely by my mum. I feel so awful being so ridiculous when I really am fussing over nothing, but this has . . . *done me in*. I just want to be married to you, when we want, with a great party for the people we love. Why is that so hard?' I cried for almost ten minutes, while Thom gave me a hug and rocked me a little, then he said, 'Listen. We can make this day – or days – into exactly the fun we want. The more our friends and family are involved, the more they'll enjoy it. Think how boring the Nose wedding was, and think how much fun we had at Jim's barbecue. Imagine if Jim had just got married at the beginning of that day. How much fun would that have been? You can choose to let this stress define your day, Kiki, or you can laugh at people who spend £20,000 and *don't even get tiny toilets*. Mmm? Am I right?' I said he would be more right if he mixed me a Band on the Run so I could think about all of this. He brought it through – Amaretto, milk and ice in perfect harmony – and I'm writing this slightly mellowed by its excellence. He's so right. The tiny toilets! Just don't tell him I said that.

TO DO:
Underwear – cleaned and freshly pressed
Rings – check someone has them
Write vows
Marry the man I love

August 20th

So here we are. Our wedding day.

At 8.30 we got up and showered, dressed – trousers and a jacket for Thom, my favourite summer dress for me – and I headed to the register office with Susie and Rich in Susie's battered old Ford Fiesta with crumbs all over the back seat. Thom was travelling with his mum and dad so we could make the token gesture of him seeing me arrive, so Susie, Rich and I sang along to Jay-Z's '99 Problems' at full blast and pulled up to the register office with it still pumping out, like naughty teens on their first day at sixth form. Waiting for us when we got there were Mum and Dad, Pete and the kids, and Thom and his parents, each in various stages of put-togetherness.

By 9.52, Thom and I were married.

Outside, our group threw handfuls of confetti at us and Dad popped a bottle of champagne which we took turns to take little swigs from. Before any of us could get giddy with excitement (or champagne), we all headed back to the house (us newlyweds crammed into Susie's crumb-laden back seat), took our semi-finery off and got stuck into full preparation. Thom's mum and dad followed Mum into the kitchen to complete any chopping, peeling, mixing and stirring that hadn't been finished the day before, and Dad, Susie and Thom headed over the road to work on the décor. There were more cars out there at this earlyish hour than I'd expected, but Mum explained it was her team of worker bees hard at it, with jars and vases and ribbons. I helped Mum for a while, but she said I was so distracted I'd cause myself an injury and imagine how cross Thom would be if he had to marry a bride with a bloody stump where one of her fingers had been only that morning, and sent me away to check everything was OK with my vows and the Orders of Service. My vows! Oh no. I made my face look as un-panicked as possible and went up to my room. With notepad and pen in hand, I tried to think how I could possibly bind my life to Thom's with words. How could I capture what I felt for him? What words could I put down to begin to say everything he meant to me? I flicked through these pages for a while, and found some inspiration. Just how much I loved him. Next step: saying those words in front of all our friends and family. Gulp. After I'd spent half an hour tweaking the vows, Mum shouted upstairs and said I was wanted over at the school, so I put the notes away and headed across.

It was . . . *beautiful*. Mum and her friends had covered the front gates with ivy and white stocks, and Rich and Thom had lined the way from the gates to the school field with white ribbon on low posts to guide people to the ceremony. Dad and some helpers had put up the huge white big top tent from the school fairs; Mum's sidekicks had festooned it with more ivy, stocks and some full blooms of hydrangea and sweet peas. Inside, the roof of the tent was filled with helium balloons of every colour, and big paper honeycomb balls in white and red hung from the poles at each corner. Tables were already groaning with dishes at 11am, being kept cool by a battery of fans, and the trestle tables of the local village hall had been transformed by vintage linen tablecloths and floral arrangements thrown together by Mum's friends, with well over three centuries of expertise between them. The tables were laid with lovely old school dining room cutlery, and the long benches along one wall of the tent were piled with mismatched plates, Pyrex school glasses and big glass jugs. In one corner, furthest from the speakers, was a cluster of shabby sofas in brown leather and red velvet and turquoise corduroy, plus a heap of oversize beanbags and a few soft comfy rugs; along the same side was a long table on which were stacked battered wooden market boxes, half filled with bottles of red wine and half with white, the latter about to be delivered to the fridges.

Mum appeared in the doorway of the tent and stood next to me, looking around. I gave her a hug, holding her for ages, stunned at everything she'd done.

'Mum, this is . . . perfect. Thank you so much.' She smiled at me.

'Much as I'm delighted that you like our flowers, the rest of it is entirely down to Eve and Susie.' She saw my surprise. 'Well, Susie was really only Eve's dogsbody – I'm sure you can imagine. They were here all night, you know, after Eve and her boyfriend arrived with a white van full of this stuff. I thought you'd been discussing it with her for weeks, but Susie couldn't believe when Eve said it was just some last-minute things she thought you could use.'

I looked around, mouth agape all over again. Eve was involved in this? She'd done all this for me? After all that happened this year – well, particularly after all that had happened – but with everything she felt about us, and everything I'd said to her . . . It was like she'd waved her wand and made what was in my brain become solid, present and delicious. Some of those things had been in this book for months, tucked into an envelope at the back, and she'd remembered from that night I'd been at her house, gloomy and over-dramatic and ungrateful, describing in lavish detail the wedding party I thought I'd never have but pined for like only the truly un-needy can. Tiny details: vintage tea tins filled with summer wildflowers on the food tables, Eve's collection of snow-globes clustered together on the table for the wedding cake, little figurines and animals spray-painted yellow and blue and pink and green, nuzzling up to the flower arrangements on each picnic table. Everything was so thoughtful and so perfect. I was suddenly glad that I hadn't asked Clifton Black to rub her out earlier in the year.

Inside the school kitchens, I peeped my head around the door and saw her being taught by Mike, with infinite patience, how to ice the cinnamon buns for one of the desserts. She looked at him with such sweetness and . . . gratitude . . . that I thought maybe she'd actually be nice to this one, and maybe we *all* might be a bit grateful. They were so happy together, so sweet that I wanted to creep off without breaking their moment, but Mike saw me and waved, and Eve smiled shyly at me, caught being happy in love. 'Eve,' I said, coming towards her, 'that is one *nice* tent. Thank you.' She threw her arms around me, and we swung one another round and round, giggling like anything, until I saw the cake over Mike's shoulder. I gasped: a giant multicoloured three-tiered

281

Greek-pillared monster cake of chocolate gateau at the base, coffee and walnut in the middle and a light, pale yellow lemon and poppy seed on the final level, topped with a bright golden crown. It couldn't have made me happier, and it must have shown because when I looked over, Mike and Eve were beaming at me. Eve said, 'Mike did that,' as if I didn't know, but she was so proud of him that I gave her another hug and she hugged and hugged me back. I gave Mike a hug too and Eve said, 'Get a room, you two,' but when I looked at her she was smiling and happy, and we all hugged until Mike said, 'Much as I'm enjoying this, don't you have plans today, Kiki?' and I laughed at how happy I was for everyone and for myself and left them to it.

Susie found me and grabbed my arm, insisting if she didn't start on my hair and makeup soon then I'd only have myself to blame if I looked like Ken Dodd when I walked down the aisle. She walked me back over the road to Mum and Dad's house and plonked me in front of the dressing table in her old room and covered the mirror, so I couldn't see what she was doing until she was done. She sprayed my hair and combed it, feathering it upwards and sticking hairclips in slowly and steadily, occasionally standing back to admire her work. Then she told me to close my eyes, and began slathering my face in all the unguents and pastes in her bag, using fingers and brushes at a brisk, confident speed. Far sooner than I'd expected, she smiled beatifically at me and told me I was ready. When she whipped away the cloth on the mirror, I saw she'd transformed me hastily but effectively into a perfect jungle-ready tiger.

Me: Thank you, Susie, this is perfect.
Susie: You are *more* than welcome.
Me: MUM! It turns out Susie won't be coming to the wedding as she'll be too busy falling down the stairs.

Susie: [shocked] *Kiki!* And me, a mother of two! Wait. Three!

Me: Fine. Redo my face or I'll put Lily in a frilly pink bridesmaid's dress. It's not too late. You *know* Mum has one.

Susie: I'm doing it I'm doing it I'm doing it . . .

She did a wonderful job in the end. Fortunately I have all the good genes anyway, but she covered the blemishes that had stress-bloomed overnight and made me glowy and dewy in all the right ways and smoothed my hair back down, and bundled it up into a scrappy bun into which she stuck some tiny rosebuds. She was just patting (or rubbing or dabbing or whatever it is you're supposed to do) some highlighter onto my browbones when there was a scuffle behind the door, some muttering, the sound of Mum twittering and Dad laughing, then the door opened to reveal a smiling Jacki, and Pedro looking sheepish.

Jacki: Happy wedding day! I've brought you a present.

Pedro: [waving like a member of the Royal Family] Hello! Sorry I was such a shit! I'm here to take photos of your special day and make everyone look wonderful but you most wonderful of all.

Susie: Aren't you . . .?

Pedro: You must be Susie! My delight knows no bounds.

Within moments, Susie was won over by his charm and I was won over by his working for free (or at least that's what Jacki insisted – heaven knows how much she shelled out for him) so we were all friends, and he snapped away madly while Jacki brought out a bottle of champagne from her giant Mulberry handbag and foamed it into four paper cups they'd snatched from the kitchen on the way up. Jacki wouldn't be in any of the photos, but instead made Susie and me laugh wildly by telling us stories of all the famous people she'd met so we'd look like laughing cover stars in all Pedro's shots. Then he said he wanted a photo of me with my dress before I'd got into it, so we squeezed into Mum and Dad's room where the dress was hanging in Mum's best dress bag on the outside of the wardrobe. We were all giggling by then – having Jacki Jones and Pedro in my childhood house was weird enough, but a glass of champagne on an empty stomach made me giddier than would be legal if someone had the sense to legislate these things. The others were giggling even more than me. Then Susie unzipped the dress bag with a huge flourish and I didn't know whether to laugh or cry. That wasn't my dress. The dress Mum had found was fine enough now I'd got used to it – strapless, clean-lined, not hugely memorable. But this wasn't that dress. This was THE dress. It was beautiful. Susie told me that Mum had been up all night rejigging that classic strapless dress into my beautiful dream; she'd layered a frosting of organza and tulle over one shoulder and down to the floor, to create an asymmetric frock with a huge flower on one gathered hip. It was so clean, so perfect. I gave a giant sob and Susie had to grab me in a Chinese burn to stop me from ruining all her good makeup work, but Pedro kept snapping away so I was laughing too. He paused long enough to get me out of the dressing gown and into most of the dress (with Jacki shouting, 'Stop shooting for a minute, Ped! This isn't bloody *Heat* magazine – we're not after a cellulite snap. Sorry, Kiki') then got more of Susie positioning the wide soft strap on one shoulder and adjusting the flower, putting the shoes on my feet (I mime kicking Suse, she mimes rolling over on the floor, yelling, we both find ourselves hilarious and laugh even harder) and tidying my messy-chic hair (cost: £0.50, for one hairband and Mum's can of hairspray).

Then suddenly it was noon, and Dad was poking his head around the door saying, 'You ready, love?' and I could hear Mum in the background shooing Thom and his gang out of the house and over the road, and everything seemed to suddenly be very quiet. Jacki said, 'We'll see you outside, yeah, Kiki?' and shoved Pedro out in front of her, while Susie fished into the bedside drawer for a folded paper choice-maker. She made me pick a colour and a number, then worked it and lifted my chosen flap to say, 'You will have a wonderful day and a brilliant marriage.' Blimey. That's weirdly apt. 'Come on, time to hit the crowds.' She gave me a peck on the cheek and a wave, and she was gone too. Dad came and took my shaking hand. 'It's not too late, love. You don't have to marry him. I'm sure we can find you a rotter that I can worry myself sick over, rather than some fellow who loves you and wants to treat you right. What do you say, Katherine? Shall we jump in my car and I can drop you off at the station?' I gave him my best smile, then thought of Thom waiting for me and gave him an even better smile, and said, 'Thanks, Dad, but I really do have plans. But I'm incredibly glad you're here to offer.' We walked downstairs together and he gave me a bear hug at the front door, then Susie and Eve and Dad and I crossed the road to the school.

Over the way, the school had been transformed still further. The paths were lined with more multicoloured helium balloons at waist height, tied to the ribbons along the path edges. They bobbed in the breeze, and in the distance I could hear some Nina Simone. A few latecomers were sprinting onto the school fields, and gave me a wave. Pedro poked his head around the edge of the building, then must have given Jim a signal, because as we turned the corner onto the pitches, the music changed. It was 'Cheek to Cheek', picked out on the school piano by Jim, at the front of the gathered crowd. Thom was at the front, next to Rich, standing with his back to me. Everyone was watching my end of the aisle, so when he turned round to face me no one saw the fake fangs he'd put in at the last moment, but – hugely gratifyingly – his mouth fell open when he saw me. I smiled at him, so happy, worried that I might just fall down or fall over or fall back into the arms of those people around me who loved me, all because it was overwhelming to realise how much the person in front of me loved me too.

Dad took one arm and Mum the other, and Eve and Susie linked arms and walked ahead with Edward leading them while Lily stood with Jim, turning the pages. We walked down the aisle, this procession of fondness, and smiled and smiled (or at least I suspect they did – I could do nothing else but smile and smile and smile at Thom ahead of me). They led me to the front, then stopped, and I walked the last few steps to Thom on my own, and thought of everything that had happened, how we'd met, where we'd been, how we'd changed, and I thought that more than anything – more than Louboutins and designer cakes, more than toastmasters and the perfect favours – I wanted to wake up every morning next to him, and make him laugh for the rest of our lives. 'Hello,' he said. 'Touché,' I said, which didn't really mean anything but still made us both laugh a bit. Then the service began.

Considering how many hours of my life I'd spent thinking about this event, I don't really remember anything of the ceremony. It was a happy blur. I know Alice welcomed everyone, and Susie read a poem she'd written herself that was unbelievably sweet and funny, and we all sang 'God Only Knows' by The Beach Boys as Jim played along on the piano, and I couldn't stop laughing, and I know Thom and I promised to be nice to one another As Long As We Both Shall Live, and I know everyone cheered when we kissed, which was lovely but a little bit unnerving like being in a pantomime, and Thom's mum and dad said a lovely little blessing speech, and the next thing I knew we were walking back down the aisle, and Jim was playing Billy Idol's 'White Wedding' in the hilarious style of a lounge singer, and we were all being handed glasses of champagne by Mum's lovely friends who didn't seem to mind at all that they weren't proper guests as it meant they could be Useful and Appreciated, instead of glaring at one another's hats. I saw Carol and Norman together, holding hands and looking like they'd just discovered sliced bread. My Aunt Pepper and Uncle Joe were playing with their grandchild while Emma and Rocky chatted to Zoe, Alice and Greta. Thom's hand didn't stay in mine for long as we chatted to different people around the field, but I kept feeling a hand at my waist or on the small of my back, or would hear, 'Don't you publishers scrub up well,' muttered in my ear and see him drifting away from me again, deadpan, and it would make my face-splitting smile creep back on. Then Rich tapped a glass and let everyone know that Dad and Thom wanted to say a few words, so we filed into the tent and stood around under the balloons with glasses of champagne while they gave short speeches, brief and full of love, thanking everyone and making me incredibly proud of both of them and of myself. They were lovely.

Everyone had a few minutes of milling around, then Thom called us all back outside, and we saw that he and Rich had laid out a rounders pitch on the sports field. He announced that they were the team captains, and that he picked me. Thank God. Rich called Pete, then Thom called Greta and Rich went for Suse. Norman and Carol pleaded old age, and sat in deck chairs with Mum, Dad, Rich's girlfriend Heidi (looking from her shape as if she might go into labour any minute) and Alan and Aileen, sipping fruit punch and calling out suggestions. The picking went on for a couple of minutes until we were all divvied up, while Thom tucked my skirt into the dipped neckline at the back for me to take up first base. Jacki was bowling, and it came as a fantastic surprise to find that she and Pedro (as backstop) made a killer pair, with me as an only-slightly-weaker member of the vital fielding trio. Uncle Joe, Mum's younger brother, was caught out almost instantly, but Rich made it to second before being run out by Pete. Thom's old colleagues were astoundingly good, but other Tom and my old boss Fiona managed to nearly knock each other out trying to catch a high ball. We managed a whole innings fielding and batting before we realised that more important than the score was the fact that we were absolutely starving, so Mum declared we were now free to tuck into the food: plates of tomato salads and potato salads and pasta salads, and piles and piles of sausages and hamburgers and tuna burgers and veggie burgers, and tray-loads of bread rolls and little iced bowls of butter. Oh, that was *one good-looking spread*, suitable for the most fairytale of weddings. Thom and I stood back for seven whole minutes until we agreed that if anyone hadn't taken their fill yet it was completely and totally their own fault, then we piled up our own plates with the feast before us. Salad niçoise with tiny anchovies! Filo parcels of feta and mint! Asparagus quiche cut into little squares! *Miniature burritos!* Yes. You understand. Once everyone had eaten most of their meal, Rich stood up, tapped his glass with his knife and opened: 'I can't begin to tell you what an honour it was when I was asked to be best man at the wedding of Tim and Kelly. I enjoyed it so much – and figured the names were close enough – that I thought I could probably use the same speech for this occasion too. Keep me posted with how this goes.' He went on for twenty minutes and – as with the best captive and willing audiences – we had tears of laughter running down our faces by the end. He gave away none of our dark secrets, but instead said that while most people find organising a wedding a living nightmare, 'Thom and Kiki have brought everything everyone loves about them to make a magical party for all of us that we'll never forget.' High praise indeed from someone with one-and-a-half eyebrows.

As the toast applause was settling down, Mike and Eve paraded over to our table with the cake, and Mike produced a cake knife from up his sleeve. 'Wow,' I said. 'A magician too?' Mike winked at me (which was somehow totally heart-warming, rather than cheesy. Can this man *get* any better?) and said, 'And you haven't even tasted it yet.' To a chorus of 'CUT, CUT, CUT, CUT' started by Susie, we cut into the base tier of chocolate gateau. Thom licked the cake knife.

Thom: Holy cow . . . Is it too late to trade you for Mike?
Me: Ask me something I'm not seriously considering. If we divorce and you marry Mike, you'll be paying me your settlement in cakes.

As we pondered the legal mechanics, Pedro came over with a shoebox-sized parcel, with a big bow on it. 'One more peace offering,' he said, and put it in my hands. Thom looked at me, and I shrugged, and began unwrapping it: inside, an old Polaroid camera and, miracle of miracles, a bundle of old films too, like gold dust since the company stopped making them. 'They'll look good in your guest book, you know,' Pedro said, then turned on his heel before I could express any gratitude. I heard Jim give a whistle, and when I looked at him I saw he was standing behind his turntable grinning at me expectantly. The music started; it was Sinatra, crooning 'I've Got You Under My Skin'. Thom passed the box from my hands into Susie's, took one of my hands in his, and put his other arm around my waist, and we were turning and stepping around the dance floor like we were Fred and Ginger themselves. Fine, maybe not Fred and Ginger, but we certainly enjoyed ourselves and when he dipped me we got a whole barrel of 'oooooh's. Which, let's face it, is one great reason to hit the dance floor. We shimmied and twirled, and waved everyone on with us, and soon the tent was full of movement and laughter. I saw my Dad and Mum, dipping and prancing so you would never have guessed Dad's state last month, Mum laughing so much and Dad whispering little jokes in her ear as they worked their way around the floor. He looked so well again. Eve and Mike were dancing too, a slow dance in the corner, just the two of them swaying together with their eyes closed; Susie and Pete were jiving like they were trying to out-injure one another, while Frida slept in her car seat in the corner and the Twins arm-wrestled at their table. Pedro and Jacki sat on one of the giant squashy sofas, whispering to one another; I knew exactly how mean Pedro was being and how nice Jacki was being right back at him, and I knew that they both really meant us all well and even though Pedro would take all this back to his East London hipsterdom as a snarky anecdote, he did look happy right now, slugging back gin and tonics with his best gal-pal at his side. Thom's mum and dad had gone for a walk outside, the old romantics, and would almost certainly be canoodling under the stars and wondering how it had all gone so right for that gawky son of theirs. All our friends, from school to now, sat together laughing & drinking, or danced with one another happily; Dan was making tiny paper cranes as he chatted to Jim, Greta, & their plus ones, who I would definitely learn the names of, soon. And Zoe sat with Zac, her head on his shoulder, happy in their own world and not working for Pedro for one night. I saw Zac get up and offer her a drink, and I saw her mouth, 'No thanks,' with a little stern laugh, and as Zac walked away she touched her stomach, and she suddenly saw me see her, and she looked so shocked and frightened, but I laughed out loud and mimed locking my lips and throwing away the key. All this life in one tent!

It didn't go on all night, though, although it felt like it. Around half past midnight, Jim turned the music down to some Miles Davis, and Mum and her gang brought out trays of bacon sandwiches and big W.I. urns of tea, and soon we were all sitting and chatting quietly and comfortably, full and tired and happy. Thom was next to me by then, and when we'd eaten all the sandwiches and they were bringing out another round of wedding cake, he took my hand and said, 'Shall we go?' and rather than resorting to my old line I decided to just follow and see what happened. He took me outside, where beside that lovely old school and lovely old school field there was a truly lovely old pair of bikes, with tin cans tied to the backs. He hitched my skirt up and tucked it up again, said, 'Your carriage awaits,' and we were off, our friends and family pouring out of the tent to wave and cheer us on our way. I didn't know how long we'd have to keep it up, aware that my skirt (even hitched) wasn't the ideal cycling outfit, but we'd only got around the corner when he rang his bell and said, 'And your bed awaits.' It was the Queen's Arms, quiet and warm, where they must have been waiting for us because the door opened the moment he'd rung his bicycle bell. Sheila the Landlady greeted us with great formality and with the finest butlering accent she could muster, said, 'The Brrrrridal Soooh-heet,' and pointed us upstairs. Our luggage was already up there, delivered by one of my crafty friends, and the room itself was cosy and perfect, and all Thom and I could possibly have wanted. I noticed on the bedside table a little plate with three slices of cake on – one coffee and walnut, one chocolate, and one lemon and poppy seed. 'If there was ever a day when three slices of cake were not just permitted, but compulsory . . .'

Thom said, then we jumped full length on the bed and ate that cake without even taking our shoes off. When we'd finished, panting slightly with greed, Thom said, 'Hang on. This doesn't feel quite right. Something's . . . missing.' I said, 'Is it all the thank you cards we're going to spend the next six months of our lives writing?' He looked thoughtful. I fished down the front of my dress, and pulled out a small golden card with looping writing on it. 'Do you take vouchers, Mr Sharpe?'

'*That's* what it is,' he said. 'Ms Carlow? I do.'

Kiki Carlow & Thom Sharpe

....

request your presence at their

Wedding

on 20th August at 2pm

at Redhood Farm

RSVP

Kiki Carlow & Thom Sharpe

....

regret to announce a lack of

Wedding

on 20th August at 2pm

at Redhood Farm

Our Apologies, But No Need to RSVP

Kiki Carlow & Thom Sharpe

....

are forced to announce a slight re-jig of their

Wedding

on 20th August at 2pm

now at St. Margaret's Primary School, N4

Please do RSVP all over again

Order of Service

··

PROCESSIONAL (JIM ON PIANO)

WELCOME BY ALICE HAMILTON

READING BY SUSIE CARLOW

'GOD ONLY KNOWS' BY THE BEACH BOYS (ALL) –
LYRICS OVER

VOWS

BLESSING BY ALAN & AILEEN SHARPE

RECESSIONAL

Cast List

Bride . . . Herself
Groom . . . Himself
Father of the Bride . . . Steve Martin
Mother of the Bride . . . Martha Stewart
Best Man . . . Rich Fleming
Worst Man . . . Pete Miller
The Twins . . . Themselves
Music Maestro . . . Jim Woodward

*Thank you to all of you for coming.
This day would be nothing without you.*

Acknowledgements

A huge thank you to Alan Trotter and Phillip Birch, who sent me home from the pub to get on with writing this book, and to Jessie Price, latecomer, but enormously welcome member of our Gang. The suggestions and help from the three of you were invaluable and I still can't believe how kind you were.

Thank you to Liliane and David Binnie, parents and babysitters extraordinaire, who let me sit up in my teenage bedroom in their house to write bits of this, wrapped in my grandma's old fur coat and undisturbed but for meals and cups of tea. They never even dared ask to read any.

Thanks to Hannah Duncan, Mark Rowlands, Lija Kresowaty, Rachel Tracy, Alice Berry, Sarah Topping, Hannah Beatson, Jenny Price, Jessica Read, Kitty O'Lone, Laurence Festal, Caroline Craig, Madeleine Collinge, Jack Faulkner, Sarah Hammond, Jess Kim, Jenny Fry, Emily Cox and Louise Willder, for all the stories, suggestions and anecdotes you shared so trustingly.

Huge thanks to Clau Webb, best agent ever and lovely human, Claire Bord, wonderful editor and brilliant deadpanner, and Caroline Hogg and Becke Parker, editor and publicist at Avon respectively; all women I'd love to spend time with anyway but who have been essential in getting this game on the road. You are all top dames.

Finally, thank you to J, M and F. A nice bunch, and by golly, you make me laugh.

⸺ ❧ *Welcome* ❧ ⸺

I can't plan your wedding for you (oh, if only I could. It would be the best wedding ever) but I can give you some of the top tips that I wish someone had given me. And these aren't necessarily wedding-only: there's always a moral to be taken when that moral is Stop Thinking Of Yourself For One Single Moment, No One Cares About The Difference Between White And Ivory.

Sam's Wedding Guide

Top Five Wedding Essentials

∽ Food & Booze ∾

Anyone who's a human will be able to tell you that these are the most important things of any party, ever. Across countries and cultures (although the alcohol thing might vary a bit) the heart of hospitality is Plenty: plenty of everything, your guests are your concern, you want them to have anything they could possibly need (and then seconds, too). If you've got a specific diet or weird palate (you hate eggs, meat makes you retch, gasp: you *don't like dessert* – I've actually met people like this), just think: if I force these eating habits on my guests, will they mind? *You're* inviting *them*: don't just feed them sliced tomatoes with a cracker for pud because that's what makes you most happy. Or they will almost certainly refuse to attend your second wedding.

Autumn

Getting married in the autumn means a) you're canny, unwilling to pay crazy summer prices but hoping to catch a little good weather, or b) someone needs to get married in a hurry and took the first date they could. What is it? A visa? A pregnancy? I promise, I won't say a *word*.

That crossover season means that food-wise, you're laughing: there are so many fresh fruit and vegetables that come in then, plus you've got an excuse to start getting the colder weather stuff out too, like sloe gin and warm Pimm's. The nights are just beginning to draw in but mostly we live in denial at that time of year, occasionally looking up from our desks in the office to say ruefully, 'God, two weeks ago I was playing football in the park/reading in my garden/being kicked out of the beer garden at this time. It's bloody *night-time* now.' But we still want to believe evenings are for fun! The mains don't matter so much for autumn weddings; you need to focus on getting loads of crackers, grapes and amazing cheeses, and putting them in clear view of everyone but away from the wild dancing that your live band is going to inspire. If you insist on giving your guests something slightly fancy, might I recommend a brilliant soup?

Spicy sweetcorn soup

This soup is so easy and so easy to do in bulk. It's thick and hearty but not heavy – serve with loads of bread, or late in the evening to soak everything up.
(Serves 4)

> 4 sweetcorn cobs
> Dash of olive oil
> Tsp turmeric
> Tsp ground nutmeg
> Tsp ground coriander
> Tsp ground cumin
> 40g butter
> 1 large onion, finely sliced

1 leek, finely slices
2 cloves of garlic, crushed and chopped
2 pints of vegetable stock
Dash of white wine
Salt and pepper

* Run a tablespoon of olive oil around a large saucepan on a medium heat. Put the cobs in, and, turning regularly, let them cook through (about 7-10 mins). Sprinkle over the spices and cook for another minute or two, then, once slightly cooled, cut off the sweetcorn from the cobs.
* In another saucepan, melt the butter, and add the onion, leek and garlic. Cook until softened.
* Add the hot stock and wine, simmer for 10 minutes, then add the sweetcorn. Simmer for another couple of minutes, season to taste, then cool and purée.
* To serve, reheat and swirl through a little crème fraiche.

Sloe gin fizz

Double shot of sloe gin
Lemon
Lemonade
Fresh mint
Blackberries

* In a low glass, put in a couple of cubes of ice. Slug in your sloe gin, a squeeze of lemon and the lemonade. Top with fresh mint and blackberry.

Winter

A winter wedding means you can go into full-on Pagan Fantasy Land – swags of mistletoe and ivy, fur wraps (faux, if you prefer), and BARRELS of mulled wine. An old boss of mine got married in deep winter, and was pulled from the church to her reception in an actual *sleigh* stuffed with real furs, and pulled by two huge horses. It had been specially arranged by her sisters as a surprise. I wish I had sisters like that.

I think winter weddings are really lovely for the hyggeligness of it: everyone you love wassailing and dancing like they're chasing the darkness away. You need loads of hot booze, big Henry VIII-amounts of meat, and if you share my deranged passion for Christmas, a karaoke machine loaded with carols, like your wedding is one of those doomed-from-the-outset affairs in a Christmas Day Eastenders episode. Here's some nice grub for a freezing wedding day:

Macaroni cheese

Such a wonderful warmer for a cold night, and so easy. You can cook it the day before, and bang it in an oven to heat through and crisp on top.
(Serves 6 with a big salad, or 12 as a side dish to a big meaty hog roast)

> 500g dried macaroni
> 40g butter
> 40g flour
> Pint of full fat milk, plus a few tablespoons extra
> Salt and pepper
> 300g extra-mature cheddar
> 100g breadcrumbs

* Put the macaroni on to boil, in a large pan of salted water with a dash of olive oil.
* While that bubbles away, melt the butter over a gentle heat.
* In a bowl, stir a few tablespoons of milk into the flour, until the mixture is smooth and free from lumps.
* Add the pint of milk into the melted butter, then spoon in the gloopy flour-milk mix gradually.
* Let that thicken. If it forms into lumps, don't panic, just put your electric handwhisk in there and beat them out of there. No one's watching. It does the job.
* Grate the cheddar and drop it into the white sauce, a handful at a time. Let it melt in. Add a bit of salt and pepper.
* When the macaroni is al dente, drain and put in a big ovenproof casserole dish.
* Pour that delicious cheesy sauce over the macaroni, and stir well.
* If eating immediately, scatter the breadcrumbs over the top and put in the oven at about 190C/375F for 15mins. If reheating the next day, wait until then to scatter the breadcrumbs, then cook for 30 mins at the same temp, until crispy and golden.

Hot punch

Bottle of red wine
Dash of fresh orange juice
Dash of brandy
1 orange, finely sliced
1 cinnamon stick

1 star anise
2 tbsp brown sugar

* Mix in a big pan with ½ pint of water, boil then immediately lower to a simmer, for 15 mins. Serve.

Spring

Oh, lovely spring. Things start to warm up again, you can start making plans for holidays (although if you're getting married in the spring, I suspect you'll be using all yours up; we'll be seeing you man your office solo in the summer months, as everyone else fucks off to warmer climes and you regret that four-week trip to Malaysia in April) and weddings begin to fill every single weekend of most 25–40-year-olds' diaries.

This is a tricky time. You're really going to need to pull something out of the bag for this one, to convince people they really want to start that annual round of time-suck occasions again, so your food, music, booze and transport is going to need to be spot-on. Now's the time to break out… the *Themed Wedding*.

Come on, what have you got to lose? Everyone's weddings are so samey – white dress, serious-sounding music, tables with white and accent colour. Go crazy! Let's go Mexican! Under the Sea! Bonnie and Clyde! God, it would be amazing. You should do it. Really. Do it? Are you going to do it? You should. You'd be realllllly cool.

My one caveat with this is, Don't Tell the Guests. I absolutely hate surprises with a passion, so it's definitely not so each guest is forced to gasp and freak out when they walk in, but it does mean that they don't have added pressure *on top* of finding somewhere to sleep, something to wear, something to give you and some way of getting there. God, I really hate fancy dress parties. But I would love – *love* – to walk into someone's wedding and find they'd decked the whole place out as a Speakeasy, or an Ocean Palace, or Acapulco. If you think friends might *like* dressing up, get some costumes together in a big basket, so once the tequila's done the rounds everyone can pile in. Oh, this is such a good idea. You should totally do it. And while you decide on just what you'll do, here are some great recipes for Themed bashes:

Old-Fashioned (for Speakeasies)

> 1 sugar cube
> Angostura bitters
> Double shot of whiskey (rye or bourbon)
> Wide piece of fine lemon peel
> Ice

* In a heavy-bottomed glass, crush up the sugar cube with a teaspoon of water, and add two dashes of the bitters. Mix in the whiskey, stir, drop in a couple of cubes of ice and the lemon peel. Because it's a wedding, I would definitely go for the maraschino cherry on a stick that so divides drinkers of Old-Fashioneds. Period accuracy be damned.

Potted crab (for Aqua Romance)
(Serves 4)

> 300g cooked crab, white and brown meat
> Butter
> Nutmeg

Ground pepper
1 lemon
Fresh dill, chopped

* Melt the butter, and add the nutmeg and ground
  pepper. In a bowl, mix up the meat, a little grated
  lemon zest, the juice of the lemon and the dill, then
  pour over ¾ of the butter. Stir. Stuff it into a little pot,
  and top with the rest of the butter as a lid. Eat with
  buttered brown bread.

Mexican

There are few occasions that can't be improved with a
huge bowl of fresh guacamole.

3 ripe avocados
Lime
2 mild chillies
1 red onion
Fresh coriander
2 tomatoes
Maldon sea salt

* Mash up the avocados. Grate in a little lime zest, and
  squeeze in the lime juice. Finely chop the chillies and
  red onion – don't touch your eyes! OH GOD. Did you
  touch them? Man, that *hurts*. Never mind. Remove
  and eat the tomato seeds. Chop up the coriander and
  tomatoes, and add them, the chillies and the onion to
  the avocado. Sprinkle in a little salt. Try not to eat it all
  before anyone else gets to it.

———♡———

Summer

For some reason (it's not like we can rely on the weather) we in the UK tend towards summer weddings, thus gambling either on everyone being blue with cold in their summer frocks, or sweating and dizzy on a freakishly sunny August day. But it does mean that there's loads of nice food that's so easy to prepare. My favourite thing at summer weddings is the barbecue: it's easy enough to run (as long as you get someone managing it who doesn't just stick a chicken drumstick in a flame until it's black outside and bleeding within), cheap and mostly un-mess-up-able. Just bang loads of sausages, burgers, corn on the cobs and sweet peppers, plus some fish wrapped in wet newspaper (really, you'll never go back once you try this) on the grill, cobble together a few salads with some edible flowers in, and Bob's Your Uncle You Didn't Originally Plan On Inviting But Your Mum Went Crazy And Insisted On It. Summer desserts are so easy too – if you've got access to a freezer, stuff it full of tiny ice creams, and if you haven't, a couple of Eton messes or fruit salads with lashings of cream make anyone's day. Here's my favourite salad, with a few other things:

Favourite Salad

Obviously you'll need loads of salads, meats, cheeses and whatnot, but when summer comes around I feel like I could eat this every day.
(Serves 2 as a main with some bread and butter, 4 as a side)

1 pack of smoked mackerel
Lamb's lettuce
1 avocado
Handful of radishes
1 orange
Olive oil
White wine vinegar
Salt and pepper

* Cut off the peel and divide the orange into 20-ish
pieces. Flake the mackerel, chop up the avocado and
slice the radishes; mix all of that and the orange pieces
with the lamb's lettuce, position tastily on two/four
plates. In a little jug, whisk up the olive oil, vinegar and
salt and pepper to taste, then drizzle the dressing over
the salad.

Summer Mule

So delicious, so summery:

Cucumber, sliced into fine strips
Ice cold vodka
Ginger beer

* Over ice and 5-6 long fine strips of cucumber, pour a
double shot of vodka. Top up with ginger beer and add
a parasol. Just because you can.

Music

Can come in any form at a wedding: a rock and roll outfit, some jazz quintet, a country dancing or Ceilidh band (absolutely brilliant at getting even non-dancers on their feet), a DJ you once snogged at a club years ago and have somehow remained friends with, even an iPod plugged into the venue's sound system – as long as you've got something that people can shake it to, everyone will be happy. Although if your favourite music in the whole world is banging Dutch hardcore house, maybe – just maybe – you can have some crowd-pleasers on earlier in the evening for Auntie Sue and Nana.

Here are my absolute stone-cold top tens for each part of the evening.

Cocktails (afternoon – meal):

'Where or When' – Peggy Lee
The song is magical, and I think Peggy Lee's is the best recording. If you insist on having a first dance, this is pretty good (also as a last dance, too).

'Band on the Run' – Wings
The song after which mine & Kiki's favourite drink was named. Also: a great song. But v difficult to dance to, hence in an early slot.

'My Baby Just Cares For Me' – Nina Simone
My friend Jack always seems to be there when this song is playing, and dances with me in the nicest way. Find a friend who'll do you the same favour, and put this on.

'Easy Living' – Billie Holiday

If this track needs justifying to you, you probably shouldn't have music at your wedding.

'Cape Cod Kwassa Kwassa' – Vampire Weekend

Summer in song form. Lovely, even if your wedding is on Christmas Eve.

'Stolen Car' – Beth Orton

One of those Proustian madeleines of a song – I'm transported back to being at the start of a relationship, so happy it seems that the pavement is dancing beneath my toes. Another gorgeous summer track.

'Tiny Dancer' – Elton John

A singalong classic. If there's someone *not* singing along (albeit quietly, as it's still early), throw them out of your wedding.

'Borderline' – Madonna

One of my favourite Madonna songs. Who wouldn't want to go to an event where people drink cocktails while Madonna sings 'Borderline' in the background?

'Baba O'Riley' – The Who

I nearly walked down the aisle to this. Great track.

'Jump in the Line' – Harry Belafonte

A great one for warming up the crowd. Impossible to listen to without tapping your toe and swinging a little.

———♡———

Dancing (after meal – about 10pm):

'Good Fortune' – PJ Harvey
Because a party's not a party without some PJ Harvey (= not a catchphrase I expect to catch on).

'Mis-Shapes' – Pulp
Isn't it funny when all those men and women who have always been beautiful and popular sing and dance along to Pulp songs like they know anything about alienation? Oh, leave them alone. It's your wedding day.

'I Wanna Dance with Somebody' – Whitney Houston
Oh, Whitney. Mums (and all other people with ears) love this.

'She Bangs the Drums' – The Stone Roses
Such a great intro. See those former indie kids suddenly flock to the dance floor.

'If You Wanna Be Happy' – Jimmy Soul
The consensus on this song seems to be 'Never play this at a wedding', but I think it's a handy sense of humour test. If anyone, including and especially the bride, finds the lyrics inappropriate, they'd best be off.

'Toxic' – Britney Spears
Floor-filler. No question.

'Blaze of Glory' – Bon Jovi
You might think that 'Livin' on a Prayer', classic of many a sweaty ironic club night out, would be better, but I actually hate it. There. I've said it. 'Blaze of Glory', though – that's basically Warren G's 'Regulate' for ten-year-old girls. Oh *yeeeaaaah*.

'Oliver's Army' – Elvis Costello
Even if it gets you into trouble with writers of military fiction, this is a bloody brilliant tune.

'Smooth Criminal' – Alien Ant Farm
While we're in full-on iconoclasm mode, I... I think this is a really good version of the song. Whoah. That feels a lot better.

'Beautiful Stranger' – Madonna
A controversial choice, I know, but I think it's an absolute kicker to dance to. Even the middle-aged will want to shake it to this.

--------♡--------

Everyone's gone nuts (10pm – taxis/the police are called):

'Twist and Shout' – The Beatles
The best wedding I ever went to played this three times. I'm unable to say if the two things are related. But it should be a legal requirement of weddings that you have to play this at least once.

'Burning Down the House' – Talking Heads
Yeah. Like you need me to explain why this is here. Come on.

'Ça Plane Pour Moi' – Holly Golightly
Banging guitars and miles better than the original (sorry, Bertrand). If you don't dance to this your ears are broken.

'Infinity Guitars' – Sleigh Bells

Sometimes I fantasise that I'm about to be swept up in a huge dance routine, and everyone on the street will know all the moves and carry me off somewhere fabulous. If anyone truly loved you, they would organise a huge choreographed number to this track, all the women at the wedding sweeping around the dance floor, clapping and stomping and snarling, and looking as if they're about to eat the world. That would be an *amazing* wedding present.

'Smells Like Teen Spirit' – Nirvana

It doesn't matter where I hear this: petrol station shop sound system, someone's tinny headphones, a funeral. I will be DANCING. *Hard*. As will your guests.

'Sabotage' – Beastie Boys

Amazing. Even better if everyone can sing along (please provide song sheets for those new to the Beasties).

'Fell in Love With a Girl' – White Stripes

I know not everyone digs Meg White's drumming, but I think this is bloody wonderful. Dance time!

'Rock Star' – Hole

Say what you like about Courtney Love, but back in the day she sure could rock. A classic jumping-up-and-down number.

'212' – Azealia Banks

Proper mind-bogglingly filthy lyrics, but an absolutely unstoppable tune. Brilliant.

'Dancing in the Dark' – Bruce Springsteen

This should be used in hospitals to test lower brain function. Impossible to hear without moving.

———— ♡ ————

DO NOT PLAY

For some reason, people seem to think these are acceptable songs to play as they walk down/up the aisle (all bets are off for actual party music – you can play D.I.V.O.R.C.E. for all I care). If you don't know why they're not, take a minute to look at the lyrics:

'The One I Love' – REM
'I Will Always Love You' – Dolly Parton/Whitney Houston
'Every Breath You Take' – The Police
'When a Man Loves a Woman' – Percy Sledge
'Kiss the Bride' – Elton John

Having said that, the two songs that played as our ceremony finished were The Lemonheads' cover of 'Mrs Robinson', followed by Billy Idol's 'White Wedding'. So really, the world's your lobster.

Flowers

If I was a millionaire, I'd buy fresh flowers every day (although if I was a millionaire, I suppose I'd actually be getting my butler to do that kind of menial work while I lay in my bath of goat milk for all the hours the sun was up). I think they are the loveliest thing, and the nicest way to make a room or occasion feel special. And wedding-wise, it's the kind of thing that your mum/aunt/bridesmaid/the girlfriend of one of the guests might really enjoy helping with, and thus feel even more involved and in love with your whole bash.

I think anything is acceptable, really, besides lilies (death), orchids (corporate office decoration), sunflowers (you're not eleven) and gerberas (everything that's wrong with wedding flowers). All of the flowers below are, of course, just suggestions; their seasons come and go and it may be that they just aren't around for your wedding. If you feel capable of growing something (or have someone else to do it for you – *perfect* mum job), you can just buy a few plain pots and plant away. If you can find some nice old plant pots in a charity shop, these can be really nice gifts for the wedding party/in-car soil dispersants on the way to the venue/things to clutter up your home for months after your wedding day. But they can cost mere pennies per table, and look pretty smart. If growing flowers is beyond you, you can always do herbs, in scrubbed-out tin cans. Edible plants at the table look wonderful and smell totally delicious (because there'll always be some idiot muttering to their friends, 'I simply cannot stand the smell of Sweet Williams/marigolds/lilacs/ hyacinths'), particularly mint, basil and coriander, and even I can grow those.

Fortunately, flower-fashions are such at the moment that pretty much anyone can bang some flowers in a vase and make it look nice (although I'm sure a florist would do it better), but weddings seem to make flower arrangements – as with so much else – so over-elaborate and eighties-ish. You can go down that route if you want – really, it's your onions if you want to pay hundreds of quid to have a wedding that looks like a conference – but you can also be sensible, and find a nice florist to help you pick and buy a few tip-top condition flowers, prep them so they'll last through the day, present them in an unfussy manner to show them off at their best in as many places as you can (buttonholes, table tops, windowsills: wherever stays still long enough to have a vase/milk bottle/

jar/tin can/plant pot put on it), and they might even give you something to clasp in your shaking hands as you walk down the aisle.

March – early May: sweet pea, lisianthus, love-in-a-mist, stocks, astrantia, forget-me-nots, lily of the valley
Grow: Sweet William in a pot

Late May – August: peonies, phlox, ranunculus, ornithogalum
Grow: Marigolds in a pot

September – early November: cosmos, craspedia, helleborus, tanacetum
Grow: Lilac in a pot

Late November – February: mimosa, anemone, carnations, chrysanthemum, delphinium, freesias
Grow: Hyacinth in a pot

***

Games

I personally think weddings can be deathly dull if you're just standing around waiting for things, like you're stuck in a doctor's surgery in your absolute smartest clothes. I am *all* about the games, but if anything team-based fills you with a cold, sick horror, you can always just put a few games in a corner; either things like skittles (which is a really effective way of making sure all the children are in one place, as they'll all just want to smash the skittles with the ball as hard as they can) or a pile of board games on a table, making sure people know they can use them at any time. Depending on how you've arranged your tables (mixing up the groups or friends together) people might really welcome that ice-breaker activity, or if all they want to do is definitely not play games, they really don't have to. But give people something to do – it's horrible to feel like you're just an extra at someone else's Ego Show. Give 'em a game and they'll be so busy calculating that it was Miss Plum in the Library that they'll never have time to realise.

Best one by far, that I was introduced to by my lovely in-laws at our wedding: the Hat Game – like musical chairs, but with hats. You stand in a circle, everyone wearing a hat. As the music begins and you all slowly start walking around in the big circular conga line, one (or two or three, depending on the size of the circle) hat is removed, and those without a hat must grab the hat from the person in front of them, who, bare-headed, must then grab from the person in front of *them*. It's an insanely good ice breaker, as within minutes everyone is chasing around, trying to evade the clutches of the hat-needer behind you, while always keeping the hat-wearer in front within grabbing distance. The final round sees two players, back-to-back on chairs, one hat between them. Wrestling a hat off a stranger's head has never been so much fun (but make sure the bride removes her veil).

A Sense of Humour/Sense of Perspective

Absolutely the the the *most* important thing. You might have planned for months and saved for years, or you might have decided to do this last Tuesday and invited only your cousin along. Either way, keep some perspective. Here are just some of the things that could go wrong:
* Your mum wears the wrong-coloured shoes.
* Your flowers aren't the ones you agreed with the florist.

* The groom has got a black eye.
* Your bridesmaid wants to wear her hair down, instead of up.
* Your bridesmaid wants to wear her hair up, instead of down.
* The dog ate your wedding cake.
* The vicar keeps referring to divorce rates (I've been to a wedding like that).
* Your venue suddenly and inexplicably smells of chip fat.
* Your brother-in-law gets drunk and knocks over a table.
* Your now-husband's ex 'accidentally' spills red wine over your wedding dress.

Now here are the things that might matter:
* You don't show up.
* Your groom doesn't show up.

That's pretty much it. Get that into your skull and you'll enjoy the day so much more.

Wedding Inessentials

❧ Favours ❧

I have never, ever, ever, *ever* been to a wedding where anyone commented on the favours. You could hire someone to hand-carve each guest's likeness into a diamond biscuit flaked with gold, and not one person will give a shit. No one cares about that stuff. I have been to weddings both with and without favours, and no one has ever said, 'Do you know what that beautiful ceremony and wonderful party was missing? Sugared almonds with the couple's initials on. I just don't feel like they're *really* married yet.' And if you know anyone who would ever say that, then you absolutely must not invite them to your wedding.

❧ Seat covers ❧

It's a chair. We know it's a chair. You know it's a chair. Please don't spend hundreds of pounds buying dresses for the furniture because they are 'ugly'. Do you what's ugly? Spending hundreds of pounds on furniture clothes, when you could blow that cash on several meals at Arbutus in Soho instead. Who will care about the naked chairs? See above, for people who care about a lack of favours.

~ Table confetti ~

Are you kidding? Table. Confetti. Confetti for the table. If there was one single item that showed Capitalism as a busted economic ideology that had now started to eat itself, table confetti would be it. (See also: table beads, table gems, table crystals.)

~ Anything mini ~

If it's worth having, it's worth having full-size. If full-size would look ridiculous, think how much more ridiculous it is in dinky little miniature. So, miniature buckets in which to stuff sweets: no. Giant buckets full of pick and mix (if you insist on treating the whole thing like a children's party): better. Mini champagne bottles: no. Normal-sized bottles of champagne chilled to within an inch of their lives: sure, why not.

~ Crackers ~

I can't believe the manufacturers of these have managed to expand their market into weddings, and I can't believe poor befuddled newly engaged women are falling for it. If you're getting married in December by someone dressed in a red and white suit and your meal is turkey and all the trimmings, by all means, cracker away, but if your theme is Country Garden Chic or Hawaiian Cocktail Party, don't start panicking about finding the exact shade of crackers for your place settings just because you saw them once in a bridal magazine and the woman on the front in the veil was really smiling.

～ Disposable cameras ～

In an age where every Tom, Dick and Harry has a spectacular camera right on their phone, it boggles my mind that anyone would still be buying disposable cameras for weddings. Here's what happens: you spend around a hundred pounds on disposable cameras (one for each table and a few spare). Most people are too sober to use them at the start of the night (or are just taking photos on their phones, as they have now done for *years*), then once they are drunk the cameras suddenly seem like hilarious retro fun. There will be six blurred photos taken of friends they've just made grinding on the dance floor. No other photos will ever be taken with them. They will stay undeveloped in your home for the next three house moves, and in the future someone will find them and bring them to *Antiques Roadshow*, where, since they are mostly unused, they will be worth thousands.

～ Everyone and everything colour matching ～

This is really where the myth of it being 'The Bride's Special Day' is at its most evil and pernicious. Somehow brides are sucked into this belief that this means the wedding day will look, sound, taste, smell and feel as if it's been put together by Mario Testino, Nigella Lawson and Sophia Coppola. This is never going to happen. Ever. You might look the most beautiful you ever have done, because even my bed looks particularly delicious when dressed head-to-toe in fresh, clean white, but everyone else may be tired, drunk, ill, may forget their lines, may have children who have no care for perfectly lined up centrepieces, may have changed their mind about which dress they're wearing at the last minute, or may just have started smoking today apparently to piss you off, because you quit for the wedding and this isn't making it any easier. When you take all this into consideration, the idea that you can make all these things match: bride's bouquet, bridesmaids' posies, bridesmaids' dresses, bridesmaids' shoes, bridesmaids' hair jewels, the napkins, table cloths, flowers on the tables, flowers in the church, car, buttonholes for all men in the party, balloons, table decorations, ribbons, bunting, mother of the bride's hat, mother of the bride's clothes, mother of the bride's eyeshadow, groom's cravat (I totally hate cravats anyway, utterly and completely – isn't a smart suit and tie about 4,000,000 times smarter?), groom's *socks,* groom's pocket square, best man's tie (or cravat), best man's socks, best man's pocket square, flower girl's basket of petals, guests' *confetti…* when you're trying to dictate the colour of the biodegradable rice paper your loved ones are throwing at you, I think alarm bells should start ringing. Not only because I share Anna Wintour's alleged disdain for matchy-matchy, but also because with all those objects, complete colour meshing is never going to happen, so I think it's JUST MUCH EASIER if you just give up and go with the flow. Let some disorder in. This is life, joyful and chaotic and real, not a Cher music video.

Hen parties –
Dos and Don'ts

DO: Ask all the people you really like. Don't worry if they aren't all coming to the wedding, or don't know one another: the more the merrier.

DON'T: Go abroad. Unless you are a wealthy heiress and your guests will never once have to reach for their wallets, keep it local. There's now some terrible arms race for hen parties, where, because *she* made *you* go to a French vineyard, *you* have to make *her* go to Sweden. Why, just because you're getting married, do you think anyone wants to blow their entire annual holiday budget just so you can have company in Disneyland Paris/Ibiza/Las Vegas/the Moon? It's *crazy*. And however much all your friends say they don't mind, they really, really do. Days off work, flights, hotels, extra clothes, ridiculously-priced cocktails – it's insane. If you love these people, find a comedy club in your local area, paint one another's nails (or whatever floats your boat), get some ridiculously-priced cocktails (locally) and enjoy the night before staggering home to your respective loved ones. If you don't love them and feel since it's Your Wedding they should support Whatever You Want To Do, then, frankly, you don't deserve a hen bash and should go and sit in the corner and take a good long look at yourself.

DO: Find out what your friends like doing, rather than just assuming you all have to go to a chocolate workshop then sport L-plates in a filthy but brilliant bar. You might all turn out to be secret Terry Pratchett freaks, and you can sit around dressed as trolls and wizards and form a new lifelong bond with Christine in HR (who you originally only invited so you could get more time off for your honeymoon).

DON'T: Get so drunk you make tired-and-emotional phone calls to your fiancé (this applies to grooms calling their fiancées, too). This is just a handy rule of life – no drinking and dialling – but weddings are fraught enough, without anyone spilling the beans about a workplace crush that actually Means Nothing, Darling, when it really does mean absolutely nothing. No one wants that.

DO: Dance, and do karaoke. It's just about the best thing in the world, whether you go to one of those tiny, freaky underground bars in Soho, or hook up some console to your TV and invite the neighbours round to join you and your friends. I've known very, very few people who genuinely haven't enjoyed themselves once it's there in front of them.

27

Stag parties – Dos and Don'ts

DO: Indulge your inner child. From asking around, the best stag parties have involved driving, shooting, paint-balling, building a massive campfire and/or killing a pig (personally, I'm *desperate* to go on a Hen night like this), so why not do something other than go to a bar with seventy other super-drunk men in busy city centre? Think how rarely you'll get all your best mates together in one place. Then think of all the brilliant stuff you can force them to do if you hire a narrowboat together and you declare yourself Captain.

DON'T: Seriously consider a lapdancing joint, really. Do you remember when Iceland's first female Prime Minister, Johanna Sigurdardottir, confirmed the ban on stripping and lapdancing bars in the country, saying, 'I guess the men of Iceland will just have to get used to the idea that women are not for sale'? Not that it seemed there was much getting used to: fewer than 10% of Icelanders were opposed to the ban. Doesn't that sound nice? Isn't that *better*? So if you want to claim it's ironic, or someone else is arranging it, or it's 'your last time before you get married', just remember: urgh.

28

Family

❧ How to Handle Family ❧ Before and During a Wedding

Mother: Where do we start. Are you two best friends? Do you tell each other everything? Can you not imagine a world where you don't speak to your mum six times a day? If that's the case, there is absolutely nothing I can advise you on here. She'll probably be in the other bed in the twin room you've booked for your honeymoon, so don't sweat it. You don't need to 'handle' her.

1. If that's not the case – if the second after you told your mum about the engagement, you started googling 'Las Vegas wedding' – here are some tips you might find useful.

    Give her something to do. The bigger the job seems, the more she'll be off your back. Something like 'find napkins' might seem like you're throwing her a bone, but she's no fool. It's such a rubbish bit of un-delegating that she'll swamp you with constant emails and calls every single time she sees anything remotely *like* a napkin. But give her something bigger – say, 'flowers' – and you might not see her for *months*. She'll be researching and reading up and asking around so she can present you with the best

29

possible options for you to pick from. And since it's so often much easier to edit than create, it's pretty hard for her to fuck this one up.

2. Let her have between one and three guests of her choice. You'll have to use all your negotiation skills here: pretend you're not going to let her have any, then (as you judge) allow her one little window of hope. She's not inviting Deborah from accounts just because she went to *her* son's bash last year, but if she has three best friends who were your surrogate mothers, you'll probably quite like it if she gets to ring them up with news of their invitations. But don't let her drip-drip-drip passive-aggressive comments into your ear until suddenly your numbers have doubled and you don't know who any of them are. That's rubbish. Just because she gave you life doesn't mean it's now open doors on the guest list.

3. On the day, recognise how much this must mean to her. It's not particularly feminist to think your child's shining moment is to be married off, but it is another major step in your life, and if she choked up on your first day at primary school, she can damn well be giddy about you actually leaving home (or whatever it is you do once you're married). Let her have a little slice of that wedding specialness. And make sure she doesn't wear that bloody awful hat she insists is vintage.

Father: Doesn't care. As long as you don't make him decide anything, he Just Wants You To Be Happy (and for you to pick a cheap wedding).

Sister(s): Tricky. Is she the supportive sort? Can you trust her with all the boring but essential jobs? Would the wedding not be able to go ahead if she couldn't make it, or are you praying that there's a two-day traffic jam on the M1 and you have to wait to Christmas to see her again? Is she your Maid of Honour, or is she a fucking pain?

1. Work out which of the two, and handle accordingly:

     Maid of Honour: Thank her for all her support and kindness. Ask her if she'd like to do a few things, but don't put any pressure on her. Constantly remind her that you know she's busy, and you appreciate anything at all that she does for you. You know it can't be the most important thing, but you're so happy she could be involved at all. Thank her again. Give her a nice bunch of flowers on the day.

2. Fucking Pain: As above. It will mess with her mind and you will have the higher ground FOREVER.

Brother(s): Doesn't care. If he does, there's something wrong with your relationship. I'm just putting it out there.

Aunt(s): If she has daughters, she will be secretly competitive, constantly whispering passive-aggressive comments to your mum. Before the wedding, ask her if you can see her hat, and say it's the nicest hat you've ever seen – you almost got a white version yourself for the wedding day. If she's not eating out of your hand when it comes to it, tell your mum later that you think your aunt's hat is shit. It'll make your mum feel better, at least.

Uncle(s): Doesn't care.

Cousin(s): If your girl cousins are getting married the same year as you, want their boyfriends to propose, or have just been to their best friend's wedding, you could hand out solid gold favours and sit them next to Colin Firth and they would hate your event. Your boy cousins will never, ever give a shit.

Grandparents: Can you think of anything more moving and amazing than seeing your child's child marry someone they love? That must be nice. Invite your grandparents and don't think twice about whatever hassle they might be. They gave your parents the neuroses that you would rebel against to make you the person your fiancé fell in love with. Think about *that* when your grandma's telling all your friends at the wedding how much she always liked Jeff (your ex).

Children: If you're one of those people who believe children add to the sense of family and community at a wedding (i.e. it's unlikely you have them), invite them. If you can't bear the thought of sticky, shouty children touching everything and/ or you're extremely thoughtful and suspect banning them is the only way their parents, with faux-begrudgingness, can get a night away from them to share adult conversation and drink themselves sick, don't invite them. Just decide which one you're going to do and stick to your guns. Don't let your aunt bully your mum about it. Just pick your side, give your reasons to anyone who seems to need them, and enjoy your day. The only children who *really* care about attending your wedding (except for maybe your own) are little girls who have watched too many Disney princess films. And you should ban them just for that anyway.

Decorations

I really think this is the most fun thing in the world, but I can understand how it might be a living nightmare, particularly if you aren't that confident about your taste, have been to some expensive-but-extremely-ugly wedding that may have influenced your preferences, or are marrying someone who has bad taste in their blood line. Really, all that matters is that a) you can afford it, and b) you like it. Who cares if no-one likes your holographic banners? You definitely shouldn't. This is a party hosted by the two of you, so as long as there are comforts in abundance where it matters, you do *whatever you like*. Here are some things you might enjoy pulling together, so just grab them whenever you see them:

Balloons	Storm lanterns
Bunting	Family photos
Candles	Cushions
Vases	Rugs
Milk bottles	Placemats
Tin cans	Mobiles
Jam jars	Platters
Ribbons/streamers	Teapots (for late at night)
Paper lanterns	Cheeseboards
Jugs	Blankets
Paper flowers	Gig/film posters
Paper pompoms	Maps

Wedding Lists

I've come around to the idea that wedding lists are a good idea. Unless you can really and truly convince your guests not to buy you anything, people *will* get you gifts – even if they aren't coming to the wedding – and it *is* really grim to see people spending money on something that is useless/repugnant/both to the recipient. How are they to know that you already have a cupboard full of cheeseboards at your house? Or that a pair of 'Keep Calm and Marry On' mugs will serve only as the catalyst for that clear out you've been meaning to have for the local charity shop? So go ahead, set up a wedding list. But I pass on the advice given to me: put lots of affordable things on ('affordable' will, of course, vary, but I think lots of £20-40 things is safe enough for most people) but not things that you could buy for yourself in single trip to the supermarket. I've seen wedding lists with such forlorn items: oven gloves, soap dishes, *brooms*. Who would ever want to give those, to mark the start of a new life together? So think of nice things that you would want to buy for someone you – I hesitate to say love, but at least will have to see again – and remember, too, that this isn't some giant claw-grab for everything you can't be bothered to buy yourself. I've heard couples argue that since they're hosting the event and providing (normally hugely overpriced) meals for everyone, they *deserve* to get Vera Wang dining sets and silk and cashmere cushions. That's a bit mean and greedy, and the guests at those weddings know it.

Table Plans

Of course, without warping the space-time continuum, not everyone can sit next to everyone else. If you insist on having table plans, big groups of friends might need to be split up, and unpopular relatives have to sit with *somebody*. But remember, this wedding thing is a two-way street: your guests are honoured to be invited, but they're still doing you a favour in joining you. Don't split up friends who never get to see enough of each other as it is. Don't put a single couple all by themselves on a table of your overwhelming family. And – absolutely key to being allowed to stay in the human race – don't separate couples because one of them hasn't earned their way onto the top table. This seems to be more and more common, and I think you might as well wear a badge saying, 'I couldn't give the smallest fuck about whether you enjoy my wedding.' All your guests would like to have a nice time too. Let them.

Honeymoon Destinations

The Cotswolds
There's so many nice places around here, it's like a parody of English beauty. I'm a huge fan of Cirencester, particularly the open-air swimming pool that only opens in the summer and is still mostly freezing, and the lovely spaces in which there always seems to be cream teas in the summer. There's a lovely B&B called No 12, which I thoroughly recommend.

Paris
Do I really need to say more? It's Paris, people. Have you *seen* the diaries you can get there? (Particularly Bookbinders Design, 130 Rue du Bac.) And the *bread*? (See Du Pain et des Ideés, 34 rue ves Toudic, although really any bread in Paris is embarrassingly good bread.) Just go. Don't even wait to get married. And if you've been there plenty of times before, just go again. *Anywhere* is good. It's *Paris*.

Rome
Absolutely wonderful if you're looking for an autumn or winter honeymoon. You can wrap up warmly and between the Colosseum, the Pantheon and the Trevi Fountain, you can get tiny thick, syrupy cups of hot chocolate and giant, crisp pizzas. If you were so inclined, you could even order some spaghetti and recreate that whole *Lady and the Tramp* moment, but I suspect you'd look a bit simple-minded. I loved the Hotel Pantheon (www.hotelpantheon.com) – it's right in

the middle of everything, cheap as gelato, and friendly as anything.

Devon

Such a lovely, lovely county. Throw a scone and it will land somewhere beautiful. You can't go wrong, particularly south Devon and Dartmoor.

Anywhere; stick a pin in the UK and have an adventure

I can't understand this mentality that your honeymoon must be absolutely the most expensive holiday you're ever going to take, as if once you are married you are *never allowed a holiday again*. Isn't the point just to stay in bed together, occasionally eating, reading, and maybe noticing where you actually are? So why not just pick somewhere in the country completely at random? There are so many ways to find great stuff to do, and so many wonderful places in the UK that you are bound to find *somewhere* good. You can each have one pin and one veto, so you don't end up going a) in the middle of the ocean or b) what a coincidence, to his team's football ground (or equivalent). If you get into the spirit of it, you'll have just as much fun investigating and planning a holiday in Nottingham, or Somerset, or Manchester, or the Highlands, as you would booking your Luxury Mango Pedicures at $400 a pop at some exclusive resort in the Maldives. And, if all else fails, there are spas all over the UK, so you can get a couple of days of face rubs and foot massages if that's what makes you most happy.

Money

⌀ Top Money-Saving Tips ⌀ for a Wedding

1. When buying a dress, ask for bridesmaid dresses, not bridal ones. They can often be just as pale, floor-length and delicious, but are a fraction of the price.
2. Cakes: look at 'non'-wedding varieties of these too, or at least off-the-shelf. For something that's mostly just going to go into people's mouths, M&S's wedding cakes are perfectly fine – delicious, even – and look totally wonderful when sparked up with some ribbons or feathers from somewhere like MacCulloch and Wallis (www.macculloch-wallis.co.uk).

That's it, really. Ultimately, you could have 100 tips about saving money and will find them in any bridal magazine, but the only ones who can actually save it are the ones making the decisions. If you decide you MUST have designer shoes for your wedding day, I'm sure you can find a discount branch, an import shortcut, a voucher online. But you'll save so much more when you realise how much people are willing to share with you, and how little you truly 'need'.

Here are some things you could buy if you don't blow £20,000 on a single day:

One unforgettable trip to anywhere in the world
Pretty great holidays for a few years
Simple holidays for a decade
A swanky gadget-filled new kitchen
A new Mini
Four Hermès Birkin bags
Carpeting for the walls, floor, ceiling and windows of most
    homes (inside and out)
A lifetime's supply of paperback books

Of course, you can spend your money on what you like. And of course, it's your wedding. But, seriously. £20,000? That's deranged.

———————————— ✣ ————————————

Finally, my attempt to lower your chances of future marital discord

I once read the ten questions every couple about to marry should discuss. I can't remember most of them (it was ages ago) but I do think it's worth considering these:

If one or both of you got very rich, what would you do with it?

Do you want children? How would they be educated? Would either of you give up work?

Do you both expect the same thing when it comes to your roles? Do either of you have a very 'traditional' (read: backwards) view on husbands and wives in the home?

If one of your parents needed care and couldn't live in their home any more, where would they go?

Do you want to live abroad? Where do you see yourselves in ten years' time?

What are your views on religion? Saving money? Eating things straight from the fridge with your fingers when really they need a spoon at the very least, if not a bowl as well?

Also:

How does your fiancé/fiancée treat waiters? Shop assistants? Cabin crew? Your siblings? Their own parents? If there's anything other than kindness and respect, don't be surprised when they turn out to be someone you – to quote *Singin' in the Rain*'s Lina Lamont – 'keeen steeend'.

That's it. Enjoy yourselves. Be kind to one another. And good luck.

Read on for an exclusive extract from

The Baby Diaries

out in Spring 2013

October 31st

Have you ever had that feeling you've forgotten something? Something nagging away at the back of your mind – until just the right movement in your memory triggers something else, which knocks another thing down, and like some Indiana Jones death trap, you can feel the clank-clunking of motion in the hidden rooms of your brain, gradually bringing the forgotten memory swinging like a battering ram into your conscious mind. You know that feeling?

So that's what I had yesterday.

I've been so busy since the wedding. Tony, my boss and head of Polka Dot books was as good as his word with my promotion, giving me six new authors before disappearing off on a three-month 'travelling sabbatical' to God Knows Where.

Thom's been settling into his new life as a trainee teacher: to no one's surprise, he's loving it. But as his enthusiasm has spilled over into our evenings, we've spent a great deal of time together marking papers – him, clunky essays on *Wuthering Heights*, me, swathes of mostly unreadable fiction: thirty-somethings who have always dreamt of writing, aiming for Heathcliff and hitting Cliff Richard. So we've been dog tired, and when we've had time off we've been with my parents (half an eye always on my Dad to check he's taking care of himself after his heart attack earlier this year), my nearly-new niece Frida, or our friends (those we hadn't had to uninvite from the wedding). It was still great to be spending *any* time together where we weren't arguing about money, or the importance of decorative accessories, or the social rules of such a complex endeavour as a wedding. But something kept nagging at me. Did we pay the register office? Had we thanked everyone? Was anyone still locked in the primary school reception venue? None of these nudged anything, although I worried at it like a tongue at a wobbly tooth. It would give eventually. And when it did, I just had to hope I didn't have a huge apology to make to anyone.

Then, yesterday morning, Thom and I were comparing our weeks. Thom said he had me over a barrel, since I spent my time lunching authors and picking my favourite colour for a book jacket, while he was at the coal-face, earning every penny trying to hammer basic English in the heads of his students.

Me: You love it really.
Thom: I might love it, but I'm a hell of lot more tired at the end of the day than I ever was making spreadsheets all day. Surprisingly.
Me: Can it really be that hard?
Thom: Kiki. I dare you to try dealing with a room full of hormonal teenagers.

That was it. Clink, clunk. Brrrrrrrrrrrrrrrrrrr. Click. Click. Ka-dunk. *BOOM*.

I must have just frozen while my brain went into its noisy activity, because Thom stopped laughing at the mental image he'd conjured and looked at me, puzzled. 'What's up?' he said. I stood completely still, calculating over and over, mentally flicking through the pages of my pocket diary – dates, dates, dates. Dates. When I managed to reconnect my brain with my voice box, I just said, 'I think we need to go to the chemist.'

Thom got it immediately. We rushed out, no coats, no scarves, into the freezing October afternoon, hurrying to the chemist around the corner. Outside, it felt like Before for a moment – we teased one another about who would go in and buy it, until I remembered what the whole thing was about, and my face collapsed. Thom went in while I read the notices in the window again and again. A Great Time To Give Up Smoking! the sign read. Or, indeed, start, I thought. Then he was out, and we were hurrying home again, and I thought, is this time included in the three minutes you have to count off? If I walk home slowly will I know the result immediately? Then we *were* home, and Thom was bustling me upstairs, and I went into the bathroom and locked the door. When I took the little test out of the box, my hands were shaking so much and the adrenaline was coursing through me so I couldn't read one word of the instructions.

Me: How does this even work?

Thom: [through the door] Haven't you ever watched TV? Piss on the stick, then we can find out who the father is later.

Me: *Please.*

Thom: [quiet] Sorry, Kiki. Pass the instructions under the door.

Me: [hands shaking, takes several goes]

Thom: OK. It's the bit on the end. Then stick the lid back on and leave it three minutes. Do you want me to come in?

Me: Come in? In here? I don't really know. I don't know. I don't *know.*

Thom: It's OK, Keeks. I'm right here. We can do this later if you want. We don't have to do it right now. We can talk about it first, if you want.

And just for a moment, I thought: 'we'? *We?* If a little plus sign appeared in this window, it wouldn't be Thom squandering his recent promotion. It wouldn't be Thom who was the only one of his friends changing his name to 'Mummy'. It wouldn't be Thom pushing a large ham-weight through his tiny little birth canal. We? Me me me me me. Then I thought: oh, fuck it. Just take the test.

So I did.

I was still shaking so managed to wee all over my own hands, but I clicked the cap back on and let it sit. I opened the bathroom door, and Thom rushed in.

Thom: How are you doing?
Me: You're holding the hand that's covered in my urine.
Thom: I'm going to take that as a 'good'.

He hugged me for a long time, not even commenting on how much the bathroom stank of piss, then we went in together to check the result. A giant glowing plus sign greeted us.

Me: Well.
Thom: That's unambiguous.
Me: Best of three?
Thom: It was a two-pack. I don't think you'll need me to go out again.
Me: Oh. Shit?

Thom took me into the living room, where we sat for ages in silence.

Thom: But... when?
Me: Our honeymoon.
Thom: How?

45

Me: Remember that night? When we agreed to start trying because it could take years? The night before we sobered up and realised our mistake? That one.

Thom: Wow. Honeymoon baby.

Me: [breaking down] It's so taaa-aa-aa-ack-y-y-y-y.

I cried for half an hour, then calmed down into a state of steady shock. Pregnant. I'm pregnant. As if reading my mind, Thom said in a ridiculous over-the-top voice, 'I can't believe we're pregnant already!' which managed to get a laugh out of me; it's always been one of my all-time worst phrases, and my laugh stuck around until I remembered that it was, at least in one sense, true. My catatonic state returned.

Me: How did this happen?

Thom: Oh Keeks. When a man and a woman love one another very much –

Me: Thom, please! *Really*!

Thom: I don't know Kiki, these things sometimes happen, don't they? I do love you very much, if that helps.

Me: I just don't know what to do. I don't know what to do. [whispering] This is ridiculous.

Thom: Shall we go to bed? Sometimes these things feel better in the morning.

Me: [staring at him]

Thom: Sorry, I don't mean it like that. I know it's not going to go away, and I know that no matter how much I say I love you and I support you and I feel for you, I know that it's your body and I can only begin to imagine your panic and your fear. But I do love you, and loving you also involves knowing that sometimes you deal best with things by vanishing in a cocoon of sleep to work out what you have to do. Is that true?

Me: Yes.

Thom: Right. So let's do one decision at a time. Would you like me to make you a drink before bed?

Me: Whiskey.

Thom: Uh…

Me: OH GOD I CAN'T EVEN DRINK. Oh God! How much have I drunk in the last month? The last two months? OH GOD I DO NOTHING BUT DRINK.

Thom: Kiki. It's fine. Let's forget about the drink and just get into bed.

So we did just that. I amazed myself by falling straight to sleep – as Thom said, it's how I cope with most things, but it meant it was an extra struggle this morning, having a mini version of the click-clunking remembering all over again. Pregnant. Pregnant. Pregnant. It still doesn't make any sense. Yes, we both want kids very much, and yes, we look forward to having them, but now? Right now? I have *just* got my promotion, Thom has just started a mind-bogglingly poorly paid job, and we're not ready for this. I feel so strange.

At work today, Alice noticed something was wrong, but only asked me once. She kept her distance for the rest of the day in the nicest possible manner, her excellent breeding (or lesbian superpower) knowing exactly when to press me and lavish me with attention, and when to leave me in peace. In Tony's ridiculous absence, I managed to get my head down and do work for most of the day. At lunchtime I needed to get out of the office, so took my sandwich round the corner to window shop, and found myself in front of the giant Topshop on Oxford Street, facing the maternity wear entrance.

They had some lovely clothes. Gorgeous slim-fitting jeans with fatty pregna-panels in the sides, lovely tops to show off pregna-busts and delicious high-waisted dresses. Not to mention the mini-me baby clothes: t-shirts and sweaters with the wildlife of

47

the season embroidered on the front, so the infant can be just as sharp as the mother. Could I live like this? Is there hope? I started walking back to the office feeling better, feeling hopeful. Maybe we could do this. It's not the seventies anymore: I wouldn't have to wear huge frilly tents and give up my job. I could be like Rachida Dati, returning to work at the French government five days after having this baby. Only, not the French government. And not five days. Women do this all over the world, all the time. And this wouldn't just be my baby. It would be Thom's as well. And who's going to make a better baby than me and Thom?

So I went to the beautiful stationery shop below our office and bought this diary. I had a sudden urge to keep a record of everything, all our decisions and mistakes and joys. It felt like the first good step in a long road ahead. But I felt good.

Then I left the shop and almost tripped over a woman screaming at her child.

Woman: Didn't I tell you, Nicholas? Didn't I say no?
Boy: [incoherent screaming]
Woman: No, don't keep crying. Pull yourself together and answer me.
Boy: [screaming, but down a notch or two] I... want...
Woman: Nicholas, if you don't behave right now, not only will Daddy be hearing about this, but you can fo get about your skiing lesson with Joshua on Saturday.
Boy: [silent for a moment, weighing up the options, screaming recommenced even higher and louder than before]
Woman: [crouching down next to him] Please, Nicholas, please, darling, just calm yourself down. What it is you'd like, Nicky?
Boy: [sensing his advantage, upper the screaming again]
Woman: Calm down, darling. You know Mummy loves you.

48

Calm down. Shall we go back to the shop to get you the little car?

Boy: [pulling back the screams a little] Ye-ea-aah – [hi cupping sob]

Woman: Alright, darling. You were very good last night, weren't you? You only got out of bed four times! I think you deserve a nice little treat, don't you, darling?

Wait. I'd forgotten. OH GOD I hate children.

So my mood overall was unchanged this afternoon, and when I came home. Thom saw my face and pulled me into another big hug as I walked through the door, and took me to the sofa where he sat me down and smiled at me.

Thom: Do you know what I thought today, as I tried to convince a room full of thirteen-year-olds to not show one another photos of women's breasts while I talked about Jane Eyre?

Me: What.

Thom: Whether it's now, or whether it's in a few years: our kid is going to be brilliant.

Me: Ha! I thought the same thing today. Just before I tripped over a woman being emotionally blackmailed by her four-year-old.

Thom: You know we don't have to be like that, don't you? You can pick your parenting style: we can be Aloof Edwardian Parents. Or Distant Army Parents. Or Caveman Parents, who feed any spare children to their pet dinosaur.

Me: That's the Flintstones.

Thom: I hardly think the Flintstones would feed a *child* to a *dinosaur*.

Me: [silence, thinking] We could be alright as parents. Maybe.

Thom: Maybe we could. But maybe… you're too *chicken* to have a baby.

Me: [laughing] If ever that ploy was going to work on me…

Thom: Kiki, we will do whatever you like. For now, I'll make us something to eat.

I sat, and I thought. God, if we can deal with Thom's redundancy and Dad's heart attack and my previously-very-badly-paid-and-very-high-stress job, all while planning a wedding that took over our lives, we should be able to manage a baby. Thom's baby. And we might just be OK parents.

Me: [calling to the kitchen] Go on, then. Let's have a baby.

Thom: [running back in] Wooohoooo!

Me: You can't make noises like that in a labour ward. And *I'm* not telling my mum.

Thom: Shit. We have to tell people about this, don't we.

Together: *Shotgun!*

Me: I called it. You can tell them.

So I'm happy. But I still blame you, Paris. I don't know how this is your fault, but it is.

TO DO:

Grow baby
Have baby
Raise baby